THE LUTHIER'S PROMISE

Cathie Hartigan

Copyright © 2025 Cathie Hartigan

The rights of Cathie Hartigan have been asserted by her in accordance with the Copyright, Designs and Patents Act 1988

The characters and events portrayed in this book are fictitious. Any similarity to real persons, living or dead, is coincidental and not intended by the author.

All rights reserved. No part of this publication may be reproduced, or stored in a retrieval system, or transmitted in any form or by any means, electronic, mechanical, photocopying, recording, or otherwise, without express written permission of the author, or a license permitting restricted copying.

In the UK, such licenses are issued by the Copyright Licensing Agency, Shackleton House, 4, Battle Bridge Lane, London SE1 2HX

ISBN-13: 9798282250763

Cover design by Berni Stevens

For Margaret James

CONTENTS

Title Page
Copyright
Dedication
Luthier:
Historical Characters

Chapter One	1
Chapter Two	9
Chapter Three	14
Chapter Four	23
Chapter Five	31
Chapter Six	45
Chapter Seven	54
Chapter Eight	73
Chapter Nine	84
Chapter Ten	93
Chapter Eleven	102
Chapter Twelve	113
Chapter Thirteen	122
Chapter Fourteen	137
Chapter Fifteen	147

Chapter Sixteen	154
Chapter Seventeen	161
Chapter Eighteen	170
Chapter Nineteen	176
Chapter Twenty	189
Chapter Twenty-one	199
Chapter Twenty-two	209
Chapter Twenty-three	220
Chapter Twenty-four	229
Chapter Twenty-five	237
Chapter Twenty-six	248
Chapter Twenty-seven	258
Chapter Twenty-eight	270
Afterword	282
Acknowledgements	285
About The Author	287
Books By This Author	289

LUTHIER:

a maker of stringed instruments, particularly lutes

HISTORICAL CHARACTERS

London:
John Dowland: 1563 – 1626
(Jane?) Dowland
Robert Dowland: c.1591 – 1641
Thomas Morley: 1557 – 1602
Sir Robert Cecil: 1563 – 1612
Robert Devereux, Earl of Essex: 1565 – 1601
Henry Noel: d.1597

Germany:
Henry Julius, Duke of Brunswick: 1564 – 1613
Maurice, Landgrave of Hesse-Kassel: 1572 – 1632

Italy:
Alfonso II d'Este, Duke of Ferrara: 1533 – 1597
Margherita Gonzaga, Duchess of Ferrara 1564 – 1618
John Skidmore/Scudamore: 1542 - 1623
Lord Gray
Josias Bodley: 1550 – 1618
Friar Bailey
Laux Maler: 1485 – 1552
Magno/Magnus Tieffenbrucker 1580 – 1631

CHAPTER ONE

London 1594

It was time for a most delicate task. When bracing the ribs of a new lute, any gap between the strips of wood, however small, would be disastrous, and even if the instrument didn't spring apart, there would most likely be a vibration on certain notes.
This lute, I'd determined, would be my best yet, and fit for a fine musician such as John Dowland to play at Court. That's if a favourable breeze blew this morning and he got the vacant post. Her Majesty liked him well enough, but whether she could put up with his changeable moods was not so certain.

I bent to my task. If I could hold this one fast for the next few—

'Will? Where are you, Will?'

A draught roared through the house as the front door slammed, rattling all my tools hanging on the rack and my temper alongside them. The man in question was home and not closing the door with his usual considerate hand.

'Here,' I called, letting the clamp slacken. It was best I went to him, rather than have him throwing himself about, but he was quicker than me and by my side, before I could stop him.

'Pack up,' he said. 'Quick as you can. We're to catch the tide.'

At once, I blew out the flame beneath the gluepot. 'What's happened,' I asked, hastily gathering my tools together. 'Is there trouble? Tide's not right for upriver until tomorrow.'

He stopped still and stared at me.

'Upriver? But we're going to the Continent,' he said it as if I was already party to the idea. 'No, wait,' He looked at the ceiling, whilst counting something imagined on his fingers. 'First,' he said, pointing one finger and nodding as if to convince himself, 'we will sail to Flanders. Second,' another finger, and more vigorous nodding, 'ride to Brunswick. The Duke knows me by reputation. *Then,*' his mood so altered that he broke into a broad grin and gave me a playful punch on my arm. 'Why then, William Totman, from there you and I will go on to Italy. To *Rome.*'

I swallowed hard, not knowing what to make of this new venture. Whether the notion was a spark that would be out by tomorrow, or meant an uncomfortable journey and months away from home, remained to be seen. Why now, was clear.

'You didn't get the position then?'

He sighed, and the force of it flared the candle so his face was in full light. Apparently, some of the young women at court reckoned him the handsomest in the land. Perhaps it was the glowering brow and half-starved look they liked. Everything the opposite of my dull features.

'No, I did not. Her Majesty is not inclined towards me at present.' He leaned closer. 'And do you know why?'

I pretended to think hard. 'Because the Queen likes her musicians cheery?'

He reared back from me. 'Cheery? What do you mean by that? Am I not cheery?'

'I meant the *songs*, John, you can't say there's a lot of merriment in your songs. Or perhaps Her Majesty wasn't happy with some of the sentiment? *Thy love will be thus fruitless ever* for example?'

Understanding flamed across his face. Then, with a twitch of one shoulder, he shrugged away my reason. 'Her Majesty says I am an obstinate—' he stopped suddenly, his gaze settling on the bench where I'd been working on the new lute. 'An obstinate—' His voice trailed off and I knew he was wondering when it would be ready.

'Is there such a thing as *an obstinate*?' I asked. 'I thought obstinate was how you described a thing, not the thing itself.'

He ignored me, no doubt already playing the

instrument in his head. The lute was progressing well, but it would be a while yet and not at all if we were off to the Continent.

'Papist,' he said, vaguely. 'An obstinate papist. That's what she said.'

'Ah.'

'Master Byrd favours the Roman church, doesn't he? Her Majesty has no difficulty with him being at court, so why would I not do?'

He had me there. Master Byrd was well-liked despite being a papist. He was also sober, several years the wrong side of fifty, and quite without any appeal to Her Majesty's ladies.

'Of course, it's not true,' he said, sweeping an arm dangerously close to the gluepot.

It was opening a wound, talking church matters with John. He'd taken to the Roman church when in France, on a youngster's whim it had seemed to me, but he had stuck to it, albeit quietly. How far Her Majesty's leniency stretched in that regard, it wouldn't be wise to discover.

'What are you going to say to your mother?' I asked. 'And the mistress? Young Robert will miss you even if the baby will not?'

His wife wouldn't hear of him going alone, nor would old Mistress Dowland and I owed her far too much, my life most probably, to refuse her anything. Besides, John could be bold and adventurous in many things, but apart from losing himself for hours in his music and poetry, he could also lose himself by turning the wrong way out of his own house. At the mention of family his excitement drained away and it was a more measured John Dowland who spoke next.

'It will be a hard conversation with them all. In truth, I hoped most fervently that Her Majesty would employ me, but now she has not, there is a great need to go.'

'Is it so very great?'

A shadow passed over his face. 'She preferred a foreigner. A talentless fop of an Italian. Instead of *me*?' He threw back his head and addressed the ceiling. 'God in

Heaven! How could she?'

'It is unbelievable,' I said, shocked. 'Do you think Her Majesty was ill?'

'How could I tell? It is hardly a question to ask. Perhaps and perhaps not. But much more pressing, Will, is my abject humiliation.' He struck his forehead. 'Dear Lord, I won't be able to show my face in London ever again.'

'Surely —'

'And even if I did, without a court position nobody would pay more than a pittance. A man cannot support his family on pennies.'

'But I cannot believe it would come to that, and your mother most definitely would not allow it.'

'No,' he said irritably, 'and if I was still seventeen, instead of nearly thirty and didn't have a family, I might feel easy about dipping into my mother's purse, but what sort of a man does that?'

If he hadn't sounded so aggrieved, I might have smiled, but I knew his disappointment cut deep.

'A great many men do exactly that, John,' I said. 'But if it is that bad, you know I will always help. This lute could fetch a very good price and I will make many more. Is such a journey the answer?'

I began hanging my chisels back on the rack.

'Ah Will,' he said, placing his arm around my shoulder. 'It was the best of days when you came to us, but it won't come to that. Indeed, I do believe such a journey is the answer to all my present woes. Abroad, I may well be able to overcome my disappointment much more quickly and besides I'm reminded of Tom Morley and his travels. He always returns with his pockets full.'

'But *Rome*, John. Why so far?' Merely crossing the Channel was too far for me and the mention of Tom Morley sent a shiver of anxiety across the back of my neck.

'It is indeed a long way,' he said, 'but I have been thinking. If Her Majesty desires the Italian style, then I must be at least as able, if not better, than the best and most famous Italian composer alive, don't you think?' He didn't wait for my reply. 'Master Marenzio is that man, and he is in Rome. I will write to him. My understanding is that he is not young, so it's best we don't leave it too long.' He sighed then whilst biting on his lower lip. 'Ah well. I'd better go and tell Jane. Wish me luck.'

'Luck?' I raised my eyebrows. 'You may not need it. Have you thought that maybe your wife would be pleased to have some peace and quiet for a while?'

'Really?' He was taken aback. 'Do you think so?'

'Go on,' I said. 'They will all miss you. As would I, if only I could remain.'

Now, looking down at the half-made instrument in front of us, we both sighed. I was keen to finish it. The separate pieces lay on the bench ready and waiting: the rest of the reinforcing parchment strips all in a neat row, the fingerboard – I must say the mother of pearl inlay worked very well in the end – and the pegs were worth the carving too. John wanted it made, but it wasn't only the look of it for him. He could go beyond my thinking into another world of melody and sweet voices singing along with this fine instrument. They would all have to wait.

'Will it take a long time to finish?' he asked.

'Another week or two at least, and even longer if the weather stays damp. I can pack it away though. It won't come to any harm as it is.'

'Thank you, Will. I rely on you more than I should.' He gave the inlay a quick stroke. 'That's very fine.'

'Yes,' I nodded. 'I'm pleased with it.'

He was already whistling a new tune as he went to the door.

After the initial flurry of haste, John had calmed, recognising that a trip of such distance required more than a box quickly packed. Safe passage was necessary, and it was a while before an invitation was received from the Duke of Brunswick. Permission for John to travel to the Continent then had to be sought from at least two members of the Privy Council.

Yes, a further delay, but it was enough time for me to finish the new lute. John was pleased, as all it took was a strum and a verse before he gave the belly a tender stroke, kissed the fingerboard and announced we were to take it with us. Hardly played before it was to endure all manner of violence on a long journey. I prayed to be forgiven my pride as I laid it in its case amongst the folds of velvet cloth.

The wind rose in the night before we were due to leave, and when at first light I looked out, the shutter was wrested from my hand and flung back against the wall with a bang. My stomach turned at the thought of being on the sea.

Molly was already up and preparing breakfast when I got downstairs.

'I've packed you both bread and pie,' she said, pointing to a cloth-wrapped bundle. 'I thought it might be a while before you get some proper food in you.'

'That's a kind thought. Thank you, Molly.' I picked it up and wondered where I could stow such a weighty item. 'I'll save mine for once we're in Flanders as I've a feeling my stomach won't be my own until then.'

She gave me a sympathetic smile. 'I'm sorry you're going.'

It was said so earnestly, I was surprised. Like me, Molly had been taken into the household as a child, but for a long while I thought she resented John's mother favouring me like a son. It took some years before she would smile or speak to me unbidden.

'I am sorry too,' I said. 'But I've promised old Mistress Dowland that I will bring John home safely, and that I will do, even if I have to lay down my own life.'

We were all still at breakfast when a knock came at the front door and Thomas Morley was shown in. He had no instrument with him so I imagined it would be a short farewell visit, but he said yes to a beaker of ale. Then, when he and John went into the parlour and closed the door, I didn't know what to think. I wasn't usually shut out.

I couldn't quite warm to Tom Morley. Perhaps it was

the way his gaze roved elsewhere when he spoke to me. I wasn't singled out in that respect as he did the same to everyone, but that didn't stop my suspicions about him.

The squat figure of Sir Robert Cecil came into my mind. He looked upon Tom most favourably. No doubt he appreciated his music, but even more he appreciated how Tom kept his eyes and ears open when he went abroad. Every plot or treasonous act, whether deed or whimsy, was of interest to Sir Robert, and he was known to encourage travelling musicians to report back directly to him. The very notion that John could be drawn into some dangerous spying chilled me to the bone, so I hovered in the hall, hopeful that I might hear some of their conversation. They spoke too quietly though, and I soon went away, not wanting to be discovered with my ear pressed to the door.

Later, once the porter had arrived with a cart for our travel boxes, I said goodbye to my workshop, checking the tools were clean and giving the floor one last sweep. Both were merely soothing tasks to quell my worries about the weeks and months to come. Eventually, John came to find me, took the broom from my hand, propped it in the corner and shoed me out of the door.

'Come along, Will. It'll still be here when you come back. We're all sad to leave this morning, but now we must look to the future.'

When we were all assembled, I bowed to old Mistress Dowland, but she grasped me by the arm and drew me close, so I quietly reiterated my promise that she should have no fear for I would keep her son safe. My heart was not so confident. He would be a difficult man to contain if a fancy took him elsewhere.

John then kissed his mother and the baby and we said farewell to Molly. I'd no doubt it would be a tearful young Robert that Jane took back to the house, but he was allowed to accompany her down to the quay.

We often had a sunlit flash of water between houses, but when the great Thames opened up before us, and I saw how the wind was whipping up the water into frothy waves, I felt more than a little queasy. It whistled through the arches under the bridge and set even the big ships tethered at the quayside creaking and straining on their ropes. No wonder the oarsmen were directing passengers to cross by foot.

Our ship, the *Christopher*, looked sturdy. It was still being loaded when we arrived at the dock, and we stood back as large bolts of cloth were stowed away below deck. I was quite taken with the ease with which the men hoisted them aboard, and it came to me that the captain and sailors were similarly skilled in their work and knew the ways of the weather and sea as well as I knew the crafting of a lute. The nerves that curdled in my stomach eased then, for it would be in nobody's interest to endanger a ship and all its valuable cargo.

Whilst John bade his wife a sorrowful farewell, I kept Robert distracted with promises that I would tell him all about climbing over mountains and our adventures in far-away lands. Then it was time for us to set sail. Gradually the strip of water between ship and land grew wider and Jane and Robert became small as toys. With a lump in my throat, I turned my gaze away and watched as the great walls of the Tower slipped by. By the time we reached Greenwich the sails were trying to escape their rigging and once out on the open sea, there was so much going up and down I could only lie groaning, whilst John sat by me, enjoying not only his portion of Molly's pie but mine as well.

CHAPTER TWO

I'd imagined that such was our haste to get to Rome, we would only stay a short while at the Duke of Brunswick's castle at Wolfenbüttel, but his generosity persuaded us to remain. One evening, John returned to our lodgings triumphant.

'Prepare yourself, Will,' he said, removing his cloak with a flourish. 'Fortune has favoured me with gifts.

'Good Lord.' I gasped at the sight of a hefty gold chain around his neck glinting in the lamplight.

'And these,' he said, loosening the leather pouch at his belt and tipping out a great number of gold coins onto the bed.

Words wouldn't come to me.

'*And*,' he said, laughing at my amazement.

'You mean there's more?' I could barely croak.

'Indeed there is, but I thought it best if I left it there.'

'What? And yet you walk through the streets with all this?' I swept my hand over the treasure.

'Mmm,' he said, stroking his chin. 'Perhaps it was rather rash, but I was so looking forward to seeing your face when you saw it.'

'What did you leave behind?'

He sat down whilst easing the chain over his head, letting it fall so it nestled in a bright heap.

'It was a goodly length of the best velvet, enough for a new doublet and—'

Distracted by the coins, he began to count.

'And?' I almost squeaked, being quite lost for what to say next.

'Twenty-six, twenty-seven! Oh yes, and another length of satin for lining and gold lace for trim. You'll hardly know me, Will, I'll look so fine. It's a wonderful colour too, blue as the sea on a sunny day.'

So, of course, we stayed. There weren't many sunny days left that year and an invitation from Maurice, the

Landgrave at Kassel, reaped similar rewards. Eventually a parcel was made, and a tall gilt cup, ring and gold chain were sent back home, as possessing such expensive items when travelling seemed foolhardy. We kept the money, and nothing would part John from his new doublet. If there were to be more performances in palaces, I agreed it was a good idea to take it with us. That he might refrain from parading it quite so much like a peacock, I did not say.

In truth, I looked forward to Italy with a particular eagerness. John was well-liked in every town and city along the way. We stayed in many great houses, palaces and castles, as well as the more usual lodging houses, each with its own style of comfort and welcome. I learnt that every country has its charms, whether it be the landscape, the customs or the victuals, and I counted myself lucky to have been to them all.

But Italy? The merest mention would see a faraway look and a slight smile on the faces of those present, even when a complaint or difficulty was the subject of conversation. Oh, but the food, would be the end of it. Or the wine, or the beautiful women, cities, country. The art was sublime, the music heaven sent and such elegance! All would finish with a little sigh. And this was while we were still in Bavaria.

Our time in Brunswick and Hesse had been mostly cold and with an east wind that bit into every patch of bare skin. Once we're over the big mountains, it'll be warm, I'd thought, perhaps even hot. We were to stay first in Venice. A beautiful city built on water sounded like the stuff of stories, but I was assured it was true.

It *was* warmer, and my doubts about the city being built on water were quite unfounded. Venice was far more beautiful than I could possibly have imagined. I'd also never seen rain like it. We stayed a week, and it poured in grey sheets the entire time we were there. Every small journey brought the misery of sodden boots and clothes and although I would like to have seen more of the city, we were confined indoors for most of the time. When we left the misery of the Venetian rain soon faded, and instead the city shimmered in my memory as if it were made of the water upon which it stood.

John was building his reputation with every note played and there was always much excitement when he arrived in a new town. Often, we travelled by coach rather than hiring horses. Not that a coach was always preferable. After only a mile or two with a family whose four children did nothing but bicker and strike each other, I regretted the fare. John began to resemble a caged beast.

'I cannot go another minute with them,' he said, when we stopped at the next inn. He was already pink from the effort of holding back his irritation.

My enquiry about horses established that there were none available until the next day which I thought might irritate him further, but I found him outside dozing on a grassy bank and suddenly, the chance of resting awhile on something that wasn't tipping us this way and that, seemed very attractive

The bank was clad with flowers I'd never seen before, and those I did know seemed to be richer in colour than the London variety. Far above us, larks sang, but the sky was too bright to see them and although I shielded my eyes, when I looked back down, everything took on a yellow hue. We dozed until slow clopping hooves and the creak of wheels interrupted the chatter of swooping martins and our peace and quiet.

Leaving John with our belongings I went to find out if the waggoner could take us and our boxes. He looked at me so suspiciously that I laughed. The coin I offered was well received but as I fetched our belongings and loaded them up, I realised why. Any payment would have been too much, for the wagon was ill-made and the mule's friskier days were long gone. John took one look and decided to walk. I worried about the instruments being so jolted about, but it was a pleasure to walk unencumbered.

Not an hour passed before we both had doublets slung over our shoulders. We wore our caps too as the sun burned and the country about was very flat with no shade. John's cap seemed to enhance his features, but mine had never sat well on my stiff, upright hair and in such heat, I felt the irritation of it keenly. A sip or two from the flagons of ale we'd bought at the inn was always welcome, although we never stopped for long. Ferrara beckoned, and John was twitching with anticipation.

'It's quite a place, Will.' John said, whilst kicking a pebble from one side of the road to the other. 'To play at the Duke Alfonso's court will certainly mean higher respect wherever we go in the future.'

'And higher pay, I hope.'

In London, I could make my own money, and this journey meant not only that I was reliant on John, but we were both at the mercy of our hosts. If music was esteemed, all well and good. The Duke and the Landgrave had certainly paid handsomely but I was very glad it wasn't all gold chains and apparel. Money has far broader uses.

We entered a grove of grey-leaved olive trees where the way ahead was lined with lavender and little white flowers I didn't know the name of, but whose perfume stuck sweetly in the nostrils. Contentment soon began to settle over me. The ale I'd consumed, however, soon had another effect, so I paused to empty my bladder by the side of the road where the grasses grew quite densely to waist height. I was readying myself to re-join the others when, out of the corner of my eye, I saw something glint and thinking it may be of value, I bent down and reached towards it.

I blame the ale, but that's what I did, and next thing, pain shot through my hand as if I'd plunged it in fire. In my life, I've been nipped by a dog and stung by a hornet, which was very bad, but never had I been bitten by a snake. A hundred times worse.

'Help!' I yelled, pulling my jerkin roughly into place as the snake slithered speedily away. 'I've been bitten! Dear God have mercy!' In ten strides I'd said as many prayers. 'John...I'm a dead man!'

He threw away his stick and ran over. 'You look very much alive to me, Will,' he peered at the twin wounds. 'But best you keep praying, I reckon? Hey! Come and look at this.'

The waggoner turned his head but made no move, so I stumbled to him. Already it was throbbing.

He gestured for us both to get back on and we set off. I remember the frown of worry on John's face and thinking that it was our speed of travel making the wagon so rickety and the world all up and down. As I watched, it seemed my hand grew twice the size and sported any number of fingers. I blinked, trying to see clearly, but what with the jolting, every rock and rut we hit encouraged the flames in my hand, and before long they began creeping up my arm.

What a hot country Italy is, I thought.

So very hot...

...and how the night comes on at such a pace.

CHAPTER THREE

'Are you back with us, Will?' John loomed over me, concern knitting his brow.

A sharp stabbing pain when I moved my right hand reminded me. He laughed out loud when I croaked that I thought so but didn't know where.

Out of my sight, a girl spoke. 'Ferrara,' she said, wrapping the name of the city around her tongue with an arpeggio as good as any John might play. *Ferr-ar-a*.

The world began to swim away from me again. *Ferr-ar-a*. It sounded like a long sigh.

It may have been the same day, or several after, when I came back to my senses. This time it was a melody, hummed in an easy pattern that roused me. I felt nothing like my usual self and determined that someone had brushed my lashes with glue, but I willed my eyes to open so I could see the source of such a sweet song.

Except she was sitting at a small writing desk and turned away from me, so all I saw, before the world grew dark again, was a cap edged with red and black stitching and a long plait of hair the colour of polished ebony.

When I next awoke, a blade of moonlight sliced the room in two. My hand felt better when I flexed it, but not yet fully recovered. The door was ajar and as I lay listening to the noises of the night it seemed to me that music was coming from all quarters. Singing of every kind, the playing of instruments, whistles and drums, as well as the more commonplace shouts and laughter that accompany food, wine and company. John was no doubt seducing some and making enemies of others.

Standing came with a great wave of dizziness so, like a wary fledgling, I perched on the edge of the bed. When the door opened with a great crash, I reached for the nearest thing with which to protect myself.

'Goodness, Will,' said John, holding the lantern high enough to light us both. 'I do hope you're not going to throw that. It'll do terrible things to my doublet and it's the blue velvet from Brunswick, my favourite.'

I placed the pot back under the bed.

'So,' he held the lantern close. 'Are you better now?'

We both inspected my hand. It was the right size once more although inflamed around the wound.

'I think I'll live.'

'Excellent. That's exactly what I hoped you'd say.'

'Oh?' A warning bell was ringing. I knew that tone of voice well. Warm and persuasive, making light of a problem that was about to fall upon my shoulders.

'It's only that—' he began, stopped, then began again. 'It's only that there's a small errand that I thought you might like to do for me. A very small errand. Tiny really.'

'I'm not that well.'

'No?' he said, putting down the lamp and handing me a beaker of wine secreted in his other hand. 'Here, this will revive you.'

I took a little sip and coughed feebly.

'Now, now,' he said. 'I can tell a sorry excuse when I see one. What you need to do is get up and explore.' Saying this, he first sat down, then lay across the bed so there was little room for me. 'You'll feel much better standing upright, and besides, Ferrara is a wonderful place. They adore musicians here and they love me already, so you have absolutely no need to worry about anything.'

I eased myself upright, this time holding on to the nearby chair.

'So,' I grunted. 'What is this errand?'

John moved into the space I left, put his hands behind his head and made himself comfortable. There was only one narrow bed in this attic space, but I didn't ask where he had slept. I'd probably find out soon enough.

But then, an idea came to me that the girl with the honey voice may feature in the story of his recent nights, a thought I found altogether vexing. The sound of her singing, that little tune lightly hummed, it was only three or four notes repeated and I could hear it clearly. With it came a strong desire on my part not only to hear her sing again, but to see her face. Could John really have seduced her so soon? Surely not, but—'

'Have you heard anything I've just said?' Startled, I looked up to see John searching my face, as if a great pustule had sprouted there. 'Well? Have you?'

I sat down again, so that he had to move his feet.

The following day, I felt much better and well enough to leave. Apparently, it had been thanks to Her Grace, the wife of our illustrious host, Duke Alphonso, that I had been put to recover in the castle. A kind woman who, by God's mercy, heard our less than orderly arrival – two foreigners in a wagon at the gate, both raving, one with fever and one with worry. The waggoner had satisfied the guard we were neither mad nor contagious, and our letters from London and Brunswick were proof enough to warrant attention. I have no memory of our arrival or, as it transpires, John sleeping on the floor.

'I could hardly leave you by yourself,' he said, as he led me down several flights of stone stairs and along a warren of passages. 'Supposing you'd died in the night? Can you imagine?'

'No,' I said, 'I can't and don't want to, but thank you anyway.'

All my wonder at the immense castle, with its neat stonework covered with patterns and pictures, the business of building work going on with its clatters and bangs mixed up with music and singing, it all receded far away as my own mortality fingered the back of my neck.

'Besides,' he said, 'Molly would never forgive me.'

'What?'

'Ha!' He was pleased with how much he'd startled me. *Molly?* I hadn't given her a thought since we'd left London. I was about to draw him out further when he said. 'Or mother, for that matter.'

And then, of course he was sad. We both were, and I forgot my recent step towards the afterlife as I remembered old Mistress Dowland, her chin quivering as she tried, but failed, not to shed a tear when we left.

A pang of fondness for my workshop struck me then too, the dry, planed wood stacked off the floor, bench cleared, tools cleaned and hung up in a row, and John's remark that the chisels in such a descending order of length, could almost be a musical instrument without any effort on my part. I'd offered to make him a pair of sticks to hit them with if he had in mind to forsake the lute.

'What do you mean Molly wouldn't forgive me?'

The stairwell turned at this point, and John, two steps in front could see around the corner. Whoever was there suddenly demanded his full attention and I nearly fell into him as he stopped, removed his cap, and bowed low.

'*Buongiorno*, Signorina Sofia.'

And there she was, looking straight at me while I was trying to recover my balance. Prettier even than I thought she'd be, with peach-soft dimpled cheeks and dark eyes sparkly as a good gem. The same quiet giggle that I'd heard before came from her lips, and here was I, with another girl's name on mine. My face burned with heat enough to toast a bun. With luck Molly wasn't a name common in Italy, and besides, I comforted myself, she wouldn't have understood.

'B...b...bongig,' I spluttered, pulling myself upright.

'Ah,' she said. 'The patient is better.'

'Oh!' In my amazement at hearing English, even with such a strange lilt, I had stumbled again.

John put his arm around my shoulders. 'Now now, Will. You wouldn't want this charming young lady to think you're missing a few strings. Let me introduce you to the mistress of our tongue, Signorina Sofia Biscaldi.' He gestured politely from me to her and back to me. 'Signorina, may I present William Totman Esquire, of London, England.'

I'm not a man of many words ordinarily, so following John's example I took off my cap and bowed very low.

'Your servant,' I began well enough, but then curiosity and amazement overtook me, and out of my mouth burst: 'You speak English?'

Then they both laughed. Sofia shyly behind her hand and John guffawing like a donkey. I was sorry that I had yet to remove my sickbed stubble.

'I do,' she said. 'Not so well as I'd like, but enough.'

That was a lot to comprehend, especially for me, who struggled often enough in my native tongue.

'Sofia is an extraordinary girl altogether,' John said, with a familiar gleam in his eye so that a second flush made me cold all over, rather than hot. 'The mistress of a musical instrument and a fine copyist's hand as well as many languages.'

Then I noticed that in her hand, somewhat hidden by her skirts, was a lute. She held it out.

'No, no,' she dismissed John's words. 'I know where the notes may be found, but they do not sing for me. I have this because I have been sent by my father. The Duke was keen to see our latest instruments and this one was left behind this morning.'

I was mystified by this, but it was clear that hurry was required, and with a nod and farewell, she brushed past, skipping up the stairs behind us. I couldn't help turning my head and was rewarded with the glimpse of an ankle beneath a froth of pale blue.

'Close your mouth, Will,' murmured John, as she disappeared round a corner. 'Or start singing, else you look a fool,'

'*Fa la la*,' I muttered. 'So, who is she?'

'I told you, Sofia Biscaldi.'

'And? Is that it? Does Ferrara educate all its women in such a manner?'

'Ha! Where would we be if that were true. Come, I have found us good lodgings, and that's where I'll introduce you to her father. He'll be pleased to meet you.'

I didn't press him, as everything I heard seemed to confuse me further. I wondered whether the snake's venom still ran in my veins and contributed to my muddle, but then in my mind's eye, Sofia Biscaldi's pretty face appeared, and I decided if that was due to poison then I'd gladly drink a full goblet.

A visit to the barber by the castle gate resulted in a new look for both of us. I wasn't sorry when most of the bushy beard I'd accrued fell to the floor, as the heat once we had stepped outside struck us with great force.

Our lodgings were above a glovemaker's shop in a room heavy with the smell of leather, and so close to the castle that one of its four great towers loomed above us. When I opened the casement, the air that came in was warm and sweetly scented. A small lemon tree grew directly out of the adjoining wall with the neighbouring property, and it appeared to be both in flower and fruit. Italy was surprising me at every turn. I flexed my hand and remembered that some surprises were not so pleasant.

'Signor Biscaldi has gone out.' John announced when he came back from settling the advance with our landlord. I didn't know whether to be disappointed or relieved.

'Why would anyone be pleased to meet me?'

He glanced at me and nodded. 'Hmm, yes, it does seem unlikely.' But then I received a slap on the back. 'I jest, Will. Well, in part. Your new face is going to take me some getting used to, but Signor Biscaldi will assume you always look like that. He's interested in what you do, rather than who you are, and that's because I showed him your latest lute.'

'Oh?' I was always keen to meet someone who appreciated my work.

'He was very impressed.'

Is there anyone who does not glow inside on receipt of a compliment? That it should come from the father of the lovely Miss Sofia was doubly pleasing, although he might not be quite so impressed if he knew the same man also had an eye for his daughter.

Signor Biscaldi's absence meant the afternoon lay before us. John was already tuning up the lute in question, which would leave me with time on my hands.

'That errand—' I began.

'Ah yes. Are you off to it now?'

I was very hesitant. John humming and looking at the ceiling was a sure sign there was something he wasn't telling me.

'It isn't like you, John,' I'd said.

'Isn't it?'

Of course, what I'd meant was that it wasn't like him to spy on a *man*. Especially not royalty.

I asked him again.

'So, why are you interested in this Prince Ges...Ges—'

'Gesualdo. Prince of Venosa.'

'Yes,' I said, levelly. 'Him.'

'No particular reason. I've heard he's rather eccentric that's all,' he paused, as if unsure what to say, before deciding on, 'not the sort of person to upset.'

Ah, I thought, swift to rage and easy with a weapon. Further questioning would be in my interest.

'Is he married?'

'Yes. Quite recently, I believe, or was it last year—'

I interrupted, recognising the sort of musing could lead him away from the matter in hand. 'So, who is the unfortunate lady?'

'Mmm? Oh her? She's not the unfortunate one, it was his first wife he murdered.'

'What? You want me to spy on a *murderer*?' I took a step back and swallowed hard but he waved away my horror as if it were a speck. 'Oh, don't worry about that, his wife is Duke Alphonso's sister-in-law, so I don't think there'll be any murdering going on while he's here in Ferrara.' He began strumming the lute for tuning, then added. 'Leonora is her name, the present wife.'

Lord, have mercy, I thought. That John could consider wooing our gracious hostess's sister was surely madness. And could the lady in question really be silly and imprudent enough to cast even the quickest of glances at John when she was married to someone who had murdered her predecessor? One snake nearly killed me, and now here we were in the middle of a nest of men far more dangerous than vipers. An icy chill raised the hairs on the back of my neck.

I must have looked quite comically aghast, for John couldn't suppress a smile.

'I'm playing with you, Will, for I have not the slightest interest in the Lady Leonora.' He took on that familiar aggrieved expression. 'How could you even think that?'

I looked for something to do whilst trying to remain calm, so began untying the fastenings on one of our boxes.

'My interest in Prince Gesualdo,' he went on, 'has nothing to do with a woman, I solemnly swear.'

Relief flooded through me. There was only one other subject that exercised John Dowland's sensitivities, and mortal danger wasn't usually one of its components.

'I hear,' he went on, in his most portentous, nose-in-the-air manner, 'I hear that he has been known to be *very* unpleasant about his fellow musicians.'

'I see.'

'No, I don't think you do see, Will. The thing is, he can be *most undeservedly* rude and unpleasant about his fellow musicians.'

'Ah.'

Then I remembered John's own rude remarks about Gregorio Howet's playing when we had been in Kassel and the subsequent row that threatened. It was fortunate for us that Maurice, the Landgrave, had been so tactful, and I was about to say so when we were interrupted by a knock and the landlord's voice.

'Signor Biscaldi is downstairs.'

'Excellent,' John replied. 'Tell him we'll be down directly. Come along, Will.'

Now, there is no question that the Dowlands are a kind and generous family and have never made me feel the worse for the poor orphan state I was in when they first adopted me. Outside of the Cheapside house it was a different matter. I was not his equal. On all our journeys together, I was his servant, and whenever it was necessary, I became an errand boy once again. This wasn't something that ever needed explaining to me. Indeed, there would have been more difficulty explaining had our manner been otherwise.

A whisper of apprehension accompanied me as we went downstairs. Yes, I wanted to impress Signor Biscaldi, and not only for my lute-making skills, but I was intrigued too. What sort of man fathered such a pretty girl, and then had her educated to speak so many languages? I was certainly taken with her ability to speak so freely to *me*, but really, was it wise? It was all very well for Her Majesty, and the young ladies at court whose expectations lay abroad, but what husband would want his wife able to converse with those he couldn't? I found that a conundrum. Most men would wish to keep her from ever leaving the house.

CHAPTER FOUR

Signor Biscaldi was a well-fed man with a face familiar with smiling, and, although my knowledge about such things was scant, his features and garb led me to believe he was a Jew. Surprise and confusion shot through me as I had not had any thought of race or religion about Miss Sofia.

We were greeted warmly with shakes of our hands and beckoning to us to follow, Signor Biscaldi picked up a case, the like of which would normally hold a lute, and with many smiles, nods and gestures, led us to a small wine cellar, opposite our lodging. Once we were sitting in the courtyard behind the street, he ordered a generous flagon of wine. I was very glad to be shaded from the hot sun by a vine growing over a wooden scaffold. The ruby grapes were already hanging in hefty bunches and were altogether something of a marvel. I had seen vines in London but never had they produced the like. I was tempted to help one from its companions, but Signor Biscaldi shook his head.

'No, no,' he said, pulling a face. 'Not for eating.'

I was warned off and drew my hand back quickly. Instead, we all gave due appreciation to the wine, after which Signor Biscaldi clasped his hands together and earnestly nodded in my direction.

'I need help, Signor Totman.'

I was taken aback. 'Certainly, sir. If I can help, I will.'

He picked up the case and gave it a pat.

'Fine musical instruments. We have little shop in Florence.' He nodded to himself. 'Actually, not so little. There is nice big room upstairs where people play instruments before they choose. But travelling to buy and sell is happy pastime for us both. Sofia, that is. My wife, she die many years ago, and I not want to leave my only child.' He smiled at the thought of her. 'What skill she has! All those languages!'

'Remarkable,' I murmured, thinking of how her dark eyes shone, and the soft skin of her—

'Please,' he said, 'look.' The case was thrust upon my knee but even before I opened it, I could see there would be a problem. I hadn't noticed before, but one corner had been badly damaged. Dropped from the roof of a coach probably or else hit with something substantial.

'We bought from *Tieffenbrucker's* in Venice. They are very good makers of course, but is not one of theirs, it is even more special.'

When I lifted the lid, with difficulty because the hinges were badly bent, I couldn't help but groan. A broken neck is nearly always fatal.

Signor Biscaldi leant forward to look. 'Can anything be done?'

'Will's your man,' said John, after he too had peered at the problem. 'That's if anyone can mend it. Did I not show you the quality of his workmanship?'

I looked closer and realised that the neck itself was unharmed, but it had become detached at the nut, and the release of tension in the strings had pulled the head and pegs completely askew. Luckily, the body and soundboard had escaped harm, and the intricately carved rose was intact. Catching the rose in a bright shaft of sunlight, I could just see a name below the hole, neatly inked across the parchment strips: *Maler*. That didn't surprise me. *Maler of Bologna* was famous across the Continent. Was it made by the father or the son? Ah there! I caught sight of the letter X. Laux Maler, the father, it must be and a costly instrument without doubt. It was an honour to hold it in my hands.

If I'd been at home, the repair would not present a problem. I did have some small tools with me, but there was no question that clamping would be required at least for a day. That's if I could find a glue pot and clamp for the purpose.

'Perhaps we could ask at the castle,' I said. 'If the Duke has as many instruments as we're told, he will surely have some means of keeping them in good repair.'

'Ah yes,' Signor Biscaldi sighed. 'There is excellent workshop for all instruments there, but this is for Duke Alfonso, and well...I not want to upset him, as I sure you understand.' And then he said as an afterthought. 'If only it were not for Lady Anna.'

John was quick to respond. 'Lady Anna?'

'You not know her?' He saw our blank faces and smiled. 'Ah, but you will very soon. The duke has many fine lady musicians. They play and sing every day – sometimes into the night. Lady Anna is one of special *Concerto di Donne*,' he went on. 'It is her birthday on Saturday, and this is gift from Duke Alfonso.'

Always keen to find out about fine ladies of any sort, I spied a familiar gleam in John's eyes.

'Do you know where I may acquire and heat some glue?' I said, before he could take a breath. 'It'll need clamping for a day at least?'

Signor Biscaldi shook his head. 'The castle is the best place, but I rather not—'

'There you are!' Miss Sofia appeared at the door, once again taking me unawares. My beaker clipped the edge of the table with a loud crack as I rose, but thankfully it did not break or spill. I tipped my head in greeting, whereas John bowed with his usual flamboyance. She nodded at each one of us in turn. Did her gaze remain very slightly longer on me? I believe it did.

'I see you have been looking at our little disaster,' she said. 'Do you think there is any hope?'

'I do believe so, Miss Sofia. We were just talking about where I may go to repair it, if not the castle.'

I gestured towards its high walls.

'Oh no, not there!' she said, clapping her hands together. 'You must take it to the palace.'

'Of course! Yes, my dear. That is a very good thought.'

'Duke Alfonso has a castle and a palace?' John said.

'Don Cesare, the Duke Alfonso's cousin lives there,' said Sofia. 'We should all go. The *Palazzo dei Diamante* is a marvel. There is no other building like it anywhere, is there, Papa?'

'No, and we have been many places.'

John was thinking much the same as me. 'The Duke and his cousin,' he asked, 'aren't they at odds with each other?'

At home, the Queen had a cousin who caused her all kinds of trouble.

'At odds?' Signor Biscaldi looked confused.

'Are they enemies?' said Sofia. 'No, not at all. I think they are sad for each other though.'

Sad seemed to me a strange word to use about anyone rich and powerful, and especially as my sense of the Italians I had seen so far was that they were quite noisy, and so excitable with their gestures that I couldn't tell if the next would be a blow.

'It is because the family will lose the castle and all of Ferrara to the Pope if,' Signor Biscaldi leant forward and lowered his voice, 'or *when,* Duke Alfonso dies. He has no heir.'

'And that's why,' Sofia continued, in the same hushed tone as her father, 'Leonora, the Duke's sister, married the strange Prince Gesualdo. His uncle is a Cardinal, and an alliance would keep Ferrara in the family.'

John and I both started at the name of Gesualdo, jogging the table and almost upsetting the flagon of wine.

Sofia continued the tale of the sad Duke and the probable loss of Ferrara. Perhaps the conversation reminded John of the travails in the English court. Her Majesty's life had been a long one, and I doubt she had a subject who hadn't wondered who would take her place when our sad day came. Whether those were his thoughts or not, I could see John getting restless, so I wasn't surprised when he slapped his knees and stood up.

'Forgive me. I must leave you. It has been a while since I practised for any length of time.' He wiggled his fingers, while I quickly swallowed the remainder of my warm wine.

'No, you stay, Will.' He pressed down on my shoulder. 'Perhaps you could arrange to accompany our good friends to this palace. To see about the lute's repair of course…and anything else, whilst you're there.'

Rain had washed the streets in the night, and only small puddles remained where the sun was yet to reach. There was a welcome freshness in the air, and I was a happy man walking alongside Sofia and her father. They were quite at ease. How different from London, where the few Jewish people that I knew kept very much to themselves, and even walking about in the city, as we were then, drew ridicule and abuse.

While the strange Prince Gesualdo was to be the subject of my errand for John, the broken lute provided an excellent excuse. It's not wise to approach strangers with nothing but curiosity lest you were assumed to be a spy. *Spy*. A sudden tightness in my chest took me by surprise as I remembered Tom Morley's visit before we left.

'You're looking very pensive, Mr Totman.'

My worry dissolved into nothing at the sound of her voice. 'A small thought of home, Miss Sofia, that's all.'

'Are you wishing you were there?'

'No indeed. Quite the opposite. London is a fine city, but— I hesitated as London crowded into my head, too complicated to describe.

'But?' Sofia smiled up at me.

'It is very busy.' I said, lost for any better words. Lord above, what a dunce I felt then, but Sofia brightened.

'How exciting!' she said. 'I hope to go one day. Papa, we must put it on our list.'

'I hope you do,' I said, rather too fervently.

It had been in my mind to gently interrogate my new friends about Prince Gesualdo, but when we came to the next corner a clear view of the *Palazzo dei Diamante* was revealed.

'Oh!' I stopped in amazement.

'There,' Sofia laughed. 'Did we not say it was a marvel?'

'Yes, but—' Again I was lost for words.

I had seen sights well beyond my imagination on our journey from England. Venice certainly, but there I didn't once feel warm or dry. Here in Ferrara, the sun shone. The façade of the *Palazzo dei Diamante* wasn't encrusted with diamonds, but I could see exactly why it should be so named. Close to, I realised that each piece of pink and white marble was hewn to a point creating a clever play of sun and shadow to trick the eye.

At the door, Signor Biscaldi asked for Count Fontanelli, and when I raised an eyebrow Sofia whispered.

'We've known him for a long time. He used to come to our shop when he was in Florence and is very learned about music and musicians. I think he would like to be among the best, but I'm not sure he is.' She sighed then, before adding, 'I can understand that.'

'It is the same for all of us who are close to the best,' I said. 'Sometimes I think I could be quite a good musician but for knowing John.'

It wasn't meant to be an entertaining remark, but father and daughter both found it very amusing.

Count Fontanelli looked surprised to find them both laughing but following our customary bows, he greeted Signor Biscaldi cordially enough. It only took a glance at me and the broken lute for him to understand the situation. He led us into a grand room painted with fine pastoral scenes which would have deserved attention had I not been alert to the company and the task. What I couldn't ignore was how the room was so strewn about with musical instruments. In the centre of the room stood a magnificent harpsichord all over decorated with gold and painted panels but propped up against the walls, laying at any angle on the chairs and even on the floor were lutes, viols, pipes, a shawm, and drums of various sizes. I was quite appalled that the instruments were treated so casually.

In the farthest corner two young ladies played a lively duet on flutes accompanied by another on a virginal. They sounded very competent to my ear, but when they finished the Count harangued them at some length so that they began again at a much faster speed. John always cautioned against speed at the expense of clarity and the conveyance of emotion, and indeed, I found the resulting flurry of so many quick notes baffling.

At a table by the window a copyist scratched out parts for an ensemble, and the Count paused to pick up his work as we passed by. Clearly, it was not well done as there was much pointing at blots and errors. There, there and there, the Count's finger jabbed the paper. The page was to be put aside and begun again. The young man flushed crimson, no doubt feeling the reprimand sting all the more for being in front of an audience. As the last in the party, I was singled out for a particularly sour stare. I was affronted and glared back but forgot all about it when the Count showed us the adjoining workshop. A much smaller room, in a similarly untidy state.

'All you need?' asked the Count.

'I believe so,' I said, 'but the lute will have to remain clamped until the morning.'

'We put my name on it,' the Count replied. 'Then no one touch it.' He pointed to a shelf where a bundle of unused quills lay next to an inkpot. 'Loreto has paper.'

I went for it at once and was regarded by the young man with the same sour expression. I had no idea why, but perhaps in his mind, I was in some way not only responsible for the blotting but also for stealing his valuable paper.

'There,' said the Count, once he had placed his signature on the note.

I bowed my thanks, and he strode to the door, but then, just as quickly, he came back and leant down to inspect the lute more closely. I looked at Sofia and Signor Biscaldi and we all held our breath. The front of the instrument was tipped towards the window, so that to see the name on the label would require either leaning right over or picking it up. I prayed he would do neither. News of an expensive *Maler* lute in the workshop would be of interest to most lutenists, and to Duke Alfonso in particular.

To my surprise and huge relief, he straightened up, slapped me on the back and spoke in rapid Italian to Sofia and Senor Biscaldi. I bowed very low as he left.

I thought he had been simply admiring the instrument but when I looked back up, Sofia and her father were staring at me with an identical expression of anguish.

'He thinks *you* made it!' whispered Sofia.

'No, surely not. I thought...' My mouth went dry.

Her father looked as if he might weep. 'I go to the castle and confess to the Duke,' he said, locking his fingers in prayer.

'But what about Count Fontanelli?' Sofia interrupted. 'He will think we have misled him. Shall I run and tell him the truth?'

On the bench Count Fontanelli's note fluttered, almost as if it heard us. I remembered him criticising the musicians and the copyist, and the thought of Sofia or her father being found at fault in any way—

'Wait,' I said. 'I have a suggestion.'

'Oh?' they said in unison.

With Count Fontanelli's compliment still loud and keenly felt, my own pride surfaced like a worm popping up from damp soil.

'It is a slight deceit, that is all, and of no consequence once the glue is set. The repair will be invisible. If anyone asks, we will say this *Maler* belongs to John. Everyone will believe that.'

For a little while both were silent and I did not press them, but then, after much chewing of her lip, Sofia nodded and her father's agreement followed soon after. Signor Biscaldi, however cast one more look of concern at the instrument. I knew what was in his mind.

'Don't worry,' I said.

He placed a hand on my shoulder. 'Thank you, but worry is something I live with all the time. If you ever meet a Jew who does not worry, send him to me.'

CHAPTER FIVE

Once alone, I took my time, glad to breathe in the scent of sawn wood and be with all the tools of my trade. I was tempted to put them in order, but instead pushed them to one side. My first task was to remove the strings from the pegs. Fortunately, the instrument only had six courses and as there was no need to untie them at the other end, I left them to dangle over the edge of the bench like strands of long hair. It was a miracle there were no deep scratches anywhere, and those on the surface would polish out without much effort. Having made my close examination, I lit a flame under the gluepot and looked about as the familiar stench cloyed in my nostrils.

As with any job that includes glue there's nothing to be done except wait for it to heat, so I allowed myself to dream a little. Sofia had taken her father's arm as they left, but she'd looked over her shoulder and given me such a smile that I'd felt my blood quicken and a strange weakness came over me, which took several deep breaths to right.

I told myself to be careful in front of John. I'd often seen him far away in his thoughts as if with a pleasing secret, and it was obvious for everyone to see. He would be delighted to learn I had a secret of my own, especially if it entailed such a hopeless cause as the fancy for a Jew. I resolved to thrust away such thoughts and bent to my task.

The neck repair went very smoothly, and when I stepped away at last, it was a relief to stretch and free the stiffness in my shoulders. Nobody would know the lute had come back from the dead, except perhaps Signor Maler. It's a pity that a man's neck did not mend so easily.

Out in the music room, all was quiet except for the copyist still scratching his paper. Before leaving, I thought to admire the golden harpsichord more closely, and spent several minutes marvelling at the workmanship, but when I reached out to lift the painted lid, the young man barked at me a warning not to touch. It was my turn to scowl, and I did so with as much scorn as I could muster.

I had been ready to leave, but instead I returned to the workshop. There lay the lute, and until the glue had properly set, in a very fragile state. I wished then that I had not been so hostile towards the copyist. To leave it so near to him, even with the note from Count Fontanelli, suddenly seemed rash and I resolved to remain until he had gone away.

It wasn't long before the workshop was put to rights, the tools oiled, cleaned and hung in their places. I even began whittling a clothes peg from a discarded piece of ash whilst the copyist scratched on. I checked the lute once again and it was whilst admiring the signature of Laux Maler that I had the notion that I could improve my own. In London, I had always felt that if a signature was legible, that would be enough, but now I realised that a beautiful lute required proper attention right down to that last detail.

Count Fontanelli's note only took up a small section of the blotted paper so I cut away a piece that was still plain. I had enough room to write *William Totman, Luthier,* five or six times and although the letters were uneven in first and second attempts, I did improve. The fifth and sixth attempts I decided to keep, as they would serve perfectly as labels in any future instruments I made.

It was while I had the scissors on the paper that Loreto came to return his inkwell and music copies to a shelf. My friendly goodnight was received with a nod and a look of suspicion as he glanced at the lute. Perhaps he thought me too pink-skinned, or too short, tall, or the colour of my hair was wrong. Maybe the style of beard wasn't appropriate for the likes of me. I was a foreigner, and for some people, that was enough cause for hostility. I counted Loreto, the copyist, amongst them.

After waiting a while in case he returned, I left the Count's note in an obvious position and made my way back to our lodgings, hoping John would be keen for us to seek out a good dinner. When I arrived, however, I knew immediately something was wrong. The landlord wasn't one for wringing hands and shaking his head without good reason. He indicated upstairs and I took them two at a time.

John was lying on his bed, curled up like a child and facing away from the door.

'What's happened, John? Are you hurt?'

All he could utter was a long shuddering sob. The room was gloomy, so I threw open the shutter and the sun fell full on his face. Groaning, he turned away, but I spotted the tears that streaked his cheeks and the handkerchief he held was clearly sodden. At least I couldn't see any wound or blood, so the hurt was of another kind.

'Tell me,' I said, sitting on the edge of his bed.

'There,' he said, feebly gesturing towards a small table. 'I've had word from home.'

Cold dread drenched me. The letter had acquired a collection of creases and stains on its journey, but they were outward only. The seal looked newly broken. That it contained bad news there was no doubt.

'May I?'

'Oh yes, you better had.' He sat up, grasping his legs and slowly lifting them over the side of the bed as if grief had thickened his blood to a paste. The effort took it out of him, and he bent forward, elbows on knees looking at the floor. 'I'll need you to help me, Will.'

My hands were trembling as I unfolded the letter and found Jane's signature beneath a crowd of small words. Not Jane then. Please not the children. Please not any of them.

My reading is not fluent, so stood in the sunlight and spoke the words under my breath.

My dear husband

I am sincere in hoping that this letter finds both you and William well. I have some unexpected news that I know you will find hard to bear.

Your dear beloved mother died yesterday, which was 15th May, from a sudden fever. She did not suffer unduly at the end, in fact, sleep took her, for which I am very glad. She was in a good mind most of the while despite the discomfort I know she felt in the preceding days.

I paused my reading and closed my eyes feeling the blow of sadness strike hard. I remembered my last day in London, her sorrow when I'd gone to say goodbye and my promise to bring John back home to her. Dear lady, even though she would never know it, under my breath I vowed to do so even more vehemently.

Just before I left, I'd bent down to stroke her aged terrier, whose tail could only twitch in response. Time was he wagged his tail the whole day long. It was that tail first caught my eye all those years ago, when the little puppy darted away and nearly got itself trampled. I was on the corner looking for a message to run so it was easy for me to grab it. A hoof knocked me though, and next thing I was gazing up at stars in the midday sky with a mighty pain in my head. There are some, mean-spirited and selfish, who'd have ignored me and stolen the dog home for dinner; that's what life up to that moment had taught me. John Dowland's mother was not like that. After giving me thruppence and a thank-you, she took me home to dinner and a comfortable bed. I sighed heavily and took up the letter again.

I am sure that she was knowing when her last breath was near as, two days before, she bade me fetch a clerk and the priest. It was written down that nothing in her life had given her such gladness as her fine son and, more lately, his family, especially as I ran the household so well.

Ah Jane, I wondered, did she really did say that? If not, it was true. Jane was a good wife and I wished John was as good a husband.

She also asked me to retain the servants, which I promised, although I may not tell them, as I don't want their work to slacken in any way. I have made all the necessary arrangements with the priest and your dear mother will be buried tomorrow. It is fortunate the plague has abated this year and we will be able to have proper service. Robert is sad as are we all, but he and the baby are in good health, although missing you, as am I.

Your loving wife.

Ps I am wearing the ring sent from Hessen. It is a little big for my fingers so have made it smaller with thread. I have thought that you may like to wear it, so will not ask the goldsmith to alter it for me. The Landgrave is a very generous man.

I refolded the paper and turned to John, who looked, with his face so hollow and long, like a man condemned.

'I shouldn't have come away,' he said.

'With all my heart I wish we had not.' I sat down beside him. 'But we could not have known what would happen and besides your mother gave her blessing to this journey.'

'But what am I to do now, Will?' He put his head in his hands and barely whispered. 'I fear I have not the slightest ability to stand.'

John taking to his bed with sorrow was nothing new. Sometimes he seemed to wake with it for no reason, it would last a day or several, then he'd be back to his normal self. It was no good trying to shake him out of it with jesting or berating him for sloth. Indeed, some of his best songs had come directly following such a bout. This heavy sorrow though, had good reason behind it, and the truth was, I felt it myself.

'If you think we should go home, but...' I hesitated, then let the word dangle.

He looked up. 'But what?'

'But nothing. I don't know what is for the best, John. If we do go home, it will not bring her back.'

'No.'

We sat in silence for a while, then John took up the letter again.

'Jane does say she didn't suffer.'

'Yes, I'm glad of that.'

'It was a while ago now.'

'Yes, indeed.'

He stood up suddenly and with such a jerk that I was almost tipped off the bed.

'Am I very wicked, Will?'

I was taken aback by that question. 'No,' I said. 'Of course not.'

He stared at me, face awash with anguish. 'Have I been the most selfish man alive?'

'No, no, not at all. Look at the letter again. You are a fine son. You gave your mother more gladness than anything. Go on, look.'

There was nothing else to say. Our situation could not be undone. I wish I had been there to pay my respects to a dear lady who'd saved me from a perilous future, but here we were, weeks away from home.

I could only think that a drop of wine would steady us both, so went to the wine merchant, after warning John not to do himself any hurt.

As I approached the door on my return, I heard Signor Biscaldi's voice. Yes, and there was Sofia too. Clearly, they had only just returned and not yet learned our news, as their faces were cheerful, and they greeted me with broad smiles.

'Good afternoon,' I said.

'Well, Mr Totman,' Sofia said. 'Did you complete the task to your satisfaction?'

'I did, Miss Sofia, but it remains to be seen whether the glue will hold.'

'When will you know?'

I was about to answer, when something behind me caught her eye, and with the slightest shake of her head, I was warned not to speak further. I turned to discover Loreto, the copyist from the palace coming directly towards us, now looking both smug and sour-faced.

Sofia took charge of the conversation, and as I was still holding the jug of wine, thought I might as well take it upstairs, but as I moved to go, my way was barred. He wasn't brash, but he was stubborn. Now it wasn't exactly threatening, but I do know a hostile gesture when I see one, and I stood up straighter. He was taller than me, but not so wide and I doubted whether holding a quill all day strengthened the arm as much as a wood saw.

'Wait,' Sofia said. 'He has come with a message. You have to go with him back to the palace.'

A chill came over me. 'Why? What's happened?' I could only think that some mishap had befallen the lute, or my subterfuge may have been discovered.

'Count Fontanelli wants to see you. That's all he knows. But it must be now.'

I held up the wine. 'I should deliver this first. We've received word from home that John's mother has died. He has taken it very hard.' I took a deep breath. 'In fact, it is a very sad day for us both.'

Sofia and her father were as shocked as anyone being told bad news about a distant stranger and exclaimed their sympathy. In the face of their kindness, my own upset suddenly became difficult to hide, and having the copyist standing too close only flummoxed me further. I was at a disadvantage in every sense.

Signor Biscaldi stepped forward and directed me to go to John at once. The couple of coins that flashed from his pocket would no doubt ease Loreto's wait as I did so. Perhaps a little wine in the meantime? I left them as they headed across the street.

John was in the exact same position that I had left him. Hunched over, elbows on knees, hands holding his head.

'Here,' I said, holding out a beaker of wine. 'It'll help.'

'Nothing can help,' he moaned, but with a sigh and slow stretch he reached out and took it from me.

Sometimes, when he's in a melancholy, I've been short with him, or tried to leaven his mood. The household got used to waiting for it to be over, when John became even more merry than ever, but here and now, having had such terrible news I only wished to share our sorrow together.

'I have to go,' I said.

He lifted his head and peered, as if seeing me through a fog. 'Go? Go where?'

'Count Fontanelli wishes to see me, and I have to go straight away.'

'Count who?'

'John,' I said, with a firmness in my voice that startled him. 'I might be in a fix. I don't know yet, but the Count thinks I made that broken lute, and I didn't disabuse him of the notion. Now he's sent a servant to fetch me, and I don't know if it's for good or ill.'

I think I saw a glimmer of sense cross his face, but then it became cloaked in shadow once again.

'I'm sure it's nothing.'

I felt my jaw clench. If ever I had wanted to give him a good shake it was then. Instead, I sat down opposite him.

'Listen,' I said. 'All our reputations may be at stake. Yours as well as mine.' Even then he merely shrugged. I tried again. 'Don't you see? Firstly, Count Fontanelli thought I made the lute and if he has since discovered that I did not, then it could be construed that I was committing a fraud,' I took a deep breath, 'and second, the fact that Signor Biscaldi agreed to the repair at all, rather than confess to Duke Alfonso that his present to Lady Anna was damaged, sullies his reputation. Don't forget his livelihood is here, whilst we're only passing through.' A chill ran down the back of my neck suddenly. 'Unless, that is, I am restrained here.'

John looked up then. 'Restrained?' he said, as if the word were foreign.

'Yes, restrained. It may be that I will have no choice in the matter,' I said. 'Do you understand?'

'Yes, yes, but that won't happen. Nobody ever thinks the worst about you, Will.' He took a long draught of the wine, then waved me away. 'Try not to be long.'

I waited for a moment or two, willing him to do or say something more. In London, his faith in me may have been reassuring, but here, where the customs and language were unknown, I felt nothing but apprehension. When I found Sofia and her father with Loreto, I could also see it on their faces. Loreto's, by contrast, looked almost amiable, if rather more flushed than usual. He also didn't appear to be in quite so much of a hurry, so I sat down.

'Now,' said Sofia. 'This is what we're going to do.'

'We?' I said, trying to contain the cough that threatened.

'Yes,' she said, with a slap of her small hand flat on the table. A gesture that clearly meant she would have no argument. Even in my anxious state, it almost made me smile.

'Papa must stay here,' she went on, 'and I will accompany you and Loreto. Count Fontanelli will look upon me kindly.' She said it with such a pretty lift of her eyebrows that I nodded, meek as a lamb.

Her father gave me a sterner look.

'I am not so happy leaving my daughter with you, but—' He shrugged as bells clanged across the city, then swallowed the last of his wine and stood up. 'I have business. Be good and be safe.'

I shall never forget that walk through Ferrara to the Diamond Palace. Loreto walked behind us, perhaps he thought I may try to abscond down one of the narrow passages that led off the main street. A laughable idea. I hadn't quite realised it, but an invisible tether had already secured me to Sofia, and I would always want to go where she led.

Count Fontanelli sat in the large music room listening to another gentleman playing the archlute, and with due respect, we waited at the door for the performance to finish. Loreto slouched away to I don't know where, no doubt unwilling to be found less than sober.

We stood and waited. And indeed, waited some more. I have known plenty of long renditions from John, but there is a beauty in his music that soothes the mind into forgetting the time that passes. It wasn't the case with this musician. Several times, Sofia and I shared a glance, and I soon sensed that she was shifting from foot to foot with increasing frequency. Perhaps it was the lack of melody? Or how the harmony twisted into knots? I decided it was just as well he didn't sing.

A discreet, and I'm sure unavoidable, cough from Sofia caught Fontanelli's attention, and he glanced over his shoulder. At the sight of us, he came over at once. My stomach felt as twisted at the lute player's notes. I hadn't been summoned by anyone since I was a lad, let alone an Italian Count.

Sofia curtsied, while I removed my cap and bowed with deep flourish worthy of John.

Count Fontanelli engaged Sofia in conversation, and he appeared in good temper. They spoke quietly together as the lutenist didn't seem to have any intention of stopping, but amidst the rhythm and melody of their speech, I caught a name, Gesualdo. As if by magic, the musician stopped playing and put down the archlute.

'Ah,' said Count Fontanelli. 'The Prince is ready.' He hastened back across the room, beckoning us to follow.

So, that was Prince Gesualdo and whilst I know it was sometimes a mistake to judge too quickly, I didn't like the look of him or the sound of his music.

'He said Prince Gesualdo wants to buy the lute,' Sofia murmured as we did as we were told. 'But that would make it very difficult for Papa. Be careful what you say. The Count may understand more English than he can speak, and the Prince even more than that.'

The worry in her voice clutched at my heart, and I realised what a foolish idea my subterfuge had been. Not that I blamed myself at that moment, instead laying it on the more illustrious shoulders of the Prince, who wished to buy an instrument before he'd even played a single note on it. What could be more reckless than that? I knew the lute looked good, but I was yet to discover whether the quality of the sound had been affected.

It was a curious thing to see the Count Fontanelli and Prince Gesualdo together. Whereas Fontanelli was a man of vigour, broad and with a healthy complexion, hearty voice and good teeth, Gesualdo, although taller, appeared weak and drained of colour, except for the dark purple-grey shadows that settled in the caverns of his face. I'd expected the usual look of disdain, well-practised by the rich and royal, but the glance from his limpid fisheyes was much more disturbing, and when it passed over me and settled on Sofia, my blood ran cold.

Can you tell a man from a glance? As a boy I could spot a generous soul at twenty paces. Such a one sees others like himself, notes the sky and flowers in bloom, laughs from his belly, and converses with ease. He tips well.

Men of meanness and cruelty are all opposite and Prince Gesualdo did everything to make me suppose he was of such character. His greeting barely stretched his thin lips, and there was a lack of rise and fall in his voice, the timbre jarring, much like an untuned course of strings. Mostly though, he scared me. I perceived that Count Fontanelli could menace, but this man was far worse. I thought of another type of man, far from predictable, violent and enraged for scarce reason. Fine instruments and music lay scattered on the floor. No sane man would treat them so. What exactly had John heard about Prince Gesualdo? Not only had he murdered his wife, but once she was dead, he had returned to the corpse to stab her several times more. I had to suppress a shudder.

Sofia's poise and calm responses to his questions filled me with admiration. After a short while, she turned to me.

'His Illustrious Highness Prince Gesualdo would like to...' she paused, looking at me intently, as if willing me to understand the meaning beneath her words. 'He would like to examine your lute with a view to making a purchase. He *trusts* you would be honoured.'

I bowed at once, placing my hand over my heart and looking I hoped, very honoured.

'I'm most grateful, honoured and humbled, that his Highness, the most illustrious Prince should be interested, but please inform him that the lute is not mine to sell.'

Sofia addressed him with all manner of proper titles because her explanation of my words seemed to take twice as long. All the while I held my breath. There were no exclamations of rage when she'd finished though. Instead, he cast another chilly glance in my direction and set off with stilt-like strides for the workshop door, where the lute lay clamped and silent.

We followed, the Count chatting amiably to Sofia, as if this was an ordinary day. In the far corner, another lutenist took the prince's exit as his cue to begin playing. A more cheerful tune would have suited me better, but he was not so knotty in his playing as the Prince Gesualdo.

I was glad to see not only was the lute still as I left it, but also with evening approaching the light in the room had considerably dimmed. Prince Gesualdo, however, was bending over to inspect it so closely that the end of his nose was only an inch from my repair. Was his sight poor? I prayed it was. Certainly, he seemed far more interested in the exterior rather than the interior, where Maler's signature could be found.

Sofia and I exchanged glances, and I think we were equally uncomfortable. What would he say? Would he take no for an answer?

I took to berating myself for being so foolish. Would the truth have been so bad? Yes, Signor Biscaldi would have lost face, but it wasn't as if the lute had gone up in flames. He could get a good price for it even with a repair.

Then I thought about Duke Alphonso. What did I know about the man? Nothing. He might well be furious to discover his present to the Lady Anna had been damaged, and it was in his power to reward or punish in whatever way he pleased. It was no surprise that Signor

Biscaldi was worried.

If Prince Gesualdo wanted something however, it was going to be impossible to refuse him. I felt hot. My clothes were made for an English summer, not the stifling heat of Italy. I glanced at Sofia, only to discover her gaze on me. We shared a brief smile, before she looked away, but with a lift of my heart I saw, and didn't merely fancy, that her cheeks became a little rosier. What a fine pair we were, standing like statues on a plinth. One slender and delicate with a blush in her cheeks, and the other solid and sweating.

A moment later Prince Gesualdo clapped his hands and announced that we were to meet again the following morning for the removal of the clamp. Then he and the Count returned to the music room. I winced, as the Prince began to play again but, when Sofia suggested that perhaps we might take a longer route back to the lodgings, I forgot all about lutes, princes, and anything else of worry.

'I thought you might like to see a little more of Ferrara,' Sofia said. 'It is very beautiful.'

I felt something squeeze my heart. Whatever the beauty of Ferrara, to my mind it would be nothing in comparison with Sofia Biscaldi. That she would actually *want* to be in my company…for a moment I felt like a king, and my chest swelled, but even as I agreed to such a pleasant proposition, I said to myself, you fool, William Totman, it won't be you she's interested in, she probably wants to practise her English.

Before we left, I checked the lute. It still sat in its clamp appearing perfectly well despite the close inspection. How Sofia and I were to escape from the palace was more of a problem. Should we wait for Prince Gesualdo to finish? Or walk purposefully out while he was playing? There were only half a dozen other people in the big room, but they were quite still and apparently paying attention to the unruly plethora of notes.

'Listen,' Sofia whispered, 'I will go first, then it will look as if you had no choice but to follow me.'

We were half-way across the room when the sound of a commotion came from the opposite door and then, to my horror, we heard raucous laughter and a familiar voice.

'Lord, have mercy! What a terrible row! It sounds like someone needs my help.'

CHAPTER SIX

The next moment he was there. John, with fingers in both ears, looking to see who was playing. Horror stuck my feet to the floor. It was an insult of dreadful proportions! Dear God, I prayed, please save all of us. For a moment I could only gawp. With his doublet only half hooked and his ruff askew he looked utterly disreputable.

'Ah,' he said, too bright about the eye and strolling towards us. 'There you are. How goes it? All well?'

I had seen this reckless behaviour of his before. Sometimes it would come upon him as if a key had been turned and unlocked this John from another room. The wine should not have been enough to inebriate him to such an extent, but poor Signor Biscaldi who scurried in after him, could only shake his head. No doubt he was mystified as well as alarmed by this change.

I tried to fix John with my fiercest glare, but he was as oblivious to my effort as he was to everyone else. They, however, had not ignored him, and a collective gasp gusted through the room. Those nearest doors scurried away.

All eyes turned to Prince Gesualdo. He'd stopped playing and sat as if he were made of stone rather than flesh and blood. Only his eyes, hooded and set deep, betrayed any sign of life, and I looked hastily away, lest the icy fire in them found my person.

Count Fontanelli was on his feet at once.

'Signor!'

If John heard, he made no sign of it. 'How's the lute, Will? Mended yet?'

The spell holding my feet was broken. Darting past Sofia, I grabbed his arm, and tried to steer him back towards the door. When he protested, I hissed in his ear. 'For God's sake, man,' I said. 'That's Prince Gesualdo you've just insulted! What were you thinking of? We must leave. *At once.*'

'Wait!'

With a strange high-pitched bark, Prince Gesualdo commanded the room. It would have been a miracle had we escaped. As he rose from his seat still holding the lute, the seconds stretched as if pulled on a rack. Once at his full height, Prince Gesualdo slowly surveyed the assembled company. I've no doubt we all trembled.

What he did next shocked me almost as much as John's outburst. I had seen fights aplenty in the streets of London, but the violence with which the prince then threw his archlute to the far side of the room drained my blood to my boots. It whined through the air and with a great clatter landed amongst a huddle of music stands, all of which tilted, toppled, then scattered in every direction across the polished floor.

Even John was cowed by the noise of this outlandish act and shrank beneath my grip. Once the resulting echo had ceased, a terrible moment of silence opened like a chasm, far deeper than the inbreath of an infant before a great wail. Prince Gesualdo's wail however, came sooner, much louder and with deadly venom.

I clutched John even tighter. 'We're dead men,' I murmured. 'Dead.'

But the Count, Signor Biscaldi and the brave and beautiful Miss Sofia were quick to act, and rushed to quell his rage, with many bows and fulsome apologetic explanations. Well, at least, I imagine that's what happened. It was Fontanelli who signalled us to leave at once, and without giving John any opportunity for further error, I hustled him away.

I took one last look over my shoulder and catching sight of Sofia's stricken face, I felt the pain of it like a blow. What a mess. What a dreadful, dreadful mess.

'I'm so sorry, Will. I'm so very sorry. Had I known—'

'Yes, yes. Too late for knowing anything now. We need to be away from here as soon as we've gathered our things.'

John, thank the dear Lord, was back to his more

equable self, and understood the urgency of our situation, but all the way along the darkening streets, I expected us to be apprehended. If not by the Prince Gesualdo or Duke Cesare's men, then by any number of ruffians that may have been lurking in the shadows, but in the event, trouble avoided these two grim-faced hurrying foreigners. As soon as we arrived at our lodgings we began frantically packing.

'Oh, damn this thing.' The latch on the box refused to shut. Irritated and weary, I sat down on my bed. Now, it came to me that we couldn't leave.

'John,' I said. 'We can't go rushing off like the naughty children. What about my promise to help Signor Biscaldi? And the lute I'm supposed to be repairing? I can't leave it like that. Both you and I have reputations to look after.'

John sighed and sat down beside me.

'Yes, and I'm supposed to be playing at the castle tonight.'

He picked up the letter from Jane and placed it inside his doublet.

'Don't forget,' I said, 'London is not a mere step away. If it's home we're going, it'll be as well to make something of a plan.'

'Yes, I suppose...' At a noise from outside, he stopped still as a startled rabbit. I could hear little but have always suspected his ears were sharper than mine. He leaned close. 'Hey ho, Will. I fear we may not have time for plans.' I cursed then, only under my breath, but John dug me in the ribs. 'Come on,' he said, straightening his ruff, and dusting himself down as he stood up. 'At least let's look presentable.'

I opened, then closed my mouth. It wasn't the time for a pert reply so all I could do was smooth my beard. The knock on the door was rapid, but light. John was nearest, so he had the good fortune to see Sofia first.

'Excuse me,' she said. 'I'm saving Papa from climbing the stairs. Would you come down?'

'Miss Sofia!' I blurted, unable to control my relief. As my fists unclenched, John glanced back at me, wiping imaginary sweat from his forehead.

'Have you saved our lives?' he asked.

Sofia cleared her throat. 'I hope so,' she said. In the gloom, her eyes were wide and shining but, I noticed as she looked at each of us in turn, without their usual laughter. 'It rather depends on what you both do next.'

At once, a more sombre mood settled round our shoulders.

'Then we'd best get to it,' said John, gesturing towards the stairs. 'Lead the way, Signorina.'

Downstairs, Signor Biscaldi waited by the front door, swatting a swarm of invisible fleas on his cuff. While not so obvious, my habit when feeling ill at ease was to grind my teeth, whereupon my jaw would ache quite badly. Already, I could feel it.

Not wanting our conversation to be overheard, Signor Biscaldi forsook the wine shop, and asked the landlord if we could sit in his courtyard. He was perfectly agreeable, and even went so far as to offer to fetch us some wine, which suited me very well. Ferrara seemed to me to have more than its share of biting insects, but they kept away from the lamps. It was a pleasure to sit out, even though we were preoccupied. I swear the scent of lemon trees could make drunkards of us with no wine at all. In the sky, the first stars were twinkling.

'So,' said John, keeping his voice low. 'Why am I still a free man?'

'Ah,' said Signor Biscaldi. 'We must thank my daughter. She persuade the prince very well.'

Sofia waved away his remark.

'No, Papa, it was really Count Fontanelli. But,' she went on, with a cautious glance at John. 'I did say, Mr Dowland, that you were not yourself since receiving unhappy news.'

She said it with such gentle sympathy that nobody could take exception, but John did not know I had revealed his mother's death to them, so I rushed to explain. He interrupted me after I'd only said two words.

'Of course. I am forever grateful to you, Signorina.'

He tilted his face to its best aspect and delivered one of his most attractive smiles. 'It does not surprise me that he succumbed to your charms.'

I bit down hard then, almost taking a lump out of my cheek. Sofia, bless her, took no notice.

'No, no,' she said. 'That was not it, although perhaps it helped. The Count was *much* more persuasive. He told Prince Gesualdo that you were a special guest of the Duke and Duchess and that they were *especially* looking forward to hearing such a famous musician play.'

Signor Biscaldi nodded vigorously at this and added. 'We also assure the Prince that you definitely *not* refer to his playing when you—' he paused, and I was glad he didn't repeat John's earlier insult. 'I not remember what you say exactly, but no matter. We just say, it *impossible*, for Prince play *equal* as well as Signor Dowland.'

'No, Papa,' Sofia said, firmly, almost like a teacher to an errant pupil. 'What we actually said was that the Prince played *even better*.' She shrugged. 'It's not true, as we all know, but...well, it was necessary.'

Poor John. I almost felt sorry for him as the pain of his playing even being compared to that of Prince Gesualdo darkened his expression. But after a deep breath, he managed a smile.

'Well then,' he said. 'I must get ready and let everyone at the castle decide which one of us is the best.'

'Wait.' Signor Biscaldi gestured for him to stay. 'There is more. Sofia, you tell.'

'Ah yes,' she said. 'There is a price to pay, of course, and Prince Gesualdo has decided that the price is to be our lute. It will replace the archlute that, he says, you broke.'

'What?' John slapped his chest. '*I* broke it? But—'

'As good as,' I interrupted. It wasn't the time to be indignant. 'Let's just be glad he didn't break all your fingers, or even your neck for that matter.'

'Oh yes.' He shrank at the thought. 'Yes, I suppose you're right.'

Sofia turned to me. 'You must have the lute ready for him to play as soon as possible. Tomorrow morning, he said, although the Count says it is rare for the Prince to rise before midday. Is that possible?'

'Yes, I can do that easily but—'

That was only the half of it. I didn't know what to say, but it was clear from their faces that Sofia and her father were trying to hide their distress. For them, the situation was now much worse. What could they possibly say to Duke Alfonso now? It had been promised for the next day, the appointment had been made, it was expected.

The night-time noises of Ferrara swirled around us: a dog howling, loud voices and laughter close by in the street, further away the beat of drums, a procession perhaps, or the practice for one, as the citizens were fond of marching about. Everything sounded ominous, and even more so when a nearby bell began tolling.

'I have it!' At John's sudden exclamation we all jumped. 'Don't worry, I know exactly what to do.'

'You do?' Signor Biscaldi squeaked. I thought for a moment that he might be taken with a bad turn. After all, he'd witnessed one of John's good ideas only an hour earlier.

'Don't worry,' said John, starting up from the table. 'You can trust me. Lady Anna, she will be there this evening?'

'Yes,' said Signor Biscaldi. 'It is certain.'

John smiled, more to himself us. 'Then everything will be well.'

'Are you sure?' I said, questioning his plan and his trust.

He opened his mouth as if to speak, hesitated and murmured to himself instead. 'Yes...no...yes. Then I can... hmm. Yes.' All the while he paced this way and that as we sat like children at their lessons, waiting to be told what to do.

'It's better if I don't say,' he eventually announced. 'Signor, if you would accompany me to the castle, I'm sure that by the end of the evening all will be well between Duke Alphonso and your good self.'

Had John invited Signor Biscaldi to his own funeral

he may well have assumed the same expression.

'But if I go,' he said, 'he will surely expect to see the lute.'

That was true. Even John looked vexed for a moment, but then he shrugged.

'A small lie will have to do. Tell him the strings were poor and it is being restrung. Indeed,' he turned to me, 'it is not even a lie, is it, Will?'

'I suppose not. It could be restrung. I was going to put the same ones back, but I don't have to.'

'Excellent. Are we agreed, Signor?'

Poor Signor Biscaldi. Alarm pleated his forehead as he looked to me, but it was Sofia, of course, who sprang to his aid.

'Don't worry, Papa. I'll come with you.'

'Ah,' John said, clearing his throat. 'I think it really would be best if Signor Biscaldi and I went alone. A woman's presence, especially one as fair as yourself, Signorina, may well distract us.' He delivered another of his winning smiles and bowed low.

Even in the dim light of the lamp, I could see two spots of colour bloom on Sofia's cheeks. I expected some resistance from her, but in the event it wasn't forthcoming. Signor Biscaldi appeared as perplexed as me by her silence and he became increasingly flustered.

'This most unusual. *Most* unusual.' He said, picking and pulling at his lace cuff again. I began to worry that the effort of so violently shaking his head might lead to seizure, but after a deep breath he calmed down a little. 'Signor Dowland,' he went on. 'I worry very much. Please tell me what you think to do.'

John smoothed the air in front of him and spoke in his most placatory manner. 'All will be well, Signor it will not be like...like earlier. I will explain on our way. Now, I must fetch my lute, and yes, I do believe this evening demands the blue velvet doublet. Will?' He turned to me. 'Come up with me. I'll need your help.'

The landlord lit the lamp and would have led the way, but we were in a hurry, and I took it up to our room. The open window overlooked the courtyard where the Biscaldis still sat below. I felt it may look suspicious to them if I closed it, so when I rounded on John, it was in a sharp whisper.

'What the devil are you up to?'

With fists on his hips, John struck a pose of defiance. 'Oh, not you too, Will. Have you no faith in me?'

'Of course, I have, when it's only you or me at stake, but not now. It isn't just us, is it?'

He looked at me askance. 'And whose fault is that exactly?'

I sat down, weak suddenly as if winded. He had me there. All this was my fault.

'You're right,' I said. 'I should have been honest from the start.'

'Come, come,' he said, more gently, and with a tap on my shoulder. 'We're all to blame. Let's not worry about that now. Can you check the lute for me?'

I opened the box containing my new lute and thought again how right John had been to say the inlay was pretty. In the soft lamplight, the mother of pearl gleamed. All was well with the strings and after a tuning, it needed nothing more.

He strummed a little and nodded.

'Yes, that's very good. That pretty inlay of yours will be quite a talking point.'

'As will your performance?'

He sighed. 'Of course, *my* performance. That goes without saying.'

'So why—'

'Look,' he said. 'Everything will become clear later. There is a price to pay, as you heard Signor Biscaldi say, and unfortunately, it will have to be a high one. With luck we will all escape with our heads, fingers and reputations intact. Here, help me with these hooks, otherwise we'll be here all night.'

More than a dozen small hooks were sewn on the inside front facing of his blue doublet. Plenty enough to try the patience of us both every time it was put on and taken off, but when done up, it did mean the join could hardly be detected. The tailor had done well to trim with gold brocade as it drew the eye away from any sign of the making.

'There,' I said, when it was finally done. 'You look a good deal more of a gentleman than you did this afternoon. Please John, for God's sake be on your best behaviour this evening.'

'Yes, yes,' he said with a measure of irritation, but then he looked at me with a sidelong smile. 'And I should say the same to you.'

I did not ask his meaning.

Once dressed, John was keen to be off. Signor Biscaldi tried to look cheerful, but it was a thin disguise. He spoke to Sofia sternly, and she replied with a kiss on his cheek and by whispering something I couldn't hear. His response was to sigh, but it was with a smile and nod of the head. To me he gave me a fierce stare, so I endeavoured to look harmless, whilst trustworthy and capable. It wasn't an expression I'd ever rehearsed, and John's raised eyebrow didn't give me any confidence in the result.

He, of course, bore himself with impatient nonchalance and held my precious lute in a casual manner, swinging it back and forth. With more fervency than ever in church, I prayed that he would be at his most charming and brilliant in the company of Duke Alphonso and his Duchess.

CHAPTER SEVEN

'There is to be a procession,' Sofia said, turning to me once they were out of sight. 'When you were upstairs, I asked Papa if we could go and see it.' She looked up at me, and if I had any words to reply, they deserted me then. Perhaps she thought I didn't want to stay because she added. 'We don't have to be long.'

'No, no,' I blustered. 'Let us go. If you like. I would like...I mean...yes.' Lord, what an imbecile I was.

'Let's wait and see,' she said. 'We don't have to stay.'

'No,' I said, but then thought I saw disappointment in her eyes. 'Or yes! I...Oh, listen.'

The approaching rumble of drums saved me from further spluttering. We made our way towards the steady beat and found ourselves amongst crowds.

'Can you see?' Sofia was craning to get a glimpse over the shoulders of those in front.

'Come,' I said. 'There's a better place further along.'

Even with the distraction of Sofia standing only inches from me, the spectacle drew my attention. I'd seen the Queen's procession in London twice in my life, but here it seemed to be a common occurrence amongst the people. Taking part required skill in the beating of a drum, or the blowing of a trumpet, or more peculiarly, the wielding and throwing high in the air a huge flag brightly decorated in red and green. At least a dozen men undertook this feat, and all performed the same pattern of movement. Like tacking sails that flap and slap in a breeze, the flags fell back down. Would they all be caught? Yes! Many people squealed and Sofia clapped her hands with pleasure. It was a joyous event and when the procession passed the crowd followed.

'We should return,' I said, leaning close to make myself heard. 'I think you father would not be pleased with me if we took advantage of his leniency.'

She nodded. 'Yes. Let's go back. It's so noisy.'

Her eagerness to leave surprised me, but when we turned away from the crowd into the quieter piazza, I was very relieved. It would be a while before my ears didn't echo with the blasting of trumpets.

'Isn't that better?' Sofia said, patting her ears. 'Now we can talk to each other. Tell me about yourself, William Totman. I am keen to know.'

It's amazing the things that can strike a man dumb. I had met many women in my six and twenty years, and none so forward in their nature had such sweet and innocent charm.

'Miss Sofia,' I said. 'I believe John might say I am a dull man excepting for my work which is, I am told, of some good quality.'

I was surely made of the same wood as my lutes.

'Is that so?' she said. 'But my experience of Mr Dowland tells me that we can't always believe what he says. I don't believe you are a dull man at all, and your workmanship is not of *some* good quality it is, in fact, of *excellent* quality and—' I had begun to protest, but she wouldn't have it, wagging her finger at me, as if to scold a child. 'Don't forget,' she went on, 'Papa and I have seen a great many musical instruments, and our view of these things matters a great deal in this part of the world.'

'In that case,' I said, sweeping my cap from my head, 'I bow before you.' And I did, adding a little twirl of my hand to finish. When I stood up, she was hiding behind her hand, but even in the gloom of the church lantern, I could see her eyes were merry.

'Listen to me,' she said, trying not to laugh. 'Of course, I am not *always* right, but I think in this instance I am.'

'Thank you for the compliment, but I have no doubt that yours is a more interesting life than mine, unless you want to hear about how to bend wood over a hot iron or carve a pretty rose, but believe me, both those things are better seen rather than imagined. Besides, as you have said, the finished result of my labour is something you are very familiar with, whereas I have almost no knowledge of this country, and *none at all* about how a young lady such as yourself should find herself here.'

I gestured at our surroundings, but I couldn't help wondering at her being with me.

'Are you very shocked?' she spoke seriously, and was perhaps, a little hurt. I could only mumble in response.

The truth was, I had never made such a long and candid speech to anyone before, except perhaps John. Embarrassed, I tried again.

'Forgive me, Miss Sofia. I am a stranger to myself as well as to this land. At home, it is unusual for a man like me to be alone with a young lady who is not his wife or sister, but that is not to say it is wrong. I am learning more every day, and if this is customary here, then I am very glad of it. Very glad indeed.'

We walked on a couple of paces, and I knew by the silence I'd said the wrong thing. You fool, I thought, and was about to try and make amends but she got there first.

'It isn't customary here,' she said, speaking with such a crack in her voice I feared for tears from both of us. 'You are right to be shocked. I'm sorry if I have misled you. It is true that Papa is very indulgent towards me, and I take advantage. We should go back now.'

'Miss Sofia,' I said, hoping she could hear in my voice the anguish I felt. 'Wait just a moment. Please. It is I that should apologise.'

Not that I had the opportunity then. As the sound of trumpets and drums faded, another sound, that of voices and laughter, grew louder. I was uneasy, recognising its raucous and bawdy nature, and when four men turned the corner, my worry became acute. The first of them carried a flaming torch and, as the shadows leapt from the walls around us, we were lit as if it were day. At once a lewd cheer went up and I knew exactly what they were thinking.

Beside me, Sofia uttered a small cry of alarm and having no time to consider my actions, I did the only thing I could.

'Quickly,' I said, taking her hand.

We stumbled to a dark recess where the torchlight didn't reach, and I sheltered her from their gaze with my arms wrapped tightly about her slender body. Remarks were hurled at us, of course, and I was sorry it was Sofia and not I who understood them, but to my great relief, the men did pass us by. I told myself that it was important to wait until they had gone some distance, but there was a glorious moment when I enjoyed the unexpected delight of holding Miss Sofia in my arms.

'Forgive me,' I said, releasing her quite suddenly. 'I did not mean—'

'Please,' she said, holding up her hand in a firm gesture despite trembling from head to foot. 'I understand.'

I was silent while she gathered her decorum together, smoothing her hair and clothes. There was a catch in her voice, and she cleared her throat before saying with more certainty. 'You did what you had to do. Let us say no more about it.'

It wasn't far to our lodging, and we were soon back. I said goodnight, expecting Sofia to go straight up, but once again, that was not her plan at all.

'Will you join me in the courtyard, Mr Totman?' She spoke shyly, while twisting her hands together as if for want of knitting. I wondered at the sudden formality with which she addressed me, and prepared myself for an admonishment, but then the little frown on her forehead cleared. She covered her mouth, although they couldn't hide the dimpled smile. 'I am sure you want to find out what has happened at the castle as much as I do.'

How my heart lifted. 'Why yes,' I replied. 'I had it in my mind to wait there too. If you are sure, that is.'

'I will ask Signora Vittoria to join us, although she may be in the courtyard already as she usually waters her flowers in the evening. Papa will be happier if he sees her with us when they return and,' she gestured towards me with the familiar wiggle of her forefinger, 'you won't have to worry about me either.'

Molly once shook her finger at me and I hadn't

spoken to her for days, but the repertoire of dances that Sofia's hands played in the air was entirely captivating. Perhaps it was the graceful arc they travelled that reminded me, but into my mind came the picture of a serpent being charmed from a basket that I'd once seen at a fair.

Nothing could persuade me away from how beautiful she was even though I had heard that witches could often hide behind a seeming lovely face. As we sat beneath the arbour Signora Vittoria watered the several dozen pots of blooms that brightened the rather plain square of pavement. She also tended two large lemon trees, two olives and a climbing bush I didn't recognise. With leaves easily as big as my hand, it grew against an adjoining wall ten feet tall at least.

'It's a fig tree,' said Sofia. 'Let's see if we can find one.'

She lifted a leaf, and from the twig beneath hung a small fig, smooth as a piece of planed timber and, unfortunately, just as hard.

'I'm sorry it isn't ripe,' I said, 'as I have yet to taste one.'

'Then it is settled then,' said Sofia. 'You will have to stay here for a while longer. I shall request that Signora Vittoria saves the first fig for you.'

At the mention of her name, the Signora cleared her throat. I couldn't understand the joke that was then shared between her and Sofia. Whether I was the butt of it, I don't know, but the melody of it was very pleasant on the ear. Even so, the turmoil in my mind would not stay quiet enough for me to listen. I was all division. My eyes could see, my hands could feel the rough knot of wood on the table, and my heart was definitely beating but, in my head, it was if a gaggle of squabblers had mustered, all vying to have the loudest voice. By turn they scolded and scorned me, but a verse of John's whispered closely as if in my ear:

Who thinks that sorrows felt, desires hidden,
or humble faith in constant honour arm'd,
can keep love from the fruit that is forbidden.

And I always thought he exaggerated in his songs. And yet Miss Sofia, an impossible match for someone of my ilk, a wealthy lady of a different race and religion, had taken my feet from under me in just such a way. My sensible wits had completely succumbed to one of Cupid's darts, and here I was, in exactly the state I'd always found so tiresome in others.

'—don't you think, William Totman?'

'I beg your pardon, Miss Sofia, I—'

'You looked rather pained.' She smiled, but gently, rather than with the teasing lift of her lip. 'Do you think we should be worried about what is happening at the castle?'

'I don't know,' I said, grateful for the digression. 'Perhaps, but it will not help for us to worry. Why not tell me a little about your life, Miss Sofia? Then I might learn the sort of thing I could say about mine.'

'That is a very good argument,' she said, 'and now I am wondering where to start. With my dear mama I think, but first, wouldn't it be nice to have a little something to drink, and eat maybe?'

She spoke with the Signora for a minute or two, before the matter of what was settled, and Signora Vittoria disappeared into the house. We were alone again, except for a moth that fluttered dangerously close to the flame in the oil lamp on our table. Sofia waved it away.

'My mama was only a girl when she came to Italy. Her family lived in Spain, but her mother died and then one day the Inquisition took her father. Everyone in the town was scared, so they did not help.'

I could well believe it. There's not many who would put their head into a furnace.

'But Papa's uncle,' she went on, 'he was a brave man and took her into his family. He traded in stringed instruments, and for a while they were safe, but when the life for Jews was made so difficult that they could not thrive, he decided to sail for his brother's home in Italy. It was about thirty years ago, I think. Mama was very young, and so was Papa, but he knew straight away that he wanted to marry her.'

She turned her face away, as if to look for Signora Vittoria, but I could see by the blush on her cheeks, she had ventured into a subject of some awkwardness.

'Was it very different for them here?' I said, by way of a change.

'Oh yes,' she said, cheerful once again. 'Florence was a friendly place then, which is why we have the shop there. Now though?' She shook her head. 'It is getting more difficult. When Cosimo de' Medici became the Grand Duke, he built the ghetto and the family had to go there. It is not *so* terrible. There is a synagogue and we can still trade, but it is not like here in Ferrara, where we can be the same as everyone.'

I should not have been shocked to hear of a ghetto. Hadn't John and I been advised against finding ourselves in such a quarter in Venice? But here was Sofia, sitting right opposite me. It was almost impossible to imagine her shut away every night.

'I...I'm sorry.'

'Thank you, but there is no reason for you to be sorry. Besides, it is not the same everywhere.' She brightened. 'Duke Alfonso is a very kind and generous man. It will be bad for us when he dies, but for now there is no ghetto in Ferrara. Indeed, he is a great friend to us, so you see, there's more than one reason why we don't want to upset him. A letter of safe passage from him is worth far more than its weight in gold.'

I understood, but there was so much more I wanted to know but my tongue was in a tangle, and I had no words that sounded polite enough to speak out loud. And yet...and yet, she was still Sofia, and how my heart jumped when I looked upon her face.

'Papa's uncle and his wife always spoke to me in Spanish,' she went on, oblivious to my disquiet. 'But we were living in Italy, so I spoke two languages from when I was very little. I liked the different sounds for things.'

The moth, a creature easily ten times the size of the pest I was used to, was still fluttering about and chose that moment to land on the table. Sofia encouraged it to crawl onto her hand. 'This little thing is called a moth in your tongue, but here it is *la falena*, and if we were in Spain now, then it would be *pollila*. All different. Isn't that wonderful?'

She lifted her hand and tipped the creature away.

'Indeed,' I said, 'but confusing too. Our journey here has taken us through so many languages, I find it more baffling than wonderful.' Was there too much complaint in my voice? I didn't want to sound as if I was disagreeing. 'Although,' I added hastily, 'it is wonderful that you are so skilled, and I am able to have a conversation with you.'

'In English!' She sat up straighter. 'How I wish to visit London one day. And there you will be. Is it a fair city?'

My mouth fell right open. Did I hear correctly? In London with Sofia? Why would she even think such a thing? I was a nobody, an orphan picked up from the gutter. My saving, only putting out my hand to help a puppy! If it had been another day, I might have had that same hand removed for stealing an apple.

'Miss Sofia,' I said, having taken a deep breath. 'I do believe you are having a little fun at my expense.'

She looked pained and an awkward moment ensued until Signora Vittoria eased the situation by arriving with a tray of pretty sweetmeats. Sofia clapped her hands together and even I cooed with appreciation. Once the different flavours, ingredients, perhaps entire recipes had been explained to Sofia, the Signora wished us enjoyment, then picked up the tray and gone back into the house.

'Please forgive me once again, Mr Totman.' said Sofia, as she considered her choice from the plate. 'I am so used to being with Papa and talking freely. This is a new situation for me, and I am afraid I have no manners.'

Then she made her choice, picking it up between her thumb and finger. Holding it to her nose she murmured, 'Hmm, rosewater,' before taking the most delicate bite out of the small pink sphere. I said nothing, unable to stop staring as her lips closed over the morsel. It took a great deal of effort to choose something for myself.

'All my life I made friends with the customers in our shop and on our travels,' she said, having swallowed the rest with more alacrity. 'Papa said it was good for business.'

How bright she looked at the memory, her expression completely untroubled. In the lamplight her eyes took on the glow of a chestnut newly unwrapped from its spikey shell. I could not look away and remained transfixed even when she turned her gaze to me.

'Now, William Totman,' she said. Her voice thrillingly soft. 'It is definitely your turn now.' And like a blackbird probing for breakfast, she tapped her slender finger on the table right in front of me. I didn't know where to start. There were worms aplenty in my background, and they'd always wriggled uncomfortably when I thought about them.

'Well...' I said. 'As for parents, I never knew them. My father anyway. I was told my mother died of the sweating sickness when I was very small, two or three years maybe, although I can't be sure. I do have one memory of her, although nothing that I can be very precise about.'

'That doesn't matter,' she said. 'I don't think a memory can ever be exactly as it was. Besides, you can be certain I won't correct you.'

I smiled at that, but how could I possibly describe the intensity of the feeling I had when trying to focus on something as slippery as a fish. John was the wordsmith, not me.

'I remember her humming,' I began. 'A sweet sound, but no tune I could put a name to. Lying in long grass that swayed above me. Sun warm on my face, the scent of grass and animals nearby, cows mooing and there were ducks quacking too.'

I took up one of the sweetmeats, but changed my mind, toying with it rather than putting it in my mouth. For Sofia, I found I wanted to put my memory into words. I *wanted* her to understand. 'A meadow it was,' I went on, 'full of flowers, daisies, cockles, heartsease, all sorts I've since come to know.' But that wasn't everything. 'It wasn't only how it looked or smelt though...' I hesitated. 'It was more than what was out there, I...' Without my realising it, an intensity had crept into my voice and I'd put my hand to my chest. Across the table, Sofia's face had acquired a new and serious expression.

'Forgive me,' I said. 'I'm babbling.'

'No, no,' she said, gently. 'I think you should say more. Especially as I'm going to help myself to another of these, so will have my mouth too full to speak.'

I thought this a ploy rather than desire on her part as she had already eaten two and although delicious, they were very sweet indeed. But I did continue.

'I feel it almost like a real place,' I said. 'One that I can go to for solace when the world seems dark.'

Sofia put a finger to her mouth and swallowed. 'Does it often seem dark to you, William Totman?'

I smiled at the alarm on her face. 'Not so much now, but when I was a boy, yes, it did. I was just glad that—' I hesitated but knew better than to stop there in present company. A twitch of her eyebrow was enough. 'I was glad that I could remember that one time, to know that, to feel that she—' Embarrassment took over. I couldn't say the word, and especially not while looking at Sofia. Between my fingers the almond paste, had become misshapen and warm from being squeezed too tightly. It needed eating, so I put it all into my mouth at once.

'To feel that she loved you?'

With my teeth glued together, I could only nod.

'Well then,' she said. 'That is why you remember it so well. But tell me, if your mother died, who looked after you?'

'Quite a lot of people, I think. No relation stepped forward to take me on, and I was passed from one to another. Eventually I fetched up at an orphan house run by a woman who everyone called Ma Perks.'

Sofia coughed and put her hand to her mouth to conceal a smile. 'Is that a real name?'

'It is, but you need to know it is Ma, as in mother, then Perks.'

'Ah, I see. Did she have a lot of children?'

'A dozen or more,' I said, and without any effort all their grubby faces appeared before my eyes. 'What a motley lot we were. Girls and boys, aged from barely walking to past grown up. I reckon we would have starved or drowned in the river had it not been for Ma Perks. None of us were her own, but there was food most days, and we had somewhere to sleep. We worked as soon as we were able, taking laundry to and fro. Lucky for us, washing wasn't something she liked and only did for a few people.'

'Did she work you very hard?'

I had to think about that.

'There were far worse places to be, but yes, we worked hard. Mainly, she was well known in the neighbourhood for having a trusted gang of message runners, and that's what I did when I was old enough. Any trouble or thievery and we'd be out the door, but the promise of dinner usually kept most of us honest. We always—'

I was about to say more when both of us started at the sound of a familiar voice. Everything else was forgotten and next thing, we were both on our feet.

My sense of hearing may not be musically refined but I know John's voice, and how he's feeling, from quite a way away. Now he was near, but we heard no more as close by, the city gate bell began to ring.

'I think it's gone well,' I said.

Sofia was already on her way to greet them. I was not so quick and stopped to tip my cap and bow at Signora Vittoria. Her presence had enabled something precious, time spent in almost private conversation with Sofia. As I got to the door, Sofia and her father appeared before me. John followed and he was looking extremely pleased with himself.

Signor Biscaldi's expression had entirely changed. His furrowed brow was now smooth and shiny, his nose and cheeks crimson (probably with wine as well as relief,) and instead of clawing at the lace on his cuff, he clapped both hands together.

'A complete disaster then?' I said, as they all beamed at me.

'So, you're a jester now, are you Will?' John threw his arm around my shoulders. 'Let's drink to our good fortune. If *you* have any jolly songs in your repertoire then now is the time for them, as *I* am quite sung out.'

He flopped down on the seat I had occupied with great flourish, sweeping his hand across his brow as if to wipe away a good deal of sweat.

'Signor Dowland is wonderful this evening,' Signor Biscaldi hopped from foot to foot, his eyes popping with pleasure. 'In everything he does, is *excellent*!'

'Thank you, thank you,' John murmured. 'You're very kind.'

'But you must tell us what happened,' Sofia clutched at her father's arm. 'We have been so worried. Haven't we, Mr Totman?'

This small deceit, said with such guile, came as something of a surprise. 'Why yes,' I blustered. 'Yes, indeed.'

John saw through me straight away and raised an eyebrow, but Signor Biscaldi was too distracted to notice.

'The Duke and Duchess *very* pleased. Signor Dowland so charming and gracious, he play and sing *so* beautiful, everyone stop in whole castle to listen.'

'I doubt that,' I said, thinking of the army of servants that patrolled the hidden stairs and passages, fetching and carrying all hours of the night and day. Then I regretted sounding so mean spirited. After all, John could charm the birds off trees when he so desired.

The evening was growing cooler but clearly there was much to tell. Sofia sat down at the table once again. There was a seat next to her, which would have been my favoured place, but I thought better of it and leant against the wall by the fig tree.

'And we best not forget Lady Anna.' Signor Biscaldi raised his eyes to heaven and sighed. 'She *most* beautiful lady and,' he waggled his finger at John, 'she *love* Signor Dowland, I think.'

'Oh?' said John. 'Do you think so?'

We all laughed at this, even me. I'd never seen him look more delighted with himself.

'And Prince Gesualdo!' Glee exploded from Signor Biscaldi almost lifting him from his feet. 'He so *rude*!'

Sofia gasped. 'Rude, Papa?'

'He arrive with Count Fontanelli and make lot of noise. Signor Dowland is playing. The Prince see Signor Dowland and his face go very dark. Then he begin push the chairs here and there, talking even more loud! Everyone turn around and see Duke and Duchess not pleased at all. It seem Duke and Prince not like each other.'

'Not like each other?' John, increasingly twitchy at the slowness of Signor Biscaldi's tale, lurched forward in his chair. 'Hah! They *loathe* each other. The Duke is most formal and polite. He may be an old man but there's no question he's used to commanding respect. Does Prince Gesualdo care? Or even notice? Who knows?'

I had to smile considering John's earlier behaviour.

'Anyway,' he said more levelly, having spent his outrage. 'The Duke was furious but could hardly admonish his new brother-in-law in front of everyone. I simply bowed and sat down – next to Lady Anna, I should add – and waited. The Duke spoke quietly to Count Fontanelli, and out they all went, Duke, Prince and Count, in that order. Which left me in their absence in the perfect position to advance our cause.' He sat back, giving himself a congratulatory slap on the chest and time, no doubt, to appreciate our rapt attention.

'Our cause?' said Sofia. 'How did you do that?'

I knew what was coming. If Lady Anna didn't feature very shortly, I'd eat my cap. I pushed it back off my forehead and waited. Before John could say anything, Signor Biscaldi clapped his hands together again.

'The Lady Anna,' he said. 'When Signor Dowland sing, she have tears in her eyes. Fan her face. Then he sit by her! Oh, she is very happy!'

I don't think Signor Biscaldi's acting of the lady would have satisfied the playgoers at the Rose or Curtain, but I had watched a similar scene many times and knew it well. What troubled me, was what John had planned for the solving of our friends' predicament with the lute.

Sofia, though, was not familiar with all John's caprices and she frowned. 'But I still don't see how—'

John waved her disquiet away. 'Do not concern yourself with how, Signorina. Let it be enough to know that our little problem is solved.'

He glanced at me then, and I knew then that my fears were justified. I looked about, even stepping into the hallway between the outer door and the courtyard to check, but no, there was no sign of a lute.

Anger flushed through me. It wasn't only the weeks spent making my finest instrument, or that he had lent, or worse, *given* it away.

'What have you done with it?' The harshness in my voice shocked us all. I didn't mean to sound quite so rough, but it was too difficult to disguise how I felt.

'Now, now Will. Don't be like that.'

'Have you lent it to her? Or given it away?'

John held out his hands and patted the air in an irritating gesture aimed at placating me. 'It was the answer to everything. Lady Anna simply *loved* your pretty lute, as we all knew she would. I mean to say, who wouldn't?'

It was supposed to flatter, but I still wasn't prepared to give way. 'And then?'

He shrugged. 'Of course, I said I would gladly present it to the lady but couldn't because it was on loan from Signor Biscaldi.'

A small cough from behind me confirmed this deceit.

'So,' John went on, 'I impressed on her ever more firmly that it was quite the most superior instrument I had ever played. Far better than the *Maler* lutes everyone thought were so wonderful. Oh, she said. Do you think so? Only the Duke has promised me a lute made by Signor Maler which I believe is to arrive very soon.'

With the merest tilt of his head, John's Lady Anna almost appeared before me despite my having no idea what she looked like. His long study of women did give him a considerable expertise for such a role.

'So *I* said,' he continued. 'A *Maler*? That's a great shame. Perhaps the Duke and Signor Biscaldi could be persuaded to change their minds and consider this one instead. Well —'

'It very good plan of Signor Dowland,' Signor Biscaldi interrupted. 'But if Prince Gesualdo hear talk of lutes, then maybe trouble. I wait by door and when Duke come back without Prince,' he broke off and beamed at us all as he slapped his chest. 'Then I breathe again.'

'Of course,' John said, 'when the Duke left it to the Lady Anna to decide, the outcome was inevitable. But Will, what would you have me do instead?'

Did he expect an answer? I don't think so. His attention was now focussed on the remaining sweetmeats on the table and after a moment's dithering about which to choose, he stabbed at one, two, and ate them in quick succession. Always a man of appetite, did he even taste them?

'You might have told me beforehand.' I said, sounding like a petulant child.

'Why would I?' He shrugged. 'I had no idea whether it would be possible,' he stopped to swallow, before continuing 'or whether Lady Anna would even be there.'

Signor Biscaldi stepped forward and helped himself to the last sweetmeat, although he did offer it to Sofia first. She declined, but his gesture gave me the opportunity to glance at her lovely face, where I saw the little frown line that dented her forehead when she was perplexed. All the churlishness I felt shrivelled at once. I'd sounded so gruff and ill-tempered. Would she think badly of me?

'Ah yes,' I said. 'I see that now.'

This acquiescence of mine, I think, quite surprised John, and instead of his usual triumphant response when besting me, he was quite sympathetic.

'I am sorry to say goodbye to the lute, Will. It was my favourite too.'

Yes, I thought, it was. I remembered how delighted he'd been with it and had spent a long time inspecting every inch of my work, caressing the silk-like smoothness of the surfaces, the boxwood pegs carved into shallow spoons to perfectly fit his thumb and, of course, the pretty inlay.

'You'll have trouble finding another lute even half as good before we get to see Signor Marenzio in Rome.'

At this, John and Signor Biscaldi started, and both began to speak at once.

'Papa?' interrupted Sofia. 'Surely not the Maler?'

He shook his head and laughed. 'No, no. Prince Gesualdo *very* not happy if we do that.'

I was very not happy about the Maler lute altogether, but John was smiling too, which made me instantly suspicious. 'You haven't done anything to that lute, have you?'

'Good Lord no,' said John. 'As far as we know, it's still where you left it. The Signor and I were talking about it on the way back and we both agreed the best thing would be for you to go there early in the morning to do whatever needs to be done, then leave it with the Count. Prince Gesualdo rarely gets up before midday, he told us, and by that time…' He thrust out his arm, pointing directly at the very fig by which I was standing.

It was a surprise gesture, but Signor Biscaldi clapped his hands together yet again and this time said with considerable satisfaction.

'We are all gone far away!'

I was stunned for a moment. In the distance, I could still hear the blaring of trumpets and close by, on the other side of the wall, a horse very slowly clopped past pulling a hefty load by the sound of the squeaky wheels that followed. We all looked at each other.

'Gone, Papa? Gone where?'

Sofia's voice contained a slight tremor, and I wondered if she was thinking the same as me. For John and Signor Biscaldi, the problem had been solved. There was no question that a few miles between us and the peculiar Prince Gesualdo would be no bad thing.

'Signor Dowland to Florence,' said Signor Biscaldi. 'Then he choose any lute in the shop he want. Yes?'

'Yes, indeed,' said John. 'We'll have to pack this evening Will. Then we can be off as soon as you come back from making sure the Maler lute is mended. I'll arrange the horses while you're there.'

I nodded like a dumb animal. Leave Ferrara? Leave Sofia? So soon? I was not prepared, not ready. I didn't think I'd ever be ready.

'And us, Papa?' she said, her face now as troubled as I felt. 'Are we going to Florence?'

'No, no, my dear. There is business in Mantua.' Signor Biscaldi turned to us. 'Signor Monteverdi is at the court. Music is very much there, and Sofia, you will see Jakob too. Why you look sad? He is good friend.' He laughed and patted her arm. 'Now, goodnight. It is late.'

'Yes, Papa.'

She left us then after bidding us all goodnight. John was hearty in his reply, but I could barely grunt such was the sticking of words in my throat. Did I see a tear glistening in her eye, or was it just the lamplight reflected? I feared I would never know.

John was jubilant. For him, everything about the evening had been a success.

'And Will,' he said, in between humming to himself while I unhooked his doublet. 'There is another good reason for going to Florence, apart from acquiring a new lute.'

'Oh yes?' I said with about as much enthusiasm as a man on his way to the Tower.

'Yes, indeed, so cheer up. Your lovely lute is in safe hands. Besides, if we behave ourselves in the right and proper manner, there may well be an opportunity to get it back.'

The real reason why I was so downhearted had not entered John's head, but this new announcement jolted me from misery to surprise. I stood up straight and looked him in directly in the eye. 'Get it back? How? Please don't say you're expecting me to steal it.'

'Hah! There's an idea.' He pulled at the hooks still fastened. 'I wish you'd hurry up with these. I can't see what to do.'

I bent to the task, the last few under his chin. I took them slowly, so he'd have plenty of time to explain.

'No,' he said. 'If all goes well there'll be no need for thievery.' Despite my efforts, he wouldn't be drawn any further. Instead, he turned the conversation to an altogether more uncomfortable place. 'And how was *your* evening?' He smacked his lips together. 'Good Lord, Will. Chances like that don't come very often, soft as a peach ripe for plucking and you, not even a novice. Well? Did she succumb to your charms?'

Something like a fury tore through me then and if it hadn't been for the suddenness and unfamiliarity of having clenched my fists so tight, I might have struck out. I knew John thought this way, and I'd seen his charms often enough, but had viewed them as if amongst the audience at the playhouse, only from the outside. With Sofia, it was completely different. She was real to me, and like a fine instrument to be treated with care. Why even then at the mere thought of her, my anger blew away like seeds from a fairy clock.

'Heavens, my dear friend,' said John. 'Have you succumbed? Don't tell me you've lent your heart to the young lady?' He grasped my shoulders tilting me towards the lamplight so he could view my expression more clearly.

'I...I don't know what you mean.'

'Aah,' he said, gently enough, but I knew he was holding back laughter. 'I think you know very well indeed.' He let me go and I turned away to hide my discomfort, and any obvious signs of blood rushing to my face.

'But my dear Will. Now you've had your eyes opened, you'll soon see that there's a whole world simply *full* of beautiful women. They won't all fall at *your* feet admittedly, but with a little help and advice from someone more experienced—' He coughed, but I determined to feign ignorance and bent to remove my boots.

While John, such was his content with himself, slipped almost at once into sleep, I lay awake for a long time. The memory of holding Sofia in my arms remained most painfully clear. *Soft as a peach*, John had said, but as each night bell struck, they began to chime a rhyme: *out of your reach, out of your reach*.

In the dead of night I remembered Signor Biscaldi telling Sofia they would see Jacob in Mantua. I lay in a restless state whilst casting characters to the name: an old friend, a child, an elderly relation? Although Sofia had made no mention of him, always my thoughts returned to that of Jakob, the handsome young suitor.

CHAPTER EIGHT

John was still asleep when I hauled myself up from a shallow slumber. It was early still, hardly light. Close by, birds twittered then flew, a cloud of fleeting shadows.

It wouldn't take long to unclamp the lute and I'd be back in plenty of time to say farewell to Sofia. I crept down the stairs as quietly as I could, but the treads creaked and, even though I carried my boots, they weren't going to let anyone pass in silence. It wasn't surprising then, that at the bottom and with only one foot shod, I heard someone else on the stairs. Our landlord, I thought, or more probably their servant girl. But when I stood up, I saw it was neither. Signora Vittoria held a lamp before her, and in its glow, I could see very well who followed her down.

'Miss Sofia!' I said, shocked to see her at this hour. 'What—

'Shh!' Both women put their fingers to their lips, but it was Sofia who whispered.

'I am accompanying Signor Vittoria to the market this morning. Papa and I need some provisions for our journey.'

'Ah, I see.' I couldn't quite keep the disappointment from my voice. At the sight of Sofia, my heart had leapt. Even though every sinew, every sensible part of me said that any hopes I had for her would without doubt come to nothing, I could not deny my heart. I prayed the marketplace was near the palace.

Only a trio of pigeons occupied the street when we stepped out into the cool morning. A round nut was their object of desire and they worried it with their beaks. Tap-tap-tap against the stone flags as it rolled, sounding not unlike my careful hammering of a nail into an awkward joint. At the sight of us, they took to the air in a great flapping and lost the nut forever to a narrow gully. I remembered the pleasure of scavenging after a public gathering. Not so much for the food, as vermin soon saw to that, but there was usually a coin or two somewhere. Once, I'd found a whole sovereign.

'Are we to go in the same direction?' I asked.

I'd never seen Sofia lack the gift of speech before, but a small nod was her only reply. We'd only walked a little way, before I realised that Signora Vittoria was not keeping to our pace.

'Should we not wait for her?'

Again she didn't speak, but this time, shook her head.

'Miss Sofia,' I said, gently. 'Are you really going to market?'

'I...I'm sorry,' she said in hardly more than a whisper.

'Sorry? But why?'

She had risen and dressed in a hurry. Her long hair wasn't tied in its usual neat plait, and from the looseness of her garments it was apparent she had not had help. Now, both haste and embarrassment flushed her skin. To my eye, she had never looked more desirable.

It was just as well that Signora Vittoria was behind us. With a deep breath, Sofia stood up straight and cleared her throat.

'I meant that I'm sorry we're going our separate ways, William Totman. Yes, the Signora is going to the market, and I will also go, but not yet. At this hour and on your own, I doubt the guard will let you through the door at the palace, so I shall come with you first.'

This change of tone and subject was a suitable quell to my fears. She was right of course. It was very unlikely that the night guards would allow in a dubious foreigner with no papers, but I was equally aware that they would be very surprised to see a dubious foreigner with a young lady such as Sofia. The coarse remarks made about us by the drunkards in the street yesterday came back to me then.

'If I explain our early presence,' she said, 'then there may be no need to rouse the Count. I can say we are catching the river boat and have not much time.'

'I don't know, Miss Sofia. The guards will want to know who we are, and they may well not be polite if we tell them the exact truth.'

'Should I say we are cousins?'

I could only laugh at this. 'No! They will not believe that for one moment, I am quite sure.' Dear Sofia, I thought, and John considers me naïve. 'It is better you say I am your servant, and we are on the Count's business. His note should still be in the workshop if they want to check.'

That idea seemed to please her and all the early disquiet in her face cleared. 'Come then,' she said. 'I'm looking forward to seeing the lute freed from its imprisonment.'

As we made our way to the Palazzo Dei Diamonte, Sofia gathered her hair into three long strands, and in a seeming trice had it plaited and tied with a blue ribbon so that instead of down her back, it fell before her to one side.

'Well now,' I said. 'That is a skill and something I have never seen before. Or rather, I have seen plaited hair before, but not so that it snakes,' I hesitated, not wanting to say quite how it accentuated the line of her breast. 'Umm...thus.'

It was my turn to colour, but she laughed. 'Are you suggesting my hair resembles a snake? Take care then. You know better than most how they can bite.'

'Indeed I do! And I hope never to experience another.'

'Then let me reassure you. Mine is entirely harmless.' And with that she flicked my arm with the end of her plait. 'See?'

What could I say to that? Everything I had wondered about Jakob seemed ridiculous now the world was awake and we were walking together. When we reached the palace, Signora Vittoria said farewell and smiled at us from behind the fabric of her headscarf. Women, I decided, were all mysterious.

Fortunately, the palace guards assessed us as harmless with hardly a glance. Inside, it was still quite dark but of course the servants were up, and one or two eyed us with suspicion. Although the tuner plinking on the harpsichord nodded in a more friendly manner. I quickened my step, suddenly anxious for the lute, but in the gloom of the workshop there it lay on the bench, just as I had left it.

Beside me, Sofia held her breath as I slowly released the clamp. It was a tense moment, but not one unfamiliar to me. Now though, my heart beat a little faster on two counts. My skills were such that all should be well, but the glue was not my own and it was so much hotter here compared to London. Perhaps I hadn't given that enough thought yesterday. Would it hold? I swallowed. It was one thing to witness a failure by myself, but not with another, and especially not with Sofia.

'There,' I said, lifting the lute free after the final turn. 'All is well, at least, so far.'

'Oh,' Sofia breathed out at last. 'That is such a relief!'

'I still have to restring it though, that'll be the real telling.'

A brief inspection showed that the main joint was indeed fast, so I set about tightening the pegs.

'This is a mighty gift for such an unpleasant man,' I said, holding it up for a final inspection. 'And I'm glad it doesn't bear my name. Perhaps when he finds out the true maker, he'll be less likely to throw it about.'

'I doubt that,' Sofia said, with more than a little bitterness. 'Now, we must write a note.' She found the Count's instructions and turned it over. I retrieved a quill and ink from a shelf and passed them to her.

'*For His Highness, the Prince Gesualdo,*' she said. 'Is that enough, do you think?'

'What else is there to say,' I said, weaving the note between the strings. 'I'm not going to sign it. With luck, everyone will soon forget my name, if they haven't already.'

'I won't ever forget it.' Keeping her eyes down, Sofia spoke in hardly more than a whisper. 'Thank you, Mr Totman. I'm sorry that your generous good nature led you so close to trouble.'

Her apology pained me. 'But you have nothing to apologise for, Miss Sofia. Although John will always have my loyalty in his palm, you and I both know that if it hadn't been for his rudeness to Prince Gesualdo, all would have been well.'

Taking a great liberty, I placed my hand over hers and for a long moment, she didn't pull back.

We left then, and I saluted the harpsichord tuner as we passed. Another day, had I time and more of the language, I would like to have stopped and asked about the instrument. I knew the principal of a quill plucking the string to make a sound, but I'd never been close enough to see the working. Maybe one day I would make one myself. There'd been talk before we left London of acquiring a clavichord for young Robert, but nothing was done. Jane may have purchased one, although I doubted it would be like the gold and finely painted harpsichord here. An instrument like that could cost her entire fortune besides taking up the whole parlour.

Outside the palace, we found the city stirring. Although relieved the lute was repaired, my heart could not have been heavier. We stood for a minute or two, looking towards the marketplace, before Sofia broke the silence.

'I think you will like Florence.'

'I hope so.'

'It is a busy place.'

'Ah.'

'Our shop is behind the Cathedral and that is very easy to find.'

'Good.'

'It is Antonio that you must speak to. Papa has written a letter to say that John is to have a new lute, but if there is any suspicion, then you can tell him everything that's happened. Papa has not put the whole story in his letter, of course.'

'I understand.'

'And you can ask him about lodgings as well. Antonio is a good man and not a Jew so it will be easy for him to help you with everything. And yes, there may even be room above the shop. There is—'

'Wait, Sofia, please wait.' I held up my hand. 'Thank you for all the advice but we should and can, although you may not believe it, look after ourselves.'

She almost protested, I think, but then looked abashed.

'Of course. Forgive me. Papa is wonderful at business and travel, but not always so good at remembering we must eat and sleep somewhere. And besides, you will be strangers in—'

'Miss Sofia, please stop for a moment.' We were approaching the end of the street and the market was ahead. There was so little time left before the Signora would be coming towards us and we would have to go back. I felt I would burst if I did not speak my mind. 'Please Miss, Sofia, soon we will be saying our goodbyes, and this is the last chance I will have to speak freely.'

In front of us, a wagon laden with baskets came to a stop. A heated exchange ensued between the driver and one to my eye with an almost identical wagon of baskets coming the other way.

'Come,' I said, guiding her into a small piazza. 'Let's move out of their way. We will still see the Signora from here.' I was glad the street was full of activity and haranguing voices so that I could not be overheard. As for speaking freely though, that was quite another matter.

'Miss Sofia,' I began, but the words wouldn't come. I tried again, this time not looking directly at her stricken face. 'Miss Sofia, may I say that it has been the greatest pleasure—' Oh no, no, no. How formal that sounded. How trite. I took a deep breath. 'We have to say goodbye.' A glance at her pink face and shining eyes told me tears threatened and I felt my own did too. Had I the world I would have given it, to take her in my arms just that once. 'My dear,' I said, more gently. 'If it could be any other way, if we lived elsewhere perhaps, if I were a better man—' She shook her head at this and brushed an escaped tear from her cheek. 'A better man would have a handkerchief to give to the lady,' I said, fumbling for my own and finding nothing. 'But even if he had one, there would still be a great many obstacles between us. We are not equals in this life. Your father would wish for you another, a far better man, no doubt. Besides, that I am not a Jew, is no small matter.'

She would speak at that point, but I continued without interruption.

'It is not to be, Sofia. You are going to Mantua this morning. I am away to Florence, and there is nothing to be done about it.'

From somewhere I heard John's voice in my head. *Now, oh now, I needs must part.* This was his territory and he exulted in it in his songs. I, though, had never made such a speech before and had never felt more wretched.

Sofia turned her face away.

'You are right,' she whispered, wiping away a tear. 'But there is always a slim shred of hope in this life, is there not? What else is hope for?'

'Sofia,' I said, as firmly as I could. 'You have taught me that the world is full of marvels and there is much to be grasped but I would not have you waste your life in false hope.'

'Is it false?' she said. 'Will you not remember me, William?'

Unable to resist, I took her hand then and kissed it.

'Always, my dear. Always.'

There's no denying I was miserable company on a difficult journey. On the outskirts of Bologna, we met with two English pilgrims who told us the city was full of disease, so we took their advice to avoid the city altogether. Even then, many a pale half-starved fellow appeared at almost every turn in the road. We'd seen sign of the famine when in Ferrara, but there was worse hunger away from the city, and the cry from beggars was for food first, even before money.

Had we not been in the good company of a merchant train, I suspect we may have come to harm, or lost our way, but at noon on the sixth day, we came within sight of Florence. Nestling there, in the broad valley, with its towers and the great dome glowing rose pink, it was a welcome sight. Not that it did much to lift my spirits. Plodding, rather than riding, had become my habit. Perhaps it was the fine views and scent of flowers that were too much for me, but I found the stony ground beneath my feet more amenable to my state of mind.

'Oh, do cheer up, Will.' John jumped down and came to walk beside me. 'Look, there's a fine city ahead. New opportunities for me to play, and who knows? Perhaps new opportunities for you, too.'

The wink and lecherous gesture didn't help me feel any better and I made no response. He began kicking some of the larger stones, and I grumbled at him, reminding him that if he wanted me to clean the dust from his boots, then he'd better desist. We walked in silence for a while, until high above us, the harsh cry of a bird cut through the air and we both looked up. It was big, an impressive sight against the clear blue, wheeling around in large circles, flying ever higher. A hawk perhaps, or falcon, I don't know. Another day I might have asked John. Several times he'd witnessed displays of falconry at court and had expressed an interest in owning such a bird. Jane put a stop to that. Quite rightly, seeing as he was so rarely at home. Beside me, he kicked one last stone and sighed.

'I don't know why you're taking it so hard. It's been nearly a week now.'

That did it. 'A week?' I countered. 'Is that how long love lasts for you? A *week*? Are you so fickle?'

He looked almost shocked at my outburst and remained quiet for a while. I imagined he was thinking up some sort of retort and it wasn't long before he spoke again.

'You know, Will, this moping is all very well in a song or a verse.' He placed his arm across my shoulders. A gesture I wasn't keen to accept but had not the energy to shrug off. 'And it is true,' he went on, 'that now there's quite a fashion for wailing and gnashing teeth over some tryst or other. Certainly, at Her Majesty's court the ladies love to see us brought low by their designs and I'm very glad of it, having such a gift for the conceit. It goes so well with all my other talents.'

The moment of self-flattery seemed to warrant a slight skip to his step. I opened my mouth to speak but he was there before me.

'You see, my dear friend,' he said, in a wheedling tone, 'although I am *very* sorry that you have received a bad bruise to the heart, what you must realise, is that such bruises are all part of the great game. Love is nothing but a *joust*!' He flung his arms in the air so violently I jumped and so did his poor horse who, with a whinny, nearly bolted. Not that John noticed. 'You're *bound* to be poked with a pike early on,' he went on, 'but you can't lie about on the ground weeping. At least, not unless you want a kicking. *Actual* weeping is for women, Will. What sort of man are you?' He looked at me and frowned. 'Or horse more like, with a face that long. Now, be a good man, and start thinking about the future.' He took a deep breath and rubbed his hands together. 'I'm liking the look of Florence already.'

My heart was doubly bruised by this speech of John's. What irked, wasn't the idea that I might be feeble, but that there was more than a little truth in what he said. Straightening up, I made up my mind. The past was done with. I'd had my first foray into love and would be forewarned if ever a woman looked at me with such bright eyes ever again. To John, however, I neglected to convey any of my thoughts on the matter, and he had to make do with a grunt.

Our letters from Duke Alfonso assured our safe passage into the city, and finding the cathedral presented us with no difficulty at all. I was reminded of working along the grain of newly sawn wood as we rode along the busy streets, to go in a different direction would be hard work and fruitless.

We'd arrived in the heat of the day, and after such a long time on the road, where the only assault on the nose was from wild rose and honeysuckle, the smell of a multitude confined by high walls proved very strong indeed. Smoke from the many roasting braziers pricked at our eyes, but our stomachs complained about the length of time since breakfast, so we stopped for a slice of tender mutton cut straight from the spit. Down from our horses, we were at once mobbed by street sellers hoping these foreigners were easily parted from their money. Of course, *we* weren't, the bread, apricots, roasted almonds and wine being deliberately purchased and most welcome.

After this feast we were on our way, down the straight road busy with wagons, pack animals, church folk and families blessed with many children, that led to the marvel at Florence's heart.

I'd already seen one or two cathedrals and plenty of large churches whilst on this journey, so I'd thought I was getting used to the papist way of gaudy display. Here in Florence though, I'd neither breath nor words. John, I believe, was similarly struck with the wonder of it. Or rather them. We found ourselves gazing at three separate buildings. Rising above the muddle and noise of human life was the huge cathedral itself, beneath the red tiled dome we'd seen from hills. Something of a miracle, I'd been told, seemingly held up only by the air beneath. Directly to the front of the steps stood another building faced in black and white marble which, on counting, I discovered had eight sides, but clad in stripes of pink and white, the bell tower stood alone, and we were right beside it when a great booming sound from above echoed all around the square, rattled the innards and near deafened me. John too, by the way he rubbed his ears.

Once we'd recovered, he set off down a street that led away from the piazza.

'But,' I asked, looking over my shoulder, 'are we not going to find you a new lute?'

'That'll have to wait,' said John. 'I've other things to do. We'll go to the other side of the river first and enquire at the palace about lodgings.'

When John had *things to do,* I always felt a twinge of worry. At home, this meant a meeting, perhaps with

Tom Morley or one of Her Majesty's courtiers. I'd not given any thought to them while we'd been in Ferrara, and my worries about religion had only concerned Sofia.

John knew me too well, I thought sometimes. Mostly he was happy to share his plans but, when he thought I'd disapprove, along would come these vague pronouncements. Of course, I also knew him very well. All I had to do was wait a little, and he'd be unable to resist telling me himself.

CHAPTER NINE

John had a specific destination in mind, the Palazzo Pitti, home of the Grand Duke of Tuscany, Ferdinando Medici. It was probably the grandest but not the most beautiful palace I'd seen in Italy. The stone was brown and rough cut, nothing like the careful cutting of marble for the Palazzo di Diamonte in Ferrara or the smooth facing of the bell tower. Even so, it was an impressive palace and no doubt impregnable.

A guard at the gate gave John's letter from Duke Alfonso a desultory glance and sent us to our best lodgings yet. Cool and clean, we had to cross back over the river, but once we had rid ourselves of the horses, paid the landlord and a boy to bring our boxes, I sat on the bed.

'Oh, that feels very comfortable,' I said, taking off my boots and stretching out. 'Much better than last night's plank. Good to be out of the heat too and a welcome relief for my backside.'

John laughed. 'Anything else you want to complain about, or are you saving it for later?'

'No, no,' I said, letting drowsiness take me. 'No complaints at all now.'

John was nowhere to be seen when I awoke but out in the street people were going about their business. I was keen to find a certain instrument shop, and after a good stretch to rid myself of leftover sleep, I set off.

The day had cooled to a most pleasant temperature and strolling through the city gave me considerable pleasure, despite the constant pulling on my sleeve from skinny children. I had resolved to harden my heart, but it wasn't long before my purse was empty of small coins and all the remaining almonds purchased earlier were gone.

Once in the great square, it was the many sellers of papal trinkets that clamoured around me. I would have hastened away from the cathedral, but curiosity made me peep inside the octagonal building opposite when I saw one of the doors was open. The exterior appealed to me well enough, but inside I could only gasp at the vast depiction of Christ and his many saints and angels on the dazzling gold ceiling panels. I stood long in admiration of the marvel until into my mind came the story of Moses and the Golden Calf. Weren't all these fine pictures some sort of idolatry? I hastened away. Not that such sights could easily be erased from the memory.

The sun, having sunk low behind the great Cathedral, plunged half the piazza in shade, but almost like an arrow, the straight line at the dark edge pointed to the doorway where I spied a sign painted with two crossed lutes. A sharp memory of Sofia pierced me then and I saw her clearly, running up the stairs in her blue gown, that very first time we spoke.

Perhaps it was fortunate that a familiar laugh diverted my attention, for there was John, in the company of a gentleman, descending the Cathedral steps. Seeing me, he waved. I could hardly ignore him, and to my surprise it was another English voice I heard as I approached. The gentleman was no older than me, he looked genial enough and there was a welcome in his expression. Another Englishman with whom to converse was a very pleasing thing, so I removed my cap and bowed.

'Henry Kemper,' he said. 'Kinsman to my Lord Gray.'

I gave a deferential nod.

'Allow me to introduce Mr William Totman,' said John. 'My good friend and the best maker of lutes in all London. Will, this is a pleasant meeting. I met Mr Kemper at Sudeley Castle, what was it, two years ago?'

'It's three years now,' he said, laughing at the memory. 'But I well remember your heartfelt song. A plea to the Queen, I think?'

One of many, I could have said.

'Mmm, *shee saide my love was choaked*,' John murmured. He looked rueful and a slight shadow passed over his face, but he took it in good heart. 'Ah well. Had she loved me better, I may still be in England. Are you a musician, Mr Kemper?'

'Not of your merit, Mr Dowland. I am a clumsy player of a keyboard, best heard only by myself.'

'We are to the instrument shop now. Do you know it?' John gestured in the direction. 'I will play some lutes there, if you care to come and listen.'

A broad smile lifted Mr Kemper's expression and he bowed low. 'That is an honour indeed, but I have another meeting for which I am already happily delayed. I wish I could accept your kind invitation.' He clearly was conflicted in his mind, seeming loathe to leave us, and even when he did, he turned back before any of us had taken a step. 'May I mention to Lord Gray that you are here?'

I knew what this meant. He couldn't extend an invitation himself, but it was another way of saying, are you looking for playing opportunities?

'By all means,' said John. 'I would be most honoured to make the acquaintance of Lord Gray.'

We were saying our farewells again when Mr Kemper's eye was suddenly caught by something behind me, and he stiffened.

'Oh, look out,' he said, 'here comes a more unwelcome meeting. Allow me to introduce you to another Englishman. He is a priest. Skidmore is his name although I do not know him well. As yet, I would advise a little caution.'

A little caution? At once I shifted my weight to the front of my feet as if ready to run. One Englishman in Florence was unlikely to be a threat to me, but it was something I'd often had to do as a lad and the habit remained.

John, though, had none of my fears and it was a friendly smile and bow the stranger received from him. For an Englishman, let alone a priest, he had the strangest appearance. Besides being a very tall, narrow-shouldered man, with a large nose and a long dark beard, his garb, cloak, breeches, even his stockings, were all the colour of a ripe orange. Although the cloak looked to be of fine quality, it wouldn't be something I'd drape from my shoulders.

I wondered if I betrayed my thought, because he took what was only a small step, but it did mean all three men stood facing each other, whilst I was left admiring the back of Skidmore's hairy neck. Although I was used to being ignored or even considered invisible, it's never agreeable and whether the person in question be man, woman, high, low, cleric or heathen, I never warmed to them, however generous their subsequent behaviour. Mr Kemper had eyes sharp enough to notice this affront though and kindly tipped his cap to me as I backed away. I returned the gesture, raising my eyebrows as well, before leaving all three and making my own way towards the sign of the crossed lutes.

I wasn't sure why I felt so irritated by this man Skidmore's rudeness, but I told myself it was because, apart from the chilly indifference of Prince Gesualdo, I'd grown used to the general civility of all those we had met in Italy. To be so ignored by a fellow countryman, a priest indeed, smarted in no small measure.

I was soon distracted though. The frontage under the swinging sign did not signify a large or ostentatious place, but it belied the surprising depth to the premises. Standing in the doorway, I could see that instruments of every kind lined the walls. There were plenty of lutes, and what I thought was only one theorbo became several when I took two more steps. Six! I had never seen so many in one place. One day I will make one, I thought, as I examined how the second set of pegs took the longer strings. I couldn't resist plucking one and the sound boomed like the cathedral bell. Thrilling it was, and I began a long trail of imaginings about how I would extend my workbench to accommodate a six-foot neck.

Above me, I heard the creak of floorboards. Heavy footsteps descended stairs, and a young man appeared from a doorway at the back of the shop.

'Antonio?' I said, and he nodded. For some reason, I was expecting someone older. Perhaps it was Sofia's assurance that he was both honest and reliable. For a few minutes we conducted a stuttering conversation, more gesture than words. My mention of Signor Biscaldi drew forth a big smile and clap of hands.

'Signorina Sofia?' he asked.

I nodded vigorously, not knowing how else to reply. I picked up one of the lutes and began examining it closely.

'Well?' said John when he strode in a moment later. 'How are you getting on? Chosen one for me yet?'

It didn't take long. Antonio knew his stock well and after reading the letter from Signor Biscaldi, he brought out two for John to try, both from the Tieffenbrucker workshop in Venice. The quality of sound was true in each, but as one had eight courses and the other twelve, it was thought best to take both.

Excited by the new instruments, John took to playing for hours each day and I knew when a song was burgeoning in his mind, as it meant every interruption was an irritant. My days took on the habit of taking a stroll towards the shop, where I always found a welcome. Any misgivings I had about Antonio quickly subsided and an agreement was reached between us; I would help in the workshop, and he would teach me to converse more ably in his language.

That first week in Florence passed by almost pleasantly. I sighed too much according to Antonio, but he didn't press me to explain. Having a job to do and learning so many new words provided good distraction.

Towards the end of the week, John ventured outside once again and sniffing the air, he proposed we took a stroll out of the city. There were few other people walking alongside the river. Although it looked pleasant enough, the water was low and with the bubbling scum glistening on the muddy banks it gave off a very rank and sour scent.

We were nearing the gate when the priest Skidmore appeared from a narrow side street almost directly in front of us, his orange cloak radiant in the sunlight.

'Dowland!' he said, greeting him, with an open palms gesture of beneficence. 'This is well met indeed.'

'Oh?' said John. 'I am honoured to—'

Skidmore interrupted, waving away the pleasantries. 'I have had you much in my mind since we last spoke.'

John bowed. I, being invisible suddenly, stepped back and fixed my gaze at a high open window on the far side of the river, where a woman was hanging out washing. I knew from my time in Ma Perks's laundry the great weight of a wet sheet, but this woman's skill and strong arms made it appear light work. I admired her for it and would have watched for longer, had not Skidmore's next remark alarmed me.

'I have yet to write the letter for you,' he said, 'but it will be done without delay. Now tell me, how was your quest for a new instrument?'

Whether he noticed the sudden stiffening of my sinews, I don't know, but John showed no sign of surprise.

'Very well indeed,' he said. 'I am now in possession of two very fine lutes perfectly suitable for my first appearance at the palace.'

'Your first appearance?' Skidmore twitched a smile. 'Then you are planning on several?'

It wasn't really in John's gift to look abashed, but he did his best.

'I trust in my art,' he said, 'and pray it pleases His Excellency.'

A glint of something I couldn't quite understand appeared in Skidmore's eye at that point. Was it amusement? Or cunning?

'And I,' he said, 'shall place my trust in our Lady and pray to her for your success. Are you on your way to church?'

John nodded. 'Yes, of course.'

We certainly weren't. Antonio had recommended a tavern.

A silence opened then and for a moment I wondered if Skidmore was waiting for an invitation, or he might decide to join us anyway. We didn't expect the stream of loud, high-pitched vitriol that erupted from across the river. Had I not a word of the language, I would have understood the meaning. We all turned to see the woman I'd so admired leaning far out of her window, and there in a heap on the muddy bank below was her clean sheet. No wonder she cursed.

There was little likelihood of my retrieving it for her, but I stepped onto the riverbank to see if there was a narrow channel where I could cross. Luckily for me, a door opened on the ground floor of the house and a small boy ran across the mud to gather the sheet into his arms. I felt some sympathy for him having once been sent to retrieve a chemise that had blown from the line, only to discover it had fallen into the foul street drain.

Behind me, I heard a loud gasp from Skidmore.

'Call your man back, Dowland. What does he think he's doing?'

John coughed a little, but I was on my way back anyway. Perhaps Skidmore feared I might behave in such a reckless way again, as he assured John the letter would be sent very soon before bidding him a hasty farewell.

We'd only taken a few steps before John slapped me on the back.

'What were you going to do?' he said, keeping his laughter contained while he checked over his shoulder that Skidmore was out of sight. 'Walk on the water? Sprout wings and fly across?'

He gambolled ahead, flapping his arms, and looking so ridiculous, I played along and we were children again. I almost forgot about the letter until we reined ourselves in.

'But why?'

'For Rome,' said John, catching his breath. 'We'll need safe passage.'

'But why from him?' I sounded more aghast than I meant. 'Surely it would be better to have assurances from the Grand Duke.'

'Oh yes, much better, if that was the only possibility, but I hope to get a letter from the Grand Duke as well.'

'So why engage the priest?'

He didn't reply straight away. We'd reached the city wall and there was a crowd at the gate. Once through, we found ourselves in a very pleasant orchard of cherry and plum trees. I welcomed the cooler air after the thick heat within the walls and my mouth watered at the thought of a cherry but like the figs and grapes I'd hankered after previously, they were not yet ripe. The orchard soon gave way to vines and then, as Antonio had said for us to do, we headed away from the riverbank, up the slope towards the ring of tall cypress trees.

The tavern was nothing like any such place in London as it appeared little more than a stone hut in a clearing, but as we approached, the smell of something delicious tickled our noses and my stomach began to rumble.

Apart from a woman tending the cooking pot, and two old men who barely nodded at our arrival, we had the company of a pig, three cats and an old dog who ambled towards us. One eye was blind, but his tail still worked, and it wagged a greeting before wandering away.

We settled at a table which was little more than a roughly-hewn plank laid on a stump and nothing was said while we savoured a feast of bean stew. It was flavoured very strongly with garlic and rosemary, and we uttered plenty of appreciative grunts. Eventually, once we'd wiped our bowls clean with a hunk of bread, our conversation resumed.

'I just thought—' John looked about, almost as if the thought had alighted on his tongue, then flown away.

'Yes?'

'I just thought that it would be as well to have letters suitable for those receiving them.'

'And who,' I said, trying to fix his gaze, 'would not suit a letter from His Excellency and yet be pleased with one from the priest?' I knew the moment it was out of my mouth that my demand would only reap a sullen response, so I mollified my tone. 'John, I am no fool. An English priest in Italy, in close contact with powerful people in Rome...' I shook my head. 'Are we never going home?'

At this, he looked at me sharply. 'Never going home? What do you mean?'

'It will be *known* there. John Dowland, England's finest musician, keeping friendly company with enemies of the Queen. What will people think? More importantly, what will Sir Robert Cecil think?' And with a quick slice, I drew my hand across my neck. 'John Dowland,' I said. '*Lately* England's finest musician. *And*,' I paused for effect. 'Mr William Totman. *Lately* England's finest maker of lutes.'

This did get his attention and he looked alarmed for all of two seconds before shaking his head and raising his eyes to the sky.

'What a gloomy fellow you are, Will. Always thinking the worst. We're a very long way from London, and Skidmore is here to study at the Abbey of Santa Maria Novella. He told me so.' He swallowed a mouthful before continuing. 'We, however, are going to Rome. Yes, there are English Catholics who want to harm Her Majesty, but I'm sure Skidmore is right when he told me they are Jesuits of the Spanish faction. It's unfortunate for us that Rome welcomes all without reserve and I hope to avoid them but, if in their company, I'd far rather be thought friend than foe.'

It sounded like a dangerous game to me, but the truth was, I'd mostly taken against Skidmore for reasons of my own, not liking his manner or his garb. That didn't make him an enemy of the Queen, although if asked, I'd wager he was.

'What about Mr Kemper's warning?'

John shrugged. 'Warning about what? He merely said be cautious. Perhaps he meant keep your purse close or your sister out of sight.'

CHAPTER TEN

Two invitations awaited us when we arrived back at our lodgings. A call for John to play before the Grand Duke and Duchess on Friday evening, and two days following, a request for him to join Lord Gray and his gentlemen friends for dinner.

At last. Playing at the Pitti Palace was even more prestigious than at the Duke Alphonso's castle in Ferrara. In the minutes when he wasn't practising, John hummed and skipped about like a schoolboy. With a faraway look in his eye, he tapped rhythms on the table at dinner and shushed me when I spoke.

I was happy for him and happy for myself that I knew such a respected man. At least, I was, until he accompanied me to the shop the next morning.

'What is it you want?' I asked. 'Surely I could have fetched it for you?'

'Hah, I think not,' he said, leaning close. 'Now Will, you need to be on your best behaviour today. Lady Anna is a most talented and beautiful woman.'

'What? Lady Anna is *here*?'

'Didn't I say?' he said lightly. 'Oh well, now you know. I'm sure she'll be interested to meet the maker of her birthday present.'

I was incredulous. He'd schemed behind my back, and I'd been such a dunderhead as not to suspect a thing.

Amusement creased the corners of his eye. 'Don't look so aggrieved, Will. That I happen to meet Lady Anna here is nothing more than a happy coincidence. It'll be a meeting of great musical minds and nothing more. We shall be discussing music, and in some depth I expect.'

Did I snort then? I believe I did.

'Oh, and another thing,' he said as we got to the door, 'I was wondering if you could entertain her maidservant while I'm with Anna. We'll be upstairs, you see.' We'd entered the shop by that time, and he gestured towards the rows of instruments. 'Show her all those lovely lutes. Why you could even play her a tune if you're very brave. Besides,' he said, leaning close, 'I understand she is quite pretty.'

Sometimes, I almost despised him and might have said something, but already he was bounding up the stairs. I followed, determined to satisfy my curiosity about the lady's beauty, whilst ignoring her servant. A glance at Antonio saw him shaking his head. I suspect he disapproved of hosting the tryst but could hardly turn away two such stars of the musical firmament, however badly they behaved.

I remembered when we were in Ferrara, thinking that I'd know Lady Anna simply from John's description but really, his was a woeful effort. At the sight of John, she rose from her seat and while I bowed low, I endeavoured to have sight of her, taking in the embroidered hem of her skirts, and the ornate brocade of her bodice with its gold and silver threads twinkling in the light of an oil lamp set upon the mantel.

Ornaments such as these and the pearls threaded in the net that contained her lustrous black hair, I had never seen so close before, and indeed while her face, serene, even-featured and full-lipped, was more than pleasant, it was the sum of every aspect of her, the slight sway as she stepped towards us, the melody in her greeting, and most particularly, her expression, which seemed demure at first glance, but then became coy the second, and even bold the third, that provided the fascination. How well practised was this performance? Didn't I know that a fine instrument can take years to finish? The craftsman must hone his skills; good materials and the rude assembly are no small thing, but the finish? All those hours spent with a cloth and polish? That's when the shine appears, not from the surface, but from deep within. Lady Anna was similarly polished in every aspect of her being. I had no doubt that for brilliance, John Dowland had met his equal.

A movement from the corner nearest the window, attracted my eye. The maidservant. Was it the dazzle of her mistress that made her appear so pale? I wondered if John had seen this slight, moon-faced woman before he described her to me. I felt the warmth of annoyance and pulled at the neck of my tunic. Later, I would have something to say.

After the formalities, during which I swear John's forehead near touched the floor, he sat on the chair nearest to Lady Anna.

'Why,' he said, holding up empty hands as if they were playing a lute. 'I am in need of an instrument. Will, can you request from Antonio the best he has in stock?'

He turned to Lady Anna. 'Mr Totman is the maker of your lute. Is it not a fine instrument?' He gestured to where my lute lay on a large trunk.

'Why yes, indeed, it is,' she said, with a slight but very gracious nod to me. 'Rosa, let me have it.'

Immediately, it was placed it in her arms, whereupon Lady Anna looked directly at me and smiled. I could only gasp. The lute was a fine-looking instrument, but the Lady Anna's beauty enhanced it a hundredfold. I was an insect locked in the amber of her gaze, and when she plucked a small phrase, something akin to the vibration of the strings ran through my entire body. Yes, those few notes were all that was required for me to know that she was John's equal in every respect. But me she had floored with a glance.

After a long moment, I came to myself and bowed very low, the blood ringing in my ears as I fled downstairs.

'Lady Anna,' I whispered, wiping my forehead.

Antonio laughed at my discomfort, but it was a sympathetic laugh, and he nodded in agreement.

There were several lutes on the rack, all of which looked well enough made, but Antonio knew his stock and chose two which I would have taken up had not the maidservant descended the stairs.

I thought perhaps she should take up the lutes, she shook her head and although the light was quite dim, I did notice two spots of pink appear on her otherwise pale cheeks when she informed us that her mistress did not want to be disturbed. I glanced at Antonio who was trying not to laugh.

Two days later, another meeting with Lady Anna occurred. Afterwards I spoke with John.

'Please tell me you are not going to continue this.'

He looked at me as if I were mad. 'Why ever wouldn't I? Is she not marvellous?'

'I can't deny that, but it is only a matter of time before it is noticed. What of her husband? I imagine he would not take kindly to this dalliance.'

'Oh, Will,' he said, sighing like his doom had come. 'Why do you always have to be so serious about these things?'

'These *things*?' I was aghast at his flippancy. 'And what if her husband is like Prince Gesualdo? Is that the sort of happy end you want? You told me yourself he stabbed his wife *and* her lover to death.'

'Oh yes,' he sighed again. 'There was that.'

'Besides,' I went on, thrusting the point home with my sharpest weapon. 'I don't want to return home and break such news to your wife and children.'

He was silent then, nursing the wound.

No day went by without John playing the lute at some point, but a palace performance required more intense practice. Such an event also meant extra effort from me as well. Saturday was only three days away and John had not only to play and sing but look his best as well. It would be a blue velvet doublet evening, but I needed to make sure all his apparel was in good order. I'd meant to grease the hinges on our travel box but hadn't, due to the haste of our departure from Ferrara, and they complained loudly with every inch of opening.

John was not best pleased, stopping in the middle of *Can she excuse my wrongs,* he said. 'Haven't you done something about that yet?'

'No, but when I next see Antonio, I'll ask if he'll spare me a little grease.'

'Well, make it soon. It sounds like someone's taken a knife to my ears.'

He didn't begin playing straight away but watched while I took the doublet out of the box, gave it a good shake, then held it up to inspect for moth or stain.

'This is beginning to show the number of times it's been worn, packed and unpacked,' I said. 'The stitching has come away in three places. Perhaps if His Excellency proves to be a generous man, it would be a good idea to find a seamstress.'

'Or find a new doublet,' mused John. 'I have a fancy for something a little brighter.

'Not orange, I trust.'

'No indeed.' He laughed at the idea but a moment later, looked thoughtful. 'What about you?'

I looked up. 'Me?'

'We can't have you looking as if you've just walked out of the workshop when we go to the palace. It's time you had another jerkin and we both need fresh hose.'

Which is why, a few days later, I was very aware of my new jerkin when we walked to the palace. I'd never had such a garment. Not that it was bright or bold in any way, being a much darker shade of red than John's crimson doublet, but it was skilfully sewn, the wool cloth was finely woven and the leather piping soft to touch. I blamed it for making me walk with a little more skip than step.

Plenty of ne'er-do-wells liked the look of us too and they called out, but we strode with purpose and fierce frowns. Mine, I hoped, would ward off chancers; John frowned more with worry. Carrying a musical instrument usually gave safe passage, as most musicians weren't worth the effort of an assault. Anything more than a couple of farthings to their name was unusual and most earnings were spent on their next meal. John's charm, talent and connections had elevated him in some circles, but the good villains of Florence had no idea who he was.

Antonio had suggested we take two lutes. It was only reasonable for the renowned and brilliant Englishman to have instruments of differing tones and numbers of courses. Yes, I thought, but kept to myself, what a wonderful showcase for the Biscaldi business.

'His Excellency avoids all this,' John said, as we skirted half a dozen men shouting and waving fists at each other. 'Lady Anna tells me there's a passageway built that leads all the way from the state offices on the other side of the river to the Pitti Palace. Look up there.'

On top of the buildings on the Ponte Vecchio was a wall dotted with small square windows that ran from one side to the other. My eyes followed these windows until they turned at an exact right angle on the opposite bank.

'How very convenient for His Excellency,' I said. 'Just think how dry you'd keep on a wet day.'

My purpose with this remark had been to make John smile as the closer we got to the palace, the more his face became strained. Although he relished performing and had told me many times that once he began playing all worries went away, beforehand was a different matter. With an occasion of this magnitude that was not surprising, but I wondered also whether the message from Lady Anna could also be at the forefront of his mind. He was yet to tell me what it had said, but she was certain to be at the palace. *Meet me later?* I wondered or *Take care, my husband has arrived?* Worries like these went round and round in my head all the time, and I often wished I could hang them out like washing from a window, and have the wind blow them away forever.

Fortunately, this time, I was wrong about the message being the source of his concern.

'Did you think that peg was all right?' he said, as we neared the palace gate.

'All right?' I didn't know which lute, let alone which peg.

'Yes, on the smaller one. I thought it looser than the others.'

'It's fine now,' I said. 'I checked them both over before we left.'

Trying to veer John away from worrying about

the instruments, however, only led to worrying about something else.

'I do hope the air will be good,' he said as he cleared his throat and gave a feeble cough.

My own worries were more to do with unwittingly drawing attention to myself. Easily done in a foreign country when you don't know the rules and customs, and a Grand Duke's palace has plenty of those. Then I remembered my arrival at the castle in Ferrara when, I'm told, I raved in a delirium. Some things you can't help. A tune came into my head as we strode across the bridge. Not one of John's, I was sure, so for a moment I couldn't place it but then, yes of course, it was the same melody I'd heard when I first woke up after that horrible snake bite and the sweet voice I could hear belonged to Sofia. Would I ever see her again?

Once in the palace, we were directed along a passage and told, not very politely, to use our ears to guide us the rest of the way. It wasn't difficult, and eventually we arrived at a room full of musicians unpacking their instruments, noisy with the cacophony of conversation and tuning up.

Just before we went in, John took a deep breath, cleared his face of worry and replaced it with a confident smile. I stayed a step or two behind him, but when John strode in, it was obvious that his arrival had been anticipated. One, two, then everyone turned to look, and the noise level dropped away to nothing. All those faces, and not a smile or acknowledgment on any of them. Musicians are a curious breed. There are a few who are resentful or harbour grudges same as anyone, but mostly they respect skill and talent. I held my breath.

It was a familiar voice that broke the silence.

'Signor Dowland,' said Antonio, stepping out from behind a theorbo. 'Welcome to the Court of Ferdinando, Grand Duke of Tuscany.' He bowed low, and then turned to the gawping assembly, swept his cap in a great arc, and announced. 'Signor John Dowland, the musician renowned in every court of Europe.'

Then came the smiles and greetings. Did John grow a little taller? I believe so. It was exactly the right thing to happen, and a surprise, as I didn't know Antonio would be there.

'Oh yes,' he told me a few minutes later, once the crowd had taken John to its bosom and we were standing next to a table laden with victuals prettily set out in blue and white bowls. 'I am here with strings, reeds and tools to fix any small injury that may have befallen an instrument on its journey here.'

I was reminded of the lute I'd mended back in Ferrara. Was it still in one piece or had the mad Prince Gesualdo thrown that one in anger as well?

'Today, it was a simple job.' Antonio went on as he picked up a roasted almond from a half-empty bowl. 'I had to remove one of these from the belly of a bass-viol.'

'How did that happen?' I said, almost choking on the one in my mouth.

'I didn't ask. All I know is that it took a steady hand.'

'And a flat knife?'

He nodded. 'Though it didn't help having everyone looking.'

I thought about how I might manage such a problem.

'I'm impressed, Antonio.'

'You?' He shook his head. 'But you are a master. Signor Biscaldi said so himself. Talking of whom, I have word from him today.'

My heart gave a sudden thump. 'They are well,' I asked, apparently turning my attention to the table. 'He and the Signorina?'

'Yes, and busy too.'

'Are they away for much longer?' I had to ask, popping an apricot into my mouth.

'Another two or three weeks I think.' He paused then shrugged his shoulders. 'Or they come home tomorrow, there's no knowing.' A dish of green olives distracted him. 'But—' he said, toying with one between thumb and forefinger, 'if Sofia wishes to come home soon, then soon it will be.'

There was a twinkle in his eye as he gave me a searching look. I wasn't going to admit my feelings. Had he an interest in her too? I was very glad when John appeared at my side, clutched my elbow, and steered me away to where I had left the lutes.

'Listen,' he said, thrusting an instrument into each of my hands. 'They want me to play next, and when the call comes, I'll go first, then I want you to follow carrying both the lutes.'

'Me? Why?'

This was a new idea, and one that straight away raised the hairs on the back of my neck. Me? In a room full of Italian nobility?

'It'll look good,' he said. 'Besides, it's something different, foreign. For all they know we do it in England all the time.'

'And it'll make you look important.'

'Well, yes,' he said, as if he hadn't already thought it. 'There is that too. But aren't you pleased to be able to see me perform properly at last? And in a palace! Just think what stories you'll have to tell. Come now. Try to look a little more excited?'

I grunted at this notion. 'I'm not exactly known for my storytelling.'

'Not yet, Will. Not yet. One day though.'

'But what do I do once we're in there. Should I put the lutes down and then leave?'

'No, you can't leave. Who will carry them back for me once I've finished if you leave? Stand to one side or somewhere out of the way.'

'But what about my cap?' I held up both lutes. 'How will I be able to remove it when I bow? And I must bow.'

He tutted at this and then stood a moment staring at my cap as if it might fly off my head by force of his will. Nothing happened, so he lifted it off instead.

'Here,' he said, shoving it under my arm. 'You can replace it after you've bowed. When you've put the lutes down.'

There was no time to argue.

CHAPTER ELEVEN

Perhaps, years later, I would tell the story of how the room so dazzled me, I could barely see. It was close to the truth. I had seen marvels in my life, in the rain-drenched city of Venice, in the castle and palaces of Ferrara, but this single room forced a gasp from my lips which caused John to glance over his shoulder. I tried to look calm even though I felt nothing of the sort.

The walls rose as high as a church, and like the inside of churches here in Italy, they were covered in pictures. There was no Madonna, no angels or seraphim to be seen here though. These were outdoor scenes of forests, lakes and rivers, much like I had seen from the high views in the mountains, with little pink towers on the hilltops. Above our heads, sheep and cattle grazed in flowery meadows, dogs bounded all about, and people were hunting, feasting, and frolicking in a way most would describe as unseemly. Amongst them, creatures of dreams and fancies, dragons, griffins and grinning beasts with wings and horns. I had never seen the like before.

But it was the living people below these pictures who glittered and shone so much that I was afraid for my sight. Most were standing and what I remember about those few steps, while I tried to fix my gaze on the back of John's knees, was a great swirl of colour, the twinkling of jewels and the rustling all around me of something that sounded like autumn leaves lifted in a squall. Now I believe it was the movement of skirts and trembling of fans. As nobody was speaking, I can think of no other explanation.

My hands felt damp against the wood of the lutes, and I had to tell myself sternly not to drop them as we approached our hosts. The Grand Duke and Duchess sat on raised seats of polished walnut, with carved figures of satyrs appearing to ascend the legs. I kept my eyes down but had seen enough to know that the Grand Duke Ferdinando of Tuscany was not as aged as Ferrara's Duke

Alfonso. With pronounced eyebrows and fleshy cheeks above his beard, he had a gentle and learned expression, rather than a handsome appearance. I was reminded that while he enjoyed music, he had more fervour for books and business.

John's bow to their Excellencies was as fluent as his music, even though it contained more elaborate gestures than I had ever seen before. I, of course, could only tilt, somewhat stiffly. Not that it mattered, as I was merely a hook upon which to hang the lutes.

There were a few pleasantries, but it was clear that they were keen for John to play and sing rather than converse. Once he'd relieved me of the twelve-course lute, I retreated to a less crowded spot near the door.

I'd need to have many hands, to count the number of times on my fingers that I've heard John play, yet that performance will stay in my memory forever. Despite the number of people in the room, forty or fifty I estimated, the opening strum on the lute sounded loud in the hush.

He'd spent a long time deciding which song would make the best impression and judging by the reaction to *My Thoughts are Wing'd with Hopes* he could not have chosen better. Despite the heat, all the ladies closed their fans and the only other sound to accompany John was the soft squealing of swifts in the far distance.

For those deaf to words, the music enchants, and for those who have no ear, the story within captures their attention. Even I have looked up at the moon with thoughts of love, but now?

Thoughts, hopes and love return to me no more
Till Cynthia shine as she hath done before.

That's what he actually sang, but it wasn't the name Cynthia that I heard, but Sofia. John's skill I realised at that moment, as my own feelings threatened to overwhelm me, was to remind everyone present, of what we hold most dear. A mere glance at the faces of the assembled company told me that they were all touched in a similar manner. Not only did the plucking of his strings pluck those of our hearts, but it was as if his voice arose out of our own souls, a pure thing, lovely as a young boy's and just as angelic.

When John was a good way into the next song, *Can She Excuse My Wrongs*, and all eyes were turned to him, I risked more than a glance around. It was then I saw, seated hardly an arm's length from where he stood, Lady Anna. She was next to the Grand Duchess Christina who, despite her jewels and finery, appeared as a cloudy day compared to the radiant Lady Anna. It was hard not to be captivated by her beauty and in truth I spent much of the second and third verses ensnared. When the song was finished and she smiled, I followed her gaze which, of course, led straight to John.

It was clear to me at once, that Lady Anna and John had eyes only for each other. After he had sung another song, she had leant across to the Duchess and whispered something behind her fan. It was greeted with a smile and much nodding, which is when John gestured that I should come to him.

'Here,' he whispered, but with a sharp urgency. 'Go and put both these lutes away. Anna will be accompanying me for the rest of the evening.'

Shock raced through me, but there was nothing I could do or say, as he thrust his lute into my free hand. Yet again, I had fallen into another little trap of John's without having the slightest suspicion. After I gave another stiff bow to the Grand Duke and Duchess, I did as I was told.

In the waiting room, many of the musicians who had already performed were still there and I knew they would not leave until the last morsel on the table had been consumed and the last drop of wine drunk. Antonio was replacing a string on a viola da gamba, so after I put the lutes away, I decided to greet the only other person I knew.

'Hello, Rosa,' I said. She didn't see me approach and I startled her rather badly, but she soon recovered as her expression quickly brightened.

'Signor Totman,' she said, with a slight nod, which

I returned. We exchanged greetings, but it wasn't long before I had to ask.

'Did you know about their performance together this evening?'

She gave a small nod but looked as pained as I felt. 'I think,' she said, lowering her voice. 'No, I fear there will be trouble.'

'And I fear you are right. Did you know what they had planned?'

'No, I found out on our way here. Anna told me she didn't want Signor Dowland to be like all the other musicians who come in, play and sing, then go out again. She wanted him to stay with her.' She glanced over to the half dozen drunkards struggling to fasten their capes. 'It was her idea that they should practise something together for this evening. At the shop they didn't only...' she looked down, blushing.

'But she is a married woman.' I fumed at their stupidity. 'It will be clear to everyone present that when they play together, it isn't only the music. What happens when her husband finds out?'

My voice had risen too much and despite the noise from the revellers, I had given them cause to glance over. I grinned weakly, which seemed enough to dissuade them from any further interest, and turned back to Rosa.

'The Grand Duchess,' she said, in a low voice. 'I know she has given approval to this...this playing together, but even so, if her husband, the Count Bonizzi, does find out —' Fear flashed in her eyes. It wouldn't only be Lady Anna that suffered. I knew her situation exactly. 'He is not at all a reasonable man' she went on, 'so we must pray he remains in Ferrara.'

'If he does not, is there somewhere you could go?'

'Possibly. I know our father would look kindly on us. He has never accepted that his favourite should be married to such a pig.'

There was so much to comprehend in that small speech, that it took a moment to muster some words of my own and then they all came out in a rush.

'You mean—' I couldn't disguise my surprise. 'Lady Anna is your *sister*?'

She nodded. 'It is hard to believe, I know, but yes, she is. I am the one with no beauty or talent.'

I was too slow to contradict her, but my manners eventually prevailed. 'Oh, Rosa, don't say such—'

'You are kind, Signor Totman,' she interrupted, 'but it is true. In Ferrara, the Duke and Duchess will help everyone who has musical talent, it doesn't matter who you are. If you are a woman like Anna, low-born but beautiful and talented, then she will marry very well. Duke Alfonso arranges it, and now Anna has a husband who is a Count. He is very old and fat and every touch of his is torture to her.' She half-smiled at this. 'I am the lucky one, for I did not have to marry. Anna is a kind sister, and I am happy to be her servant.'

'But, Rosa,' I said. 'What if anything should happen to her?'

'Please,' she said, stepping a little closer. 'We do not tell everyone that we are sisters and I'm not sure why I have told you, except I believe that both you and I wish to protect those we love.'

My heart went out to her. She was a kind woman, not so plain as I had first thought, especially not when animated in conversation, but still, pale as a ghost compared to her sister.

'Thank you for your trust, Rosa. You are right that we share a similar problem. Both you are I are bound in love and duty to very charming, talented, and beautiful people, who revel in reckless behaviour. We can only hope that our fears are not realised. Certainly, I will do my utmost to persuade John that we should start for Rome at once.'

I have never seen a face clear so quickly.

'Are you leaving us then?'

I had to laugh. 'Please,' I said. 'Try not to look so delighted, but yes, it has always been the intention to go on to Rome.'

Embarrassed she began to stumble an apology, but I

was far from offended and, in no time, she began to laugh with me.

'Come,' I said, 'let's get ourselves a little wine, I think we've earned it. Besides, it looks like Antonio has finished his task.'

Rosa returned to her quieter self when we joined Antonio, but she did smile when he told her about the almond rattling about in the bass-viol.

It was a while before John returned and whilst we were a little flushed with wine, he was drunk with success. I couldn't stop thinking about Jane Dowland at home and Lady Anna's husband. He may be the nearer and the most dangerous, but I felt more anguish at the thought of Jane and the children hearing gossip about their beloved John while he was so far away. Musicians travelled freely, and at speed, all over the Continent and they traded news and information like coinage, as Tom Morley had often informed us.

Later, I mentioned to John the plan to go to Rome whilst I yet again wrestled with the hooks on his doublet.

'Oh, there's time yet,' he said. 'They seem to like me here, and the Grand Duke is very generous.'

It was true. Our new clothes were all paid for and apparently there was plenty left over. I would have asked how much, but John closed his eyes and began humming quietly to himself. This meant one of two things. He'd either had a moment of inspiration, or much more likely, he didn't want me saying anything about what had transpired earlier that evening. I'd nearly done with the doublet hooks and was about to broach the subject when his eyes flashed open, and he announced.

'I am thinking of sending something home for Jane. Perhaps some cloth? Or a jewel? What do you think?'

I didn't say anything to this notion, born I dare say, out of guilt.

'Although,' he went on, 'she didn't seem very keen on the Landgrave's ring, did she?'

To chide John would do no good and if anything, it

would make him worse. Most women, he seemed to think were to be toyed with, but I feared Lady Anna may have had a quiver of Cupid's darts about her person when they first met.

'I'm quite sure,' I said with heavy emphasis, 'that your dear wife would be pleased to receive anything from her husband.'

At last, the doublet was undone, and we both sighed with relief. I stepped away, and began to attend to my own fastenings, but felt John's hand on my shoulder.

'Let us stay awhile, Will,' he said, with a note of pleading I'd rarely heard before. 'I will write to Jane, and believe me, I do miss her and the children. They seem so far away though, and everything here is so...so...'

His skill with words and poetry seemed to desert him, but the lifting of his features and faraway gaze told me exactly *who* everything was. He swept the memory away with a wave of his hand, as if to say not now, not now.

'Besides,' he said firmly, 'Florence is a city that suits you and me almost as well as Ferrara. I am sorry that the Signorina Biscaldi is not here, but perhaps she will come soon and then how would you like to rush away to Rome?'

'I wouldn't like it at all. You'd probably have to drag me with force, but then, I do not have a wife and Miss Sofia does not have a jealous husband.'

He sat down on the edge of the bed, holding a leg out straight so that I could pull off his boot.

'True,' he said, frowning, but after a long moment he shrugged. 'But there's nothing to be done about that. All we can do is be on our way at the first sniff of him.'

'And Lady Anna? And Rosa? What do you think will happen to them? A knife in the heart? The same fate as Prince Gesualdo's wife?'

Then he looked truly grave and more hollow-cheeked than ever as he gave a sharp intake of breath.

'That is very much in my mind. Trust me, Will, I did not want to play together so publicly. I cited the wife of

Prince Gesualdo to her just as you have.' He shook his head. 'But Anna is persuasive. *Life is to be lived*, she said, *and the Grand Duchess is fond of me and not at all inclined towards the Count.*' He sighed. 'We can only hope that Duchess Christina's favour is enough.'

What good is hope and favour against a sharp blade? I didn't ask, knowing full well already, so I pulled off the other boot and set them next to mine by the door. Ready in case we had to depart in haste.

John remained asleep, even while I rose and dressed the next morning. The smell of new baking coming in through the shutters encouraged me into the street and I had the thought of taking some breakfast back for him. I was looking for the soft doughy buns which contained sweet, dried fruit, but John had a great liking for the hard bread flavoured with olive oil and garlic. My stomach would complain vigorously if I ate that so early in the day, despite there often being more hole than bread beneath the crust.

The mornings in Florence were cool and clear. Like most cities we'd visited, the air wasn't very fresh later in the day, but I took a few good deep breaths as I strolled towards the market and felt much better for them.

Most shops were still closed, but from every side came the clatter and bang of shutters and doors opening, the clop of hooves and creak of wheels and the now familiar cry of *buongiono*, as neighbours greeted one another.

I wasn't expecting to recognise anyone, but even from a distance and without the vivid cloak, being so tall and with such a long thin beard, he was unmistakable. Stepping from a doorway, I hoped he wasn't about to walk in my direction, but then he turned to speak to the figure who remained inside. I feigned interest in a table laden with great rounds of cheese, but the merchant was equally interested in persuading me to part with more money than I possessed.

I had no argument with Skidmore though, and as he was still deep in conversation, I walked quickly on, hoping to pass unnoticed. A few skills learnt in my boyhood on the Cheapside streets came back to me; adopt a different stance, gait and keep your head down. I had more hair then though, which was good curtain to hide behind.

I passed by safely, as Skidmore's attention was entirely caught by what proved to be a smiling young woman in the doorway. A sinful liaison? Or a hint of treachery? Nothing surprised me about the behaviour of men and women. Indeed, I'd seen and heard many men of the church, vehement in the pulpit about my sinful behaviour, only to be discovered indulging themselves. So different from John, who, if he was asked, had to be stopped from confessing to everything.

The baker I favoured wasn't far from the Palazzo Vecchio, and where I'd discovered that whilst my breakfast buns were still warm and plentiful, John's olive bread wasn't yet ready

My first plan had been to sit in the piazza before returning to the baker's stall, but I found myself heading down a street towards the Cathedral. Not that I was thinking of going to prayers. Despite my worry about Lady Anna's husband arriving at any moment and stabbing us all, whilst wandering through the streets eating a very good bun, I felt almost content. I liked this city, its people, and their noisy ways. There was a lot of laughter and every day one saint or another had to be celebrated. I could only think that Heaven was packed so tight with saints, there'd hardly be room for any faithful followers. I tried not to think of what happened to the doubtful and hesitant, like me.

I swallowed down the last mouthful and rinsed my sticky hands at the feet of Neptune in a fountain. John would have to get his own breakfast. If Antonio had some work for me, it wouldn't do to coat an instrument in honey.

I hurried along congratulated myself on avoiding John Skidmore but when I turned the corner, there he was, right in front of me. He didn't greet me with any kind of cheer or smile, but I was acknowledged – if you can call a pointed finger an acknowledgment.

'*You*,' he said, composing himself by taking a deep breath and standing straight which, made him about eight feet tall.

'Me?' I said, looking over my shoulder.

'Of course, you. You're Dowland's man, aren't you?'

Such an easy man to dislike, I thought, inclining my head only slightly.

'You'd better tell him—' he sniffed, looking at me down his long thin nose, I swear was sharp as a chisel. 'Tell him I have heard the gossip.'

'Gossip?' I said. 'What gossip would that be?'

'Don't be a fool. You know very well. Your master would do well to take care.'

'I don't know what you mean,' The words fell out of my mouth before I could stop them. 'Perhaps it's just tittle-tattle you were listening to just now. I'm sure you know how women love to gossip.'

He drew back as if scalded and sucked in his breath so hard I thought he might choke on his beard.

'And *I*,' he said, with a hiss, 'have no idea what *you* mean.' Gathering his cloak about, he turned away, but then, looked back. 'You may tell Mr Dowland, that I will not go back on my word. His letter will be delivered forthwith.'

A pity, I thought, as I walked on. Even so, I was troubled that I'd been rash. It hadn't been in my mind to try and forestall the letter even though I doubted the need for it, and it wasn't my habit to make enemies.

As I crossed the piazza, I speculated what if anything, might happen next. Did it matter so much that I had seen Skidmore earlier? He wouldn't be the first or last man of the cloth to seek a woman's company although, on reflection, such earnest and close conversation I'd witnessed was unlikely with a casual acquaintance. Would he make something of it? I didn't trust him. My fear was that his letter might contain some hidden message to our detriment.

All this ruminating closed my eyes to what was

happening about me, but as I approached the shop, a sound awoke my ears. A sound much sweeter than any made by a musical instrument, one that put away all previous thoughts, made light of my step and filled my heart with the greatest of pleasure.

CHAPTER TWELVE

At the shop doorway, as if on command, Signor Biscaldi, Sofia and Antonio all turned to see who had obscured their light.

'Welcome home,' I said, stepping in and around several stacks of boxes. 'I see your travels have been successful.'

'Why, it's Mr Totman!' Sofia exclaimed. She came over at once, and while I resisted the great temptation to gather her into my arms, she smiled up at me and said: 'What a great pleasure it is to see you again. You must tell me all that you've been doing since we last met.'

'Tut tut, Sofia,' Signor Biscaldi chided but he waved me in. He occupied the only chair and was cooling himself with Sofia's fan.

'Good business?' I said, pointing at all the boxes.

'*Very* good, but very tiring also.' His face pleated into a smile. 'My daughter has enough...enough...' he shook his head, devoid of the word. I knew what he meant anyway. Sofia had spirit and energy enough for them both. She took up the conversation.

'We arrived later than expected yesterday. There was a commotion on the road from Fiesole and we had to wait for such a long time. Then, as there was no Antonio here, we just left everything as you see it so we could get in before the ghetto gate was locked.'

I hated to think of it, but while there was nothing I could do about the Grand Duke's laws here in Florence, there was something I could do.

'May I help you unpack?'

'Yes, yes. That is very kind,' said Signor Biscaldi. 'Perhaps you say what you think of our new lutes?'

I smiled at this. 'And if I say they are all not as good as mine?'

'Ha!' he slapped his thigh. 'Then I find big thick rope and tie you to the bench, so you make lutes for me.'

That made all of us laugh, but in some corner of my mind, I thought being tied to the Biscaldi's shop might be a very pleasant thing, albeit not with a big thick rope.

Any conversation about lutes soon turned to an enquiry about John. I said he was well and the performance for the Grand Duke and Duchess had gone *very* well. The darting of glances between Antonio and myself, however, did not escape the bright, but sharp eyes of Sofia.

'Has something happened?' she asked. 'Did Signor Dowland behave badly again? I hope no more lutes have been hurled to the floor.'

'No indeed!' Signor Biscaldi sat up with a start, no doubt imagining a costly incident. 'Which lutes he choose?'

'Have no fear,' I said. 'He played a fine twelve-course lute, and one that is still very much in one piece,' I said. 'I'm afraid the difficulty is more a matter of the heart.'

'Difficulty?' Sofia and her father spoke as one.

'You may not be surprised to hear that Lady Anna is in the city. A lovely and very *persuasive* lady, she has since been very keen to...to...' I hesitated, wondering how best to explain. Antonio though, had no such difficulty.

'She and Signor Dowland, they meet together here, upstairs,' he said, raising his eyes in that direction before pointedly saying. 'On their own.'

There was no doubt about his meaning. Signor Biscaldi put his hands together in prayer and looked grave. Beside me, I heard Sofia gasp.

'At the palace, they played together,' I said. 'With the approval of the Grand Duchess, but even so, I'm afraid it was much remarked on.'

'Remarked on?' Signor Biscaldi took a sharp intake of breath and shook his head. 'There is gossip?'

I nodded. 'I have heard, but only a word, and that from a priest.'

'A *priest*?' he almost choked on the word. 'They are worst.'

With the picture in my mind of Skidmore waggling

his finger in my face, I was inclined to agree.

Signor Biscaldi levered himself from the chair and paced to the back of the shop. He stood there, for a few moments with his arms folded, all the while muttering and shaking his head.

We were all quiet, not wanting to interrupt his thoughts. Antonio began to unpack some of the boxes and move them away from the entrance. I followed his lead. As the sun rose higher, light filled the shop, and with it the noises of a busy morning. A heavily laden cart rumbled by, footsteps, snippets of laughter and conversations came and went. The hour bell rang, and I assumed that John would be finding his own breakfast by now.

Ah, John, I thought. Why did he have to make life so difficult? Not just for himself, but for so many people around him? I glanced at Sofia, who caught my eye and gave me a bleak smile in return.

'Can it be stopped?' Signor Biscaldi asked, once he'd finished pacing and returned to his chair.

'I don't know,' I said. 'I did hope Lady Anna's husband would come to Florence but then, if he's anything like Prince Gesualdo, both their lives will be in danger.'

Frowning, Signor Biscaldi took to his habit of picking at his lace cuff. Already I could see where some stitching was coming loose.

'They blame us,' he said, glancing up at me. 'Always Jews are blamed. Even if not our fault. They close shop and make us leave city. Or worse.'

We were all silent, trying to comprehend what would happen in any of those dreadful situations.

Antonio was the first to speak.

'Would it—' he hesitated. 'Would it be wrong to tell John that Lady Anna's husband is on his way?'

'Is he?' I said, sharply.

He shrugged. 'I don't know. Maybe Signor Biscaldi has brought the news.'

Sofia was quickest to grasp his meaning. 'Of course! Oh Antonio, that is a very good idea.'

'Yes, yes.' Signor Biscaldi clapped his hands. 'Very

good idea indeed. We come with news. Why not? He will arrive say, any day?'

'Yes,' I said, slowly, whilst misgivings bloomed in my mind. 'It is a good idea. Whether John would believe such a lie from me is not certain. He may well be suspicious.'

'I could tell him.' Sofia said, laying her hand upon Signor Biscaldi's arm, but then she frowned. 'Come now, are we being too hasty? If the Grand Duchess was happy, perhaps we shouldn't interfere. Let us get on with unpacking rather than plotting.'

I was surprised. Why would Sofia be reticent suddenly? The truth was that nothing good could come of our remaining here. Had I forgotten Rosa's relief at the thought of us leaving for Rome? Her fear for her sister's life? I glanced at Sofia and knew that despite everything, at that moment and at the sight of that little crease in Sofia's smooth forehead, I would give anything to stay.

'But if not me, then Papa could speak to Signor Dowland,' Sofia went on. 'Do you think he would be more likely to listen to advice rather than threats?'

'That may depend on the weather or the time of day, but leave it to me. I will find the right time to speak with him.'

Even as I said it, I couldn't imagine when that right time would be and, when I found a lute with a couple of broken strings, the subject was changed.

'This one'll need attention,' I said, lifting from the box. 'Poor quality strings, I think.' I checked all the points of contact between string and wood, but the pegs, nut and bridge all looked well-made, and with no rough edges that would have stressed the string. Besides, the break was a span's width from any of them. 'The instrument itself seems quite good. Do you have more strings, Antonio? I could change them now.'

The answer was no. All his stock had been used up the evening before and the errand for more, he'd meant to make earlier in the week, had slipped his mind.

His errand would have been to the premises of a man

called Lorenzo, who made a living soaking and tanning any fresh entrails he could scavenge or buy for next to nothing. People hurried past his shop with their breath held to avoid the stench, but it was well known in Florence that Lorenzo's strings were the very best.

All that I discovered from Sofia as we made our way there. My curiosity about anyone or anything to do with my craft, had led me to suggest that I should go to buy the new strings, and very quickly Sofia offered to show me the way.

No wonder Signor Biscaldi had grumbled. We were an odd couple to be walking the streets of Florence; a young Jewess accompanied by a man, clearly a foreigner. Of course, people stared, and we received a couple of unwelcome remarks. Sofia took no notice. She told me that Florence was a city that for the most part was tolerant of Jews, although not nearly as liberal as Ferrara, but that didn't mean every man, woman and child welcomed them.

'And how do you find Florence, Mr Totman?'

Our conversation to that point had been all politeness. This was the first question she asked of me directly.

'I like it very much,' I said, adding without a moment's hesitation, 'and even more so now that you have returned home.'

She coloured at once, but it was with a smile she couldn't conceal.

'I am glad,' she said, shyly, and in some mysterious invisible way she reached into my chest and gave my heart a squeeze.

We walked on, my feelings threatening to burst out into laughter or a great shout of joy. All the world was beautiful. That is, until a boy, not more than twelve years old, a stupid, ignorant boy, stepped from the crowd walking by us and spat at Sofia's feet. My joy became fury at once, and I was about to make chase and give him a good hiding until a small hand patted the air in front of me.

'No,' she said. 'That is not our way.'

She walked on, while I followed, with my fists still clenched and rage quietly boiling. Once we'd turned a corner, however, she stopped and waited for me with almost an amused expression on her face.

'Thank you,' she said.

'But he shouldn't do that.'

'He most certainly shouldn't, but would a beating from you stop him next time?'

'It might make him think first.'

She shook her head. 'Next time would be worse. I know that boy. He would have a grudge and blame us, not himself.'

I blustered a little, but all conviction left me when I remembered a grudge of my own.

'You're right,' I said, as we walked on. 'That's exactly what I did when I was probably the same age as that idiot. I stole a current bun. I'm very fond of them and had one for breakfast only this morning.'

'I hope you didn't steal that one, Mr Totman.'

'Indeed not. It was honestly paid for and more delicious for it. Back when I was a lad though, just before I could take my first bite, a strong hand grabbed me and there was no wriggling free. I was made to put it back. That felt so painful, I remember it clearly, plump, round and dotted all over with juicy currants, just what my hungry stomach needed.' I sighed at the memory.

'Oh, you poor boy,' said Sofia, who I could see was smiling behind her hand. 'But what happened?'

'I was very lucky. As the stallholder didn't lose anything, he let me off with a cuff round the ear and a kick up the backside as I ran away. Even so, for a long time afterwards, I blamed him for stealing my bun.'

'You were lucky indeed. If every little thief went unpunished we'd all have nothing to eat.'

I was surprised at this harsh remark until I realised, she was in jest. It had been a difficult time for me and so was the memory even though I had recounted it lightly. Now, whenever I see some poor wretch at the whipping post crying out from the pain of it, I give thanks for the stallholder's kindness.

Our way should have led us to pass close to the Abbey of Santa Maria Novella, but I asked Sofia if we could take another route. The chance of meeting Skidmore again was remote, but I didn't want to risk it. Sofia was intrigued and giggled when I described him. There could be no good reason for her to know such a man but still, I was glad she had no recollection of ever seeing him.

After a sharp turn, we crossed a strongly smelling tanning yard and hurried through a narrow passage where the stink became almost overwhelming. Even I, used to all sorts of stench from the tannery at Bermondsey, wrinkled my nose. Sofia held a lace handkerchief sweetened with lavender to hers.

Across Lorenzo's shop frontage, a line was strung, holding at one end the entrails waiting to be scraped smooth, while at the other hung a long curtain of finished strings already stretched and wound. Lorenzo knew Sofia and was pleased to see her although he looked suspiciously at me. After an explanation of my virtues however, he was happy to tell us exactly how the freshly slaughtered sheep's gut would become the source of a beautiful sound, pointing fondly at the vat of bloated entrails being soaked so it would be easier to scrape away the fat and any other spoiling matter. It would not be my choice of work, but I could see how there would be certain measure of satisfaction in the task of oiling and polishing a wound string ready for its instrument.

Our order filled Sofia's basket. Strings for six course lutes outnumbered the other instruments several times over, but something I'd noticed back in London was also true here: archlutes were becoming more popular. The long bass strings have an appealing resonance, but they're also more susceptible to breaking in spite of their thickness. Antonio had asked for them particularly.

'Please,' I said to Sofia as we left. 'Let me carry the basket.'

'Thank you, Mr Totman. That would be much

appreciated.'

She handed it over and straight away took out her handkerchief. A glance of amusement passed between us as, once we'd speedily retreated from the stench, a few deep breaths were needed. A trader selling little cherry tarts hailed us and I bought two for each of us, although Sofia insisted one was enough, which left me with three. I didn't mind, especially as I could listen to tales of her travels rather than speak of my own, and all the while I kept my eyes open for that boy, or indeed anyone, looking to insult my dear companion.

The number of people in the piazza surrounding the cathedral had swollen by many times when we got back, and it also appeared busy in the shop. At first, peering into the gloom I imagined business was going very well, but the opposite turned out to be true. Nobody was there to buy, but all wanted something.

Antonio, nearest the door, took the basket from me.

'Ah, thank you,' he said. 'More work to be done. I've a queue for these now.'

John, leaning casually against a rack of guitars and citterns, was in conversation with a young woman facing away from me. He raised a hand and waved me over, where I discovered Rosa.

'At last! There you are. And with the delightful Miss Sofia.' He beamed at us both, and I felt the heat of embarrassment rise to my face. 'You have returned at exactly the right time. Rosa has come to fetch some new strings for Lady Anna.'

A glance at their faces told me that wasn't the only reason for her visit. Another tryst? Surely not. I would have sought Signor Biscaldi's opinion but, beside me, Sofia gasped.

'Jakob!' she cried, with pleasure. 'What a lovely surprise.'

The young man with Signor Biscaldi broke off his conversation at once and greeted Sofia warmly in return. There followed much in the way of smiles and gestures that spoke of more than friendship, each one a knife that stabbed me. There were introductions and talk of wine, but John thanked them and declined. He stood by the door blocking most of the light for which I was thankful, as my expression would no doubt have betrayed me. Fortunately, the cathedral bell began to toll, saving us from further discourse.

'Come,' John said, slapping me on the back and guiding me to the door. 'Let's leave these good people for now. I see they have much to talk about and I have need of you back at our lodging.'

We bade everyone farewell but once outside, John turned to Rosa. 'Until the day after tomorrow then.'

She gave a slight nod before hastening away and disappearing into the crowd.

'So,' I said, unable to resist a glance over my shoulder for a last look at Sofia. 'What is this need you have of me back at our lodgings?'

He looked at me askance.

'Oh that? There's nothing. I just noticed your tortured expression when Signorina Sofia greeted the decidedly eligible Jakob. A very good friend of the family I discovered, and high in the estimation of Signor Biscaldi.'

'I'm very pleased to hear it,' I said, gritting my teeth.

At least John tried not to laugh. 'Oh dear,' he said. 'Come on, Will. I think a little wine is in order. Best not overdo it though, as it's important we're both on our best behaviour this evening.'

CHAPTER THIRTEEN

For dinner with Lord Gray, John decided on the blue doublet, and I was glad of that. A hole had been patched almost invisibly by the excellent seamstress who had made my new jerkin, and once on and I'd given it a brush it looked almost as good as new.

'Still no letter from Skidmore,' John said as we passed Santa Maria Novella. 'I wonder if he's changed his mind about writing it.'

'Perhaps,' I said, hoping that was the case. 'Will you enquire about him this evening?'

'I hadn't thought to. Why? Should I?'

'Well,' I hesitated, unsure of my own opinion. 'Mr Kemper was rather cautious in his appraisal of the man, but he didn't make clear why. Lord Gray may be more forthcoming.'

John didn't say anything, but I think I detected a slight nod.

Our landlord had given us plentiful instructions about how to get to the tavern, but the shadows were lengthening, and the streets narrow with tall buildings on either side. At a loud shout and raucous laughing behind us, I was back in Ferrara, just before I had taken Sofia into my arms. I swallowed and tried not think of her. I *would* not.

Even so, with the arrival of Jakob my spirits had plummeted. All my resolve to forget her had drained away the moment she greeted me again. If I was a sensible man, the incident with the street boy would have reminded me of our differences, made me see reason, put any thoughts of Sofia quite behind me, but in truth, it only made me love her more.

I clenched my fists, tight as I could, then shook them out.

'All right?' said John, startled by my action.

'Just a little cramp.' I shook my hand again and

glanced behind us in case of danger. The shouts I'd heard were friendly though and not directed at us. By chance though, I did see Henry Kemper, stepping from a side street.

'Well met,' he said, greeting each of us with a friendly slap on the arm. 'We are almost there and the door is not obvious. Here, around this corner. It's a private entrance, which means we won't have to fight our way through the crowd in the public rooms.'

We would have walked straight past it for certain. Even the man lighting a lantern above? the door wouldn't have alerted us, as there was nothing to indicate a tavern.

The company was all from England and I rejoiced to understand their conversation about the heat, price of wine and the joys (delicious oranges) and hardships (uncomfortable seats) of travelling, without any effort. Once Mr Kemper had introduced John to a portly gentleman, whom I assumed was Lord Gray, he came over to where I hovered by the door.

'Come and sit with me, Mr Totman,' he said, leading me to a smaller table at the far end of the room. 'Lord Gray is very happy to have us present here, where we can eat and converse without imposing on the other gentlemen.'

'Lord Gray is most generous, and please, my name is William, or Will if you like,' I said, surprised at such a welcome. I'd expected to be given a plate and that if I was lucky.

'I do like, and in that case, let us both dispense with our surnames. Please call me Henry,' he said, slapping his chest, as if to remind himself. 'Let us be seated. Lord Gray is most generous indeed, and especially to Englishmen when abroad. For all the marvels here, the good company of a compatriot is always welcome.'

I thought of the priest. 'All compatriots?' I asked. 'Forgive me, but I seem to recall you weren't all that pleased to see a certain English priest when we met on the Cathedral steps.'

'Who, Skidmore?' He sniffed at the name. 'Yes, well, there are always exceptions.'

I was about to ask more, but in through the door came a young woman bearing two large jugs of wine in each hand as if they weighed nothing at all. It was clear she was skilled at this feat and there was quite a cheer as she placed them all on the larger table. Before she was able to pour a drop, however, Lord Gray gestured that she should bring one of the jugs to us. She did as bid, of course, but she reserved her smiles and manners for the gentlemen. We were to pour our own wine.

'Skidmore's a strange one,' Henry told me as we dipped our first course of hard bread into a saucer of olive oil infused with garlic and rosemary.

'How so?'

'His sartorial choices?' he winced. 'Are they not strange?'

'They certainly wouldn't be my choice, and rather surprising for a priest. Do you think he is hoping to be a cardinal, and it is a step in that direction?'

He took my remark as a good joke, and almost choked on his mouthful.

'You could be right, although whether Her Majesty or His Holiness would welcome him in that role isn't at all clear.'

I was eager to find out more. 'Has he already proved himself unworthy?'

'I do not know for sure, but rumours surround him.'

He was interrupted by another course arriving and, although I was keen to hear about Skidmore, the platter of salted meats served with green beans and dotted with sprigs of fennel kept us quiet for a while. Eventually, Henry sat back.

'Skidmore has made a name for himself,' he said, 'as someone who can ease the way for the traveller, especially if they are on their way to Rome.'

'Indeed,' I nodded. 'He has said he will write letters for us. Well, I say *us*, but it is John I mean, of course. Skidmore has already taken against me.'

'He takes against many people of good character and faith,' he swallowed a mouthful of wine before continuing, 'but there was talk he was involved with Babington.'

I stiffened at the name. 'You mean the traitor?'

It was Babington's execution that I remembered so clearly. Even though it took place nine or ten years ago, it was the first and last time I'd stood so close. I put down my knife.

'Yes,' he went on. 'The same. Not that it was proved, and to be honest, I have my suspicions about most of the tale.'

'Why so?'

'Too many had told it before it got to me, but this is what I heard.' He leaned forward to speak, although there was no one to overhear and the gentlemen were very loud in their conversations. 'Babington, thinking that Skidmore was more for the Pope than the Queen, had asked him to a meeting about such matters at The Grapes.'

'The Grapes at Limehouse?' I knew it well and was rather fond of the tavern.

He nodded. 'The very same, but the peculiar part of the tale is that while they and the rest of the traitors were having dinner – ordered by Babington following Skidmore's pronouncement that he'd had nothing since breakfast – a note was delivered to Skidmore, from whom I can't say for certain, containing an order that he should *arrest* Babington.'

'Arrest him? At The Grapes? But I heard they found him up Harrow way.'

'Indeed, and so they did. It seems Babington must have caught sight of the note, for before any arrest was made, he left the company saying he was going to pay his dues, but then he never returned. Both his cape and sword were left behind on his chair. What do you make of that?'

What I made of it didn't take long to work out. 'When you said, Babington *caught sight* of the note, do you think Skidmore *showed* it to him?'

He shrugged. 'We'll never know, but it seems likely to me. And not only that,' he said, leaving the rest of the sentence hanging in the air while he skewered a particularly long bean and bit off one end. 'Not only that, but if he was for the Queen, what was he doing falsifying the signature of Sir Thomas Baskerville?'

I gaped at that. Everyone knew how much Sir Thomas was highly respected by the Queen, having commanded many battles and even voyaged to the New World on her behalf.

'Yes, and quite recently too.' He thought for a moment. 'May, it was. We were in Flanders still. A fellow there made a deposition to the effect that Skidmore signed a travel paper for him in the name of Baskerville.'

The letter he was supposed to be writing for John sprang into my mind. What falsehoods might that contain?

'Was it true?' I said, even more aghast.

'I believe so.'

'Skidmore surely can't return to England then. Is he known to be such a villain?'

'Oh no. He convinces many that he has the power to walk unscathed through any hindrances that might cross his path, and so far it seems he has. He pays no regard to Lord Gray's advice that Her Majesty would not appreciate any hint of treason.'

The next course's platter, containing a pair of pigeons, arrived with a thump on the table, but that time Henry's response, an appreciative smack of the lips before clapping his hands together, did elicit a smile from the woman.

'Do you think,' I ventured, once we were picking the last of the meat from the small bones, 'that perhaps Skidmore is for *both* sides?'

He nodded slowly, took up his napkin and wiped his beard. 'It has occurred to Lord Gray that that is a possibility, a probability even, but it is hardly something we can ask directly.'

'No indeed.'

'For my part, I find him an odious fellow who is only on his own side and best avoided. But enough of him now,' Henry took up his glass and raised towards me. 'Tell me, how this delightful city is treating you? Will you be sorry to leave?'

I sat back, picking up my glass as a rush of feeling surged through me. It would be difficult to describe how I couldn't wait to leave and yet the greater part of me wanted to stay. Instead, I suggested that all the cities in Italy I had visited were beautiful, each in their own way. Henry Kemper was not a reticent man and was happy to pursue the line of conversation, and by the end of the jug of ale, I was well informed about several fair cities that warranted a visit.

John seemed distracted as we walked back to our lodging. I didn't press him, as sometimes the muse came upon him unexpectedly, although lately the muse wore the guise of Lady Anna. Was he was thinking of her? We were both quiet and I tried my best to put thoughts of Sofia from my mind and instead consider what Henry had told me about the devious Skidmore. I'd had no success in persuading John that a letter from such a man might be more hindrance than help in Rome, and a dangerous one at that, but this new information? Perhaps it would bring him round.

The next morning was a slow and bleary-eyed start for both of us. When I opened a shutter, it was to a blade of light so bright, I drew back almost blinded. John muttered a complaint and turned over, while I took my time over getting dressed. Once out in the street, I felt a little better, but my favoured stallholder laughed when he saw me. I went back to our lodgings with a hunk of dry bread, washed down with the weakest wine, it was all we could stomach.

Eventually, when we were mostly recovered, I thought back to the conversation I'd had with Henry Kemper, but at my first mention of Skidmore, John picked up his lute. Usually that meant an end to conversation, but I was quite determined.

'Are you sure there isn't something you're not telling me?'

That incurred a loud strum of irritation.

'What sort of thing?' he said, pouting.

Irritable myself, I took a deep breath.

'I don't know, but I do know that Skidmore is someone you'd usually avoid. Instead, even though warned off by our own countrymen, you're about to—' I couldn't think of a word, 'to be *intimate* with him.'

There was a silence then, during which I had to thrust away a picture that came to mind. I looked back at John who was gawping at me with raised eyebrows.

'Intimate with Skidmore?' he said faintly. 'How *very* repellent. You quite shock me, William.'

Whether his shudder was for effect or could not be helped, it was enough to make us both smile.

'I shocked myself,' I said, 'but it was born out of worry for you.'

John was quiet. 'You're right to be worried,' he said at last. 'I'm worried for us both. I didn't think it would be difficult or dangerous. They just said, keep my eyes open, that's all.'

It was as if something crawled over the back of my neck, so real it felt, I gave it a rub.

'What is *it* and who exactly are *they*?'

'It was when I went to fetch the letters from Sir Robert.' John looked almost bashful. 'He only mentioned it like an afterthought. I was to let him know if I heard of any gossip or plots against the Queen. That's all.'

That's *all*? An afterthought? I said nothing. Perhaps Sir Robert Cecil was so casual, but from everything I'd heard about him, it seemed very unlikely.

'Then I spoke to Tom Morley,' John went on. 'I thought seeing as he'd had experience of the sort of thing that he might be able to give me some advice.'

'By *the sort of thing*,' I said, lowering my voice, although we were alone in our room and had heard no one pass our door. 'You actually mean, *spying*.' I mouthed, more than whispered the word. 'That's what spies *do*.'

'Yes, but it's not *only* what I do, is it? This is what I really do.' He strummed the lute again, winced at the sound and set about tuning it.

'What exactly did Tom Morley say?' I persisted. 'Did he tell you to get friendly with the likes of Skidmore? Or close enough to hear any rumours?'

Eventually John managed a small shrug.

I might have guessed. Tom Morley would suggest getting as close as one string to another. Could he be cut from the same cloth as Skidmore? Albeit not so garish and a mere seam rather than a cloak. Tom had a barrel-load more charm too, but there was no one who thought more of Thomas Morley than he did, except perhaps his mother.

'But Tom isn't—' I was about to remonstrate when a sharp knock on the door made us both jump. We were upright and on guard in a moment.

'Yes?' I said. 'Who is it?'

'Message for you.'

I recognised the landlord's voice with a great deal of relief. The talk of spies had made me jumpy but there was nothing threatening about the message he handed me. I'd expected it to be for John, especially as the paper exuded the faintest scent of lavender.

'It's for me.' I said, once I'd shut the door.

'*You?*'

I nodded. Had I ever received such correspondence before? It could only be from Sofia. I thought of her little hand, dancing before me when she spoke, stretching out before me to quell my anger at the ruffian in the street, that same hand that had sealed this letter to me.

'I wonder who that could be from,' John said, with a smirk. 'Go on, open it.'

He didn't have to tell me again. The lines ran straight with not a single blot, but my eye went first to the bottom of the message, and I read:

Your friend
Sofia Biscaldi

'It's from Sofia,' I said.

'Well, that is a surprise.' John said and he flopped back down onto the bed. 'Is she declaring herself?'

For John, receiving notes from ladies was almost a

daily occurrence when we were at home, a source of irritated amusement to Jane Dowland, but this was my first.

I ignored him and began my reading.

Forgive me for writing to you, Mr Totman,

I had to smile at that.

but Antonio has asked for you especially—

Oh. This was Antonio's idea. Disappointment stole all my excitement.

and of course, Papa and I will be delighted to see you.

I was very glad of that.

We have discovered that one of the more valuable instruments we purchased while away has also suffered a little damage. Antonio is certain that it is not very bad, but it would require someone with your skill to mend it. Papa and I agreed at once, so I am writing to ask if you would help us once again.

An invitation of sorts, it was hardly a declaration of love but, ever hopeful, I decided that door was not yet locked.

'Off you go then,' said John once I'd told him. 'I shall be glad of the time to practise without you moping around.'

With that he began humming *Can She Excuse My Wrongs*.

I rather dreaded being confronted with a beaming Jakob, but when I arrived at the shop there was no sign of him. Sofia and her father both greeted me with smiles and we exchanged news of our good health, although when Signor Biscaldi lowered himself onto the only chair, he did say he'd come back too fat for the clothes he'd left at home. I was glad then, that in my eagerness to see Sofia again, I had not stopped to buy currant buns.

'Is Antonio not here? I asked. 'I understood he wants me to repair something?'

They looked at each other, and Sofia coughed.

'I'm afraid,' she said, pink-cheeked with embarrassment. 'I wasn't very truthful in my letter.'

'Oh?' I glanced from one to the other. 'Is there something else wrong?'

Both looked uncomfortable.

'The subject is difficult,' said Signor Biscaldi.

'Delicate,' said Sofia.

'But my daughter insist you are man of good sense, so we think of little something that mean you come here by yourself.'

I was both baffled and worried, having had enough intrigue for one day, after my conversation with John.

'I will certainly help you if I can. What is it?'

'It's about Signor Dowland and Lady Anna,' said Sofia.

I groaned but was unsurprised. 'I'm sorry. If I can do anything I will, but my own wish is that the lady's husband would summon her home.'

It was an easy thing to say, but I recalled the conversation I'd had with Rosa and her telling me how unpleasant he was. Lady Anna was beautiful and talented, the womanly equivalent of John, yet she was at the mercy of a pig. Perhaps I shouldn't be so quick to send her home.

'It isn't good for us that they come here,' said Sofia. 'Not only because of the danger from the Lady's husband or because of any gossip. It is because of who we are.' She placed her hand on her father's shoulder. 'If we are not completely blameless, and sometimes even when we are, then we are found to be at fault.'

Signor Biscaldi took hold of Sofia's hand and squeezed. 'If the shop closes—'

'Florence is our home now.' Sofia's voice shook. 'It may well be that the Grand Duchess liked Signor Dowland and Lady Anna playing duets together, but it would be better for us if they could…could rehearse somewhere else. At the Palazzo Pitti perhaps? But not here.'

'Of course, it would be far better,' I said. 'I shall put it to him as soon as I get back.'

Signor Biscaldi shifted on his seat and shook Sofia's hand a little.

'Yes, I know, Papa.' She turned to me. 'There is something else.'

I was familiar with the little frown that forked between her eyebrows and steeled myself.

'We have heard from Count Fontanelli.'

'Oh?' I said, sharply. All that had transpired in Ferrara came flooding back. It was a name I'd not expected to hear ever again. The Count seemed a reasonable man but the company he kept filled me with dread. I would never forget the icy glance from Prince Gesualdo.

'Yes, he says he is shortly to pay us a visit.' She looked away, biting her lip and peering at a violin as if she had never seen one before. There was a long silence. When I turned to Signor Biscaldi, he fixed his gaze on the pigeons pecking outside the shop doorway.

'Well?' I asked, trying not to sound perturbed. 'What is it? I think you had better tell me because this is a most awkward situation.'

To my further alarm, Sofia clenched her fists in irritation. She gave me the quickest of glances before looking down at the floor, but it was enough time for me to see her face was very pink.

'Oh! You see, Papa? I knew this would happen. I cannot tell Mr Totman a lie.'

Signor Biscaldi wiped his forehead before mumbling his agreement. 'You are right, my dear. As always, you are right. What is to be done?'

Had I not heard Prince Gesualdo's name echo in my memory, I might have been amused at their behaviour. In London I knew not a single Jew with whom to pass the time. Indeed, I had been told more than once they were all liars and thieves. My experience of Sofia and her father though, had already told me they were nothing of the sort. Their current discomfort made that quite clear.

'Perhaps,' I said, speaking slowly as if greatly puzzled, 'it would be best if you took me into your confidence. I cannot help otherwise.'

'Go on, child,' Signor Biscaldi said to Sofia whilst gesturing to me. 'You tell him.'

'Yes,' she said. 'It is for the best. You are an honest man, Mr Totman, but I am sure you understand the predicament we are in.'

'I believe so, but please, do go on.'

There was very little room in the shop now that it was full of new stock, but Sofia paced the four steps to the door and back as she told me what they had planned.

'The Count *is* to pay us a visit,' she said, with a brisk nod. 'We have known him for some years, so that is not unusual, but of course, Papa and I thought straight away of the…the difficulty we had in Ferrara. It was with much relief that we read his letter further, and he informed us that whilst he was on his way to Prince Gesualdo's court near Naples by road, the Prince would most likely be journeying by sea from Venice.'

'But that is good news.' I said, breathing easily again. 'It would not do for us to be in Florence, let alone in your company, were they both here. Even with the Maler lute as recompense, I doubt Prince Gesualdo will ever forget John being so rude about his playing.'

Sofia's frown cleared, and she gave me the sweetest of smiles before her brow puckered once again and she turned away. I grew suspicious.

'But that cannot be all,' I said. 'What else have you to tell me?'

Signor Biscaldi slapped his hand down on the counter, impatience getting the better of him. 'We think to tell Signor Dowland not only about the Lady Anna's husband, but also that the mad prince *is* coming here.'

I started at that. Tell John a lie?

'Yes,' said Sofia. This admission put an end to her pacing, and she settled by her father with her hand on his shoulder. 'We thought he would definitely leave the city if he knew Prince Gesualdo was here.'

I understood their reasoning straight away and if it was a question of everyone's safety and telling John a little lie, I knew which I preferred.

'And how soon exactly,' I said, 'were you thinking that he may be arriving?'

We all looked at each other. It was a good plan, I could see that, even though I was in no hurry. A more lingering glance at Sofia told me tears were threatening to fall.

Signor Biscaldi sighed and tutted as he teased the lace on his cuff. This was a decision he would have to make. Eventually, he hoisted himself to standing, walked the same four steps as Sofia had to the front of the shop, before turning to face us.

'Tomorrow is too soon. Lady Anna will expect to see Signor Dowland and I would not wish—'

'—to risk her anger,' interrupted Sofia. 'We must not forget she is a friend of the Grand Duchess.'

I'd forgotten that. There was every chance that she would ask John and Anna to play together again and if John left suddenly, it would be a more than a slight, it would be a serious insult. Again, I thought. We're back here again. In such a situation that we must leave in a hurry. Usually, it didn't matter so terribly to me, but this time I had just as much, if not more to lose than John.

'Is a week too long?' I asked. A week? One little week. I felt distress tighten in my chest. The days would go by as quick as lightning. Was it such a good idea after all?

'Perhaps a few days,' said Signor Biscaldi, nodding and shaking his head by turn.

'So little time,' Sofia whispered to herself, before she cleared her throat and asked, 'But Mr Totman, do you think Signor Dowland will go? What if he decides to stay? I am sure that Lady Anna can be very persuasive.'

'That is true,' I said. 'I doubt my charms can match hers, but I will do my best.'

'You good friend to us, Signor Totman.' Signor Biscaldi slapped me on the arm and shook my hand for a long time. When he sat down once again, it was with an expression of considerable relief.

I thanked him, wishing that I could feel so resolved and took my leave. Sofia accompanied me to the front of the shop where we both shielded our eyes against the bright light of midday. A few steps took us out of her father's earshot and into the welcome shade of the cathedral wall.

'You are very kind,' she said. I was about to disagree,

but a gesture from her forbade it.

I couldn't help but smile. 'Miss Sofia,' I said, 'a little while ago, you told me that you were not a musician, but I do think that if there was an instrument to match the movement of your hands, it would play the most beautiful melodies.'

It had been a while since I'd seen Sofia laugh so freely. Oh, that we were back in the little courtyard in Ferrara and innocent of what was to come. It was only when a great bell began its loud tolling, that we came to our senses again.

'I...I wish you could stay longer,' she said.

'That is my dearest wish too,' I said, 'but we both know that would be troublesome for all of us. I have not yet persuaded John though. I will do what I can, but I cannot make him do anything if he is determined otherwise.'

She looked at me with a rueful smile. 'I feel sure you will succeed, Mr Totman.'

'Sofia!'

The shout made us both start. Jakob was waving and trying to make his way towards us, hindered only by a large wagon containing a couple of frisky young bullocks which, at the sound and sight of Jakob's greeting, began to roar against their captivity. Jakob wasn't quite the last person I wanted to meet, Skidmore had that pleasure, but I wasn't at all pleased to see him. Even so, I tried not to let my irritation show.

'Well met,' he said, having dashed in front of yet another wagon. 'I am very pleased to see you. Are you on your way somewhere?'

Was it a fancy of mine, or did I detect a moment of displeasure on Sofia's face? I liked to think so, but it vanished in a trice.

'No, no,' she said, with an easy smile. 'I was saying farewell to Mr Totman, that's all.'

'Ah yes, Mr Totman.' He did look at me then. Something of a penetrating stare too, the sort I'm not keen on.

'Now, Jakob,' Sofia said. 'There is no need to look so suspicious. Papa and I hold Mr Totman in high esteem. You must be friendly.'

'Of course,' he said, at once and doffed his cap. I did the same and his face broke into a cheery smile. 'That's all right then. You must forgive me, Mr Totman. I'm very protective towards my dear Sofia, that's all.'

'I am glad,' I mumbled whilst bowing. If Sofia and I had been saying our farewells, then it was time for me to go. 'Until tomorrow then.'

I regretted saying that almost at once. As I walked away, I heard Jakob say, 'What's happening tomorrow?'

Amidst the general mayhem and the sudden barking of a dog, Sofia's reply was lost, but having to witness Jakob and Sofia together filled me with such despair I almost stumbled as I walked back through the narrow streets. Now there was John to face with the news of Prince Gesualdo's imminent arrival. In truth, he might see straight through my planned deceit, especially if I was as inept in the telling as Sofia and Signor Biscaldi. I passed the baker's stall and purchased one herb and garlic pastry for John and an apricot tart for me. Disguise the main event with distraction, was a lesson I'd learnt when young.

CHAPTER FOURTEEN

The afternoon was so hot, I saw few people on my return to our lodgings but as I approached the river, I recognised one of the gentlemen who had been at the dinner hosted by Lord Gray. Older than me by a good twenty years, he had the bearing and countenance of a man not in the least brought down by age or care. I was surprised to see he wore a wide-brimmed hat made of straw. How sensible, I thought, and decided to purchase one for myself as soon as possible.

I caught him up.

'Good afternoon,' he said, raising the hat a little. 'I have come to the correct door then, for I believe you to be Mr Dowland's man?'

'Indeed, I am.' I said, removing my cap.

He introduced himself as Mr Josias Bodley, younger brother of Mr Thomas Bodley, who sat in the Commons. I doubted John was familiar with either, but I included both when I announced his arrival.

We found John with quill in one hand and lute in the other, which meant a new song was in the making. I apologised at the interruption but, at the sight of our guest, he seemed very happy to put away the composition.

'Mr Dowland,' said our guest, removing his hat and bowing low. 'My best wishes to you. I come from Lord Gray.' He began fanning himself. 'Goodness, it is so very hot this afternoon.'

John laughed. 'And every afternoon since I have been here.' He bowed. 'It is a pleasure to see you again, sir.'

'And you too,' said Mr Bodley. 'In fact, it is pleasure that I have come about. The pleasure of hearing you play. I mentioned to Lord Gray that it would be a fine thing if you would be willing to entertain us at some point. For a fee, of course, and he agreed at once and asked me to come straight here and, if you agreed, make the necessary arrangements.'

John was well-known for his songs of melancholia but like many who wore their long face like a costume, it could easily be cast off when a compliment came along. Even after years of adulation at home and across the Continent, there was still a part of him that feared his fame would one day flicker out. It seemed unlikely to me, but it certainly kept him from being idle.

'I am most honoured,' he said, smiling broadly, 'and will be delighted to play anytime at Lord Gray's convenience.'

But not, I thought, tomorrow afternoon when you will be meeting Lady Anna. I was about to remind him about this prior engagement when a knock on the door startled us all. The landlord announced two friars were below with a letter for Signor Dowland.

'At last,' murmured John, before turning to us. 'We will all go down. Mr Bodley, I hope you don't mind staying a short while.'

I was unsure whether entertaining these friars with Mr Bodley present was a good idea. In my opinion, any associate of Skidmore, a friar or a messenger, could not be trusted.

'Perhaps I should leave.' he said, picking up his hat.

'No, not at all,' John said. 'If you did, I'd earnestly ask you to stay. I do not know these friars, or the content of the letter, and I would be glad of your presence to witness what passes between us.'

Although I could see Mr Bodley wasn't altogether happy with this arrangement, he graciously agreed. John was right. Having a friendly witness could be no bad thing. The landlord led us all to a side room furnished simply, with no comforts apart from six chairs and a statuette of the Virgin on a small table in one corner. John and Mr Bodley entered and there followed all the customary greetings. I remained by the door thinking to have an eye to both outside and in, but I was curious about the two friars and settled to study them first.

The elder one, badly pockmarked and with the teeth of a rodent, introduced himself as Friar Bailey from

Yorkshire, not that he needed to tell us what was obvious the moment he opened his mouth. My meeting with folk from the North of England amounted to fewer than the fingers on one hand and I enjoyed the novelty of hearing English spoken perfectly well but with such a curious accent. In other ways though, I was not so keen. He produced the letter with a flourish, but instead of passing it to John, held on, casting it about for us all to see as if to show a jewel.

'It is a great honour,' he said in a voice so full of oil, it almost left a trail in the air, 'to be the bearer of a letter between two such distinguished men.'

My fists clenched at once. Mr Bodley looked almost flustered, not knowing who the letter was from, and the young moon-faced friar turned his gaze to the Virgin and remained silent.

John though, laughed.

'I am glad,' he said, taking the letter from the outstretched hand, 'that in receiving this letter, I am able to provide you with half such honour, Friar Bailey, I trust that Mr Skidmore has done *his* duty.' He flicked the paper with thumb and forefinger as one might remove a crumb or insect before breaking the seal.

On hearing the name Skidmore, Mr Bodley frowned, and the flush on his face deepened.

'Now,' said John. 'Let's see what's been said.'

The sudden quiet made every rustle and clearing of the throat seem loud. Outside a dog whined and in the solitary olive tree in the courtyard a pair of doves cooed.

My attention turned once again to the room, and the irksome nature of watching John read the letter to himself.

'—*exquisiteness upon the lute,*' he murmured, with a smile and sigh.

Baseless flattery it seemed to me.

'—*will I assure you give content.*'

Skidmore knew of John by reputation, not direct experience.

'—*inclined to the good.*' He snorted at this. 'Inclined

indeed. *Only* to the good that should read.'

It took another few moments for him to finish, whereupon he held it to his heart and thanked the friars for their trouble. Friar Bailey's acknowledgment was fulsome.

'We are always delighted to assist one of our countrymen make their way to the seat of our faith.'

I stiffened at that and in doing so, accidently knocked into one of the chairs. Everyone started at the interruption, a sign that even here in Italy, an English papist is not at rest in his mind.

'Please, forgive my man,' John said, with a smile. 'He can be a clumsy fellow but fear not, we are all friends here.'

They settled back again, and I thought to save for later any grievances about the reflections on my character. I noticed Mr Bodley's smile seemed extra strained, but Friar Bailey, hands together in prayer, looked heavenwards as if in rapture.

'I am very glad of it,' he said, 'for it is our holy duty. Indeed, Mr Dowland, you will not be disappointed on your arrival, for I happen to know that you will be *very* well received.'

'Yes indeed! There have even been letters from Rome about you.' This fervent utterance from the younger friar gave us all a surprise.

'Oh?' John looked to Friar Bailey who beamed in return.

'My young friend speaks truth,' he said, leaning forward, 'if a little too loudly. But yes, there has been communication with the cardinals in Rome. Your discontent with the English court is well known there.'

A shiver ran through me, which I found difficult to disguise, so I shifted from foot to foot as if tired of standing. All the while, I wrestled with how this could possibly have come about. Discontent? Why would they think that? Had it come from England? Surely not. John was liked and admired by those he knew. At least I thought he was. Sir Robert Cecil and the Earl of Essex were happy to write letters for him. I wondered if there had been some loose-tongued talk at the dinner with Lord Gray or, and this thought had the weight of a truth behind it, Skidmore had spread a rumour.

'You should have a large pension from the Pope,' added Bailey. 'He and all the cardinals would make much of your coming.'

That was even worse news. Did they believe John would desert his Queen, his country, his own—'

Abruptly, John stood up and walked the few steps to the window. After a moment, he took a deep breath, held it a moment or two, then let it out in a rush. 'I have a family,' he said. 'My wife and children. I could not leave them to suffer for any of my actions.'

'Ah, yes. They would be in grave peril.' Friar Bailey shook his head at the pity of it, but then smiled with such smugness, I would happily have rearranged his teeth had I been closer. 'But we have good people who would speed their passage from England,' he went on. 'Why, Mr Skidmore has brought out seventeen himself, both men and women.'

Skidmore. Of course. I thought of the woman I had seen with him. Was she one of them? I wondered what Skidmore took from her in return for his help.

'Gentlemen,' John said clapping his hands together. 'I thank you for trouble in bringing the letter and please give my thanks to Mr Skidmore. You have given me a lot to consider.'

'Oh, we can't do that,' said the younger man. 'Thank Mr Skidmore, that is. Sadly, he's gone from us now.'

For a happy moment, I thought he meant Skidmore had died.

'Oh?' said John.

Friar Bailey gave his young colleague a rather fierce glance before turning back with a smile.

'Yes, indeed,' he said. 'He left in haste, but it is understood that his studies have taken him to France.'

It is understood indeed. What was that if not another way of saying he was up to mischief.

'I see,' said John. He then turned to me, with a bland expression that I could see took him considerable effort. 'If you would show these good friars out, please Will.'

The friars, looking very comfortable in their chairs, would no doubt have enjoyed a lengthy and treasonous conversation, so it was in sudden ungainly haste that they rose and bade us farewell. I made sure that once they were through the front door they took themselves off and didn't lurk with their ears to the window.

When I returned, it was to discover John sitting once again, but now with his head in his hands, groaning as if sick, and rocking to and fro like a baby in a cradle. Mr Bodley looked grave. His happy errand had brought him all sorts of trouble.

'The letter may be innocuous enough,' he said to me, 'but they were speaking in an altogether different tone. Has Mr Dowland spoken of his discontent? Is he *really* thinking to stay in Rome?'

'Not that I am aware,' I said. 'Mr Dowland has been known to swear on his life to protect Her Majesty.'

Beside us, John groaned louder.

'And I am very glad of it,' Mr Bodley said. 'I must say that whilst I am fond of this country and its people, I'm no papist. Her Majesty is tolerant of Catholics, and I try my best to follow her example, but my own family is of the Protestant persuasion. As for that letter,' he gestured towards it with disgust. 'My advice would be to inform Lord Gray of everything that has transpired. I trust in his wisdom, and it would be for the best if you did too.'

'Yes!' John said, jumping up with such vigour that Mr Bodley fell back against the table in the corner and set the Virgin dancing dangerously close to the edge. 'We must inform him. We shall go at once!'

I did not like the idea of John going anywhere whilst in this state of upset, but fortunately Mr Bodley was of the same mind.

'I shall go first,' he said, restoring the Lady to upright. 'Lord Gray may well wish to gather his thoughts about this before a meeting. No doubt he will send word soon.'

'Do you think anyone will come?' said John, when I returned from seeing Mr Bodley to the door. 'Or am I a traitor now?'

I shook my head, but there was no small part of me that wondered the same. We made our way back upstairs to our room in silence. John was all dragging feet and slumped shoulders. I didn't know what to think. Once inside, I shut the door and sat down on the bed. John paced the floor.

'Skidmore is not our friend,' I said, 'for all his flattery. But he can hardly imagine that you would join a plot of any sort against Her Majesty.'

Or, I wondered, was he trying to ensnare John in a plot so that he could ingratiate himself even more with his papist friends in Rome? It would be quite a triumph for him, as I fancied one John Dowland might well equal more than seventeen men and women of no repute.

John said nothing but held the letter behind his back. Another, darker notion entered my head.

'You haven't,' I said, slowly, 'by any chance, given Skidmore encouragement in this matter, have you?'

I expected an explosive denial followed by some sort of reproach, not silence. After a moment or two, I gave in to my own impatience.

'Have you—'

I got no further, before he whirled around, now thrusting the letter before him as if held filth or poison.

'Oh *Will*.' He stared at me, utterly stricken, before saying in a small voice. 'I may have.'

'May have?' I was aghast. 'What does that mean?'

'I may have encouraged him.'

He looked distraught, but now *I* said nothing, glaring instead, if only because I held my jaw so firmly closed.

'I *may* have mentioned that I was ill-disposed towards the Court.'

'Ill-disposed?' I burst out, in a loud whisper. 'Towards the *Court*? If you said Court, he would straightaway think you meant *Queen*. Why would you say such a thing to anyone? Let alone Skidmore!'

'It was the first time we met.' John went on. 'He asked me why I came here, so I told him.'

'Told him what? What did you say?'

He was quiet as if recalling, then shook his head. 'I cannot lie, Will. I told him it was because the Queen had not favoured me with a position and that she thought me an obstinate Papist.'

'What?' Incredulous, I struck my own forehead. 'I can hardly believe it. Why did you not say you were going to study with Master Marenzio?' I got up and went over to the window, and almost pushing John out of the way so that I could close the shutter. It did so with a bang. 'You have said exactly that to everyone who asked since we left Cheapside,' I harangued him. 'In Brunswick, Hesse, Venice, Ferrara, to Dukes and stable boys, but now you come to Florence and tell the first man who could be a possible, no, a *probable* threat, that you're out of favour with Her Majesty, the Queen of England, for being a papist and now!' I had to swallow and draw breath. 'And now, you are looking to go to Rome! I can hardly believe it.'

My heart thundered in my ears as I shook my head, recalling the day when we had first met Henry Kemper and John Skidmore on the steps of the Cathedral. How I regretted leaving them. Would my presence have prevented such an admission? I'd like to think so.

'I'm sorry, Will.' John said. 'It was a light-hearted remark at the time. He'd asked why I wasn't at Her Majesty's Court and the sting of my rejection suddenly returned. But I did not say it with any malice. Indeed, when Skidmore suggested I had friends in Rome who would help my family escape England to join me, I told him I was a good and loyal subject of the Queen.'

John's apologies were also light-hearted and many, but this time I sensed the truth of it, and I felt my anger with him ease. Who has not made remarks out of turn only to regret them later? Even so, I did not like the sound of it.

'Was that the sum of this conversation?'

He nodded.

'Apart from my saying that like all the papists I knew in England, not one would harm even a finger of the Queen. He commended me for that but did say there were English priests in Rome seeking to overthrow Her Majesty with the help of...you can guess, I expect.'

'No doubt the Spanish, damn them.'

'Jesuits of course, although—' he hesitated, frowning at a thought. 'I remember passing the time of day with two priests. An Irishman, Pierce and another, whose name —'

'When was that? You didn't tell me.'

'Draycott, yes, that was it. They were headed for Rome too.'

'Oh?'

'Yes, by sea from Venice.'

'Were they friends of Skidmore?' I didn't remember them at all.

John shrugged. 'Skidmore, it seems, is friends with all those who wish to uphold his faith, but whether that means a serious plot against Her Majesty, who can tell?'

I realised then, that I also had a confession to make.

'Skidmore has no love for either of us.'

'Really?' John took my meaning straight away. 'And what misdemeanours have *you* done?'

I told him of my meeting Skidmore and the woman I'd seen him with earlier that morning.

'You were good to defend me, Will, although I suspect it made him even more determined to succeed in his cause.'

'Yes,' I said. 'I should have been a little less hostile. He is an easy man to dislike, with a temper of oil and pepper. Do you think the letters of welcome and a pension from Rome are a falsehood? An invention to implicate you further?'

He frowned. 'We cannot know. Lord Gray may well have more understanding of Skidmore. It was clear that Mr Bodley did not hear his name with any pleasure. We can only hope that I am granted an audience.' He picked up the lute which lay on the bed and returned it to its box. 'I will take this with me in the hope that my music commends me to him, even if my actions do not.'

Amidst all the worry, I could not help but smile. A remark containing such self-deprecation was a rare thing.

CHAPTER FIFTEEN

It was only an hour later when a message came from Lord Gray. We were to come to the tavern where we had previously dined. On the way, I reminded John of his appointment with Lady Anna.

'Signor Biscaldi suggested the palace would be a more suitable place for you both to play your duets.'

That was greeted with a derisive snort, so I determined to make their case again.

'Listen, John. They have as much, if not more reason than us to fear scandal. Even here, where the Grand Duke allows Jews considerable freedom within and without the ghetto, Signor Biscaldi believes they would be the first to be blamed for any wrongdoing, whether its cause was theirs or not.'

I told him about the ruffian spitting at Sofia. He was sorry, but not surprised.

'It's the same everywhere.'

His mind was elsewhere but I decided to press home the case for leaving anyway.

'Did I tell you,' I began, knowing I had not, 'that Signor Biscaldi has had word that Count Fontanelli comes to Florence?'

All his attention was at once restored. 'Oh?' He clutched my arm. 'Will he come alone?'

'I believe so.' I swallowed then, but Sofia's anxious face came to my mind, and I continued with the little lie. 'But it seems Prince Gesualdo may well follow him. Exactly when is not yet known.'

John has very strong fingers from all that running up and down the fingerboard of a lute, and he gripped my arm even tighter, almost to the point of pain.

'Damn them,' he said. 'Is the city soon to be *full* of our enemies?'

Hardly full, I thought, but even two is a big number when the danger is great.

We said no more on the subject as we had arrived at the tavern where we were shown to a small courtyard.

Lord Gray sat with Josiah Bodley and Henry Kemper and despite the trouble we brought with us, their greetings were warm. A jug of wine was called for and to my surprise, I was included.

'My dear Dowland,' said Lord Gray once the wine was poured and we could converse privately. 'I am glad to see you have come prepared to play your instrument.' He turned to me then. 'Is it one of yours, Mr Totman? I hear you are the maker of very fine lutes. I should very much like to have you explain the process to me.'

My tongue seemed suddenly twice its normal size, but I bowed low before stuttering, 'It would be an honour to share a little of my learning, My Lord, but as for this lute—'

'It is not one of Will's,' sighed John, 'and sadly nothing can quite compare. I gave the finest lute he's ever made away, struck as I was, by the immeasurable talent and beauty of a certain Lady Anna.'

As one, all the gentlemen nodded and cooed their appreciation.

'I hope you weren't too upset, Mr Totman,' said Lord Gray, once their reminiscences were over.

'Indeed not,' I replied. 'What man would not be proud of having something he had made in the hands of Lady Anna.'

It was only after the words tumbled out of my mouth that I realised the ambiguity of what I'd said. For a moment there was silence before they all nodded and laughed at length. Evidently, John told me later, it was the look of horror on my face that they really enjoyed. I wasn't so sure, but it helped that Lord Gray raised a glass, and we all drank to fine instruments and beautiful women.

'Gentlemen,' Lord Gray said. 'Let us be serious now. Mr Bodley was to return with news of a performance, but instead I hear we are caught up in some present difficulty. Unless we must make urgent haste away, I am sure a little music later will be most welcome.'

John bowed and professed his thanks and apologies for causing concern, but both were waved away.

'Do you have the letter from Skidmore?' asked Lord Gray.

John retrieved it from his doublet, and it was read in silence, first by Lord Gray and then by Henry. After this, John was instructed to relay to the best of his knowledge what was said by the friars, and both Mr Bodley and I were asked if we had anything further to contribute. All was recounted, even the near calamity with the statue of the Virgin.

That the situation was serious there was no doubt. Each man's frown grew deeper as they considered what should be done.

'Do play for us, Mr Dowland,' said Lord Gray, after a short while. 'I sense our time here in Florence is coming to an end, but I have no doubt some music will ease our unquiet thoughts.'

He was right, I thought, as I felt my knotted brows slacken and saw the same on the foreheads of the gentlemen. John had chosen to play a song I had heard several times before: *Sleep, wayward thoughts* which he wisely dedicated, as a most loyal subject, to Her Majesty. I expected him to sing this with his usual melancholy, leaning for some time on the words *dis-eased* and *displeased*, and sighing here and there but that was not his interpretation. Today he went a little faster, there was something jauntier about the accompaniment and he made much of the repetition.

Sleep, wayward thoughts, and rest you with my love:
Let not my love be with my *love dis-eased.*

He bowed low when the song was done, and although a small audience, the response was enthusiastic. John may not always be in control of his own temper, but he commanded with his music, and I marvelled how the earlier mood of agitation had lifted somewhat to become altogether more sanguine.

'Well played and well sung, Mr Dowland,' said Lord Gray. 'My thanks indeed. You have given me time to settle my thoughts. Now, whilst I would be more than happy to sit here and listen to you for several more hours, it is time we acted on this unfortunate news from Rome.'

He gestured to Henry to refill the glasses and, as if by magic, a servant appeared carrying a platter of bread and salt meats. Despite our present troubles, there was no sense of urgency amongst the company.

'I am of the opinion,' he eventually continued, once we had all partaken, 'that one amongst us at the dinner may have spoken with Skidmore or one of his associates. Whether by design or accident, that can't be known, so I will put aside any inference as to who the culprit may be. What I know, is that all of us here,' he paused then, and looked so directly at me that I almost choked on a morsel of ham I was finishing. He smiled at that. 'Forgive me, Mr Totman, I do not wish to offend any person here, but my understanding is that whilst we are all guests in this beautiful country, we are all sympathetic to, if not wholly accepting of, the papist cause. Our first duty, however, as loyal Englishmen, is to Her Majesty the Queen.'

He raised his glass *'God save the Queen!'*

It was whispered with similar fervour by us all.

'*Sleep, wayward thoughts* was a good choice of song,' I said, as we made our way back to our lodgings.

'Mmm,' said John. Had he heard what I said? It wasn't like him to go by a compliment without comment, but after a few more yards he added, 'Although it was Lord Gray that gave me the idea. He said he had *unquiet thoughts* and it reminded me.'

We'd come to the river, and it was lot fuller than when we'd previously walked along the embankment. That day came back to me clearly, especially the look on Skidmore's face when I'd thought to rescue a sheet from the mud. I put his face from my mind and instead tried to enjoy the late afternoon sun and the swifts skimming just above the river's green surface.

Once back at the lodgings, I wasn't surprised when straight away John took up his lute. Our belongings lay strewn about and would have to be packed again. To think of leaving lowered my spirits considerably.

The afternoon's discussions had led to the belief that all the Englishmen who had attended the dinner could fall under suspicion of plotting against Her Majesty. Why else would we meet so secretly in a private room? It was determined that Lord Gray would depart for Sienna the next day. Mr Bodley had a notion for an urgent trip to Ferrara, I think because John and I had talked favourably about the city. The other Englishmen would soon hear that their dispersal from Florence was advisable. As for us? Yes, we were to leave, and it was assumed that we would not have the slightest wish to go to Rome.

John, though, had yet to confirm where we were to go, or even whether we would go at all. I felt almost mad with sorrow and worry. Was John as truthful about Skidmore as he made out? I tried to piece together all the information I had about the papists' cause, and the request from Sir Robert Cecil that John take note of any talk or plots against the Queen.

What bothered me had only really made itself felt when John began to sing for Lord Gray. Mostly known for his music, he was also a poet. When John was not quite in his right mind, he did not always craft his speech so tightly, as Prince Gesualdo discovered to his fury. But John was perfectly well when we met Skidmore that day. I still couldn't understand why he would say something so risky unless—

'John?'

It was rare for me to interrupt his playing and he looked up, startled.

'I've been thinking.'

'Oh? That sounds bad.' He said it lightly but followed it with a sigh. 'Can things get any worse?'

'It's occurred to me,' I said, slowly, 'that if Sir Robert Cecil had asked me to keep my ears and eyes open, then it would be prudent to actually have some news to give him when I returned.' I picked up a shirt of John's that had found its way to the floor. 'I mean, it wouldn't do to appear dilatory in the task now, would it?'

John took longer than necessary to put down his lute, but then he looked at me with the face of a boy thinking about stealing a bun. Should he, or shouldn't he?

'I am not sure what you are saying, Will, but I fear it all the same. Be plain with me now.'

I folded the shirt taking my usual good care. 'It was the words in your song that made me wonder. Not what they were about, but that you had such a clever way with them. Although—' I hesitated.

'Ah, now he comes to it.' He sniffed with irritation, so I went on quickly.

'I could understand your remark to Skidmore about Her Majesty if you weren't...you weren't quite *yourself*, but that was not the case. You were altogether in your right mind on that day. We met Henry Kemper on the Cathedral steps and the conversation was perfectly amiable until Skidmore came along and turned his back to me.' With the memory, I felt my temper rise. 'And for some reason, ever since then, I cannot help but remember Sir Robert's task and Tom Morley's visit before we left London, and it's come to me that you were quite deliberate in poking Skidmore, and you didn't tell me.'

I had worked myself into such a state of hurt and indignation that I threw the shirt into a box.

'And now look at all the trouble it's caused,' I went on. 'All our English friends here being thought traitors and having to move. What about us? You have said nothing about where we are to go. Will it be to Rome with a fat pension and to hell with your home and family? Have I been in the company of a traitor all this time?'

Anger churned in my chest as I slammed down the box's lid. It made quite a noise, and I sensed John flinch.

'Hush, Will. Hush. Do not speak so loudly of such things. There's no need for temper.'

He got up and crossed the room, but I wasn't ready for an appeasing pat on the shoulder and turned aside.

'Well?' I whispered, but still cross. 'Am I right? You did deliberately speak to Skidmore, and we are to Rome?'

'No, of course not.'

There was little conviction in his tone, so I folded my arms and waited for an explanation.

'You were right about one thing,' he said, 'but not the other. I did deliberately tell Skidmore I was unhappy not to get the post at Court, but I would swear I said nothing treasonous. You must trust me on that, Will. I would never do such a thing. Please tell me you know that.'

I searched his face for any falsehood lurking but felt inclined to trust he was speaking from the heart. Even so, I still needed persuading.

'I was a fool, Will,' he said, 'and it was a very foolish thing to do. I am a loyal subject of Her Majesty. Indeed, I told him that more than once. As for Rome,' he went on after a big sigh. 'Meeting with Signor Marenzio still draws me. Would it be so very foolish to go?'

God in heaven, I thought, was there no end to his foolishness?

'I believe it would be, but the choice is yours, John. Whatever it is you decide, I would be glad of knowing when we should start.'

'Ah yes,' he said, then a trace of mischief crossed his features and he added. 'Well, it will have to be after tomorrow for I can't possibly let down the lovely Lady Anna.' He almost skipped back to where his lute lay on the bed. 'Besides, it would look rather odd if *all* the Englishmen in Florence left in haste. Some may well think that suspicious. Wouldn't you?'

CHAPTER SIXTEEN

Signor Biscaldi and Antonio were delighted with the pastries I took with me the following morning, and they weren't at all keen to save any for Sofia who was visiting her dressmaker. How long she would be they didn't know. Appointments could take hours.

'Do you have any repairs for me?' I asked Antonio trying not to sound too disappointed. 'I'd rather be busy with my hands here than idly wandering about the city.'

In the workshop a shelf of small repairs needed attention and, although I could see perfectly well for myself what was required, he gave me instruction for each one. I understood why and would have done the same in his position. He had an appointment with a timber merchant and was leaving me in charge not only of the repairs, but also of his reputation. It wasn't how I'd thought to spend the morning, but I was glad to be in a tidy workshop again inhaling the smell of sawn wood and using the tools of my trade. The repairs were easy and my mind wandered here and there, always coming back to Sofia. Could I really stay here and let John go home alone?

It was my habit, my role, and my duty to look after him. Hadn't his mother given me that very task before we left? I thought of the old lady's kindness. How she taught me my letters when John was away at school so I wouldn't suffer from his learning when he came home. I could never betray her trust. As for John, he'd always looked after me. I would be dead by the road after that snakebite, if not for him.

Thoughts such as these galloped about in my head until I heard Sofia's cheerful greeting calling from the shop. I can't deny I jumped at the sound of it, and the coiled violone string I was about to thread fell from my hand and bounced across the floor.

'Good morning, Mr Totman,' she said, a few moments later, as I was scrabbling under the opposite bench to retrieve it. 'Are you hiding under there? I hope not on my account.'

'Indeed not, Miss Sofia,' I said. 'That is something I would never do. This one, however,' I held up the errant string as I stood. 'This one tried to escape me, but I have it now.'

'So I see.'

She came closer, so that we both stood in the sunlight coming in from the large window above the bench. At the merest glance at her smiling face, so eager in expression, all my previous resolve fled away. Why not remain? John shouldn't need me; he was a grown man now. I gripped the string in my hand more tightly.

'Miss Sofia,' I began, only to be interrupted by a call from the shop.

'Sofia, are you there? We should go.'

Jakob! Damn and blast the man. Why was he here again?

I groaned audibly and for the smallest moment Sofia placed her hand on mine.

'I must go,' she said. 'Perhaps later—'

'Come,' said Jakob from the doorway. 'We'll be late for the rabbi. Ah, good morning, Mr Totman.'

Clearly, he was not pleased to see me, but Sofia did look back before she left. There was an understanding between us, I was sure of it. I began threading the violone string and gradually my conviction wavered. Why would she be going to see a rabbi with Jakob?

I did not have time to dwell on such a thought before Signor Biscaldi came into the workshop. After much mumbling and pacing about, then looking as if he might be in pain, I asked him if he would like to sit down. He shook his head, reached deep into a pocket, and pulled out a purse that clinked with the sound of coins. Then he really surprised me by holding out his hand and gesturing for me to take it.

'What errand is this for?' I asked, astonished to see such a large purse containing many gold coins.

'Oh, no,' he said waving my words away. 'No errand.

This is for you. For the work here.'

For a moment I could only stare. 'But it is far too much.' I calculated two or three ducats would be more than generous.

He shook his head. 'I like you to have it. You help us in Ferrara and now here.'

'It is still too much, Signor.'

'Please,' he said, with a wobble of distress in his voice. Taking my hand, he closed it around the purse. 'It is good currency, very useful when you travel.'

In my whole life I don't think anyone has handed me so much money for doing so little, and there was no denying the appealing glint of gold. Even so, I felt deeply unhappy about accepting it. I liked Signor Biscaldi and was about to protest once again when I saw the worried look and sweat on his brow.

'Oh no, no, no.' I said, shaking my head and suddenly very unhappy myself. 'Signor Biscaldi, my dear sir, are you worried I might decide to stay?' I held out my hand. 'Is this to make sure I go?'

Such was his obvious distress, and the way I felt, more disappointed than angry, that I thought we both might cry.

'I'm sorry, so sorry Mr Totman.' He took my hand again. 'Forgive me. It was wrong of me, but I mean only well. You must understand, I worry so much. My daughter, my darling Sofia, she is my life.'

He let go of me then and took to his old habit of plucking something tuneless on the lace on his cuff.

'Of course,' I said, 'but—'

'I have seen how she looks at you and I worry so. It would be so difficult. Jakob though, she like him well enough, and he is a good man.' He gave himself a light slap on the cheek. 'Mr Totman, forgive me again. You are *very* good man, but from far away and not, and not—

'And not a Jew,' I said.

'It is so difficult,' he said, nodding and shaking his head in turn. 'There would be trouble for her and for you.' He looked over his shoulder despite our being alone. 'Mr

Totman, my daughter, she is everything to me. Since my dear wife die, there is no one else. What would you have me do? Agree to a foreigner? A man with talent, yes.' He gestured at my workmanship. 'But also, in service to the famous Signor Dowland. A man who is very public and not always, how shall I say, calm? What life will my Sofia have with you?'

I took a breath, about to plead my cause, but he interrupted.

'And then I think of Jakob,' he glanced away and smiled, as if a conjured Jakob stood just behind me. 'A good boy, kind, cheerful and hardworking. He has friends and family to keep Sofia safe if I'm—' He shrugged off the dismal thought of his own mortality and turned back to me. 'I hope if you not here, maybe she like him more? He cares for Sofia and when trouble comes, and it does for Jews everywhere, then they will be together. Where are you, Mr Totman, when trouble comes along, and people threaten? With Signor Dowland? Or my daughter?'

I remembered the boy spitting at Sofia in the street and about how much worse it could have been. Here, Jews were infidels and mostly left alone, but that was at the whim of the Grand Duke. Another ruler might think differently. I had no words to say to Signor Biscaldi. If I'd been wearing armour, his argument would have pierced it. I would protect Sofia with my life, but would it be enough? A glimpse of hostility to me had come from that mean-faced copyist in Ferrara, for no other reason than I was a foreigner. I had no friends or family here to help if the world grew darker. Perhaps, I thought, although the pain of it almost made me cry out, perhaps Jakob would be a better choice.

And what about John? I had made a solemn promise to his mother to see him home safe. No good man would renege on such a thing, but neither would a good man accept the heavy purse that weighed down my hand.

Signor Biscaldi said nothing but continued to pluck at his cuff.

'Thank you,' I said, eventually. 'Thank you for being

honest with me, Signor. I understand that you want the best for your daughter but, I wonder, is Jakob the best? She will have an opinion of her own, we can be sure of that, even though it is for you to decide.' I took one gold ducat from the purse. 'This,' I said, holding it up so that it glinted in a ray of sunlight. 'This is enough for the work I have done. I am a rather proud man, Signor Biscaldi, and although I know you meant well, I cannot be bought.'

It was with a rueful smile and sigh that he took back the purse.

'I like you, Signor Totman,' he said. 'There are men who would kill for this. In another life—'

I interrupted him.

'In another life, *everything* would be different, Signor Biscaldi. I count myself as a man who has been fortunate so far in this life, and it has been more than a pleasure to make the acquaintance of both you and your daughter. I shall always be glad of that,' I paused and looked at him directly before continuing, 'whatever happens in the future.'

As if I had charmed it, the cathedral bell began to toll the hour.

'Ah yes,' he said. 'The future. It arrive all the time and I never ready.'

He left me then and went out into the shop. Thankfully, there wasn't anything I had to do that required too much of my attention, as my head was full of very unquiet thoughts. That Signor Biscaldi should even think to buy me off both hurt and angered me. On the other hand, I understood his turmoil. I was a stranger here and likely to suffer suspicion on my own account. Would I wish such difficulties on Sofia?

I stood doing nothing except rubbing the gold ducat between my thumb and forefinger until, a moment later, Signor Biscaldi came back.

'Forgive me, Signor Totman,' his voice thin and tired. 'I interrupt your work again, but there is something else to say.'

'Please do,' I said. 'I haven't settled to anything yet.'

He looked almost as wretched as I felt. Gone was the restless man, who blinked and twitched with worry, instead he looked as if all his good spirits had drained away through the soles of his feet, leaving a man grey-faced and shambling. Had he changed his mind? If this was the effort it took, I doubted Sofia would have me. My expression must have given away how much my wounded pride hurt, as he held up his hand and bowed his head a little.

'Do not worry,' he said. 'It is my fault. A time is come at last. It is no surprise, and yet,' he hesitated, all the while shaking his head. Silence followed whilst he found a handkerchief and wiped his brow and I waited for an answer to his riddles. 'And yet,' he went on, 'I not prepared.'

'Signor,' I said. 'I do not know the exact cause of your distress, but surely it is Sofia you should be talking to, not me.'

'No, no!' he said, with such force that I was surprised. 'Sofia does not know, that is the trouble. Oh, it is so very difficult.'

I was more than curious.

'Surely,' I said, with effort, 'if Sofia doesn't know, then whatever it is, perhaps you should tell her first? Why tell me? Please Signor, please don't say anything to further convince me against your daughter. I understand the difficulty only too well and it is most painful. You too are in pain, I can see, and Sofia would be most hurt to think you are keeping something important from her.'

'Yes, yes,' he said, 'that is true, but it perhaps important for you. It is—'

Whatever it was, I did not find out then, for the shop door opened at that very moment. Signor Biscaldi stiffened at once and drew away from me and recovering his former stature, bustled back into the shop.

'Another time then,' I said to myself.

I turned back to the bench with such confused thoughts, they would have ploughed a deep furrow in my brow, but it deepened further when I recognised the customer's voice. I put down the replacement peg for a rather inferior lute and crept over to listen by the door. Through a punched-out knot in the wood I could see Count Fontanelli and standing behind him, Loreto, the evil-eyed copyist I'd thought of only five minutes beforehand.

CHAPTER SEVENTEEN

The Count and Signor Biscaldi were partaking in pleasantries; how was the journey, weather, accommodation? An archlute was mentioned and next I heard Signor Biscaldi's footsteps approach the workshop door. I looked about for the most expensive instrument that was ready for sale.

'Good,' he whispered to me as I handed it to him. 'You understand Count Fontanelli has fine taste.'

He took it into the shop and after a few twangs from the Count, I heard Signor Biscaldi's voice.

'And the Prince Gesualdo? Is he well?'

I shuddered.

'Yes, well enough. We are on our way to his home in Naples.'

We? Did he mean with the Prince? Wasn't he supposed to be going by sea?

'And you travel with him?'

I admired how casual Signor Biscaldi sounded on hearing this alarming news.

'Yes, he was to go by sea for the speed of it, but he fears the water more than most and on seeing me make ready with horses, changed his mind. He is at the Pitti Palace now.'

Damn the man and his watery fears! When Antonio had suggested we tell John the Prince Gesualdo was coming, we had thought it a convenient lie. Now, it was the truth. What was to be done? Florence may be a city of many people, but not so many were musicians and had the fame of John Dowland. It was more than likely their paths would cross and he would hear about the duet with Lady Anna. Prince Gesualdo had traded a fine lute against John's insult, but rekindling a hurt into a blaze could be done with a mere word.

The Count was not done yet though and worse was to come.

'Do you remember that English fellow?' he said. 'The luthier. Stocky chap with coarse light-coloured hair'

If Signor Biscaldi replied, I didn't hear it, but perhaps he was too afraid even to speak because the next thing I did hear chilled me to the bone.

'A fraud, you know,' said Count Fontanelli. 'Passed off a lute made by Master Maler as his own work. A convincing trickster I must say. He would have made a considerable amount if it hadn't been for Prince Gesualdo. I hope you didn't get too involved with him, or that John Dowland for that matter. A fine musician but clearly mad.'

My jaw dropped and it was fortunate that it was a string I held, and not a hefty tool that would have clattered on the floor when I dropped it. A fraud? Me? I could feel blood pounding against my temples. How could that be? There was no fraud.

In the shop a deal was done, the Count left, and shortly afterwards I peered around the workshop door. Signor Biscaldi stood clutching the back of his chair. He looked pale.

'Did you hear?' he said.

'I did.'

'Prince Gesualdo is in Florence.'

'And I am a fraud and John is mad.'

Hand over hand, Signor Biscaldi worked his way round from back to front of the chair then, with a grunt, sat down. On a shelf nearby lay a fan of Sofia's which he took up at once.

'This is bad news,' I said trying to remember exactly what had happened that day in the Palazzo di Diamante when the Count admired the Maler I was repairing. I certainly didn't say I had made the lute, but there again, I didn't deny it. And what did happen to the paper bearing my signature that I rejected? I was going to burn it. Damn my foolish self. I don't think I did.

Signor Biscaldi fanned himself so vigorously a welcome draught reached me as well.

'Listen,' I said, with more hope than judgement. 'This may well work in your favour. When John and Lady Anna are here, I will keep watch at the door, and perhaps if we both pray that Prince Gesualdo has no desire to walk this way, we should survive the afternoon. After that, I will do my best to persuade John that we must be gone from the city as soon as possible. Once he hears about this, I think he will be glad to go.'

'And Lady Anna? What about her,' he cleared his throat, 'her fondness for Signor Dowland?'

I could only shrug. 'We should not forget they are both married. I'm sure they have strong feelings for each other, but they know they have no future.'

That brought the colour back to Signor Biscaldi's cheeks. For me though, it seemed as if the future was both dangerous and dismal. There were so many ways John and I did not belong here, and when I looked at Sofia's dear papa, I knew that despite how much it would hurt me to leave, it was the right thing to do.

'I should get back to the bench,' I said, turning away, but at the door I looked back. 'There was something you wished to tell me?'

'Mmm?' Ah yes.' He hesitated, but then turned away. 'No, no. Really Mr Totman, no matter now.'

I was curious and would have asked again had I not had a more pressing request.

'Signor Biscaldi, with your permission, when John and Lady Anna are here, may I say goodbye to Sofia?'

He looked at me squarely. Two men sizing up the ways of the world in a glance. We both knew he should say no, but he understood my desire was from the heart and well meant. After much sighing, Signor Biscaldi made his way back into the shop, his *I hope you not make it worse*, still echoing in my ears.

In truth, my repair work was done, but into my mind came the idea that I might make a little keepsake for Sofia. It was the gold coin that now rested against my heart that made me think of it. I was no goldsmith and had not the time to make anything that would reflect my skill or do justice to the light and beauty that she had brought into my world. Even so, whilst not as valuable as gold or precious stones, there was much to be said for what can be done with wood. It was just as varied in its colour and strength; it was warm to the touch and lent itself to objects of both great and small size. Besides, although I could not make any piece of wood sparkle, I could certainly make it shine. I looked about the workshop to see if there was anything discarded that could be remade in some way.

Such was the work that time went by quickly and without my knowing it. When the shop door opened, I started with a mixture of hope for Sofia and fear in case it was Prince Gesualdo, but a cheerful whistling of Tom Morley's *I will no more come to thee* signalled another particular person. It was a surprise to hear it from John's lips, not being one to promote anything but his own songs as a rule. I doubted the Lady Anna would appreciate such sentiment either, but I knew little of such a person. Perhaps she was just like John and regularly played at love. I had no idea of the rules of their game; leaving my love was going to be hard indeed.

'Good day to you, Signor Biscaldi,' I heard him say. 'I trust you are well?'

'*Si, si.* But these days too hot for me. And you?'

I was done with the keepsake already so began tidying the tools away. It was hot. The large window above the bench was good for light but when the sun arrived, I'd retreated to the shade and worked more by the feel of my hand.

'Signor, I am a man in your debt.' John was saying. 'You have been more than generous with your premises, but I'm sure you understand that love makes fools of us all.'

Now, now John, I thought, recognising a certain persuasive tone to his voice. Are you hoping the Signor will allow further use of his premises? I grabbed my old jerkin and joined them straight away.

'Aha, you are here.' He greeted me with no surprise. 'I thought as much.'

'I was happy to help out with one or two repairs.'

'And I trust you're getting well paid for your efforts?'

He laughed not knowing it was an unfortunate comment after the conversation I'd had with Signor Biscaldi. The poor man looked mortified, but before I could rectify the situation, John had turned to other matters.

'A stroll, Will? I'm in need of something to fill this.' He patted his very inconspicuous stomach. 'May I leave my lute here, Signor?'

I took it upstairs for him. When I returned, they were discussing the best place for us to eat.

'I thought the good Signor could recommend somewhere nearby,' said John. 'I passed a place behind the Baptistry. Do you know it?'

'I expect it's very busy and expensive,' I said, quickly. 'Especially being so close to the Cathedral. Perhaps there is somewhere where only those who know Florence go?'

I stared hard at Signor Biscaldi in the hope he might understand my feeling that John's presence in the city should be kept quiet. His choice of tavern, however, surprised even me, when, a few minutes later, we turned into a narrow and poorly-kept street. I didn't at all like the look of the huddled gamblers who offered us good odds or the urchins who stroked our sleeves.

On arrival, however, we stepped through the outer door into a pretty garden courtyard, and with the word of introduction sent to the landlord, we were given a warm welcome. There were only two tables outside, both occupied, but with a spoon halfway to his mouth, the bowl belonging to a lardy looking youth was whisked away and set down at an empty place on the other table. It didn't please him, but according to the landlord's gesture, it was that or out on the street.

The roasted mutton and green beans with white onion sauce tasted very good indeed and until at least half was in our bellies, we said nothing.

'So,' I said, eventually. 'Have you decided our destination yet?'

He raised his eyebrows and gave a false yawn. 'Now don't be tiresome and spoil this excellent meal.'

It wouldn't spoil mine, I thought, but tried to make light of my question.

'I was thinking of the packing, that's all.'

'Oh, don't worry about that, Will. I've seen you pack a box in a trice. It's one of your very many skills.'

A compliment to shut me up if ever I heard one.

After we'd eaten our fill and were walking back John did tell me of his new plan.

'I am thinking that perhaps we should move our lodgings.'

My heart sank.

'What do you mean *move*? Don't you mean leave? Especially now we need to avoid Prince Gesualdo. He's here in Florence at the Pitti Palace. Doesn't that settle it for you John? It's surely time for us to go.' I left out the accusation about me being a fraud. That would need too much explaining. 'The last thing you need,' I went on, 'is another invitation to play at the palace. Then what would happen? It's unlikely the Grand Duke Ferdinando will be as forgiving as old Duke Alphonso if Prince Gesualdo causes trouble.'

'Maybe,' he sounded petulant, so I said nothing. It was a tone of voice I knew meant he was unsure of himself. 'But Lady Anna is rather special.'

'You say that every time.'

That wasn't strictly true and if asked, I would be the first to agree that Lady Anna was very special indeed.

He shrugged but didn't say anything. I had to control a surge of irritation. How I wished I could impress on John that sometimes there were other factors at play, more dangerous and even more important than his own feelings.

He would have laughed, I think. Not at the content of my speech, but the manner of it. Too serious, too boring, always telling him off. There was a lot of truth in that, so I contented myself with a sigh.

'Don't *you* want to stay here?' he said suddenly. 'Or

are you bored with Miss Sofia now? You still seem to spend every spare minute seeking her company.'

'Never,' I spluttered. 'I would *never* be bored. She is my, my—'

'Yes, yes,' he interrupted, holding up his hands. 'Spare me the detail. I can tell by your face.'

We'd only taken a few more steps when he put an arm about my shoulder.

'My dear brother,' he said, sweet as warm cream. 'You really are the best of men. Mother was right. Honourable and true. Where would I be without you?'

So much for him laughing. He *was* sincere, my beloved brother, and the irritation I had felt for him vanished like a bubble had burst.

On arriving back at the Biscaldi's premises we found Antonio had returned as well as Sofia and Jakob. The latter was describing the visit to meet the rabbi, and he had everyone rapt and smiling at his tale. Including, I noted, Sofia. I must be happy for her, I told myself. I will be happy for them both. I would absolutely ignore the dragging pain of such an effort.

After a brief round of greeting, I bundled a grumbling John straight up the stairs.

'The less you are seen, the better,' I said. 'If the gossip has menace, it may well be that Lady Anna will think better of coming here, but if she does, then it should look as if it's for her own sake and not for a tryst with you.'

I left him and went back downstairs to find a sorry Jakob saying his farewells. I tried my best not to look too pleased. His glance lingered on Sofia as he left, resulting in a near collision with someone arriving when he reached the doorway. The light was such that at first, I couldn't see who it was, but after Jakob had apologised at length and gone on his way, I recognised Rosa. My heart lifted to see her especially when she said she had a message from Lady Anna.

'Is the Lady not coming,' I asked, with rather too much eagerness.

She shook her head. 'I've come to say that she *is*

coming. My apologies, Mr Totman. It would suit both you and me for that not to be the case, but yes, she is. I am to warn you that she is bringing her lute here to be restrung. Apparently, there was an accident with her sewing scissors and one or two have broken.'

So that was the excuse and a rather thin one too, considering Rosa could have brought the lute with her. I raised an eyebrow though and she smiled, although her gaze wandered over my shoulder.

'Hello Rosa,' Antonio said.

She coloured at once and I upbraided myself for ever thinking she was plain. I am not always quick to see the motives of others, but her sudden shyness and looking at the floor told me that she was not averse to the handsome Antonio.

'I have to go now,' she said and bobbed us both a curtsey before disappearing into the throng going to prayers.

'Never mind,' I said, having noticed Antonio's disappointment. 'She'll be back soon. They're both coming here later.'

He nodded. 'Ah yes, but with Lady Anna here, everything will be different.'

'Indeed.'

We stood for a moment considering Lady Anna and the difference she might make, but my thoughts soon sped in another direction.

'Antonio,' I said, glancing over my shoulder to where Sofia and her Papa had their heads together peering at a ledger. 'Would you mind remaining in the shop for a while?'

'Of course,' he said, following my gaze. 'I understand.' He touched his hand to his heart in a swift gesture that spoke more than words.

It was time for me to say a final goodbye to Sofia. I think Signor Biscaldi found the sight of our obvious attachment to each other quite distressing. It was nothing, however, compared to our distress when we were alone. Even in the shadowy afternoon light, I could see Sofia's eyes were bright with tears. With my right hand I held on fast to my left wrist as I could think of no other way to stop myself taking her into my arms so great was the temptation.

'Oh, Mr Totman,' she said. 'What must you think?'

I was taken aback. 'Must think? I hardly know.'

She glared at me. 'About my going to see the rabbi with Jakob?'

'Ah. I don't—'

'It was not what you must think.'

'Miss Sofia,' I said gently. 'It does not matter what I think.'

'But it does—' she hesitated then and lacking the words, shook her head and in a childlike gesture, raised clenched fists to her face.

I felt the same frustration and before I knew what I was doing, covered her little fists with my hands. She did not pull away and there we both stayed, enchanted by the wonder of a touch, until a quiet cough from the doorway startled us and we stepped apart.

'Later,' I whispered. Her smile was enough reply.

CHAPTER EIGHTEEN

John stood in the doorway, no doubt tired of his own company upstairs. All my desire to shout at him I controlled by gritting my teeth, although the ensuing sharp pain caused my eyes to water. Had I driven a sharp nail into my jaw it may well have hurt as much.

'Ow!' I said, clutching at my cheek.

'What's this?' said John, with a look of feigned horror. 'A slap? Well done, Miss Sofia. I'm sure he deserved it.'

Poor Sofia. I could see she was appalled by John's assumption, but before she could protest, I reassured her that John's sense of humour wasn't always easy to perceive.

'Forgive me,' he said, bowing low to Sofia. 'Will is quite right. I am most known for my songs of love, sadness and despair but I am not without wit, although sometimes it may miss the mark.'

Sofia smiled at that. 'Oh yes,' she said. 'I remember well how you *missed the mark* with a certain prince in Ferrara.'

John struck at his temple and groaned. 'Indeed, Signorina, and I am forever in your debt as a result. Prince Gesualdo was the worst—'

'Enough about him,' I interrupted quickly. 'I fear his ears will grow warm, especially as he may well be hereabouts.'

With a fearful start, as if about to be struck, John glanced over his shoulder. That's good, I thought. He's not so breezy about the danger after all.

'Besides,' I went on. 'You should speak with Antonio. He has had a message from Rosa about Lady Anna.'

Although he smiled at my mention of her name, something like a shadow also passed over his face. He too had a goodbye to say at some point and I wished both it would and would not be this afternoon. I had never felt so divided in my thinking.

'Oh?' said John. 'Do we know what was in the message?'

I looked at him blankly even though I knew quite well, and Sofia was also quiet. He looked from one to other of us, not fooled for a moment.

'I had best go and find out then,' he said with the smallest twitch of a smile and then he was gone.

'Make sure you keep out of sight,' I called after him, before turning to Sofia. 'Miss Sofia, I—'

'He is not for me,' she said, waving a dismissal. 'Jakob. I know what Papa thinks, but I was only taking him there. That's all. Introducing him to the rabbi. He is new to Florence. Jakob, that is. I don't want you to think—'

'Please, Miss Sofia. Please stop.'

She looked up, so shamefaced I had to smile.

'Let's not speak of difficulty,' I said, 'or what may or may not be in the future. For my part, I will always cherish our time together and I hope you will think of me with joy in your heart rather than sadness.' This was quite a speech for me, and I stopped, suddenly afraid my words sounded forced or rehearsed from a song of John's. 'I mean that most truly, Sofia,' I whispered.

She held my gaze, and I could not draw it away from her lovely face. So solemn and so very near it was, that I leant forward and gently placed my lips on hers. I pulled back almost straight away, shocked at myself but also because so swift a thing could wield such power. Were we equally amazed? I think so. Sofia still did not look away, but with a finger touched her lips and then put it to mine. It was as if we were alone in the world.

Had a call from Antonio not warned us, our state of trance may have persisted, but shortly afterwards we heard the Lady Anna's rich and melodious voice greeting Signor Biscaldi.

'I must go,' she whispered, pulling away.

'Wait,' I said. 'I have something for you.' I wanted to give her the keepsake, but then Antonio appeared at the door, and he beckoned to me.

'The Lady wants *you* to restring her lute,' he said. 'I

am not skilled enough it seems.'

He hung his head, but I caught his wry expression and slapped him on the back.

'I'm sorry not all of us are so blessed,' I said, 'but don't worry, I'll share my fee.' We both knew there wouldn't be one.

I turned back to Sofia before I went to the task, and raised my eyes to the heavens, or indeed, the upstairs room.

'Later then,' I said, so only she could hear. 'When she is with John. Come, make your way before me.'

Out in the shop, Lady Anna's radiance equalled any number of candles.

'Ah, Signor Totman,' she said. 'It is good to see you again.'

'Lady Anna,' I croaked, bowing low whilst marvelling at the rich melody in her voice.

'I have to say sorry to you, Signor Totman. Your beautiful lute has had a little accident.' I must have looked alarmed for she laughed. 'Don't worry,' she said, 'it is not so bad. Two strings have broken, that's all, but you may decide to replace every course. I would not like the sound to vary from the old to the new.'

Or, I wondered to myself, because it would take me longer and she didn't want to be interrupted?

'Yes,' I said, looking at the deliberately cut string. 'I should replace them all. Better a little more effort now, rather than sorry later.'

'Oh yes indeed,' she said, with another little, but utterly disarming, laugh. 'I'm so glad we understand each other. Now, Rosa, let Signor Totman have the lute and Signor Biscaldi, perhaps you can lend me another to play this afternoon?'

Surprised at being unexpectedly addressed, Signor Biscaldi stumbled a little as he headed for the rack of lutes behind where I stood. He caught hold of my arm to steady himself and a glance passed between us. We were all mesmerised by Lady Anna.

Once she was ensconced upstairs with John, I think

we breathed out. For a moment we were quiet, listening to the creak of floorboards and muffled voices before Signor Biscaldi broke the silence.

'Please put my chair outside, Antonio. Help him, Signor Totman. It is quite heavy. If any trouble come, I will see it.'

He was right, it was far better for him to be seen sitting comfortably by his own premises rather than having a foreigner, especially one thought to be a fraud, lurking at its door. Besides I had a lute to restring and as Sofia followed me into the workshop, I couldn't help but be glad of the tryst upstairs. I lay the lute down and drew the little leather pouch from beneath my jerkin before turning to Sofia.

'Here,' I said. 'I don't think John will interrupt us now. This is for you. It is such a small thing, and of no real value or skill at all.' Nothing I made would ever really convey how I felt.

'Oh, Mr Totman, I—' She slipped the trinket from the pouch and gasped.

In the palm of her hand, the plaque did not look so bad. I had chosen a small piece of walnut for the back which I polished to a shine and the gold ducat nestled tightly in the well I had carved out for it. Luckily, the ducat was an old one and the usual image of Christ holding out the scriptures was worn quite smooth. A dozen or so knocks with a hammer rendered St Mark, who adorned the reverse, almost disappeared. I was sure that when the plaque was finished it would be impossible to see that it had ever been a coin.

One of the lutes in for repair had acquired a large gash in the central rose. An accident of sorts clearly, as if someone had thrust at it with a knife or sword, and a great shame it was too, for the rose was beautifully carved. It would need, however, to be completely replaced and so what was a shame for the instrument, became a blessing for me. I was able to cut a square of the rose to fit under the rim I'd made on the darker walnut but removed certain tiny slivers so that the gold shone through, and the letter S for Sofia became obvious.

'It is a most beautiful thing!' she said, turning it this way and that so the gold glinted in the sunlight coming through the high window.

'I'm sorry it is not all my own work. There was not enough time.'

'Hush, Mr Totman. That you thought to make such a treasure for me is enough.'

Her face grew solemn and tearful as she smiled. I could hardly bear the pain of it myself and looked to the restringing instead.

'You must know,' she said, 'I do not want to marry him.'

For all her determination, she could not disguise the quiver in her voice.

'Miss Sofia,' I said, as firmly as I could manage. 'He is a good man. You could do much worse.'

'Could I?' she said. 'And could I also not do much better?'

'I don't think so. Besides, your father—

'Papa would want me to be happy.'

'Of course, he wants that,' I said, tugging a little too sharply at the first course strings attached to the bridge. 'But doesn't he know better than anybody that the price is not only very high, but the future is so uncertain?'

'Is it?' She reached towards me. 'Is it so uncertain?'

Although said softly, the misery in her voice cut to the quick of me. I put the lute down and took her hand.

'Miss Sofia,' I said. 'We both know the future is uncertain for everyone, but it is especially so for those who are not of the right family, faith, or indeed whether you live on the correct side of the street. You know that, and I know that I would not have any harm come to you.' I kissed each of her lovely fingers and drew her close. 'But perhaps, here and right at this moment, we are not in danger.'

A sudden shriek shattered that notion in an instant. It wasn't loud, but it was a shriek nevertheless, and not one made in jest. We jumped apart and I and started for the door, but Rosa, rushing from the shop, was there before me. Ghost white and trembling, she pointed behind her.

'It is him! It is him! He is coming here, I swear it.'

'Who is it? Who's coming?' New fear gripped me but through the shop I could still see Signor Biscaldi sitting in his chair. Why had he made no movement?

'Count Bonizzi, Anna's husband!' Rosa clutched at her head turning this way and that. 'The Signor does not know him but I am sure. Amongst the crowd. I saw him. I did! What's to be done? Help us, for Mercy's sake!'

CHAPTER NINETEEN

Sofia darted in front of me and took her arm.

'Quickly,' she said, pushing Rosa in front of her. 'Upstairs. We must warn them.'

I was right behind.

'No! You must stay!'

'But John—'

'No! Stay and say nothing. You must! Trust me.' Over her shoulder she said. 'Keep on with the strings.'

It wasn't easy for me, leaving John to his fate like that. In my life, I'd never done it before. With my hand curved over the handle of a sharp chisel from the workbench, I was of a mind to ignore Sofia's instructions and rush up the stairs but, at that moment I saw Signor Biscaldi rise quickly and his heavy chair toppled sideways. Then the shop door was flung open with a bang and three large men blocked the light. I retreated into the workshop, put down the chisel and picked up the lute, all the while grinding my teeth so fiercely that the pain in my jaw returned with a vengeance.

'Can I help you, gentlemen?'

How Antonio managed to sound so calm I don't know. Signor Biscaldi's querulous voice, however, reflected exactly how I felt.

'Yes, yes,' he said. 'What can we do for you? Anything, yes, anything you like?'

I heard a crash and the discordant twang of instruments falling. Dear God, would they wreck the place? I held the lute, but my hands had turned to cold stone.

'Where are they?' said a man's voice, high pitched with fury.

There was a thud and I started. Surely, they wouldn't strike an old man.

'Who...who?'

Another thud, and I decided I could bear it no longer.

Antonio was strong. Could the two of us take on three? I was about to lay the lute down and make for the door when I found it blocked by a huge brute of a fellow.

'Who's this?' he shouted over his shoulder.

'My assistant,' said Antonio, calm as you like. If he'd been struck, I could see no injury. Whilst praying that the thudding noises were other than blows to Signor Biscaldi, I held up the lute and flicked at a broken string as if it were important evidence.

'A foreigner?'

I nodded. 'From Copenhagen,' I said, quickly, thinking that London would not be a good idea if they were searching for John. Then, because he looked like a man who would not know much of the world, added. 'Denmark.'

Behind him, Antonio raised his eyebrows.

'The Danes are keen to learn our skills,' he murmured, before another man pushed past them both. When he stood in the centre of the workshop and looked about him as if from a high pulpit, I knew without doubt that this grotesque human being was Lady Anna's husband.

He wheezed heavily, most likely from the effort of moving his great bulk and already the workshop was pungent with the smell of his sweat. All it would take was a sharp shove and he'd topple over. Not so for the other man though, his flesh was muscle hard and there was another, third man, I had yet to see.

'Is there no way out here?' he said, in a pig-squealy voice, whilst looking about. 'Or is there somewhere else? I know she is here.'

I shrugged and looked at the floor.

'It will be bad for you.' He pointed at Antonio, then at me. 'It will be bad for you too.' He performed an ungainly sort of twirl then, pointing at all the instruments and the work on the bench. 'And very bad for all of this, if you do not say what you know.'

A flick of his fingers and one of the lutes in for repair crashed to the floor courtesy of the brute he employed.

This was bad. I'd been in some scrapes in my life but usually there was some way out. Here, unless you count the window, which could possibly be accessed by clambering over the bench, the only way out was through the shop. The husband wasn't the only one sweating as I held my breath, feeling the throb in my jaw worsen. What would happen next? I feared for our fingers, although at that moment even our lives seemed cheap.

An image of the room upstairs flashed into my head. The women silent and trembling. John too. He'd be berating himself for not having left the city already, for all the good that would do. Was there another door in that room? A window through which he could escape? I had no memory of either. The only window was directly above the shop door and high off the ground. A large cedarwood chest, big enough to take a man, stood against a wall, but hopeless for hiding, as it would be the first place anyone would search.

In the workshop the air crackled as if a thunderstorm was about to break. Any moment now, I thought, as the hairs on the back of my neck rose. Then I remembered the calamitous noise and upset when Prince Gesualdo had hurled his archlute across the room. I glanced about. If I threw the lute and caused a commotion, it could alert the other man still in the shop. If he came to find out what was going on, there'd be the smallest chance for John to escape. How would he know though? Surely, they could hear from upstairs as we could hear them from below. I swapped the lute from the left to my right, the stronger hand, then remained still.

The husband cleared his throat and spat generously on the floor only a yard from me. Even so, he was not my target.

I made ready, gradually raising the lute higher and another stray and desperate idea came to me; perhaps amidst the row I could leap onto the bench and make my escape through the window. But how long before a strong hand gripped my ankle? Would they even bother with me if it was John they were after. Perhaps they might think I *was* John. There was only one way to find out as I braced myself.

'My Lord?'

A voice I did not expect to hear stayed my hand. We all recognised the footsteps descending the stairs and the melodious voice calling out.

'Is that you I heard? Where are you, my sweet?'

I nearly choked. Her *sweet*? This repellent toad of a man? I couldn't admire the woman more.

Lady Anna stood in the doorway lit by a ray of sunshine, but at that moment, if you'd told me she was the sun, I would have believed you. Whatever had happened whilst she was alone with John, thankfully, it had not affected her attire in any way.

All the men present bowed before such gorgeousness, except, of course, the vile husband. He waddled over and caught hold of her wrist in such a rough manner as to make her wince.

'I hear,' he rasped, putting his sweaty face close to hers, 'I hear you've been making a fool of me?'

'My Lord,' she said, sounding shocked. 'I would never do that.'

It was painful to watch as the husband gripped her hand even harder. I remembered back to the conversation I'd had with Rosa. No wonder she'd been glad not to marry. That Lady Anna could maintain her composure with such surety showed this wasn't the first time she'd felt his violence. I wished him dead.

'Check upstairs,' he said to his man. 'And make sure you're thorough. As for you, wife,' he pushed her back out of the workshop and into the shop. 'Start saying your prayers.'

I was already praying. No doubt Lady Anna had decided that to come down may allay her husband's suspicions. It was as weak a plan as mine. John was surely trapped.

There was such an exodus, that I was left alone in the workshop as the heavy footsteps ascended the stairs. There was more thudding about in the room above.

The chest was opened and closed with a bang, and I heard protests from Sofia but, to my astonishment, no cries of discovery. Footsteps descended the stairs, first Sofia's familiar delicate tread, then the same heavy tread as before. I began to hope that a miracle had indeed occurred, but I was mystified as to how, for unlike so many houses in London, where wood panels could easily conceal secret doors and passages, this was a building of stone and in the upstairs room, apart from a small tapestry, the walls were plain.

I would have to wait for any explanation though. In the shop there was still something of a commotion as Lady Anna was doing her best to assuage her husband's temper. Another set of heavy footsteps went up the stairs and came down again, presumably to affirm the first man's story that there was no English lutenist to be found there.

I held my breath. In my hand Lady Anna's lute still sported a broken string and it quivered with some violence in the draught from the outer door of the shop being slammed shut. A very loud silence followed during which I put down the lute and eased myself into a position where I had a view into the shop.

Shutting the front door had obscured almost all the light and I could only make out the outline of Signor Biscaldi and Sofia clutching each other. Gradually as I grew accustomed to the gloom, I realised there was no one else there except for Antonio who had his ear to the door.

As for the vanishing away of John Dowland, I was desperate to discover how that had been achieved and when, after a few moments, impatience got the better of caution, I stepped into the shop.

'Hello?' I whispered.

'Oh, Mr Totman!' Sofia broke away from her father but helped him as we all retreated to the quiet of the workshop. I could see then that the poor man looked deathly pale.

'Here,' I said, pulling up the bench stool. 'Sit here now and I'll fetch your chair.'

The chair was still outside. Made of oak with a solid seat, back and arms, I was glad of Antonio's help after we checked that no further trouble awaited us when we opened the door.

'A few hours more,' he said, 'and our plan would have worked. I do not think things will go well for Signor Biscaldi now, but for you, I have a little good news.'

'Oh? About John. He is safe?'

He shook his head. 'It's from Rosa,' he said, after we both lifted on my count of three. 'She said Lady Anna wants you to keep the lute.'

I nearly dropped the chair.

'Rosa also said,' he paused as we manoeuvred the chair around a large box. 'Lady Anna is very sorry but such a gift is too dangerous to keep.'

I was both sorry and not sorry. A gift from John Dowland would be a colossal affront to the husband and, even considering the Lady Anna's friendship with the Grand Duchess, that she could still suffer the same fate as the Prince Gesualdo's first wife didn't bear thinking about. The lute had felt good in my hands though, and a large part of me was glad to have it back.

My face must have reflected these mixed feelings as Antonio smiled.

'Maybe,' he said, 'it does not like to leave its master.'

'Maybe.' I said, with as near a shrug as I could muster holding the chair. I didn't say anything about John's prophecy back in Ferrara, that the lute would indeed come back to us.

Back in the workshop. I put any thoughts of lutes and trysts right out of my mind. That the danger had passed was a relief, but we did not know if it would return.

'The door is bolted?' Signor Biscaldi asked as he lowered himself into the chair.

'Very tightly,' Antonio said, as he checked again.

We all took a deep breath.

'So,' I said, once Signor Biscaldi was settled and looking a better colour. 'We have survived this afternoon but please, before we say anything more, is someone going to tell me what's happened to John?'

After a shared smile and glance between Sofia and Signor Biscaldi, he nodded.

'Come,' said Sofia. 'I will show you.'

She led me upstairs while I determined to look very closely at every aspect of the room to see if there was a hidden door through which he must have fled. Then it occurred to me he may still be hiding.

'I hope he is not locked in a very small place.'

'No, no. He will be far away from here now.'

I was yet to be convinced and remained doubtful even when we reached the top of the stairs and especially when having looked at all the walls and checked behind the tapestry with my own eyes, I found no way out.

'Can he be in the chest?'

'Don't you think we would have heard him by now?' She laughed at this feeble suggestion. 'But perhaps you'd better see for yourself?'

It was certainly large enough for a person, although probably not one the size of Signor Biscaldi. Once I'd lifted the heavy lid, the scent of cedar and lavender wafted out. The garments, mostly cloaks and hats for winter had been flung about.

Beside me, Sofia whispered, as she began to gather them up.

'Perhaps he is asleep.'

'Miss Sofia,' I gently pleaded with her. 'You toy with me about someone I hold dear. Please let me know where he is.'

'I'm so sorry. How thoughtless I am. Please, please forgive me. I will show you. Help me with the rest.'

I took the one remaining hat out of the chest, but now it was empty, I was still none the wiser. The bottom was planked tightly and strutted across. I turned to Sofia to find that she wasn't paying attention to my task but was hastily removing the lace on her cuff.

'What are you doing?'

'Please,' she said, offering it to me. 'I did not make this, but I have nothing else to give, and I would that you had something to remember me by.' Her cheeks grew pink as I held her gaze.

'Thank you, my dearest Miss Sofia,' I said, covering her hand as well as the lace and lifting it to my lips. 'I will most certainly never forget you, but why the haste? I am not going anywhere just yet.'

'But it may be that you disappear in the same way as Mr Dowland.'

I looked at her sternly. Surely she wouldn't tease me now? I hid the lace cuff safely within my jerkin before looking inside the empty chest once again. It was still empty.

'Is there some magic here?' I said, doubtfully.

'You have to get in.'

I felt rather foolish, but even so, put one leg over the edge.

'Face that end,' she gestured, 'then sit down. Don't lean back though.'

I did as I was told.

'Now,' she said, with a smile. 'We have to shut the lid, but don't worry, we can open it again very soon.'

I didn't like the sound of being shut in such a small space at all, but the last thing I saw before everything went black was Sofia's smile and then her lips pursed in a kiss. What I heard was a thud as the lid closed and then her voice, muffled but very close.

'Now lean back and push a little.'

I was glad to have something to engage my thoughts away from the unease that threatened. When I leant back, I heard only the softest of creaks but soon my eyes began to make out a strip of pale light in the bottom of the chest by my feet. I pushed it a little and it moved as if recently oiled. The strip of light grew slightly wider and I realised I was looking at a very clever trapdoor. It wasn't hinged, rather it slid back beneath the half of the chest where I was sitting.

Daylight flooded in when Sofia opened the chest again. Then I could really see what had happened. A short ladder dropped from under my feet and at the bottom I saw the passage that had taken John away from danger.

My gasp of surprise made Sofia laugh.

'There,' she said. 'So now you know the Biscaldis' deepest secret.'

'But where does it go?' I said, starting down. 'And where is this place? I thought the shop hard on its neighbour.'

I was keen to explore John's escape route, but Sofia called me back.

'Wait,' she said. 'I will tell you, and then you may think better of going. Come.'

Although resolved to venture along the passage, Sofia's warning made me hesitate and I clambered out of the chest.

'Is John in further danger then? Where is he now?'

'Now? That's impossible to say, but all going well, he could be enjoying a stroll or a flagon of wine. What I hope is that he is keeping out of sight.'

I looked at her sternly and she blushed.

'Forgive me,' she said. 'I should not jest about such a serious issue. Papa had the secret passage made by building a false wall at the side of the shop. There is a turn in it after a while so for thirty steps afterwards it is very dark, but then there is a little door.'

She paused and clutched at the lace on her remaining cuff in almost the same way as her father did when he was perturbed.

'And?' I said, feeling similarly agitated myself. 'The door opens—'

'At the back of the synagogue in the ghetto.'

I opened my mouth and shut it again. Of course, that's where the passage would go. Where else? No doubt it could serve equally well as an escape route in the opposite direction.

'It is fortunate,' she went on, 'that at that time there would be few people there when John opened the door. It is hidden, but even so, apart from those who know, the old rabbi and one or two of our dearest friends, for most it would be a surprise to see him appear. I hope he did not linger or reveal the door. He does have a cloak and hat from the chest as a disguise although—'

We both looked at the garments that Sofia had left in a neat pile on the floor. Signor Biscaldi was not a tall man, and he was rather wide. As for a hat, I supposed that for it to fall over John's face may not be such a bad thing.

'I should go and find him.'

'Yes.' Her eyes were already brimming with tears.

'It's goodbye once again,' I said softly.

And that time, our third goodbye, my own feelings would not be contained. I took her into my arms and held her as close as I had that evening in Ferrara. Her slender body trembled against mine, and when I kissed her, it was with no small feeling.

All my life long I would not forget that moment and oh, that it would have continued for longer, but at the sound of extra loud coughing and slow footsteps on the stairs we drew apart. Always thoughtful, Antonio kept his eyes on his feet when he mounted the last few steps into the room.

'Signor Biscaldi is asking for you, Sofia.' He turned to me. 'We've found a different box for the lute so that you're not seen with the same one that Lady Anna brought with her.'

'Thank you,' I said, clearing my throat and blushing almost a brightly as Sofia. 'That's well done and very kind.'

'I've also finished the restringing for you,' he said, with the faintest twinkle in his eye, 'I hope it meets with your approval.'

It was hard to feel any levity, but this was Antonio. A fine craftsman and a patient teacher of his native language. I lay my hand on his shoulder

'Thank you. There's no doubt about that.'

We were a sad procession that made our way downstairs to where Signor Biscaldi wrung his hands and looked almost as sorry at my departing as the rest of us.

'A little wine before you go?'

It was a politeness, that's all, and I shook my head.

'Once I've found John and we're on our way, I'll send

word, but it's best I don't say where we're headed.'

'Is wise,' said Signor Biscaldi, nodding to us and himself. He took hold of Sofia's hand. 'And we close shop until Lady Anna return to Ferrara. Soon I hope.'

I could give Sofia only the swiftest of glances as I took my leave. I'd seen her pretty face too often stricken with pain and whilst my own hurt lay upon me like a great sack of wood, that I should be the cause of hers, I regretted far more.

Antonio unlocked the door and we stepped into the city's noise and a shaft of late afternoon sun.

'I thought I might accompany you,' he said. 'If you'll permit me, that is.'

'Of course. Although you won't find me very good company.'

'Perhaps not, but two is better than one at preventing unwanted company and I would be very upset if that nice lute were to get damaged in any way.'

I gave his remark a hollow laugh.

'That nice lute,' I said, 'has caused us nothing but grief and difficulty. I'm beginning to think it maybe cursed.'

'Cursed?' With a sharp intake of breath, Antonio looked over his shoulder. 'You shouldn't say such things for people to hear. They will so delight in the notion that the whole city will know before we've reached the Arno. Especially if it has befallen a foreigner.'

'My apologies, and I should know better. London is the same, full of people with big ears.'

I had said the remark in all seriousness, and it was only when Antonio said he thought they must look comical and wished to see them, that I also smiled.

'You must admit,' I said, 'this lute has caused us some trouble.'

'Yes, indeed, but do you know? I have always liked to believe that an instrument as fine as the one you carry, isn't happy unless it belongs in the arms of the right player.'

I raised my eyebrows. 'My good Antonio, I had not

thought you would have such fancies.'

He shrugged and again I remembered John's notion that the lute would come back to him here in Florence. Well, it was on its way. For myself, I'd rather it had taken a more straightforward path.

To avoid being accosted by foes of any kind, Antonio led me through streets I didn't know. I was glad he kept our conversation afloat as it kept back the great wave of misery that threatened me. When he asked where I'd learnt such skill, I thought fondly of John's mother.

'Old Mistress Dowland apprenticed me with a craftsman,' I said. 'She was as loving towards me as any orphan could wish, but she was also wise. As a boy, I had always a small wooden trinket in the making, clothes pegs mostly, having lived in a laundry, but for John's mother's birthday soon after I'd joined the household, I decided to make a little box for her bobbins. I think that's when she first saw my skill. Her own son had a prodigious talent of course, but that talent came with very exacting standards about the instruments he played. Signor Biscaldi would have done very well to have a shop in Cheapside, as John paid no regard to the expense if he had a desire for a new lute. My belief is that Mistress Dowland thought putting me with an instrument maker might eventually save her some money.'

'And did it?'

I shook my head. 'Not at all. I think it only increased her expenditure as she also bought all my tools. Ah well. If I could pay her back, I would, but it is too late for that.'

'A generous lady indeed, but I think perhaps your loyalty to Signor Dowland has settled any debt.'

'Perhaps, but—'

He interrupted. 'Will you stay with him your whole life long?'

My *whole* life? I had not thought. It sounded almost like a sentence.

'I don't know. I haven't considered—'

'Listen,' he said, putting his arm about my shoulder. 'It is not my business, but maybe you should think about returning.' He spoke so earnestly I was taken by surprise, and even more so when we stopped and he fixed me in a gaze. 'With your skill, it would not be difficult for you to make a good life here, and it would be a happy one with a woman who loves you very much.' He smiled then. 'As for you, my friend, even a blind man could tell that you love her.'

I was too stunned to say anything for a few moments. That Antonio should feel inclined to speak so, moved me to the point that I even felt the prickle of tears. I took a deep breath and told myself to keep steady.

'Thank you, Antonio.' I said having recovered myself. 'You are a true friend. You can be assured that I will think on what you've said, but for her own sake and safety, she must surely marry Jakob.'

We had nearly reached the river. Perhaps he was about to persuade me otherwise, but then with an anguished look, he merely sighed. He was going in another direction and after a brief but heartfelt farewell, we parted. I forced my thoughts away from our conversation and on to the hope of finding John at our lodgings where I would pack in a trice, for I couldn't believe he would wish to remain within riding distance of Florence after such a scare.

But when I turned the corner, all such thoughts were silenced by a noisy scene unfolding at our lodgings. Three men stood in front of the landlord who stood shaking his head while barring the door. Two of the men were officials in livery, but the third, a slighter man stood behind.

I stepped back, hoping to remain unseen, but I was far too slow and a voice cried out.

'There he is! He's the one.'

CHAPTER TWENTY

I'd seen him in the shop only that morning. Loreto, Fontanelli's servant, the surly copyist from Ferrara was jabbing his finger in my direction and twirling it around in triumph.

'He's the fraudster!' he shouted. 'I saw him do it.'

There was no point in my trying to flee. I was too close and too obvious to make my escape in a city I hardly knew.

'You have to come with us.' I was told by one of the officials.

No amount of feeble protesting would make any difference. The landlord stood with his arms folded, apparently unmoved by the scene. I thrust the lute towards him.

'It belongs to Signor Dowland.'

At first, he ignored me and began to close the door.

'Please, I beg you.'

He looked at me with contempt, but his better nature prevailed and he took it with a shrug.

Never had I felt such fear and shame as during that short walk. With a glance I could see everyone looking at the spectacle of a stranger being escorted away. Jeers started soon after, encouraged by that worm of a copyist who cavorted about like a jester, taunting and pointing at me with his stupid finger. Then I remembered my dear sweet Sofia and her calm indifference to the ruffian who had spat at her in the street. I did not have her resolve and was not at all indifferent. Even so, I tried to keep my fists unclenched.

We should have left sooner. Round and round in my head it went, but better than the other thought that I wouldn't allow. The darker one about my future. Why didn't we flee at the first mention of Prince Gesualdo? A man like that would be even more fickle than John in his tempers. Yes, the new lute distracted him for a while, but he would always remember the insult, and any gossip about John Dowland at the Palazzo Pitti would surely rekindle the memory. *We should have left.*

Count Fontanelli had seemed such a reasonable man. A good customer and almost a friend? No. No Count of any race makes *friends* with a merchant, especially not a Jew. That the Count had seemed affable was maybe a veneer, one stuck with such weak glue it could be changed on a whim. Why Loreto had so taken against me, I did not know.

We should have left.

I'd thought that I would be brought before Prince Gesualdo to explain myself, but the true horror of my situation became apparent only when I was escorted down a flight of steep and twisting steps to a passage lit only by a small opening cut high in the wall.

'What is this place?' I asked, knowing only too well that underground was the domain of cellars and dungeons. 'There's been a mistake. I shouldn't be here.'

This provoked hearty laughter from my guards as they pushed me through a door and turned the key.

'Welcome to *Le Bargello*,' called one from the passage and they both clapped their hands as they walked away.

Assaulted and stunned by every echo of the last hour, I stood looking at the door, trying to make sense of what had happened.

Once my eyes had settled to the gloom, I looked about and made out that although the space was hardly large, being but three or four paces square, it was not running with damp and the air was stale rather than foul. A cellar rather than a dungeon.

Shame, hot as lava, flamed through me then, filling my head until I thought it would burst. With a groan I squatted down, covering my face with my hands. How could this have happened?

The answer came to me in the shape of Loreto, the copyist. Why though? I thought back to the first time I had set my eyes on him in the *Palazzo dei Diamonte*. I had been amazed by the rich decoration in the music room but shocked by how badly the instruments were kept. The Count had stopped to speak to the copyist and yes, complained about his work, but that wasn't anything unusual.

Then I thought he must have watched me scribe my own name. Harmless enough but didn't I know how some people see anyone who hails from another country as a thief or a villain? No wonder he'd looked at me so sideways when, on the order of Prince Gesualdo, he'd come to fetch me later that day.

I sat down on the floor and tried to remember what had happened and how it could possibly be that Loreto was now waving that same piece of paper in his hand. That was his evidence. I must have laid it aside or dropped it on the floor. Who would believe I'd written such a thing for such a flimsy reason as improving my signature? Such vanity and such a fool!

'I do have friends,' I said out loud, trying to reassure myself.

Friends. Oh yes. Dear, *dear* friends but none had the ear of the Grand Duke or were friends of Prince Gesualdo. No doubt John would have persuaded Lady Anna to help, but not now her husband was in the city. Besides, I had no idea where he was, or whether he could help me.

If only I had money, but Signor Biscaldi's ducat had gone into the keepsake for Sofia and the only coins I had left were of little value.

All my hopes lay with John. That he was not back at our lodgings worried me and I thought of him wandering lost in the city streets wearing Signor Biscaldi's ill-fitting cloak and hat. An easy target.

Even if he did return to the lodgings, I wasn't sure he'd be able to help me. Between us we were a catastrophe in the making. Would he keep the news of my incarceration from Sofia? For her sake I hoped so. For my sake, I would do anything to see her again, but all this trouble was of my own making and now more than ever I could see that Jakob was the better man for her.

I stood up, stretched a little and paced the few short

steps in both directions. Already, staring at the same view of the wall opposite set my nerves alight again and sitting once more I shut my eyes, determined to make pictures in my mind's eye that would allay my fears. I thought of London, not my workshop or the Dowland house, but the time before, with Ma Perks and all of us sweating in the laundry. What a disappointment I'd be in her eyes, and after I'd made something of myself too.

I felt the heat of tears behind my eyes and tried to rub them away. As a boy, I'd counted myself one of the canniest, always alert to trouble. How did I become such a blundering man?

Almost as if he were beside me, I heard John's voice advising me about one of his favourite subjects:

You can't lie about on the ground weeping. At least, not unless you want a kicking. Actual weeping is for women, Will. What sort of man are you?

Now I knew where the blundering man had come from. Love had blinded both my eyes and ears. Yes, I'd *suggested* to John that we leave Florence, but I could have *persuaded* him, had my heart and true conviction been present. Where were they? With Sofia at the instrument shop.

I berated myself with thoughts such as these until I was startled by the night bell. Up until that moment I had been waiting for help to come, but even if John was not in his own trouble and had discovered my whereabouts, he could not work for my release at such a late hour. The gloom soon became darkness and with it all the unfamiliar rustlings and creaks of a strange place. Sleep came fitfully and with dreams of suffocation and hurt.

I awoke with daylight in the high window and a bladder ready to burst, so I thumped on the door and shouted. To my surprise, the guard came along quite quickly, and I was pushed along to a stinking drain.

On my return, instead of being locked in again, my guard escorted me up the stone steps. How my hopes rose! Soon I would be able to explain myself. If John were there, he would vouch for me and, although we were both foreigners, he was famous across the Continent. That would be a good thing surely. Why, hadn't he even played before the Grand Duke and Duchess? I almost skipped the last few steps.

What foolishness though, to let my thoughts run wild. I was led into a courtroom where the only person I recognised, amongst the half dozen or so who weren't guards or officials, was Loreto. As sullen as ever, with a smug sneer crossing his face when he saw me. I did wonder if my honest explanation might hold sway as his appearance was certainly against him, but then, in strode Count Fontanelli. Everyone sprang to their feet. I could see he was in great haste as he patted the air with irritation to signal that everyone should sit. I was left standing, of course, and on spying me from the other side of the room, he turned to the official in charge and said with great certainty:

'Yes, that's the man.' And with that he turned and left.

All my hopes drained from me as blood from a mortal wound. It would make no difference what I said in my defence and indeed, when it came to my turn to speak, I could barely stutter. Had I better command of the language it still would not have helped. How thin my excuses sounded, even to me.

'Why would anyone scribe his name so many times if not for some wicked purpose? He was a grown man, not a schoolboy.'

Loreto added many embellishments to entertain the company. The most painful lie to hear was that I had glued a label bearing my name to a lute made by the master craftsman Laux Maler, for the purpose of deceiving Count Fontanelli and Prince Gesualdo.

The more Loreto spoke, the more drenched in sweat I became. When the scrap of paper was produced as evidence a groan escaped my lips. Why had I not destroyed it? Such a small thing, such a big mistake!

My judge, a man who looked in need of sleep and

with a frown permanently etched into his forehead kept nodding. On the wall directly above him, in a large roundel, the Blessed Virgin gazed down on us all. In my whole life I'd yet to see a prayer answered, whether one of my own or any of the many desperate pleas for mercy from others, but I prayed very hard to that serene lady.

Loreto continued, his story becoming a fabrication of enormous size. During that short time in the Palazzi dei Diamonte, he had overheard my admitting to any number of crimes. The Maler lute was for show and demonstration, while my own inferior instruments were sold. I was a foreigner, an enemy and not only that, friendly with the Jews. They were bound to be all in this fraud together.

At this pronouncement, I could not stop a gasp of protest escaping from my mouth. I had made no mention of anyone else being involved. Thankfully, the question of who owned the lute I sullied with my name was never raised. Perhaps Prince Gesualdo had already thrown it across the room. Perhaps the Count had instructed Loreto not to mention it. Perhaps it was assumed—

I started as the magistrate clapped his hands together. He'd grown impatient with Loreto and his inflating story.

'That's enough,' he said. 'I don't need to hear any more. You are too fond of the sound of your own voice, I think.'

He turned to me, and I willed any expression to my face that might prove an honest heart. Whether he'd take me for a madman though, I couldn't tell.

'Signor Totman,' he said. 'You are charged with deceiving Count Fontanelli and Prince Gesualdo. This fellow,' he proffered a dismissive wave at Loreto, 'is witness to the act. I do not trust most of his testimony, but it is your hand on the paper. You have said the writing of a label was an amusement and not for gain. Why anyone should do such a thing seems to me foolish. Your wits, however, are not on trial here.'

He paused then, sitting up straighter and giving full

weight to the drama for the benefit of his audience.

'I therefore find you guilty. 'Guilty of deceit and fraud.'

As my innards turned to water, I saw his eyes narrow.

'But,' he said, once again sitting back in his large chair, 'here in Florence, we understand mercy and no harm was done. A lesson though, should be learnt. Three months or fifty ducats.'

And with that, he gestured to the clerk to record the verdict and waved for me to be taken away. As his words tolled in my head, I struggled to understand what they would mean. The guard pushed me out of my trance and down into a cell where I was kept until it filled with the guilty of the morning. We were a grim half dozen. Only one man spoke, and that was to abuse his accuser repeatedly, every insult accompanied by an imaginary blow. By the end of the morning, I'd heard so much about the cheating swindler, I felt I'd know him in the street.

Mostly though, I paid no attention and instead, harangued myself. Three months! And I should be grateful it was not worse. I told myself I was lucky. In London, I'm sure it would have been worse. I still possessed two hands, ten fingers and all my faculties. It was three months, not years.

Such a small thing, a piece of paper bearing my name. Loreto must have gained in some way, but what? I was at a loss to know. Perhaps deceit was his first thought in all situations. Hadn't I met many such men? It wasn't usually mine but then, I hadn't disabused Count Fontanelli of the notion that I had made the Maler lute. How bitterly I regretted that.

The sun blazed on us as we were taken through the streets, but it was the jeers and rude gestures that sent the blood to my face. That, and gritting my teeth too hard again sent a stabbing pain through my jaw. I would not be cowed though and searched amongst the people in the streets for a familiar face. With my hair and pallor I stood out from the local population like a lantern in the dark.

A great square building greeted us as we turned the

corner, the featureless walls the height of four or five men and not a window to be seen, could only be the prison. Above the door an inscription read *Oportet Misereri*.

I'd never been imprisoned, but I'd heard enough tales to scare me witless when I was a boy. Rats as big as cats, lice fat from feasting on your person, and without money, a man could easily starve. As I the door loomed above me, I shivered, trying hard not to imagine what might lay in store, especially when, having arrived in front of the warden, the man who had babbled and cursed all morning produced a fat purse and a considerable number of coins changed hands.

When it came to my turn, the warder raised his eyebrows. Firstly, at my appearance and then again when he saw the slender state of my purse. I could almost see him think, who was this clean-clothed, light-skinned foreigner? And why has he no money? He folded his arms and gave me a long look. I could see by his impressive beard and the newly pressed state of his ruff, that he was a man who paid attention to details. I had no idea what he saw in me, but I hoped it wasn't someone who needed another lesson learnt. Perhaps the state of my garb signalled wealthy friends. Was it a kindness, or simply chance that I was taken to a sizable cell which I had all to myself?

'Tell me,' I asked my escort. 'If I wanted to get a message to someone, what would I have to do?'

He looked me up and down, perhaps expecting me to reveal a purse. When it became obvious that was not to be he shrugged.

'The *Buonomini* will be here soon and they are usually obliging.'

That I was ignorant of these people must have been clear on my face.

'Charity,' he said. '*The Buonomini di San Martino* look after the poor in here. You won't have to wait long. The warder keeps them informed about anyone new and without means.'

The cell was far from comfortable, but it was also

far from what I had imagined. Instead of descending to some filthy dungeon, I had been escorted up a flight of stone stairs. Half a dozen men could have lain on the floor and two wooden benches, narrow and just long enough, served for sitting and sleeping. The privy in one corner even had a board for covering and above it, a high window gave plenty of air, despite a close view of the high wall outside. I shivered to see it remembering that not so long ago I had admired the stonework in Florence.

Although I had not abandoned all hope of a rescue, I did count three months on my fingers. October, November, would December be mild? A man could freeze to death else. With a groan I sat down and put my head in my hands. So much for keeping John out of trouble. I prayed he wasn't somewhere similar hoping for help from me. When an agonised wail arose from the depths of the building, I shuddered.

Hours passed in gloomy contemplation, but eventually it was interrupted by the sound of a rattle of keys outside. I hoped it was the early arrival of the *Buonomini* and I would be able to send a message. To whom though? The landlord at our lodgings did not look at me with a friendly eye and I had no idea whether John had even returned there.

Disappointment raged through me as I received a hunk of bread and half a beaker of sour wine from a wretched looking boy.

'*Buonomini*?' I asked, more in hope than faith.

He said nothing before the key was once again turning in the lock.

The bells of the city tolled the hours as time dragged on. It wasn't only nightfall that made the world a dark place. My own humour became blacker still and during hours of fitful sleep I condemned John to a miserable and violent death somewhere in a Florentine gutter. I saw him lying there, in Signor Biscaldi's coat, now bloodied and torn. How I had failed old Mistress Dowland, failed in her trust, in her belief in me. Sofia, I saw too, her face pale as the moon, as Jakob, no wait, not Jakob. My beloved Sofia, clasped in the arms of, of Gesualdo, the mad prince. No! I started into full wakefulness and sat up.

Through the high window I detected a smudge of morning. Slowly, I got to my feet. After a night on the bench, every inch of me ached, as if I'd been given a hard beating. A stretch this way and that did little, and I sat back down. For what else was there to do?

The black humour came again, bringing its bleak forecast. Nothing would come good, and three months could just as well be three years or thirty. I thought of John. Was this how he felt when the mood took him? Never would I be fierce with him again. Again? If only there would be an again! Tears pricked and at first, I squeezed them away, only to allow them to flow freely when again they threatened.

The day was full before I heard voices outside, and when the door opened, it was to a small assembly standing in the shadow of the passage. In front, the warder and behind him, a churchman in habit and hood.

'*Buononimi?*' I asked once more, for who else would come in such a garb. But wait. My eyes accustomed to the scene. There. Yes, there at the back, taller and at once filling my heart with hope and joy, was the most excellent man in every respect, John Dowland! My dear friend and brother. Never had I been gladder to see him.

Once the warder stepped into the cell, I could see that John was finding his serious expression difficult to maintain, biting his lip to stop it from bursting gleeful laughter. We were hardly in the place for that, I told myself sternly, so I willed myself to stay staring at the floor. How I wished to shout out my relief, but it would not do to celebrate just yet. For all I knew, my freedom could be jeopardised in the blink of an eye.

CHAPTER TWENTY-ONE

I've never been one for riding a horse, preferring my own two feet. For further travel, the outside on a coach or wagon suits me best, but the day after my release from prison I'd have gladly ridden without stopping, and the next day too, had there been a horse willing and able.

Having gathered our belongings, we left Florence in haste, waving farewell to the landlord who cheered up considerably once John paid him a handsome tip. From the gate over the river to the South, we took the road to Siena, the first stop on our way to Rome. At least that's what John told anyone that would hear him. I said nothing, leaving my fate in his hands until we were well away from the city. After about half an hour we reached a tavern where the beguiling aroma of food filled the air. We ordered a jug of wine with onion stew, which I ate as if I'd starved for a week rather than a day. A ripe peach to follow sweetened the breath and was so delicious we bought more for the journey.

It was early afternoon and too hot for anything vigorous, but the Tuscan hills were wooded, and the shade made for a pleasant ride. I soon discovered our way led not to Siena after all. With advice from a pedlar about directions we turned East and headed for the coast.

When the shadows began to lengthen, and tiredness overtook us, a hayloft for comfort and a trough for washing provided good enough lodging for the night. The old couple who lived in the farmhouse were more than happy with a florin and brought us bread and a jug of wine for our supper. The day was cooling and across the valley a shepherd whistled to his dog. At any other time, I would have settled easily to admiring the view whilst eating, but John had not said a word about my release, and I could bear it no longer.

'Now tell me,' I said, 'else I go mad with guessing. How on earth did you convince the warder to free me?'

'Oh that,' John shrugged this great deed away as if it was nothing. 'Really Will, you do get yourself into some awkward spots at times. What would you do without me?'

Whether he was joking I couldn't tell, but he said no more and set about soaking a chunk of bread. The explanation would come soon enough but the moment of triumph was his to enjoy. I could prompt though.

'I suppose it was the landlord who told you where I was.'

'Mmm,' he nodded, while chewing. 'And highly suspicious he was too. It took me quite a long time to convince him that we, well, perhaps not you, but *I* was an honest man. Luckily, I was still wearing Signor Biscaldi's cloak, and he took a fancy to the fur. I could see the lust for it in his eyes, so I thought it could be just the thing to loosen his tongue.'

'You traded Signor Biscaldi's cloak?'

'Well, I didn't want to trade my own, did I?' He looked indignant. 'And he was keen to have it remade in a more suitable style. A good idea, I thought.'

Or theft, I thought, feeling both guilty and ashamed about all the trouble we had caused to Signor Biscaldi. I could not yet think of Sofia as lost to the past without a pain in my chest that threatened to stop my breath.

'And of course,' said John, emphasising the point by waving his remaining bread in my direction. 'Once he was stroking the fur trim, he was more than happy to tell me about all the excitement taking place on his doorstep.'

'I expect he was.'

'I would have gone straight round to the jail,' John went on, 'but when he mentioned Ferrara, Gesualdo and that Fontanelli fellow, I knew that my own standing, however celebrated I may be, I knew it would not be enough.'

He stood up and began pacing back and forth like an actor on the stage.

'What could I do?' he said, knocking on his head in the manner of thinking hard. 'Aha! I had it.' This came with a similarly exaggerated gesture of surprise, but then he came and sat close by me. 'What I needed to do,' he went on in a low voice, as one conspirator might to another, 'was seek help from the *highest authority*.'

Authority of any sort worried me; *highest authority* could only mean one thing, hence the appearance of Friar Bailey at the prison. He would not have been my choice, but here I was and more than grateful.

'That was well thought,' I said. 'And I'm very glad you didn't leave it to a few prayers for that assistance, although I will say mine with more fervour in future. It's a good thing it was Friar Bailey you spoke to. Had Skidmore still been in the city, I've no doubt he would have left me to rot, but surely, they wouldn't release me on the word of a friar.'

'True enough, but don't forget what I said about a higher authority? A friar would not do, but what about a cardinal? Remember the letter from Rome that Friar Bailey talked about? Full of flattery and the promise of a large pension? Who else would have the authority to offer such a thing? So—' He clapped his hands together, excited by the sheer brilliance of his tale. 'I went straight to the abbey and told the good friar how keen I was to make for Rome, and that I had already sent word to my wife to make herself and the children ready for a long journey. There was just one problem, I told him, and that was that I couldn't leave without my numbskull of a manservant who had got himself into a little trouble.'

'A *little* trouble?'

'I didn't tell him exactly what to begin with, merely impressed on him that in spite of your general stupidity, you were the best maker of lutes in the whole world, and I couldn't possibly trust anyone else to string my very precious instruments, should I be so fortunate to play before the Holy Father.'

A sudden flare of pain reminded me not to clench my jaw so tightly. John took my grimace to mean otherwise.

'I hope you don't mind my calling you such things, Will.' He slapped me on the back. 'It was all for the best.'

'I suppose so,' I mumbled. 'Was the good friar

convinced?'

'Not exactly.' He said with a sigh. 'I did have to part with most of my money for the fine, and even then, that pimple of a warder wanted to take you back to the courtroom. Eventually, I promised him a mention in the first song I played in front of His Holiness. It's easy to spot a surfeit of vanity when it's in front of you.'

The notion that John would mention the warder in a song made me laugh out loud.

'He's never heard any of your songs, of course.'

'True, and neither has the Holy Father for that matter,' he frowned. 'It's a good thing we're not actually going to Rome, as it would have been most awkward. All the mentions of Her Majesty would need to be altered.'

'And all the innuendos he may not approve of?' I'm not much of a singer but I couldn't resist humming the tune of *Come Again: to see, to hear to touch to kiss, to die with thee again, in sweetest sympathy.*

'Ah yes,' John said, wincing a little at my rendition of one of his most popular songs. 'Although I doubt he'd understand the reference.'

'No?' I shrugged. 'He may be the Pope, but he's still has the body of a man and I don't think there's any alive who has not felt desire.'

'Tut tut, Will. I'm guessing that even to say so is treasonous here. It's a good thing we're not in company.'

'I'm very glad we're not, and I would be most cautious before saying such a thing again. Prison was not an experience I care to repeat.'

'Good, for I couldn't afford to pay that fine twice.' He jumped up and took a deep breath. 'Ah, if only my songs were as sweet as this evening air. Come, Will, I'm sure it must be better than any medicine.'

He was right. Although late summer and still hot, a few heavy storms had kept the air clean and scented with rose and honeysuckle. I stood up stiffly and went to join him. As the song of a bird filled the darkening valley, I breathed in my medicine and felt its benefit. For all the wrong in the world, there was sometimes considerable beauty and balm to be had.

A thought persisted though.

'You have not told me the sum you paid, John. Whatever it is, I will pay you back.'

'Don't be silly, Will. We're in this together, aren't we? I know you can't earn any money whilst you're away from your workshop. It was very good of you to come at all.'

I almost told him about Signor Biscaldi's effort to bribe me then but thought better of it. Had I kept the money, I could have paid the fine myself. The memory of it was sharp and reminded me of something else I wanted to ask.

'How did you fare in the synagogue? I got as far as the trap door in the chest, but Sofia insisted I went no further.'

John almost choked at this. It took another mouthful of wine for him to recover.

'It was a very good thing it wasn't time for prayers,' he said. 'Otherwise, I'd have been stuck in that horrid little passage not being able to go one way or the other. I was lucky. Sofia had told me to push on the panel at the other end and listen carefully. I can tell you, Will, that I listened very carefully indeed, but didn't hear a thing, so I crept out. The door I'd come through was a panel the same as all the others and once I'd closed it, there was no going back. You should have seen me, Will. I pulled the hat right down over my face and ran like the wind!'

We both laughed then and the feeling of it, the relief and joy of freedom, made me laugh even harder, especially when I considered what a vision John must have seemed running along in Signor Biscaldi's cloak.

'I'm very glad you escaped so easily,' I said, once settled. 'I'm very sorry for Lady Anna though. Her husband was worse than anything I could have imagined.'

A shadow passed over John's face then and we were both silent for a while, in dread of what may have happened to her at the hands of that vile pig. I didn't want to dwell upon her fate but remembering that day reminded me of something else.

'Did you see what it was like in the synagogue?'

'Lord no. Why would I want to?'

I shrugged. 'I don't know, out of curiosity, I suppose.'

'My curiosity does not lean in that direction. Why do you ask?'

'No reason.'

Fortunately, John didn't pursue the conversation, but of course, I was curious. More than curious. Every aspect of Sofia and her life was of interest to me even though all possibility of being with her was over. I remembered the bright gold of the ducat I'd hammered before fixing it into Sofia's keepsake and saw again her pleasure when I gave it to her. But as for how long would it remain a treasure, would a year see it cast aside?

I couldn't help sighing.

'My goodness, Will. That was a big sigh! I hope you don't have too many regrets about our trip.'

I shook my head even as many small regrets crowded into my mind. Really, they all added up to nothing much. I only had one big regret and that wasn't to do with the past. Nothing in the world would ever make me regret meeting Sofia Biscaldi but without her, my future seemed bleak.

Sleep didn't come easily, but the night was not wasted. I whittled a small stick of hardwood into a sharp point and was able to extract from between two back teeth a shard of something jammed between them. It hurt to remove, and I tasted blood, but I was glad to have it done. If only all problems were solved so easily.

John awoke the next day, a different man. His temper had kept buoyant for several weeks and even though I knew it could quickly plummet, I was often surprised by the speed and depth to which it could fall. At home, when the blackness came upon him, we would all creep about the house waiting for it to pass. Weak wine and plenty of sleep had been my recipe since we'd been away, but here we were in a barn far from anywhere and although we had been welcome, I wasn't so sure about a longer stay. I left him on the straw, turned away from me.

After dowsing my head in the water trough, I felt

more able and looked about the yard before making my way to the house. My offer of chopping and tidying up their woodpile was greeted favourably, although I wasn't allowed to begin without breakfast of bread spread with honey. It was the most delicious I had ever tasted, and I asked if I could take a little for John. A great tiredness came upon him sometimes since the sad news of mother's death, I told them. It wasn't quite a lie, and I didn't want to frighten them with the idea that we had brought illness into their midst.

Breakfast consoled John only a little. He looked at me with rheumy eyes and a face longer than a theorbo's neck.

'We are doomed, Will,' he whispered, between nibbles.

'Indeed,' I said, rather too heartily. 'Should I begin to chop the wood or are we doomed this morning?'

'It is no jest, Will. I am very serious.'

He looked so strained and hurt, I regretted my remark and spoke more gently.

'Was there any particular reason for you to think so?'

'It is because, as fast as your strongest glue, we are stuck. How can it be safe for us to go home? Not after I committed myself to Rome. Her Majesty may have eventually forgiven an obstinate papist, but not one who has received a pension from the Holy Father.'

'You haven't gone to Rome though or received a pension.'

'But it was *offered*. Isn't that bad enough? And don't you think Skidmore will make sure everyone hears about it both at home and abroad?'

I could only nod in agreement. There was truth in that, for certain.

'I led Friar Bailey to believe that I was an ardent papist,' he went on. 'Not one who has such a weak and feeble faith as mine.'

He was wretched now and getting rather noisy in his argument.

'But you have true friends at home, John. People who love you.'

That sounded rather unconvincing, even to me. Having good friends and relations could be worse for them if it came to treason. Unless Her Majesty or perhaps Sir Robert Cecil were amongst them, we'd all be under suspicion.

'I will be tried and found guilty the moment I step foot in England. It will be the noose for me and more than likely you as well,' he clawed at his neck and pulled such a face it was truly fearsome. 'The noose and worse before it!'

I didn't like to be included in the treachery one bit, but he could well be right.

'Now, now,' I said. 'We are not there yet and I'm sure it won't come to that. Be calm and speak more softly. We are strangers and it would not do to frighten our hosts with such loud raving. There was no need for them to let us stay, let alone give us breakfast.'

As if severed by a knife, all the excitable energy fell away.

'But we cannot return to Florence.' His voice sounded thin and quivery. 'Not after what I said to Friar Bailey.'

There was nothing I could say, so I left him and went to chop the wood. It was good to have something physical to do while my thoughts churned. Oh, that we *could* stay! I felt at that moment that I would have done anything to make it possible. Sofia was always in my mind, and yet, although we were still far from the coast, I could sense the smell of the sea in my nostrils, the tip of a vessel as we sailed away and eventually, the pleasure of the familiar: London, young Robert, grown much bigger now probably, and of course, my workshop where, I thought ruefully, where perhaps I would be king of my own little kingdom again. It seemed further away every minute.

We couldn't go home. Not without reassurance of our safety, and how could we get that?

The untidy heap of wood began to turn into a decent pile, but I was slow and often distracted as I would frequently stop and examine something that I thought had potential. The warmth and grain in olive wood intrigued me. I had seen some small vessels and tools that were very beautiful, so I put to one side a piece that I thought might be enough for a set of pegs and hoped my few coins might be enough to buy it.

I'd nearly done when John appeared at the doorway of the barn, shielding his eyes from the late morning sun.

'Good morning,' I said. 'Here.' I held out the dregs left in a beaker of thin goat's milk I'd been given as refreshment. I had drunk some, for thirst's sake, but it was without much joy.

'Lord above,' he said, pulling a face after the first mouthful. 'Whenever did they milk the goat? Last year?'

I laughed, more with relief than at his joke. A remark like that could only mean that he was on the way to recovery from his black mood. This was doubly confirmed when he admired my woodpile.

'I think I've grown soft on this journey,' I said, 'but it's been wholesome work, even if tiring. Besides, it's given me time to think.'

'Oh? What's this? Nothing bad, is it, Will?'

'No, no.' I shook my head. It was an idea I'd had which I'd dismissed at first, but it kept returning, each time with more insistence.

'The opposite, I hope. If we cannot go forward or back, then we must go another way. You do still have friends in Germany, and from there we may more easily gain news of your standing within the Court.'

John frowned but didn't say anything. I left him thinking it over, while I fetched a broom from the barn. By the time I got back, his face had cleared, and he looked more like his old self.

'Yes, you're right,' he said, but then added, 'as usual.'

I recognised the tone from when he was a sulky boy, so I began sweeping up all the small twigs and leaves into a heap of their own.

'Besides,' he went on, 'I'll no doubt be able to play here and there as we go along. We'll need to earn our passage after all the expense of Florence.'

'You know I'm sorry about—'

'Yes, yes.' He interrupted, waving my apology away as

if tired of hearing it. I remembered not to grind my still sore teeth together just in time, and instead the yard was swept even more vigorously. Yes, it was my fault that John had to pay such a large fine but reminding me of it seemed a little unkind.

To Germany then, with no idea of how long we would stay there, or indeed, whether we could ever go home. The last conversation I'd had with Antonio came back to me. He was right. I did have the sort of skills that meant I could make a life wherever I went. Florence may not welcome back a felon, but the fine was paid. Besides, there were other cities. Was he right to suggest that my loyalty to John had already paid any debt of gratitude I felt to his mother? With these new thoughts it was as if the ground beneath me trembled. Oh Sofia! I almost groaned with longing for her. Yes, I was loyal to John and loved him as a brother, as, I believe, he did me, but did that really mean we had to continue along the same path for, as Antonio said, *all our lives long*?

Whilst we made ready to leave the farm, I tried to find a place for an extra burden. A lump of olive wood given as payment for my work. John bore the expression of someone who suffered much while waiting.

'I hope that'll be worth the effort.'

'So do I,' I said, giving the horse a scratch behind the ears. 'I'd hate to think we came all this way for nothing.'

We had travelled in quite the wrong direction the previous day, and anyone looking out for us on the road south from Florence might well begin to question whether we were ever going to Rome. They'd find out soon enough though. Avoiding Ferrara, in fact anywhere that might have a connection with the Este Court was more difficult, but it was already September, and if we were to pass over the mountains and into Germany before winter set in, then time was pressing.

CHAPTER TWENTY-TWO

Wherever we stopped, John was always happy to play if asked, but we didn't make much of our presence and only stayed one night. The charms of Venice, however, would not be denied and we stayed three whole days. The rain stayed away and instead the whole city twinkled and shone in sunlight. John had promises to keep with many of the musicians who resided in the city, and I had a promise to keep too, although it was not with a person.

I knew about the Tieffenbrucker family of lute-makers, but it was Signor Biscaldi that insisted I should visit their shop if ever I was in Venice.

'Shop!' he'd said, shaking his head. 'It is wrong word. This is shop.' He'd swept his arm in a generous arc encompassing the small violins and guitars at the front to the long-necked theorbo in the rack near the workshop door at the back. Then he pointed outside. 'The Tieffenbrucker shop is as big as cathedral!'

I'd not believed that for a moment, but I was anticipating sizable premises as I walked towards the Rialto Bridge. I would never have found my way had not the landlord of our lodgings been so clear with his instructions. Crossing the bridge was a small detour but more than worth the effort, he'd told me, and all Venetians were still very proud of this new and wondrous construction. I wasn't disappointed.

But when I reached Tieffenbrucker's, I was disappointed. What was Signor Biscaldi thinking? An impressive looking shopfront, yes, but hardly a cathedral. I felt the same once I'd gone inside; bigger than the Biscaldi's, but not sizable enough for a congregation. The instruments on display though were well laid out on two levels, the smaller lutes, violins and guitars on a shelved balcony that ran around each wall reached by a narrow set of stairs on wheels. On the ground level, all the larger bass instruments were placed in racks. The variety of woods and design was almost overwhelming, but I was determined to commit as many features to memory as I could. Don't forget to buy John's strings, I told myself, as I asked for help with identifying the wood of a pretty, eight-course lute.

Cypress, it transpired. I should have guessed considering the number of trees that grow everywhere. A conversation covering all aspects of lute-making ensued, and as a result I was shown the premises behind the shop. That's when I understood what Signor Biscaldi meant. Not quite a cathedral, but equally as large as a timber warehouse on the Thames docks. On one side, from racks right up to the lofty ceiling, string instruments of all kinds hung from their necks, the draught from opening the door, setting them to gently sway. The instruments being repaired, or that were still in the making, were being worked on by a dozen men on as many benches. On the opposite wall all the raw timber was stacked and clearly labelled, and the fixings too. The racks of strings alone covered the same length as the entire wall of my workshop where all my tools, timber and fixings were kept. I was completely without words and gasped like a landed fish as my eyes took in each new marvel. There was nothing like this anywhere in London.

I bought more strings than I intended, but my main accomplishment was in discovering why instruments weren't made with olive wood. I was shown some olive wood pegs, but they were expensive, and they did not have many. The raw timber was difficult to dry and fickle when worked. To my eye, though, the pegs were beautiful. Polished and richly veined, the wood gleamed. I vowed to make some as soon as I could.

My visit to the Tieffenbrucker's shop had an unexpected but pleasing outcome. During my tour of the premises, I was introduced to the great Magno Tieffenbrucker, a man as tall and broad as his name. When I mentioned that John and I were headed to Nuremberg, he was keen for us to travel together as he was returning to his native Bavaria for a family wedding in Rosshaupten.

It was fortunate for us, not only because he knew the road, but because Magno was so happy to meet the renowned John Dowland, and to boast about all aspects of his business. Slow as I am, I listened with polite interest at first, only gradually realising that he considered me as someone of equal standing. A laughable idea when I thought of my tiny workshop, but he was a craftsman as well as a merchant and had been full of praise when John showed him the lute I had made.

'I am more than impressed,' he said, running his fingers over the back seams then checking the balance and weighing the instrument in one hand. 'Well, William Totman, if ever you find yourself in Venice again, I hope you will come and see me.'

I thanked him, but I knew polite words when I heard them and thought nothing more of it.

He was an affable companion, but once he had left us, the issue of whether we would be welcomed home rode along beside us. John and I were mostly silent except for the occasional remark that startled the other out of a reverie.

'A letter!' John announced on one such occasion. 'I shall write a letter.'

'Just the one?'

'To begin with, as this letter will be most important. I shall write to Sir Robert, tell him what happened in Italy then throw myself at his mercy.'

'I see,' I said, thinking that if I had a list of people whose mercy would most likely *not* be forthcoming, Sir Robert Cecil would be very near, or even at the top.

'I will write honestly,' John went on, 'and begin by reminding him that I did speak to his good self and to my Lord of Essex before I came away.'

'Honour,' I said, under my breath.

'What?'

'Not *his good self*. Perhaps you should refer to him as *Your Honour*.'

I had spoken so firmly, that he looked at me sidelong. 'Oh yes,' he gestured agreement with a little wave, 'that would be much better.' Then after a little while he said. 'Perhaps you should advise me when I come to write it.'

I understood his remark to be in jest, but his future and mine too, depended on this letter. After we'd travelled another mile or so, I couldn't resist making another suggestion.

'Sir Robert has always thought kindly of you,' I hesitated, unsure how to best phrase my meaning. 'It will be all to the good if he hears your voice in the written words, but I wouldn't enlarge on any other subject other than the plots against the Queen.'

'Quite right,' said John. 'He's a very busy man and won't want a long letter.'

'That's very true,' I said. 'So, no mention of lutes or any other misadventures.'

It was, however, almost as if the idea of writing to Sir Robert opened our ears to more information that we could include in the letter. A rumour in Venice became the latest gossip in Germany. Perhaps it was the sight of us, two Englishmen a long way from home, that gave every innkeeper and stablehand the entitlement to tell us that the King of Spain was making great preparations for England the following summer.

By the time we arrived in Nuremburg, John was in such high excitement at the prospect of writing to Sir Robert that I thought his words would tumble out in blots and errors, but he was a skilled copyist, and the resulting pages were in small, neat script. It was, however, the longest short letter I had ever seen, and I pleaded with him to read it to me before sealing it up.

I should not have worried. Only John Dowland could describe our travels and travails so readily and with such earnest feeling. I was pleased to see he made no mention of our time in Ferrara, only that he had played and received *great favours* from the Grand Duke in Florence. Contrasting the true loyalty of kind Lord Gray, Bodley and Kemper to Her Majesty, with the treasonous words of Skidmore, Bailey and all the other papists, read very well.

I did hesitate, however, when John asked if I thought

it wise for him to send the letter from Skidmore we were to carry to the traitor Nicholas Fitzherbert in Rome, too. If scantily read, it could be considered innocuous. Sir Robert, though, as John pointed out, was a man who searched for the story that lay beneath the surface of things, and he would most likely already know the slippery nature of Skidmore.

Both letters were then sealed together and at that moment, I had no doubt that Sir Robert would understand why John had fled from the country in such haste and we would soon receive a reply.

After weeks of anticipation however, all hope of that drained away. If John was very disappointed, he hid it well. Fortunately, we were welcomed at the Landgrave's court at Hesse-Kassel, and John, when he was in cheerful mind, played often and to great acclaim. A suggestion from the Landgrave that the whole world would be grateful if he should print a collection of his songs could not have come at a better time. John with nothing pressing to do could get up to mischief or easily sink into gloom. A new project was exactly what he needed.

I was not so settled. The craftsmen who remembered me from our previous visit were happy to let me share a bench, but I felt some resentment from the new apprentices. *Who was this man pushing himself forward?* I saw all manner of questions in their sly glances. With the dreadful memory of Loreto still so recent, I determined to be polite and helpful whenever I was in their company. Thankfully, it wasn't long before I had the pleasure of their ignoring me.

When winter came, it brought snowfalls and drifts higher than a man, disguising everything I thought familiar. Our journey home wasn't going to be soon, even if we did receive the correct assurances.

One especially grim day, when the cold snipped at the tips of my nose and fingers, I decided it was time to make a start on the olivewood pegs. Having heeded the advice about keeping the wood dry, I'd wrapped it well and it seemed unharmed when I placed it on the bench, but at the first cut with the saw, I was suddenly, utterly miserable. The scent released from the wood took me straight back to Italy, to the surprise of biting into an olive for the first time, to wine the colour of plums, lemons like sunshine and always and everywhere, the warmth and laughter of my Sofia.

Except she wasn't *my* Sofia.

'No, she's not.' I said, out loud and so forcibly that the others in the workshop looked up. I shrugged and proffered apologies whilst pointing at the lump of olive wood, as if in blame. Grunts and murmurs of sympathy came my way as they returned to their own work. I sighed to myself. If I'd thought that keeping myself busy could stop my thoughts, then I was quite wrong.

It was a while later, when a bell began tolling in the chapel, that I roused myself from the exquisite torture of remembering her in my arms, to find myself still staring at the lump of wood. I turned it over and frowned. I could see what to do and it would be a task to keep me busy, but something was holding me back. The saw felt strangely small for my hand, almost as if I had never used one before.

The air seemed thick and for a moment or two I couldn't take a breath. The chapel bell seemed to be tolling in my head, on and on it went, until I put down the saw, shut my eyes and leant against the bench.

Whatever was the matter with me? My mouth felt dry, but I had no pains anywhere, except for a dull ache in the heart that lived me with all the time. I had got used to that, or so I thought, and there was no remedy unless—

Will you stay with him your whole life long?

It was Antonio's voice that first came to me. I had never questioned that before. Of course, I was loyal after such kindness from old Mistress Dowland. I did love John as a brother and had never considered my loyalty as repaying a debt. That was before I owed him an actual debt, of course, and before a more attractive way of life presented itself. Was I a man to be bidden, docile as a domestic pet, my whole life? How unlike Sofia, who was determined to burst out of the life that was expected.

I looked again at the wood. The mossy bark spotted with lichens gave no impression of what glowing objects could be made with the wood beneath. I'd learnt that over years and had a talent for finding the correct wood for the task. Perhaps people were like that. Mistress Dowland saw something in me that she liked and, to my astonishment, so did Sofia. Why, even Magno Tieffenbrucker, a man I admired tremendously, spoke to me as an equal.

The pegs would have to wait until another day. My thoughts were too jangled for making anything so precise, so I cleaned off the saw with a little oil and put away the wood. Once outside in my new woollen cloak I set off smartly for it wasn't a day for standing still. The sky was clear blue, the snow deep and in the sunlight it would surely blind a man if he stared at it for too long. Paths had been cleared leading to and from the castle for which I was glad. Nobody paid me any attention as I walked along the main thoroughfare, such are the advantages of winter garb and here my light hair did not mark me out.

Outside the inn, a bad-tempered group of travellers jostled for places within a coach. It was an unlucky passenger who'd have to ride on top so, of course, money was changing hands. The horses, already fed, watered and impatient to get going, stamped the snow into slippery puddles.

I made my way through the crowd and into the welcoming arms of the inn, where a spit roast over the fire cheered my belly inside and out. Gradually, my tingling toes returned to life and having devoured the last mouthful of a very tender hunk of mutton and washed it down with ale, I sat back. I had been both hungry and bone cold in the workshop earlier. Could that have been the cause of my agitation?

A preposterous notion, I thought, shaking my head. Half my life had been spent hungry and the other half in a cold workshop. It was more than that. I'd always thought making the finest instruments would bring me more than enough satisfaction in this life, but now I needed to make something of myself.

The voices of my friends, Sofia, Antonio, and now Magno Tieffenbrucker, all chimed in my head. There were many futures in front of me. I didn't have to wait to be told what to do, I could make my own decisions.

Through the window, I saw the coach door finally shut and a disgruntled couple make their way up to the rear outside seat. Their faces already pinched and crimson from waiting, they settled themselves as best they could, keeping close and pulling on their cloaks to keep out the icy draughts.

I imagined myself boarding the coach and how gladly I would have ridden aloft if it took me back to Italy. The notion that I could do just that, struck me then with such surprise and force that I alerted the innkeeper again, this time with a loud gasp. He looked at me warily so I decided to forego another draught of his excellent ale.

Trudging back to the castle I hardly noticed the cold as a new and fierce excitement warmed my innards. I was under no illusion about returning to Florence, but there were other cities that might suit me, and I would start with Venice. An introduction from Magno Tieffenbrucker would open many doors. First though, I had to speak to John and that would not be easy. He was much taken up with thinking about the printing of his songs and wasn't quite so keen to get back to England while he could enjoy the generous hospitality of the Landgrave.

By the time I had arrived at the castle door, my opening gambit was prepared, I would sit him down with a glass of ale and tell him that my future lay in Italy. I would thank him, indeed I'd be eternally grateful, for everything he and his mother had done for me, I would repay the fine in due course, but it was time for me to lead an independent life. Yes, that's what would happen.

I found John pacing our room in a state of high excitement.

'At last!' he said, bounding over like a young puppy.

He clutched my shoulders and began searching my face as if to check it was really me.

'At last?' I echoed in bewilderment. 'I've only been away an hour or so.'

'But when I came looking, they told me you weren't yourself. I was very worried, Will.'

He was always comic when he attempted admonishment, so I tried not to smile, thinking instead to come straight out with my plan.

'I have a plan,' he said, gleefully, before I could utter a word. He clapped his hands together and laughed. 'Yes! There now, no need to look quite so pained, it is you I have had in mind. I may have been rather occupied with my collection lately, but don't think I haven't noticed you've been stomping about like a wounded bear.'

I could only grunt at this, being so taken by surprise.

'Now sit down and listen,' he said.

I perched on the edge of my bed as John pulled up a chair and sat directly opposite me looking very pleased with himself.

'What you need to do, Will,' he said slowly and with no small triumph, 'is *go home*. Yes! It's obvious! Why didn't I think of it before?'

'Home?' I blurted. 'But—'

'Yes, home. Listen,' he leant nearer, 'there's no problem with *you* going home. It's *me* that's the problem. Just think, if you go home, you'll be back in your own workshop, with your own tools and getting on with a new instrument. Won't that be better than messing about with pegs and trinkets?'

I did not know what to say. Just as if I'd walked in with a bright candle, a vision of my workshop flared in my mind. All my tools lined up, oiled and clean. Why, even the scent of newly sawn wood was in my nose from the broom there in the corner, sitting as usual in its small heap of sawdust.

'Well?' he said. 'Isn't that a wonderful idea?'

John's face came back into focus.

'Y...Yes.' But I shook my head. Where was my resolution to return to Italy? 'I don't know though.'

'Don't know?' he said, amazed. 'What is there to know?' I must have looked distressed for his expression softened. 'You don't have to worry about me, Will. I'll be perfectly happy here without you. I'll miss you, of course,' he added quickly, 'but I'm sure it won't be long before I'm home too, especially if—'

He looked away.

'If?'

No reply. Instead, he stood up and, as if alerted by a noise outside, strolled to the window and looked out.

'If?' I said again.

With a dancer's grace and a twirl, he retraced his steps, not to the chair though, but to sit by my side and put an arm around my shoulders.

'I did think,' he said, 'that if I asked you nicely, you may be able to send word to me about how things are at home.'

That was his first thought then. I didn't doubt that he had some care for my situation but of course, it was an advantage for him that prompted a course of action. I'd never minded before. That he considered me at all was a marvel. His mother's son and equally kind and generous. I took a deep breath. I'd made a promise to Mistress Dowland before we left, that I would do my best to see us both return to London safe and sound. I would not betray that promise now. When John was home again, then I would consider my own future, but not before.

'Yes,' I said, still somewhat hesitant.

John slapped me on the back straight away. 'Excellent! You are the best of fellows, Will. Have I ever told you that?'

'I don't recall,' I said, but not without a smile.

'Then remind me to say so every day.' He jumped up. 'Now then. It's obvious you can't go today, but there's no reason to stay much longer, is there?'

The snow delayed my departure to England but during

that time I finally sent word of our safety to Sofia and her father. I decided to enclose the only two olivewood pegs I'd managed to finish, not only as a token of my affection for them both, but also to ask if they considered them profitable for me to make in the future. To be honest, I thought my suggestion a feather in the breeze, but maybe it would be enough for a reply.

CHAPTER TWENTY-THREE

I missed John on my journey home. Without him, there was merely the tedium and discomfort of miles going by. For all my complaints about his behaviour, I soon sickened of my own dull thoughts and remembered fondly how we sparred in conversation.

Every new morning reminded me why I should never revisit the flat lands. A dank mist, grey and cold as a morgue, hovered over the ground taking all the familiar lines of the world away. Buildings and trees having lost their supports loomed like monsters, and the people walking seemed to hang in the air and search for their feet as they glided along.

Whilst in a coach I slept or feigned sleep for most of the time. There was war to the south and didn't I know only too well the dangers of a loose tongue? The day came when something did rouse me though. I was so used to the sour smell of travellers sat too long in their seats that when a fresher, salty tang wafted into my nose, it could only mean one thing. I sat up and looked out for my first sight of the sea.

I'd never liked crossing water, but for once I didn't spend my time heaving over the side. Carrying a cargo of wine and oil, the sturdy barque I'd spotted at the dock sat well in the water and didn't roll from side to side. Even so, I was glad when the church towers at Reculver came into view and even more so whilst passing Sheerness fort, for the sun vanquished the thin covering of clouds and turned a dreary day into one of happy expectation.

How I wished that Sofia was by my side as we made our way into the Thames estuary. She'd be clapping her hands with excitement, gasping at this and that, pointing here and there, and when I looked down into her eyes—

No, I told myself. Look at what is in front of you and not in your mind's eye. And that's what I did. London may not have the charms of Venice, Ferrara or Florence, but as the river narrowed and voices could be heard hailing each other in my native tongue, my heart swelled. Soon we sailed past the Royal Fleet at Greenwich and, having rounded the bend at Limehouse, where I thought fondly of a jug of ale at The Grapes, the Tower and London Bridge came in sight.

I disembarked at the Custom House when the officer came aboard to inspect the cargo. He paid me little attention, but an Englishman returning home after more than a year, in apparent good health and wearing a new coat, could be someone to mark. If, however, that Englishman is also carrying a letter of safe passage from the Landgrave of Hesse, then he is someone not to hinder. All thanks to John for requesting such a favour on my behalf.

Straight home, I'd told myself, stepping onto firm ground again, but a strange reluctance overcame me I couldn't quite fathom, so I strolled, rather than strode, up towards Canwicke Street. More than a year ago I'd not wanted to leave this city and yet, only weeks ago, I had been ready to forsake it altogether. And yet, and yet. It was a bright spring day, the air fresh, and there were smiles on the faces of the market traders. Persuaded easily into buying a hunk of bread with a smear of damson cheese, I sat on the wall at St Mary Bothaws's and enjoyed it almost more than all the delicacies Italy had to offer.

It's impossible to sit and eat in any city for very long before you're joined by something with an eye to what's in your hand. Pigeons and gulls are usually quick to spot it and they bring the cats and dogs, but that day it was a skinny child of about ten or eleven who sidled up to me first.

'You be wanting all of that?' she asked.

'I had thought so when I bought it, but now? I reckon not. What's your name, girl?'

'Alice,' she mumbled, not taking her eyes from the half slice of bread that was left.

'Try not to eat it too quickly, Alice.'

She shook her head as I handed it over, no doubt as

familiar as I used to be with the sickness that came from eating too much, too quickly, after a long time of hunger.

I don't know why the sight of her, instead of any other urchin, should have pulled at my sympathy, but a sixpence I'd been polishing between thumb and finger all the way from London to Florence and back found itself a new bearer. Then I went on my way, not wanting to entertain half the urchins in London, who'd no doubt been spying.

By the time I got to the Eleanor Cross, it was clear why each step felt effortful. Much in the city was the same as I had left it, but things would be quite different at the house in West Cheap. Jane Dowland would be in charge now and, knowing her, she'd have the household running smoothly at her first bidding. Not that I had anything but affection for her and the children, but with old Mistress Dowland gone a year ago I began wondering if I still had a room or whether I should go elsewhere.

They'd not be that surprised by my arrival as John had sent word ever before I left Germany. I dithered though, as I approached the front door. Should I knock? Or walk straight in as usual?

A moment later, the decision was taken from me because the door flung open and out dashed a young lad who, had I not caught him, would have had the both of us right over.

'Oh, oh, sorry sir.' He squirmed as I held him by the shoulders. 'I didn't mean—'

'Robert?' I said, amazed at how he'd grown. 'Is it really you?'

Then he looked up at me properly. 'Are you William Totman?'

'Yes, indeed.' I laughed and let him go whereupon he ran straight into the house calling out, it seemed to me, for all the neighbourhood to hear.

'Mother, quickly! Everyone! It's William Totman come back. He's here at last.'

At least someone was pleased to see me, I thought, even though I'd been away so long, he almost didn't remember me. Then I heard the familiar squeak of the upper parlour door opening. I removed my cap, took a deep breath, and steeled myself to meet Jane Dowland.

'Madam,' I said, bowing low when she appeared in the doorway.

'William Totman.'

I knew at once by the smile in her voice that it was going to be all right. Jane has rather a thin face that settles easily into disapproval, but all that goes away when she is pleased, and now she was.

'Come in, come in.' She beckoned me into my old home. 'How good it is to see you. Robert has been looking out of the window twenty times a day for the past week.'

'I have,' he said, 'and now I must go to my lesson. Do I have to, Mother?'

'Yes, you do.'

'Oh, please?'

He looked so downcast, but I could see that his pleading would get nowhere.

'Unless you're going on a very long voyage,' I said. 'I'll still be here when you come back.'

'Robert has a music lesson,' Jane explained, 'and if he doesn't go now, he will be late.' She gave him a stern look and he did as he was told, albeit while dragging his feet. 'Before you go,' she called after him, 'ask Molly to bring in some wine.'

'Then I'll be even later.'

'Not,' she replied, 'if you hurry.'

We heard a big sigh then a call for Molly.

Jane shook her head, but I could see she was proud of her boy.

'He is much taller now,' I said, 'and looks so like his father.'

'It is just as well, as I would forget my husband altogether if he did not.'

There was a barb to her comment, for which I had every sympathy. Would John ever settle at home?

'Oh, I doubt you would,' I said. 'He's not a man easily forgotten.'

She laughed at that. 'You're quite right. Let us celebrate his success. I did not mean any harm. John is a good husband when he is here, and look, even when he isn't.'

She gestured towards a glass and silver goblet I recognised. The ornate standing cup from Hesse, with a gilt cover, almost as tall as my forearm was long.

'Ah yes,' I said. 'The Landgrave had been so well pleased with John that evening, he'd filled it full of silver.' I didn't add that Maurice the Landgrave was so full of wine he had to be carried to his bed only moments later.

I glanced about the parlour to where Jane had made changes. The settle had moved so that it was possible to see down into the street and, as well as the splendid cup, opposite me a new tapestry bordered with spring flowers and bright with musicians and dancers adorned the wall.

Moments later Molly entered the room with the jug of wine so willingly ordered by young Robert.

Molly. A good woman, an honest and almost pretty woman, but not for me. Never for me. She gave me a shy smile when I asked after her health, but it was Jane who answered.

'Molly is very well. And so she should be, for she is to be married shortly.'

Did I look relieved? I must have and I expect my congratulations were too effusive as well, but they were genuine, as I always had wished her well. Once she had left us, Jane bade me sit down and our conversation turned to more serious matters.

'How is my husband? Although he said in his letter that he was well, I wondered if this was true. Why else would you come alone?'

There was far too much to tell, and besides, I did not want to reveal that John worried he could be accused of treason. Before I left Germany, we agreed that if anyone asked why he had not returned with me, I should say he was hoping for an invitation from the Court first. In the meantime, he was enjoying the Duke of Brunswick's generous employment.

'He is very well and would have come,' I said, having completed a thinly-wrought tale of our journey, 'except he is much taken up with preparing a volume of songs. It is my understanding that he wishes it to be ready for printing when he returns.'

'A printed volume?' She gasped and clapped her hands. 'How wonderful. I am sure there will be a great demand for such a thing.'

'I have no doubt of that. I am only sorry that John's mother will not know of it.'

'Indeed.' Jane sighed but then sat looking at her hands as if they had arrived on her lap by accident.

I wasn't sure what to make of her silence.

'Forgive me' I said gently. 'You bore a heavy burden with no help. I was very sorry, and I know John regretted it every day that we were not here.' It was a small lie I hoped would do no harm.

She looked at me with narrowed eyes, tilting her head for a moment, but then she laughed.

'William Totman,' she said. 'It is no wonder that everyone thinks so well of you, for you always know how to make them feel better about themselves.'

I was rather flummoxed by this remark and blustered an apology.

'No, no,' she said. 'It is a *good* quality! But dear John, I think, will have to speak for himself. For now, I am glad to hear what you say. Death is never easy, and she took a long time over it. I think secretly hoping she might see her son again. I don't know, is that possible?' We both pondered this impossible question, but then Jane shrugged. 'In her condition, I don't think so. All I can say is that she lived a good life. A woman who loved her family and looked after them very well.'

She stood up abruptly, and while I remembered her always as a woman of swift and nimble movement, the wine had dulled me so I was slow to my feet.

'Now,' she went on, 'I have something to fetch, and I expect you are keen to see your room and workshop again. Be assured, they are as you left them.' She looked me up and down. 'Perhaps it would be a good idea to change from your travelling clothes lest you leave all that dust about the house. I will be back within the hour.'

'Yes, of course. Yes. Thank you. Until later.'

Once she had left the room, I peered at my sleeves and yes, she was right about the dust. Then I headed to my workshop at the back of the house. If it was as I left it, then there'd be dust aplenty.

How often had I trodden the dozen or so steps it took to get from the front door to the workshop? For years I'd never given that small journey the slightest consideration, and yet I found my heart beating a little faster. What would I find? Perhaps the rain had got in, birds were nesting, or a family of rats had taken up residence. All fanciful ideas that vanished the moment I lifted the latch and stepped inside.

It's true that a room cannot greet you with a word or bound towards you with its tail wagging, but I did feel that I was in the company of an old friend. Stopping in the doorway, I sniffed the familiar scent of wood and glue then remembered all the instruments I'd made over the years.

Jane was right. My bench was as clear as when I had left it, the tools clean and lined up in order or size hanging from the shelf. Even the wood I'd stacked appeared to be unharmed despite the long neglect. Someone had been in though, for the floor was swept and there was no sawdust in any of the corners.

No, the workshop hadn't changed but something had. It used to be that there was always something that needed doing. It could be a small thing, a final coat of oil, or maybe the anticipation of a whole new instrument. But at that moment I felt no such excitement.

I crossed to the stable door that opened into the small yard at the back of the house. I went out expecting to see that Molly had hung up washing, and there it was. My days at the laundry had not left me. Any dry day in spring was welcome, but one with such a blustery breeze meant working from the moment we rose. At first, I was only the peg boy, being too small for carrying or hanging, but I remember trying to avoid a slap from the cold wet sheets as I delivered a peg to whoever shouted next. Two, sometimes even three dozen sheets could be dried on a windy day and for Ma Perks and her boys that meant a special treat once we'd done. It may well be why I'm not only fond of an apple dumpling but also can whittle a very decent peg. And faster than most, if I do say it myself.

I stood downwind to shake out my cap and coat before going back inside and bolting the door. With no coat on, I straight away felt the deathly chill of the workshop and a shiver ran through me. It had always been cold, but usually my own efforts warmed me and most days I lit a fire fuelled with offcuts. A small workshop meant a small fire was adequate. Now though? I remembered with a sigh the airy and sunlit space at the Biscaldi's and the huge premises belonging to Magno Tieffenbrucker.

Once upstairs, having narrowly avoided hitting my head on the lintel, I stood in the middle of my room wondering what to do with myself. Everything was the same, but somehow completely different. The possessions I hadn't taken were still there, but apart from a cap with an embroidered band of blackwork made by John's mother and a schoolboy gift from the man himself a stanza composed and written in his best script, they were things with little meaning.

The family soon returned and not long after came the sound of many footsteps on the stairs, noisy whisperings outside and then a rattling on my door. If I had any misgivings about my presence, they vanished right away when I found Robert and his younger brother outside, wide-eyed and hopping from foot to foot with excitement. Before I could draw breath, Robert gave me an order.

'Mother said to come down at once.'

'And a very good afternoon to you,' I said, and even though they wriggled, I gathered up one in each arm and gave them a squeeze. As soon as I let go, they were off down the stairs squealing that I was strong as a bear and had tried to kill them but was on my way and would be down in a minute.

CHAPTER TWENTY-FOUR

In the parlour, Jane was smoothing her hair.

'It's such a blowy day,' she said, by way of greeting. 'You must be glad not to be on the sea now.'

'Indeed. I'm not one for the water, although I can tell you that crossing over big mountains is almost as worrying, especially when the coach creaks and rolls.'

'Mountains!' said Robert with eyes big as full moons. 'You went over mountains? What are they like? Did they have snow on top?'

'You must tell us all about your journeys, William,' said Jane. 'But I am going to insist that you begin when we are all together for supper as there is something I wish to talk about first. Robert, go upstairs to your room. Practise something of your father's, then you'll be able to play it to us later.'

He sighed but did not need to be asked twice. Once he'd left, Jane bade me sit down while she lifted the lid of the old oak chest that sat under the window. I knew it contained the family's deeds and documents as well as the good silver.

'I must apologise,' she began, 'for leaving you so hastily earlier.'

'No need,' I shook my head. Jane always was swift in speech and action.

'I had an important errand to run, and it was the mention of John's mother that reminded me.'

'Oh?' It seemed a lifetime ago when in Ferrara I'd read Jane's letter while John lay across the bed in a stupor. I remembered the scent of lemons from outside as I read and feeling a little hurt at not being mentioned. Perhaps I had been after all.

'One moment,' she said, lifting out a couple of scrolls. 'Ah, here it is.'

She put one back and the other, tied with a black ribbon, she laid on the settle. I had expected her to hand it to me, but instead she closed up the chest, picked up the scroll and said:

'Come. I have a surprise for you. It is not far.'

'Far?' I echoed, as she picked up a cloak and cast it about her shoulders. 'You know, Jane, I'm not really one for secrets, or surprises come to that.'

'Oh, but I am, William.' With a twinkle in her eye, she waggled a finger at me. 'You should remember that without John here, I keep company with my children for the most part, and they *love* a surprise.'

And with that she called for the boys, who so quickly tumbled down the stairs, I guessed that they had been waiting for the signal. Having excited children in the party as we left the house was to some extent reassuring. I assumed Jane wouldn't take them anywhere perilous and doubted she would embarrass me in front of them, but I admit to feeling unnerved. Was there a play to see? Someone to visit? I couldn't think who.

Out in the noise and chaos of a gusty day, Robert skipped and jumped his way ahead but when the wind stole my cap, lifting it high in the air, he was determined to catch it. I was glad it caught on the corner post of a wagon and not in the filth beneath our feet. Even on such a fresh day as this, the smell was unmistakably London; absorbed into the cobbles and timber, a pungent stew of woodsmoke, sewers and the warm hoppy scent of ale at the passing of a tavern.

Jane was right, it wasn't far. We turned into Forster Lane, a street I knew very well because I'd often have a few words with Joseph Tucker, the joiner whose premises lay opposite. We appreciated each other's work, and I was just thinking how I'd be pleased to see him again when Jane stopped by his door. He was a hard worker and his premises used to be open more hours than closed, but now the door and all the windows were shut.

'What's happened here?' I asked her. 'I didn't think Joseph would ever move away.'

Her expression told me everything and even though I didn't know him all that well, it still hit me. I shook my head and tutted at such a loss. A kind, quiet man, there wasn't a window in the street he hadn't either made or repaired.

'Was he ill?'

'No, it was an accident. Very soon after you left, if I remember rightly. A little knock on the head after a passing wagon turned over. He seemed all right according to churchwarden who looked in on him, but the next day a fever took him and then—' She shrugged. 'It didn't take long.'

'Well, I'm very sorry for that,' I said, removing my cap.

We stood in silence before it came into my mind that this might be the surprise that Jane had referred to. Really? She had seemed so light-hearted.

'Goodness me, what was I thinking?' she said, as if reading my thoughts, 'I'm so sorry. I really should have warned you about Joseph! Now you will think I am most callous to be so flippant about a friend passing.' An anguished frown pinched her whole face.

'Please don't fret,' I said, 'there's no need for you to be sorry. Poor Joseph. though. I used to enjoy his company, and I certainly envied all the space he had here.'

Her expression softened and she smiled. 'Did you?' And with that she lifted the keys that hung from her waist, found one about which was tied a knot of yellow thread, and proceeded to open the door that led into Joseph's premises.

'Boys,' she said, sharply once the door was ajar. 'No touching anything. Do you hear?' She held up a warning finger and I nodded with them such was my amazement that we were to go inside. 'This was my errand earlier,' she said. 'I wanted to check all was well before we came.'

Opening the door let in the late afternoon sun and despite the swirl of dust motes the clean and tidy state of the place surprised me even further. It was the same as my workshop. All the planking was neatly stacked, the floor had been swept, and even the brass pin on the vice had been polished until it shone.

'I sent Molly round,' Jane said. 'It was when I received word from John that you were on your way. She's done well here, don't you think?'

'Indeed, she has.' I was only half listening. Instead, I gazed about, remembering the times I'd leant against the bench and watched as Joseph planed the struts for a casement or set his chisel to something ornamental. *Be steady and patient,* he'd say, with a voice rougher than his rasp, *that'll do for most things.* I'd said the same to myself so many times.

'What do you think?' Jane said again.

'Yes.' I nodded. 'Molly will make a good wife. I shall tell her so later.'

'No, no.' Jane pressed her hand on my arm. 'You didn't hear me. What do you think of this?'

'This?' I echoed, like an imbecile.

'There's something you don't know,' she said, blushing a little. 'When I wrote to John with the news of his mother's death, I thought very hard about whether to include her wishes for you. Perhaps I should have done, but it was my worry for John that kept me from doing so. Like his mother, I also wondered what he'd get up to without you there.'

If only she knew the half of it, I thought, remembering the prison cell, but the news that old Mistress Dowland had included me in her wishes, and that we were standing in the workshop of a man now long dead, rendered me into such a state of bewilderment that I could hardly put two sensible thoughts together.

'We all worry about John,' she went on, 'but you must know that we also worried a great deal about you. When you were little, Mistress Dowland had it in her mind that you would remain close with John but, as your skills became more obvious, she felt it wouldn't be right for you to be in service to John if it meant you couldn't develop them for yourself. When she heard about Joseph's death and knowing he had no family, it came into her head that his premises could be the perfect place for you. So here,' she said, holding out the scroll brought from the house.

'This is the deed of ownership and, if you look, you will see it has your name on it.'

Luckily Joseph's old chair was right behind me, and unbidden, I sat down with a thump.

Jane placed the scroll in my hand as I sat utterly dumb and with tears pricking in the corner of my eyes. What a sight I must have been, so slack-jawed and speechless, for the boys giggled behind Jane's skirts. Bless her, she gave them a very fierce look.

'I...I...' I found myself only able to croak so shook my head instead.

'I can see it's quite a shock,' Jane said, gently. 'We'll go home now, but perhaps you should stay here for a little while? Here, you should have this.'

She unhooked the key from her ring and handed it to me before shooing her children out of the door.

'I'm so pleased for you, William,' she said. Then she was gone.

I'd hardly drawn breath when she was back.

'My apologies,' she said. 'We were all so excited to bring you here, I forgot to say there's something else for you at the house.'

'What?' It was hardly credible. 'Something else as well?'

She laughed. 'Yes! But don't worry, it's a small thing, and familiar too. Come back soon or I'll have to send Molly to find you.'

The door closed and I was left by myself. When I'd hoped to be king of my own castle again, I'd never imagined one so vast.

'Mistress,' I whispered to the heavens. 'I wish more than anything that you were here. Why I deserved so much from you, I'll never know. And now there's all this?' I spread my arms wide.

Joseph's workshop was easily twice the size of mine, but it had always been warmer. How I'd envied him the stone chimney with its iron fire basket. It was cold and swept clean now, but he had kept it going the whole year round.

I stood up, only to experience the world tilting, and had to sit back down again. Perhaps it was sea-legs from the Channel crossing that made me so unsteady. A deep breath and I moved more slowly. In my mind though, thoughts leapt about like sparks from a flame. Bright, but then gone, only to be followed by another, and another, and another. Most were ill-formed questions; answers would not come easily.

At the back of the workshop a door led to Joseph's dwelling place. I knew the scullery downstairs but had no idea about what lay above. I could have guessed though. A room that contained a bed, a chair, and a chest carved with a trellis of oak leaves, all his handiwork. I felt like a thief opening the chest, but it was empty except for a lavender bag in one corner. In a heartbeat I was back in Ferrara with Sofia in my arms.

I dropped the lid and it shut with a thud. No sunlight found its way into the room at that time of day so it was rather gloomy, but not so dark I couldn't see that the bed had been made up with clean linen. I opened the chest again, found the lavender bag and took it to the window. The contents looked and smelt fresh, and I was sure the pouch, tied neatly with a blue ribbon, hadn't been there long.

Then the obvious hit me. This was *my* house now. The bed was for me, the chest for my clothes. I would sleep here, work here, *live* here. I wondered that Jane hadn't told me straight away when I arrived or indeed, why all my things were still there, and not here. Perhaps she thought too many surprises might bring on an apoplexy.

'I didn't want you to think I was turning you out of your home,' she said, when I mentioned it later.

We had just finished a very good supper of rabbit flavoured with thyme and sage. John and I had eaten well on the Continent and in Italy I had acquired a stronger taste, for garlic, olives and red wine that I'd first found unpalatable. Even so, I thought, wiping my plate with the last mouthful of bread, there's nothing quite like a familiar dish to gladden the heart.

'You are too good, Jane. I will sleep there tonight and if it's no trouble, may I come and collect my things in the morning?'

Nothing was said about avoiding the awkwardness of staying in her house her husband was away, but I'm sure it was on both our minds.

'Of course, you can. Which reminds me, I still have that little something for you.'

Another surprise, I thought with trepidation, as she left the room. I was relieved, therefore, to see it was something small and certainly familiar, because I'd made it myself.

'Oh!' I exclaimed, pleased to see the box I had made for the mistress's bobbins many years ago. 'How kind of you to keep it, Jane.'

'No, no. It wasn't a kindness.' She shook her head. 'I was instructed to give it to you, but I have often considered emptying out the contents and keeping the box myself, for I always admired it. Especially —' she peered closely at the box, cocking her head on one side then the other, 'especially the way you disguised the catch. That was so clever.'

Now then, who doesn't like to hear a little praise? Dear Jane. Being married to John, she had my sympathy most of the time, but then I wondered if his being away suited her better. After all, she was a woman of restraint, who enjoyed order and calm. When John was home it was as if a whirlwind entered the house.

'Thank you for your very kind words,' I said. 'But please accept the box as a gift. It would be a great honour if you would and besides, what would I do with a box full of bobbins?'

This made Jane laugh so merrily, I wondered if I had unwittingly said something comical.

'Here,' she said, once her giggling had subsided. 'Have a look at your box of bobbins. In future, I'd advise examining gifts more carefully before giving them away.'

Once it was in my hands, I understood her meaning.

No amount of bobbins would weigh that much. I released the catch, a little button of bone I'd carved, and lifted the lid.

For the second time in my life, I was confronted by the bright shock of gold and cried out in amazement at the sight of five, six, no ten, sovereigns that lay before me. With a racing heart and ringing in my ears I shut the box with a snap. Just as before, when Senor Biscaldi had placed the purse of ducats in my hand, I'd done nothing at all to deserve it.

'No, Jane,' I said, handing it straight back. 'I can't accept that.'

Her eyes narrowed. 'Has this journey made you soft in the head, William? It is yours now. If John's mother was sitting here instead of me, do you think she would let you refuse?'

Of course, she wouldn't. For a lady with a kind and gentle heart, there were days when both John and I trembled before her, especially when we had been making mischief.

'She would not,' I mumbled. 'But, Jane, I don't deserve it.'

'Deserve it? Hah!' She scoffed at the idea. 'Dear William, look about. There's not many in this life that deserve what they get, and that's whether for good or for bad, in the hovel or the palace. Here,' she said pressing the box back into my hands. 'Why not start thinking about what can be done with it.'

CHAPTER TWENTY-FIVE

Despite the elevation to wealthy property owner, my promise to John's mother was yet to be fulfilled. Only when John was safely home could I consider my own future. Following such a generous legacy, I felt it even more keenly. Besides, whatever Jane said, the gold sovereigns in the box would not all be for me, as I was determined to repay John the money for my fine.

In the morning, Robert helped carry my things to Joseph's rooms. I say helped, perhaps hindered was more like, but his company was too delightful for me to complain. Not wanting to give him sharp tools or anything too heavy, I unpacked my travelling bag and let him carry the items one at a time. The small tool kit wrapped in a leather wallet, my spare shoes, hose and jerkin. As for my tinder box, the remaining olive wood pegs and a very important bundle of letters, they stayed in the bag, which I carried.

Before I left him, John had asked me to seek out various people that might favour his return, with instructions that I was to deliver his letters to them in person and try my hardest to wait while they were read. *Look at the expression on their faces*, I was told. *Is there a smile at first sight of my hand on the paper? Or a smirk, or worse, a yawn?* John had great faith in me that I would recognise a true or false reaction. I wasn't so sure.

Once I had shooed Robert back to his mother, I set about lighting the fire. It wasn't so much the warmth I required, but some sense of how the house used to be when Joseph was alive: comfortable, lived and worked in. Without him, without John, without Sofia, and in an unfamiliar place, after only a few hours I was already at odds with myself. There was plenty of timber that I couldn't imagine would be useful for anything I could make, so it wasn't long before a spark produced a determined flame.

I pulled the chair over, settled myself, then delved in my bag to find the bundle of letters. I laid all three on my lap, looking at the names. Henry Noel? I did wonder about going to see him first, but doubted anything he said could be relied upon. Despite being a friend of John's and his first choice for an evening in the tavern, it still amazed me Her Majesty put up with such a talentless fop at Court.

What does he do there? I'd once asked John after Noel had visited.

'Oh, you know.' He'd shrugged. 'Stands about and looks pretty. That sort of thing.'

I let his letter fall to the ground. Sir Robert Cecil was next and the very thought of him made me shudder. Of course, the chances of my seeing him without weeks of waiting were very low, so the most likely person to help would be the third addressee, Tom Morley over at Bishopsgate. He'd be keen to know John's whereabouts. Also, he would have the ear of Sir Robert. If there was any malicious gossip about John and his time in Italy, Tom should have heard it. Whether I'd be able to interpret his shifting gaze was another matter.

About an hour later I was redirected from his house to St Helen's church, and I passed a pleasant few minutes watching and listening to him play the organ as the people filed out from prayers. Unlike John's songs, which were celebrated for being melancholic, there was always a cheerful turn to Tom's music, even when serious.

'What a surprise,' he said, after our greeting. 'How goes it, Totman? Does this mean that Dowland is also back home?'

He began walking towards the door and I wondered how I could possibly assess his expression if I could not see it.

'No,' I said, catching up. 'He is at the Landgrave's Court still, but I do have a letter for you.' I handed it over and it seemed that he would put it away to read later so I quickened my pace. 'John was very keen I should wait whilst you read it.'

'Really?' He looked rather put out. 'Has he got himself

into trouble?'

I held open the door for him as he broke the seal and cast his eye over John's script. Whether I'd be able to re-enact the full cast of characters that played upon his face, I had no idea. A frown turned question as his eyebrows jumped from low to high, and a curl of the lip stretched then shrivelled. Finally, he mouthed the words, with much nodding and shaking of his head. It was quite a performance, considering John had led me to believe he'd kept all his letters brief.

'Hmm,' was all he said in conclusion.

What was I to make of that? I stood in something of a dither before he beckoned me to follow.

'Yes, yes,' he said. 'Do walk with me. I am due at a shop in Gracechurch Street and am in haste now, but we can still talk.'

'Indeed, we can,' I said, quickly falling into step beside him. It wasn't easy to stay there though. Leadenhall market lay ahead and, given that it was well past midday, the flow was against us. We were past Threadneedle Street before he spoke again.

'I don't think—' He tailed off before beginning again more firmly, as if convincing himself. 'I don't think Dowland has a *terrible* need to worry.'

'*Terrible* need? That doesn't sound very encouraging.'

'Well, these things are hard to judge.' He hummed again. 'But now I think of it, I do recall his name being mentioned not so long ago.'

'In a good way?'

'Oh yes, in a very pleasing verse. One of Thomas Campion's better efforts, although a little too gushing for my liking.'

'Thomas Campion?' I was heartened. Not that I knew the man, but I had heard his name. 'John will be most flattered. Was it read at Court? Did Her Majesty like it?'

'Hmm. That I don't recall.'

We were approaching Leadenhall and all the distractions of a busy marketplace, so I decided to take a risk.

'Perhaps you are likely to see Sir Robert Cecil soon?'

Tom's shoulders twitched and he looked at me askance. 'What are you thinking? He is not one for requests as a rule.'

I told him that John had written some months ago, reporting on the papist plot brewing in Italy, and we'd wondered if his reply had gone astray.

'Who can tell?' he said. 'Sir Robert would have been glad of the intelligence, I'm sure. But yes, of course I will plead John's cause for him. Besides,' he flicked an imaginary crumb from his doublet, 'he liked that I dedicated my *First Book of Ballets* to him, so he may well listen.'

'I thank you, sir. For John, his family and myself. We all wish he was home.'

'Indeed,' he said. 'As do I.'

He spoke warmly and I believed him. Yes, there was rivalry between them, but they were old friends and admired each other's work. I was convinced he wouldn't wish John any ill. We had reached the bookshop in Gracechurch Street, and I was about to take my leave, when he suddenly laid a hand on my arm.

'Wait,' he said. 'Now we are here, it has occurred to me that there is another reason that may well propel John back very soon indeed.'

I looked at the sign swinging above the shop door. *William Barley: Publisher and Bookseller.*

'Here is the future, Totman.' He clutched my arm more tightly before going on. 'Books for sale to anyone who can afford them. Just imagine, anyone! And not only books of words, but books of music. Look,' he pointed in the window. 'What can you see?'

I did see. Two volumes lay on a table within. *First Book of Ballets* and *The First Book of Canzonets for two voices,* both by Thomas Morley. To see such a thing displayed in a shop window, well, I have to say that I gasped.

'It used to be,' he went on, 'that Master Byrd had the patent from Her Majesty to print music, but that lapsed earlier this year. Hence these new publications.'

Now I understood why John would want his own songs printed. His fame would spread even wider. Anyone who could sing, or play, would be able to enjoy his music.

'How truly wonderful!'

'Isn't it,' said Morley, gazing at his volumes like a fond mother. 'And think what a marvellous legacy we'll leave.'

In truth, that had not occurred to me, but he was right. I had sometimes wondered how long my own handiwork would survive. I'd seen plenty of instruments that had survived their makers, but where are all the songs of the past? I could only think of the glees and catches we'd sung as children. Hardly the masterpieces spun from the minds and fingers of John Dowland or Thomas Morley.

'Yes,' I said. 'John has yet to have any of his music printed and is keen to see such a thing of his own.'

'Oh, but that's it.' said Tom, clutching my arm almost to the point of pain. 'Listen.' He drew closer. 'This is a little difficult, because William Barley has been good to me and I bear him no ill will, but when he showed me a book of music he'd only recently published, I recognised many pieces that I knew were John's.'

'By John?' I almost choked with surprise. 'But how can that be? He has had no permission, I'm sure of it.'

'No, and when I asked, Barley said he didn't think he needed it.'

'Didn't think?' I bristled at the affront and made for the door, but Thomas held me back.

'No, no,' he said. 'There is nothing to be done about that now. What good would come of a row? Besides, don't you see that you can use this to your advantage?'

'How can that be?'

'Write to John and tell him. I wager he'll be back on the next coach. I know I would be if someone had taken advantage of me in such a way.'

There, in Thomas's face, I saw the same indignation that would flush John's features when he heard. It was a very good plan.

'Yes,' I nodded in agreement, 'I shall write at once.'

'Better still, buy a copy and send it to him. It will strike harder if he sees it.' Releasing my arm, he slapped me quite unnecessarily hard on the back.

Such was the improved state of my wealth that I didn't even need to ask the price of *A New Booke of Tabliture for the Bandora*. I did not comment on the crude engraving of the instrument on the front, a surprise choice considering it was an instrument John rarely played. Neither did I smile at William Barley during the exchange. I half wished I could see John's thunderous expression when he received it, although I wouldn't want to be in the way when it was thrown across the room. In much the same way, I surmised, as a certain archlute in Ferrara.

When it came to securing safe passage for the book I sought Tom's help again, and he arranged for it to travel with an official messenger. I was glad, then, when he sought my help for a new instrument and a repair to another. Plenty for me to do whilst waiting for John to return.

Would I get used to living and working at Joseph's? It still felt peculiar to wake up and find I was sleeping in his house. When Tom delivered his lute, he admonished me for keeping the old sign. Truth be told, I had not thought to change it. Together we took it down and while I said I would think about getting another, all I did later was write *William Totman – Luthier* on paper and put it in the window. It was not difficult to see from the street, but I shuddered when I saw it, remembering the previous time I had written my name on paper.

There was considerable comfort to be had working with my own tools again, at my own bench, and at my leisure. During the day I was always occupied, and in the evenings, I might go to a playhouse if they were open. The nights though, they were long. It was then I would dream of Ferrara or Florence and always with Sofia. They'd begin joyously enough but then trouble came – floods, wild beasts, or the violence of others – and the end was always full of fear, tears and separation.

I'd wake early, go downstairs and poke the fire. Then I'd sit for a while brooding until the noise of the city roused me. I thought of all the people I cared about. Apart from Jane and the children, John's mother and Joseph were gone, Molly was shortly to be married, Sofia, Signor Biscaldi and Antonio were far away, and there was no knowing when John would be home. Everyone seemed think that becoming my own man was very desirable, but I wasn't so sure. I'd heard nothing from Italy since we left and if I went back, what would I find? I could not bear to be in the same town if Sofia had already married. Perhaps Venice and a place at the Tieffenbrucker workshop? Here, or there, I could be my own man, but I'd still be lonely.

It was a fine June morning when I opened the door and found a flustered Molly standing on the step.

'He's back,' she said. 'And I didn't know what to do. He's in something of a humour and the rest of the household are out.'

I put down my chisel and went with her straight away. John was home again and pacing about in the upstairs parlour.

'*Mistakes!*' he roared, by way of greeting and whilst repeatedly slapping the volume of music down on the chest as if it was raw meat on a slab. 'Not only was I not asked for my permission, but the damn thing is full of mistakes!'

'Yes,' I said, nodding in agreement whilst trying not to grin like a fool simply because I was so glad to see him. 'Tom Morley said he thought it was a poor printing altogether.'

'Poor?' he raised his eyes to Heaven. 'Poor, you say?'

'Not I,' I said. 'Far worse than poor. Bad, I call it. Very bad. Did you see the cover engraving? Why, young Robert could draw better.'

'Of course, he could.' At the mention of his son his expression softened. 'Has he changed? Almost as handsome as his father now?'

I laughed. 'Yes! And only seven. Imagine him at twenty!' I spread my arms. 'He will be the darling of all the ladies in London.'

'You mean England, surely.'

'For certain.'

'Ah, Will, I have missed you.' He looked at me fondly then sighed. 'There was little fun to be had in Hesse. The Landgrave was a fine man when sober, but that was not so often. He even went to *sleep* during one of my performances. Can you imagine?'

'He did pay well though,' I said, gesturing towards the fine goblet and cover.

'Not enough, I'm sure,' said John, but he did go and lift it, feeling the weight then twirling it about, better to admire the delicate glass painting and relief work on the silver base.

All John's complaints about the book, and the mistakes it contained, would come to nothing. Many copies had been sold already. What was done, was done. He could correct them in the volume he planned but that wasn't yet ready. I understood his fury, as I've no doubt I would feel the same if an instrument of mine were poorly repaired. The mere thought of such a thing reminded me again of how foolhardy I'd been with the Maler lute. Trying to absolve myself by suggesting the workmanship was equally good, merely left a sour taste in my mouth.

I had wondered whether John would resent the generosity of his mother towards me but when I offered to pay back the fine, he teased me. It was the day after his return, and he was sitting with me in front of Joseph's fireplace. Firstly, he said he'd be glad to accept it and about time too, but then, when I passed over the purse, he caught hold of my hand and turned it over, so the purse dropped straight back into mine.

'What?' he laughed. 'Do you think I would take it? Come now. How could I? You came away with me freely and I am well-aware of all the lutes and money you could have made during that time. No, no, you must keep it.

Besides, if my dear mother were still here, imagine! She would be furious with me.' He sat back and looked at me a little strangely then. 'Do you know,' he mused aloud. 'I sometimes wonder if she did not prefer you to me.'

I almost staggered, hearing such a wrong thing.

'No! Never!' I could hardly speak for the shock. 'You must never think that. Before we went away, if you'd been there that last time, when I said goodbye and she spoke of her dear son.' I shook my head. 'I can tell you, in all truth, that she'd never say such a thing. Your mother loved you more than anything in the world. Her only sorrow was that you didn't have company, so when I fetched up—'

'Yes, yes. I see.' He stood up and gave a small laugh. 'Goodness Will, that's quite some feeling from you.'

Embarrassed, I looked away but a soft cuff on the side of the head was probably just what I needed.

'Come,' he said. 'Let us seek out Henry Noel and Tom Morley. I feel an evening in the tavern would do me good. We should not shout about my presence in London, but I think one evening is not too big a risk.'

'Only one evening? Why? Are you leaving again?'

He put a finger to his lips even though we were quite alone. 'Shh. Don't let anyone hear. I promised Maurice I would return in August for—

'But it's nearly July already.'

'Yes, well. It may not happen. Come, let us go.' Then he stared at the faint glow in the fireplace. 'Are you going to dowse that ridiculous fire? What is it? Two twigs you found and thought you'd rub together?'

'It'll be all right,' I said, putting the large iron guard in front. 'Keeping it going reminds me of Joseph.'

He spread his arms wide. 'In a way that being surrounded by his whole house doesn't, I suppose.'

We were a very jovial company in The Mitre. Somewhat to my surprise, I was treated as an equal amongst them, which I didn't remember being the case prior to our journey. I wondered whether it was because I had come into property, but I also wondered whether they saw something in my face that told of a different man within.

On the way home I did my best to hush my friends else John's arrival home become common knowledge. In contrast, John seemed altogether calm about his possible arrest. Hours went by though, and then days. Nothing was heard and gradually, John became bolder in his outings. Worry wouldn't leave me, though, and I spoke of it to Tom. Had he spoken to Sir Robert Cecil? Yes, but nothing was resolved in the conversation, although Tom did say it was clear that Skidmore was not thought of with any favour. Apart from that, he hadn't heard anything since.

More work came my way. Henry Noel asked me to replace some pins on a harp and John had a list of his own, including a lute for Robert and a small robust instrument that the little one could play with.

During the day, work provided a distraction from the dilemma that kept me awake at night. The truth was, that despite John being back, despite everything I now had, even in spite of at last being my own man, my longing for Sofia was, if anything, more acute than ever. I made a little box for her lace cuff, similar to the bobbin box, but much slimmer and with her whole name inlaid on the lid.

I knew that every new job of work delayed my departure for Italy. I'd said that I would only wait until John's return. So why wasn't I making preparations to leave? Certainly, the work pulled me to my bench. London could be a violent and dangerous place, but I knew the city, knew its people, knew how to get about, and knew where things were that I might need. I felt sure that if I worked hard, I could make a success of my business and a name for myself that perhaps could even rival Maler or Tieffenbrucker. And, of course, I would miss John's family, young Robert in particular, who would like nothing more than spending a morning watching me work, all the while asking about the places I'd been and people I'd met. Often, I'd wish for such a son.

The pull to stay was strong, but truly? It was not so strong as my resolve to go. Then, a week after he'd arrived home, John received a command to play before the Queen at Hampton. Tom came with the news, calling on me first as he passed by. Together with John we went to the tavern and drank Her Majesty's health. My worries about Tom being duplicitous drained away with my ale. Indeed, all the worries that had sent us wandering across the North of Italy and then to Germany, rather than straight home, seemed almost fanciful after a few jugs. Admittedly, no official position at Court was offered but, unlike last time, John took that with a shrug. The evening passed very merrily. I'm not the best of singers but, as part of a trio, warbling on its way home, I didn't embarrass myself.

The following morning, my head was so full of sawdust I was unable to concentrate properly. I put down my tools. The time had come for me to start for Italy, and I couldn't do that until I'd had a difficult conversation.

CHAPTER TWENTY-SIX

High summer had set in, burning our cheeks and noses. Not surprisingly, the queue to fill flasks and water bottles at the Great Conduit stretched nearly all the way to the Dowland house. I liked the heat but wished for the high stone walls of Italy and their cool shadows. Soon, I thought, soon.

Molly let me in and sent me upstairs. In the music room, John was at his writing desk.

'Ah, Will, good,' said John, hardly looking up. 'I have just composed a new verse. Listen to this: *And although your sight I leave, Sight wherein my joys do lie, Till that death do sense bereave, Never shall affection die.*' As he read, he tapped along before shrugging. 'Oh well,' he said, 'You'll have to ignore the *And* so strongly stressed, but there's a verse before and it makes sense in the round. I must confess to being rather pleased with the rhyme. What do you think?'

I stood there blinking, wondering how it could be that he should touch on such a subject and speak straight to my heart.

'It's very...' I hesitated, searching for the word. 'It's very pertinent.'

'*Pertinent?*' he said, frowning. I had his full attention then. He put down his quill and stood up. 'Are you unwell?'

I was in danger of screwing my cap into a tight ball. 'I need to speak to you.'

'Good Lord, whatever is it? A sickness?' His face darkened. 'You're not in trouble again, are you?' He guided me to the settle by the window and rescued my cap, shaking it out so it resembled its former shape. 'Tell me directly, Will. I would hate for you to keep anything from me, and you know I will help if I can.'

He went to the door and called out to Molly to bring us a jug of ale. His concern made me feel much worse.

How could I leave him? My thoughts scurried hither and thither, remembering when we were young, his mother's legacy, all the times he had helped me. I had been supposed to look after him but, more often than not, it had been the other way around. I put my hand to my heart and felt the smooth surface of the cuff box beneath my jerkin.

'I have to go,' I said in barely more than a whisper.

John fetched his stool from the desk and sat opposite me.

'Come along, Will,' he said, slapping his knees. 'What is it you have to know?'

I shook my head and said more firmly.

'I have to *go*, not know. I have to go back.'

'Back,' said John, slowly drawing it out as if it was a foreign word he didn't know.

'Yes, back to Italy. To Sofia.'

For a long moment, he said nothing. Molly came in with a tray and he gestured to the table and then for her to be gone.

I'd expected him to tell me I was mad, but I wasn't prepared for the long, wounded cry that preceded his argument. It turned me cold.

'John, please—' I began.

'No. Don't say anything.' He stood up and paced about, first to his desk, then the window which he opened, then shut again. The ale slopped onto the tray when he poured himself a beaker and pouring one for me just gave him something to do. Not that he handed it to me.

'I understand—' I began again.

'Do you?' He rounded on me. 'Do you really?'

'Well, I—'

'I suppose you've heard from her.'

'No, I—'

'No?' He sat down on the stool, finished his ale in one long gulp and smacked the beaker back down on the tray. Silence followed, until eventually, he gave a long sigh.

'So,' he said, addressing me in a curiously quiet and civil tone, 'you want to go on a perilous journey all the way back to Italy, to find a girl who now may well be married to another man, a Jew, by the way, and who lives in a city where, not so long ago, you were convicted and imprisoned for fraud. Well, I must say, that sounds like a very good future for you.' I would have replied but with a curt gesture for me to desist, he went on. 'Whereas here,' he said, 'you have your own home, work, friends, me—' He stopped abruptly and shrugged, deflated, as if a pin had burst a bubble 'Oh well. I suppose that's what you've been waiting for. You're free to do what you like *now*.'

I started at that and felt a fast thumping of my heart. All my life I had done everything I could for this man and here he was, clearly wounded by what I was saying, but his emphasis on *now* implied a layer of meaning I couldn't let stand.

'Please,' I said. 'Your dear mother's generosity towards me has nothing to do with why I am going. I made the decision before I knew anything about what was in her will. Before we left, I promised your mother I would do my best to see you safely home. If not for that I would have returned to Venice there and then.'

I paused then, expecting some sort of response, but there was none. He sat with his face turned away, as if to peruse the street, but I knew by the fast beating of his heel against the floor that he was containing a great deal of feeling.

'Please, John, please understand,' I went on. 'Jane told me that your mother wished for me to live my own life, and I have thought a great deal about what she meant by that. It seems to me a house far away in Italy is not at all the same as another close by in Forster Street. I am sorry about it, but I am convinced that you should have Joseph's house back.'

A faint flicker of surprise swept across his face, but he stayed silent. Was his expression set less hard? I couldn't be sure.

'Before we left Florence,' I went on, 'Sofia said she would never marry Jakob. Is that still true? I can hardly sleep at night, John. If she has married, then I will leave

Florence and try my best to be happy for her. If not, then maybe her father could be persuaded that whilst I'm not an ideal match, I would always love and care for his daughter.'

At that, John slumped forward, put his head in his hands and groaned. It lacked all the shrill energy of last time, but in some ways affected me more.

'Oh, Will,' he said, sitting back with as big a sigh as I've ever heard. 'You do know that this idea of yours is madness. I admire your loyalty to the girl, but to go all that way on such a frail hope—'

'Strong hope.'

'Well, that's as maybe. I'll say it again. You could have a perfectly happy life with someone else. Besides, if you don't make a family quite so important to you, you can travel about and do other things without feeling all that heartache.'

'Other things?' I said. 'Like Lady Anna?'

'Ah no,' he said, gently. 'Certainly not Lady Anna.'

I didn't jolt him from the memory. The afternoon of their final tryst was as bright to me as if it was yesterday. A day of wonder and despair, from making the keepsake and holding Sofia in my arms, to the shock of Lady Anna's husband arriving, the surprise trapdoor in the trunk and then the terrible shame and horror of the arrest and prison.

'I should very much like to know what happened to her,' he said, eventually. Then, after a very deep breath, he added, 'if there had been *any* possibility— well.' He looked at me with a rueful smile. 'Perhaps I do have some feelings that could be akin to yours.'

'I'm sure you have all the same feelings,' I said. 'Look at everything you write? You may say it's all playacting, but it's a dull song that has no heart and there's not a man or woman alive that would say John Dowland writes a dull song.'

He looked a little brighter when I said that. It wasn't our habit to pay compliments but if not then, when?

'Thank you. It is good to be reminded of that, as

sometimes, even I forget. As for your journey?' He sighed heavily. 'It may be madness, but I can understand that it's the right thing for you to do.'

I felt tears prick at the back of my eyes. What a thing for John to admit. It wouldn't have been easy for him.

'And you should know,' I said, 'that I don't leave here, Jane, the children, and you, especially you, John, at all easily. I am—' I mumbled, not having anything like the correct words to convey what I felt. 'And I will be, very, very sorry.'

Was I doing the right thing? Hurting one for the love of another? John had the life he chose, a life of fame, fortune and a loving wife and children. Whether he appreciated them was not a question for me. I had a chance for love, and however much anguish I felt, I knew my resolve was not diminished.

'I should hope you would be sorry,' said John, his old self suddenly. 'How long have you been here? Ten, twenty, years, is it? And I thought you were only staying to dinner. Heavens, it's well past time you left.'

When I was at last ready to leave, it was almost two years to the day since we had set off previously. Mischievous doubt plagued me in the small hours but, during the day, it was John's new faith in my plan that kept my resolve strong. He thought I'd come back a chastened man and, in truth, I wondered the same.

Jane insisted on a feast for my last evening, and it wasn't only the eyes of the children that grew large when we sat at table. I doubt they had seen the best linen before, or the silver goblets. It was our first swallowing of mussels cooked in mead, but I could tell it wouldn't be the last in that household. Robert licked his lips and was happy to eat his brother's small share when it was pushed away. He was happier when Molly brought in the game pie that followed, but best of all was the spiced jelly and cream.

'My dear Jane,' I said, as I wiped my spoon. 'I have no doubt that such a marvellous meal would amply sustain me even if I did not eat for a week.'

'I doubt that,' she said. 'But you won't have to starve. I've asked Molly to put aside something for you to take with you.'

She blushed a little when I thanked her, and once again I wondered how John could so easily throw his loyalty to the breeze when he spied another woman who took his fancy.

In the parlour after dinner, I could feel John getting restless. We'd said everything there was to say about the journey, which route to take, the towns to avoid and those to enjoy, and now we were in danger of repeating ourselves. Either that or start weeping.

Jane saved us from that by suggesting that Robert played to us on his new lute. It was an excellent performance and gladdened all our hearts, so that when he asked if he could stay and listen to his father play, his pleas were granted at once.

Eventually though, it was time for him to go to bed. Robert's goodbye to me was a very sorrowful event, only allayed by my promise that he should come and visit me as soon as he was allowed.

'Let us have no tears,' John said, clutching my hand when it came the time for me to go. 'But I want one of your appallingly scribed letters from every city along the way. Don't forget to seek out my friends and steer clear of my enemies. And yours too, come to that.'

I nodded, unable to speak. Could my grasp convey anything like how I felt? I doubted it. All I knew when I left him, almost stumbling away, was that whenever this moment came into my mind, it would be clear, bright, and I would feel encouraged in whatever I was doing. What was it that Sofia said about the memory of my mother? I remembered it so well because she loved me. I was sure the same could be said about John.

I surprised myself by sleeping soundly and waking in full daylight. Something to do with such an excellent meal perhaps, or that everything to do was now done. After dressing, I visited the barber, then returned to wait for the cart to come and collect my box at half past nine. John had persuaded me to take a lute. He regarded any musical instrument as an object of power, able to open locked doors, or conjure a meal when required. Of course, for him, the merest pluck of a string meant everyone came running to listen. My rudimentary playing was not so commanding. Even so, I was happy to take one along, if only to prove my workmanship.

The boat was to leave at twelve o'clock. So, once the cart had gone, I checked the fire was out and took a last look around. The key felt heavy in my hand, and I remembered how Jane had found it difficult to turn, then my surprise when she'd ushered me inside. I'd oiled the lock soon after and now it turned with ease. After a deep breath, I prayed to the Lord for a day of fair weather, slung my bag over my shoulder, picked up the lute and set off.

At the corner of the street, I recognised Alice, the girl who had eaten most of my bread and damson cheese the day I'd returned.

'Any messages, sir?'

'Perhaps,' I said. 'Do you know the Dowland house?'

She pointed straight at it straight away. 'You mean that one?'

It was only yards from us, but she would know who lived in all the houses hereabouts. Just like I did when running messages.

'Here,' I said, holding up the key. 'I want you to give this to whoever opens the door. There's thruppence in it for you when you come back. Mind,' I held up the coin. 'I'll have my eye on you.'

A couple of steps and I was out of sight but could see when Molly opened the door. It touched me that she should turn so pale and cry out a little when she received the key. I squeezed my eyelids tight shut, then blinked several times to clear my tears. When Alice returned, I handed over her thruppence and another besides, telling her it was not for squandering. She smiled and thanked me nicely.

I'd agreed with John that I should go alone to the docks, and walking the busier streets suited me well. Any distraction was welcome as I was sad to leave. I was about to turn into Swan Lane when I first thought I heard my name being called out. It was strange, but I ignored it, thinking I'd misheard. The next time, however, my pace faltered. Several times I heard it, and not with the same voice or from the same direction. I stopped then as a twinge of worry crept across the back of my neck.

A further call gave me sight of a stocky boy of about eleven or twelve and another, his twin, converging from another street, and yet another at the junction of the lane close by me: three boys, until finally Alice arrived, and they all stood like a small tuneless choir calling my name. I hung back from making myself known, waiting behind a stack of barrels outside the Swan Inn, in case I could glean whilst they were there.

'He must be on the dock already,' said one.

'Or not here yet.'

'You two go on,' said the biggest boy to the twins. 'Me an' Alice'll stay here.'

'Enough,' I said, stepping forward and addressing the girl. 'You know me. What is all this urgency?'

'You must come with us, sir.'

'Oh really? On whose orders?'

The last time I'd been so addressed I was being arrested. These scruffy children did not give rise to the same fear for myself, but I was anxious to know who had sent them, and why.

'We don't know exactly,' said the boy, but Alice shook her head.

'I know,' she said. 'It was Mistress Dowland.'

This was a surprise. An idea had presented itself to me that perhaps John may have invented an obstacle to my travelling today, but Jane? She knew his moods and tempers as well as I did. If he were struck by a gloom, she would understand and wait it out, not call me back.

'Jane Dowland? I said. 'Did she ask you herself?'

'No, sir, but I did see her talking to the housekeeper at

the door.'

'And how did she seem?'

Alice frowned. 'I dunno, but they was both all flustered.'

'She didn't mention an accident or a mishap of any sort?'

'No, sir.'

'And she definitely said I have to go back?'

'We have to come with you to make sure,' said the biggest boy.

This met with a vigorous nodding from all of them.

Now I was worried. For John to insist was one thing. For *Jane* to insist was another and she wouldn't do so without great need. Telling a messenger to make a return journey was strange too. Surely, but *surely*, John wouldn't contrive this as a way of stopping me going.

Then a great fear drenched me from head to foot. Had John been arrested after all? It was possible. A treasonous yarn may have come to Sir Robert's ear at last. I tried to recall conversations I'd had with Tom but nothing untoward came to mind. Even so, my suspicions grew. Would he really betray John for his own furtherance? Surely not. Someone else, then. John wasn't a man easily missed when out and about. Was Skidmore back in England? I did not doubt his treachery.

'You boys,' I said to the twins. 'There's a carter waiting for me at Lyon Quay. Tell him to bring my box back to Cheapside. I'll pay him for both ways then. Do you know the house?'

'Aye,' they both said, although it sounded as one.

'In haste, then.' I said, parting with sixpence between them, before turning to Alice and the bigger boy. 'Come, we must also make haste.'

On another day, it could have been a pleasant stroll, but my mind was so full of questions that even the bakery did not stop me. A wagon had shed its load at Dowe Gate so we hurried all the way along St Martin's Lane before turning up Bread Street, and it must have been a good half hour by the time we reached the Eleanor Cross and the house came in sight. All the way, I pressed the children to tell me all they knew but they had little to say. They hadn't seen John. Alice said Jane seemed flustered and her hair wasn't done as usual. She thought she saw another man through an upstairs window but had nothing further to say about him as it was only a quick glance. Who, I wondered would be in the best parlour?

Even from a distance I could see the door stood open. Quickly, I paid off the children, a handsome amount in truth, but I told them to wait close by until the midday bells rang and have something to eat in the meantime. Alice might stay, although I doubted the boy, but if John was in trouble, I would need to send them to rouse some good help amongst his friends. I could think of nothing else, lest he had some ill or hurt. I almost wished that were the case. Better, perhaps, than the hand of Sir Robert striking a blow.

CHAPTER TWENTY-SEVEN

Molly was waiting for me with the door open.

'Oh, William,' she cried, clutching her apron to her face. 'I'm so glad you've come back.'

'What's happened, Molly? I cannot fathom what would bring me back so urgently. Is John hurt?'

She shook her head. 'There's a man come,' she whispered, while taking my bag from me, 'and you're to go up at once, that's all I know.'

I didn't stop to ask more about this man but took the stairs two at a time. Having already set a fast pace all the way from the docks, my breath was coming quite heavily by the time I reached the parlour. I paused for the moment and put my ear close to the door, although was none the wiser for it. Taking a deep breath, I brushed any dust from my jerkin and stood up straight.

Jane must have heard me because she opened the door as I was about to knock. Her pallor that told me all was not well.

'Who is it?' I said in a low voice, hoping to be forewarned.

'Ah William,' she said. 'What a good thing we fetched you in time.' With a small shake of her head and a weak smile she gestured for me to enter.

I was baffled. There was John, sitting easily on the settle, apparently unharmed. The other man, a slim figure who stood with his back to the window, I did not recognise at first, as the midday sun pouring in rendered him completely in the dark. There was, however, something about the way he clutched and pulled at his cuff—

'Signor Biscaldi!' I burst out. For when he stepped out of the shadow, he was perfectly clear to me, if only half the man he was the last time I had seen him. 'What are you—' I stopped and quickly gazed about. 'But where is Sofia? Why is she not with you?'

John was first to reply. 'A little patience, Will,' he said, taking to his feet and slapping me on the back. 'But I must say I am glad you are back. Come Jane, let's leave them now.'

Not a man I'd known to express concern for me all that often, I saw it in his eyes then. A little patience? Tell me at once! I wanted to yell, but instead removed my cap and clutched it to my heart while I gave Sofia's dear Papa a hasty bow.

'Signor,' I said, keeping my voice level as best I could while my heart tried to beat its way out from my breast. 'You're looking very...well.'

I wished I'd never referred to his appearance then, as in truth, he was a changed man. Instead of the round and ruddy complexion I remembered, his cheeks had hollowed, and baggy skin hung beneath his eyes and chin.

'Thank you.' He smiled at my hesitation. 'I confess to feeling tired. The journey here is very long, as you know, Mr Totman. Now? It is good to see you. I hear we almost missed you.'

We? He said *we* had missed you?

'Please,' he went on. 'Do sit down. You have no need to worry about my dear Sofia's health. Will you have wine?'

Such was my relief and the weakness in my knees, I may well have fallen down, with or without his permission. Hope flared within me. Surely Sofia had come to London with her father. She would never let him travel so far without her.

'I am very glad to hear that,' I said. 'Yes, thank you.'

While he poured the wine, I gave thanks that I wasn't at sea. But what of Sofia? And the purpose of this visit?

'Mr Totman,' Signor Biscaldi said, having handed me my wine and sat down. 'I drink to your good health.'

'And I yours and, of course, that of your daughter.'

'Yes, yes, thank you.'

We both took a draught of what proved to be the household's good wine. I was very glad of it and took another. I was fond of Signor Biscaldi, but if I could have turned him upside down and shaken his news from him, at that moment I would have done so.

'Mr Totman,' he said, with a sigh. 'You should know the reason my dear Sofia is not here this morning.'

'Yes, please,' I said. 'In every haste, sir. Please do tell me.'

I looked at him directly then, with every bone and sinew in my body yearning for news of Sofia, only to see an expression on Signor Biscaldi's face that drained all my hopes away. Like his daughter, he was very bad at disguising his feelings, and there was no hiding the anguish he felt. It was plain to me as his eyes and nose.

'What is it?' I said, feeling cold dread in the pit of my gut. 'What has happened? Is she well?'

He nodded. 'Yes. Very well in health, but her heart? I not so sure. Mr Totman, you surprised, for she refuse to come here with me. She is afraid, I think.'

Sofia afraid? I could scarcely believe it. Shock rattled through me, but with a slight gesture Signor Biscaldi prevented me from interrupting.

'*I* am afraid from the beginning,' he went on. 'We travel all the time, but this journey is very big risk. I am not talking of bandits or robbers, although perhaps I am, because Mr Totman,' he paused, raising a pointed finger and glaring in an almost frightening manner, 'I am talking about you.'

I could only stutter a reply. 'Me? How so?'

His face relaxed and he opened his hands. 'All these months, I refuse my daughter to come or write here. How we both suffer.' He sighed and took another draught of wine. 'But then,' he leant towards me and spoke with more urgency. 'We receive the nice olive pegs. They very good quality, I like them very much.'

I could only murmur thanks while grasping my knees even tighter.

'Ah yes, I see you are impatient too. Just like Sofia. When they come and the letter, she even more certain we come here. This is how she persuade me. We must come for business, she say. Signor Dowland is a good person to know. She love you, not Jakob and if I marry her mother for love, why not her? I am weak man, Mr Totman but I must tell you, I am also very selfish.'

I expressed my doubts about his assessment of himself, but he waved them away.

'There is something I do not tell Sofia all her life.' He shook his head and with a very big sigh went on. 'Something very important. I nearly tell you the day Count Fontanelli came in the shop, I so nearly tell you but, he interrupt us. Perhaps, if I did, it save us this journey.'

I didn't like the sound of that and couldn't help wishing for some sort of tool to prise the words out of his mouth. 'Oh?' was all I could muster.

He shook his head again and continued to fiddle with his cuff.

'Signor Biscaldi,' I said. 'Please—'

'Yes, yes. It is this.' He took a deep breath. 'Mr Totman, if Sofia is my *son*, it very difficult for you.'

'Indeed,' I said, slowly, not knowing what to make of such an unexpected notion. I took another mouthful of wine.

'But she is my daughter and so like her beautiful mother it almost pains me. Her mother, Signor Totman, and this important, was a Morisca. Do you know what that means?'

I frowned, remembering that Sofia had mentioned the name when telling me about her mama, but we were interrupted, and its meaning was lost to me.

'It means,' Signor Biscaldi went on, 'that her family were Moors who were made to convert to your church.'

'Moors?' I said, surprised by more unexpected information.

'Yes, they not Jews. You may know this already but what you not know, and I never tell Sofia all her life until now, is that being Jewish is from mother to her children.' He pointed at an invisible mother on the other side of the room. 'Not,' he said, drawing his hand back and pointing at himself, 'from father.'

A silence followed. I may have blinked several times.

Certainly, I heard a rushing sound in my ears as I fathomed what I had just heard.

'Passed from a *mother* to her children?'

'Yes' Signor Biscaldi coughed. 'That is correct.'

'So does that mean Sofia is not a Jew?'

It was a difficult question for him to answer. Twice he took breath to reply, but then shook his head.

'Please,' I said, feeling almost weak with waiting.

'Yes, yes,' he said, taking a deep breath. 'I understand. In Florence we live in the ghetto and I take Sofia everywhere with me.' He turned away, reaching for his glass. 'She is a child of five years only. There is no reason for her to know about this matter and when I talk with the rabbi, he agree. Jakob is a fine boy and if they marry—' He shook his head, leaving the notion to dangle. 'How wrong I am, Mr Totman.'

'And Sofia,' I had to ask. 'Have you told her?'

'I have,' he said, and a shadow passed over his face. 'When your letter come and those nice olive pegs break her heart, then I tell her. It is a very sad time for us both.'

For Signor Biscaldi it was clearly a painful memory, but for me, well, I dared to hope again.

'And so,' he continued, 'we come to England. There is much to prepare but soon we leave Antonio and the shop. But then?' he clapped his hands, stood up, then crossed the room to look out of the window. I watched him like a hungry dog hoping for food. Eventually, he turned back, and settled his gaze on me. 'But then, something happen on our journey.'

I stiffened, praying that he would get to the crux of his story soon.

'Every day,' he went on, 'instead of being more happy to come here, Sofia is not happy. What am I to do? I ask her why and she wave me away. It is worse and worse, until every day she weeps. Shall we go home? She weep even louder. Mr Totman, I can tell you that I am very worried. This is not my daughter.'

I was shocked too. 'But why? What has happened?'

Signor Biscaldi was silent and when he sat down

again, I could see his eyes were glazed with tears. He spoke quietly.

'Sofia is worried. All her life she has been a Jew. It is not like a cloak to put on and then take off. It is not something to be thrown away. Also, Mr Totman, I have to tell you, she love another man. She love her Papa as well as you.' He placed his hand on his heart. 'One Jew,' he said, then gestured towards me, 'and one Christian. Two different lives. She must choose. She also thinks, and Signor Totman, I must tell you that all the way here I hope, maybe you have a wife now, have forgotten her, or are gone away again.'

'Oh no, no,' I burst out and leapt to my feet. 'None of those things. In truth, despite my good fortune, I could not settle here without knowing if she had forgotten me.'

'Good fortune?' Signor Biscaldi's eyebrows rose.

I hesitated to explain. After all, my fortune was rather diminished, since only that morning I had insisted to John that he should have Joseph's property. It was something to think on but all of that seemed unimportant now.

'Signor Biscaldi,' I said, 'about my good fortune I will explain later, but first, you say Sofia must choose between us. But why? Is there not enough love for us all? I am quite sure that Sofia has enough for you and me. What about your own wife? Who made the choice then? Please,' I pleaded with him, 'let me see her. Even if it is for one last time.'

He sighed. 'It is an easier choice for my wife. She already part of the family and well, it may be hard to believe, but she love me as I did her.' He searched my face. 'I believe you love my Sofia, Mr Totman, but perhaps she love you in Ferrara and Florence, but not in London.'

'Do you think she is afraid to come here? What if she took one look at me and changed her mind.'

'Change her mind?' he said. 'Is not in her nature, but we must find out. Come with me to the inn.'

I wasn't surprised to find Jane and John in conversation outside the door and their glances told me they had heard every word. Jane led us down the stairs, and blushed when Signor Biscaldi said farewell and kissed her hand. John, however, followed us out into the street and put a hand on Signor Biscaldi's arm.

'Signor,' he said. 'While in Florence, you were most indulgent towards me in the use of your premises, and I thank you for making no mention of that in front of my wife. I owe you not only an apology but also a fine fur cloak. Would you indulge me one more time by selecting a suitable lute from my collection as recompense? Perhaps an instrument I have played may add a little to its value. Besides,' he went on, all the while drawing Signor Biscaldi back to the front door of the house. 'I'm quite sure, my honest and very honourable friend would have no difficulty in persuading your daughter to see him. A little time together perhaps may clarify their feelings towards each other.'

Dear, dear John. Never again would I doubt his friendship and loyalty. His attempted subterfuge would not deceive anyone, but Signor Biscaldi was a kind man and wise enough to know that his daughter's happiness was also his own, and the matter needed to be settled one way or, although I could not bear to think on it, the other.

'I believe you are right, Mr Dowland, but what need have I for a cloak in summer? And one so big? Am I not a changed man since last time we met? Come then,' he stepped back inside the door. 'I will tell you why this big change and also be happy to see any instrument you wish to show me. As for Mr Totman, do you have a servant that could accompany him to The Feathers?'

'Have no fear for Sofia, Signor,' I said, beckoning to Alice who was still waiting on the other side of the street. Despite her torn frock, mercifully, she looked quite clean. 'I will take a girl with me. She is honest despite her apparel.'

No sooner had Signor Biscaldi agreed than I turned on my heel and we were off. Alice had difficulty keeping up with me, but I was in a state of torment and could not slow. One moment, I was sure of Sofia, the next, terror took me, and I doubted her.

Outside the inn, I tried to calm myself. It wouldn't do for me, red in the face and panting, to barge inside demanding to see a young foreign woman.

'Alice,' I said. 'I need you to go in and say you have a message for Miss Sofia Biscaldi who is staying there with her father.'

'Right,' said Alice, eyes narrowing. 'Miss Sofia Bis—
'Sofia Biscaldi.'
'Sofia *Biscaldi*.'
'Good. Yes, that's right. Off you go.'

Alice folded her arms. 'What should I say?'

I groaned. What did I want her to say? How could I put the words together? With both hands I scratched my head in the hope of etching some sort of message that would do.

'Oh Alice,' I said, eventually. 'I wish I could tell you. Anything. Just say anything that will mean she will at least see me.'

'Right,' said Alice. 'Expect I can manage that.'

As soon as she'd disappeared, I regretted being so rash. Surely, she wouldn't be rude or upset dear Sofia, would she? The minutes went by, until I could pace up and down no longer and the traders nearby began hurling abuse. I started for the door, only to be met on the inside by Alice coming out.

I could tell by her face that not all was well.

'What is it? What's happened?'

She shrugged, not looking me in the eye.

'Well?'

'I did try, sir. Told her she 'ad the most good man in London downstairs.'

Despair and surprise coursed through me with such weight I could scarcely stand.

'Oh Alice,' I said, fumbling for a coin. 'You did try. Thank you. So she wouldn't even see me?'

She shook her head. 'Only for a few minutes, is all. I said she was mad but a few minutes is it. An' I was to come too.'

'Alice!' All my despair vanished.

'I wouldn't build up your hopes just yet, sir,' said Alice. 'She took some persuading. In the end I told her I wasn't going anywhere until she said yes.'

'I see.' I swallowed. If I'd had hope, then it certainly shrivelled then. 'In that case, I'd best begin with an apology.'

Inside, it was busy with noise of laughter and talk. Alice led me through the tables where men huddled over their tankards then shouted when their card play proved successful. The stairs were in a corner, and it was only when we reached the top and turned into a passage, that the noise abated enough for me to hear my own heart beating. With only a small window at one end the passage was quite dark, but when Alice knocked on a door and it opened, light flooded in.

How many times I had imagined this moment? To see her again, one more time maybe, that would be enough. But no, no, no! Once couldn't possibly be enough. As I stepped into the room, I clutched my cap to my heart and bowed low.

'Miss Sofia. I—'

'Mr Totman,' she interrupted me sharply. 'You have had a wasted journey. It was my express wish to Papa, that I wouldn't see you.'

It was a knife to the heart. When I stood back up, she was looking out of the window.

'Sofia,' I stuttered. 'Please. I am so sorry, I —'

It was then I realised that she was weeping, and I was across the room in a moment.

'No!' she cried, her small hands a shield against me. 'This is what I feared. Please! You should go. It is all wrong.'

I was aghast. 'Wrong? Sofia, please. What is wrong? You have come all the way from Florence and your father has allowed me to come here today. What can possibly be wrong? Please Sofia, I cannot bear that you are so unhappy.'

'It is *because* of Papa,' she said. 'I have not been a good daughter. We shall go home, and everything will be as it was.'

'How can that be?' I said, desperate to understand her. 'Your Papa loves you and wants every happiness for you. How can that be wrong?'

'Did you not see him?' she turned on me with such a fierceness I'd never seen from her before. 'How thin he is? How tired.' She paced back and forth dabbing her eyes with a handkerchief so violently I thought she may do herself a hurt. 'He is a sick man. Perhaps dying. And I have made everything worse.'

Fresh tears came in abundance, whilst I could only stand mute as a fool. Signor Biscaldi sick? Of course. No wonder she was so distressed.

'Oh my dear. I am so very sorry to hear that. Can anything be done?'

'He will not have it. I know he does not want to worry me, but he makes light of everything even when it is serious.' She looked at me directly then, her eyes red and gleaming with tears. 'And it is all my fault.'

I was appalled. 'No, Sofia. That cannot be, for sure.'

'Yes, for sure.' She screwed her handkerchief into a ball. It was already soaked. 'Ever since Papa told me about my not being a proper Jew anymore. That's when it started, and I made us come on this long journey. Mr Totman, Papa loves his food, but he hardly has eaten anything since we left Florence!'

I held out my own handkerchief which, after a little hesitation, she took, thanking me between sobs.

'It is because of me,' she said. 'I am sure of it. All my life I have thought myself a Jew. What now though? I am not? That is a very hard thing to understand. What does it mean? I worship as a Jew. I have lived as a Jew. Now though? I cannot leave Papa. What will he do without me? I will stay with him and that means I cannot marry you. It is what I have decided. I must go home and try to make my Papa happy. Then maybe he will be well again and if not —' Fresh tears fell before she could continue. 'If not, then I shall look after him.'

I shook my head.

'My dear Sofia, I—'

She held up her hand. 'We must part again, Mr Totman. I confess to never thinking it would be my choice to do so. I hope more than anything that you will not be pained by this and that any thought of me fades quickly from your memory.'

Stifling a sob she turned away with my handkerchief once again at her eyes.

I could hardly make sense of anything I was hearing. Did she really believe that Signor Biscaldi's illness was her fault? Could I believe that? I thought of the first time I had seen Sofia, when I'd woken from the stupor caused by the snakebite. She was singing the sweet melody that so often since I have sung to myself. I remembered meeting Signor Biscaldi and mending his valuable lute too, then I remembered Sofia and her darling Papa. His pride in her, her love of him and how they laughed and were joyous together. But now, after their long journey here, they would go home and pretend that everything was the same as before. And I would not be pained? Impossible.

'Miss Sofia,' I began, trying to keep my voice level. 'I am so full of arguing feelings that I can hardly speak. Indeed, I hardly know where to begin, but please hear me. Let me say my part and then I will leave you.'

'Of course, William,' she said, her voice quiet and trembling. 'Please, go ahead.'

I tried. Once, twice I began, then faltered, but I took a deep breath and straightened myself. John's voice came to me – *what sort of man are you?*

'Earlier today,' I said, at last, 'A miracle occurred. I was about to board a ship that would take me over the sea. I would journey on across the Continent eventually to Florence, to find out whether our love was still true, for it had not diminished in my heart and I hoped it was the same for you.'

At this she uttered a small cry.

'Can you imagine my amazement then,' I went on, trying to contain my increasing disquiet, 'when I discover that you and your dear Papa are here? Surely, I think, this is a sign that we are meant for each other. Sofia, I rejoiced!' My voice was rising. 'But now, you tell me Signor Biscaldi is a sick man and that you must go *home*.' I had to take several deep breaths then, for fear of shouting. When I had hold of my temper I continued, although each word was a mouthful of gristle. 'I must tell you, Sofia, it feels too hard to bear, but bear it I will, for your sake. I understand. At least, I think I understand, although that a sickness in one should be the fault of another, especially *your* fault, seems impossible to me. I'm sure your father would not countenance that.'

'He never would.' Sofia said softly, indeed almost to herself, before turning to me. 'And that is why the reason he and I must go home, is because I have changed my mind about…about you.'

I looked at her stricken face. 'But you haven't changed your mind.'

She said nothing, so I persisted.

'Have you?'

'You know I never will, William,' she said. 'But even so, you must go now.'

We looked at each other for a long while. Which of us moved first? I don't know, but it was almost as if another William Totman bowed before the beautiful lady, another William Totman who stood straight and replaced his cap, who walked across to the door, opened it, and stepped out into the darkness of the passage.

CHAPTER TWENTY-EIGHT

Cheapside has no great incline but the return journey was a mountain to climb. Alice remained with me after I'd nearly fallen over her sitting on the floor outside Sofia's door. I said I'd no errand for her to run, but she stayed by my side. Perhaps she thought I might come to harm. Whatever her thinking, I was glad of her quiet presence. When we reached the Great Conduit, she made me sit on a step, take a drink and give my face a wash. I did as she bid without argument, although if there was any benefit, I couldn't say.

When we reached John's house, Molly opened the door. She took one look at me and gasped.

'Oh no!' she said, taking my arm. 'I can't believe it. And we all thought you'd come back cheerful.'

I said nothing about that but gestured to Alice.

'Can you give this girl a little kindness, Molly? Some dinner and maybe do something about her frock? Here,' I fumbled in my purse. 'Here's five shillings. Perhaps a new one?'

Both Molly and Alice gawped at the sum. It was probably far too much, but I hardly cared.

'Is Signor Biscaldi still here?'

'No. Didn't you pass him? He's not long left.'

I shook my head. 'No matter. It's probably for the best.'

Molly tutted loudly at that, but then, having said that John was in his music room, she told Alice to follow her, giving the girl something of a smile even as she inspected her for fleas.

Like Molly, John had assumed I would return with a spring in my step and everything right with the world.

'Whatever happened?' he said, searching my face. 'Is London not to the young lady's taste?'

'Please,' I said, slumping down on a chair. 'Don't joke. I'm in no mood for anything except a bump on the head, hard enough to send me into oblivion.'

There was already a jug of wine in the room and John insisted I took a good few mouthfuls before anything further were possible. Once that was accomplished, he pulled his chair over to face mine.

'Now then,' he said. 'This is ridiculous. Nobody crosses a continent to tell someone they don't love them anymore. Even someone as thoughtful as Signorina Biscaldi. She would have written you a letter. You would have moped about for a while and that would have been the end of it. So? What has happened? Tell me everything.'

Despite my misery, there was something comforting about John's forthright manner. I didn't mean to tell him everything, as it seemed an impertinence to divulge Sofia's thoughts, but with encouragement and a little more wine, I did. To begin with, he made no response apart from a sympathetic murmur, but as I talked on and out came the news that Sofia's mother was a Morisca, he began to frown. When I told him what that meant, his frown deepened, but when I revealed that Signor was a sick man and Sofia considered it all her fault, he was not only breathing heavily but suddenly jumped out of his chair, letting it fall to the floor behind him with a great clatter, charged over to the door, and flung it open.

'Jane?' he called out. 'Jane? We're going out. Get yourself ready.'

'Mercy on us!' came her reply from downstairs. 'Whatever's the matter?'

'Quickly, now. We don't want them to leave before we get there. Come along, Will. We can't leave you behind.'

I got to my feet despite being stunned by this sudden haste.

'What are you doing? You can't be thinking of trying to persuade Sofia otherwise? She is quite resolved.'

He turned back to me.

'My dear brother, I am sure she is, but there is something of a mystery to be solved. Don't forget, that while you were with her, *I* was with Signor Biscaldi. Both you and I heard what each had to say, but let me tell you, in my own mind, they cannot be reconciled.'

'But Sofia would never lie!' I was appalled.

'No, no, of course not,' said John, patting me on the back. 'And I do not think Signor Biscaldi was lying. Perhaps neither know the truth in its entirety though. Have you thought of that?'

'Why ever would they not?'

'That,' he said, guiding me to the door, 'is what we are going to find out.'

In no time, we were all tearing along Cheapside, with John in front, hailing all those ahead to clear the way. Jane was almost running beside him so that her skirts billowed out like sails and then came the much more peculiar sight of Alice, wearing what I assumed was a smock of Molly's, and consequently so big it had to be tied about her skinny frame with a short length of rope, not unlike that worn by the Franciscans. She was determined to come with us and would have followed had we said otherwise. Perhaps it was for a good story to tell. I desired more than anything for it to have a happy ending.

I was a dead man come back to life. Hope flamed through me like strong drink, and it was almost with a drunkard's gait that I made my way. Every thought I had began the same way – why? Why would they lie? Why would they not know if they were lying? It was so baffling I wanted to cry out with frustration.

John continued to command the situation when we arrived at The Feathers. That the landlord knew him came as no surprise to me or Jane, and it was just as well. Wine was ordered and a private room, spacious enough for us all, was arranged for us at once. We sat at a large oak table, clean and scrubbed, but marked with the wear of many elbows. Alice was sent upstairs to invite Signor Biscaldi and Sofia to come down. I had no doubts about her powers of persuasion.

At the first knock, my heart jumped, but it proved to be the wine arriving. Not since the courtroom in Florence had I felt so thrown into confusion. It seemed an age before the door opened once again and Sofia entered followed by her dear Papa. I looked closely at Signor Biscaldi. Certainly, he had lost a good deal of weight, but he didn't look like a man in pain. Perhaps he had another sort of sickness. Lord knows, they were legion. Sofia kept her gaze down. If she glanced in my direction, I missed it. There were the usual courtesies while the wine was poured.

John insisted that he should sit one side with Jane and me across from him, so that I didn't look directly at Sofia or her father. I would have welcomed the time to look upon her face although it would have pained me greatly to see her distressed. I wondered where John had acquired such wisdom and continued to wonder as he opened proceedings almost as if we were in a courtroom.

'Signor Biscaldi, Signorina Sofia,' he said. 'I must seek your forgiveness for insisting you see us.' He cleared his throat. 'My good wife and I awoke this morning believing that we would not be seeing our dear brother,' he gestured towards me, 'for a very long time. If indeed, ever again. This was a great source of sadness to me and my entire household. It was the greatest good fortune, therefore, that Alice here,' he looked about, for Alice was not immediately obvious, sitting, as she was on the floor in front of the door. 'That Alice, there,' he continued, 'fetched him back when you arrived, Signor Biscaldi.'

Both Sofia and I sat still as statues when this was said. Jane smiled and looked pleased. Signor Biscaldi remained wary, shifting his glance to each of us by turn.

'I believed,' John went on, 'that when William left my house to visit Signorina Sofia at these premises, the day would end happily. Signor Biscaldi, from the conversation we had this afternoon, I thought that may have been your understanding as well.'

Signor Biscaldi looked uncomfortable. 'Well,' he said, 'I—'

John interrupted. Casting his arm about the room, as if to capture the attention of a much larger audience, he went on. 'But it was not to be. For when Will returned to my house, it was as if his doom had come upon him. I could not let him suffer alone, of course, and begged for him to reveal what had taken place. It was not easy,' he said in a low voice, pausing for effect whilst I wished for fewer theatrics and greater haste. 'But I soon realised that what I was hearing from Will did not tally with the tale I had heard from you, Signor.'

At that, Sofia gave a small cry. 'Papa,' she said. 'What does this mean?'

'I do not know,' he said, so clearly anguished his cuff would be threadbare before long. 'Signor Dowland and myself have a little talk about instruments and the shop in Florence, that's all.'

'So we did,' said John. 'And, if I recall correctly, you mentioned that the shop has a secret passage which you may have need of soon?'

'Soon, Papa?' Sofia laid her hand on his arm. 'But why soon? Has something happened?'

'Oh, my dear,' he said, patting her hand. 'I not want to worry you.'

At that, Sofia began to weep and this time it was Jane who came to her rescue with a handkerchief. Although the room had a high casement window that was open, I was beginning to feel as if there wasn't enough air to breathe. I wished fervently that whatever the outcome of our meeting, it would come soon.

'But Papa,' she said, trying to keep her voice level. 'I am very worried. I have been worried about you ever since we left Florence.'

'Worried about me?' Signor Biscaldi said in alarm. 'Why? What did I do? It is Duke Alfonso in Ferrara that is the big worry.'

I don't know whose mouth dropped open the widest. Certainly, we were each one of us amazed and sat back in our chairs all at once as if struck by a bolt from above.

I was first to speak. 'The Duke?'

'Who?' said Jane.

'Yes, yes,' said Signor Biscaldi. 'Even now he may be dead already. The rabbi tells me the Duke is very ill before we leave home.' He shook his head. 'There will be trouble for us all once the Pope takes Ferrara. The Grand Duke in Florence does not trouble us Jews much but he will heed words against us from the Pope. Yes, I am very worried.'

Sofia had wiped her eyes and sat up a little straighter.

'Papa, 'she said, firmly. 'I am sure you are right, but what about you? You are clearly a sick man yourself.'

She looked at him with such tender care I could have wept.

'Me? Signor Biscaldi was so startled he jumped back in his chair as we all had done when he mentioned the Duke. 'Sick? Am I?' He cast his eyes about as if sickness was something hiding behind his back. 'Why should you say so when I am not?'

Not sick? Was that true? I held my breath.

'But you are so thin, Papa,' Sofia's eyes gleamed with tears. 'You hardly eat and are tired and worried all the time. I am very sorry that I have made you so unhappy that now you are ill.'

'Oh, no no no, my child.' He clutched her hand and kissed it. 'Never would you make me unhappy or ill.'

'But Papa, whenever I asked if you were in good health, you waved me away.'

'Yes, because I am in good health.'

John cleared his throat.

'Forgive me,' he said, 'but I believe there is nearly a firm understanding to be had between us all.' He turned to Signor Biscaldi. 'Clearly your daughter believes you have a wasting sickness, but earlier this afternoon, you told me that *not* eating might one day save your life.'

Signor Biscaldi nodded. 'Indeed, Signor Dowland. My dear daughter,' he kissed her hand again. 'I am ashamed for not telling you but now, I will tell you all.'

He took a deep breath and composed himself, becoming a Signor Biscaldi I had not met before, serious, and thoughtful. He rose to his feet.

'Dear friends,' he said, slowly, whilst looking at us in turn. 'My daughter's wish to come to London is hard for me. As I say to Signor Totman before, I am selfish man. I not want to lose my Sofia, but I also wish her to be happy.' He frowns. 'It is very difficult. So, I go and see the rabbi. He is wise and will help. But when I arrive, and before I speak, he say Duke Alfonso is to die and we must prepare for very bad future.' He paused and appealed to us. 'Why, you say? Duke Alfonso, he is in Ferrara. Maybe in Florence, not much different.' He shrugs. 'Perhaps. But perhaps not. All Jews in Ferrara may need new home. Where will they go? Not Venice for sure. The ghetto very bad there. Mantua? Maybe, and maybe Florence. Where the ghetto is small and full already.'

He shrugged again and took a sip of wine, before turning to John.

'Signor Dowland, if I say, you, your family, must leave England tomorrow, what would you do?'

John looked taken aback, blustered a little, but said nothing.

'Or if men come in your house and take all your possessions. Your instruments perhaps? The fine cup you have with silver lid?' He didn't wait for an answer before turning to Jane.

'I see you have fine jewels about your neck.' He leant towards her and said harshly, 'Give them to me.'

Jane uttered a small cry, her hand going straight to her throat to hide the garnet necklace.

Signor Biscaldi smiled. 'Forgive me, Signora Dowland, these are precious things to you. But what if, like me, you treasure a *daughter*.'

I started as he gestured towards me.

'Signor Totman knows, and because Sofia tells me, that in the street she is called names and sometimes people push in a bad way.'

'Or spit at her,' I said, feeling my fists clench.

'Indeed.'

He turned back to Jane, who'd paled at these revelations.

'Is true,' he said, holding out his hands. 'Jews are persecuted. Everywhere and always. This, I describe, is every day. It could be worse. If my business is taken or

I am robbed and left for dead, what of Sofia? My friends, the rabbi says we already lucky to be safe in Ferrara and Florence for such long time. *One day, he say, maybe it not safe at all.*'

It was very quiet in the room as we all considered such horror. I heard laughter outside, then Alice fidgeting by the door. She understood an uncertain future better than most.

John cleared his throat, but Signor Biscaldi hadn't finished.

'After talk with rabbi, I return to the shop,' he said. 'And now I know Sofia must go to London. If she is not Jewish and Signor Totman is a good man, he will keep her safe. That most important.'

He bowed his head and with a shaking hand, reached for his wine.

'But for me?' he said. 'I worry. I do not know London. There are some Jews there, I hear, but not many. Perhaps I cannot stay and must leave Sofia.' His voice cracked. 'Leave her for the first time in her whole life.'

Sofia reached out to him. 'Oh Papa—'

'Yes, yes, my child,' he said, softly. 'I will finish. For now, I tell why I am ashamed.'

He took another sip of wine. Yes, his hand shook, but when a tear appeared on his cheek, he hastily brushed it away as if cross with himself and addressed us again.

'How will it be in Florence when I return? I cannot know, but if the rabbi says we must prepare, then prepare I must.' He turned to Jane. 'Signora, your husband mention the secret passage in my shop. This is how Jews prepare for bad time; in very *good* time. The passage goes long way to the synagogue in the ghetto. I decide, before we leave for England, to try an escape.'

Poor Jane had no idea why Sofia and I gasped then but we knew what it would mean. I was back there in an instant, remembering the dark when Sofia shut me in, the small space, the small trapdoor, how there was very little room to move. John remained quiet. It wouldn't do to explain everything to Jane.

'Signora,' said Signor Biscaldi. 'They not surprised. Sofia show the passage to Signor Totman so they know it is too difficult for me. I not know until I look at the little door and—' he looked down at his diminished girth. 'Now, maybe I manage. Then? I much too fat.' He turned to Sofia. 'I very ashamed of myself and did not tell you. I make up my mind then. I will not eat so much. It will not be hard on the weeks it take to London. Nowhere has food good as Tuscany. When I return, I will try again.' He laid his hands flat on the table. 'That is the end. Now, a little more wine, I think.'

Jane reached for the flagon.

'Thank you for the explanation, Signor Biscaldi,' she said.

Perhaps it's a siren song that wine sings when it fills a glass as, quite suddenly, I felt a tightness in my chest, which I'd not even known was there, leave me, and I took a great breath.

John had brought us together and we had discovered the source of misunderstanding. Sofia, I think was more than a little stunned. She hadn't lied, but she had been wrong. Would that change her mind now? A glance suggested she was more of her old self, but I didn't know for sure.

'Signor Biscaldi,' I began, 'if I may—'

'Forgive me, Will,' John got to his feet. 'But I am quite certain that some of us here would be much better elsewhere.' And then, with an authority I'd last seen used by the magistrate in Florence, he spoke to each in turn. 'Jane, we must let Molly know there are two more for dinner. Signor Biscaldi, I believe you and I have further matters to discuss. Shall you come with us? We can leave Will here with Alice to accompany Signorina Sofia to our house a little later. Is that a suitable arrangement for us all?'

By *all*, he most particularly meant Sofia.

'Oh!' she said, blushing so deeply, she hid behind her hands and spoke in a small voice. 'Yes, I think that would be most suitable.'

Did it really take an age for three people to leave the room? It seemed so but leave they eventually did. If John's smile contained a slight smirk I didn't notice, for he had made a new future possible. Alice, bless her, positioned herself on the outside of the door, leaving Sofia and me alone at long last, with only a large oak table between us.

'My dear Sofia,' I said. 'I believe that John has outwitted us all today. If he has done wrong, then I promise to leave without delay and never trouble you again.'

'Oh no, William, he has not done wrong at all.' Her hands fluttered. 'But I have been a silly girl and have caused much trouble. I am a little cross with Papa for not telling me why he was not eating, but mostly I am cross with myself.' Two angry red spots appeared on her cheeks as she frowned.

'You have no need to be,' I assured her. 'Your father was ashamed of himself, and shame is a hard thing to share. I think there have been many times in his life when he has not always been as open as you, my dear. That is not a bad thing for a businessman, and I imagine, often very necessary for a Jew.'

'Yes,' she said, 'and it was hard for me to learn that I am not really a Jew. What will that mean? I am still my father's daughter and isn't it my duty to look after him? Sick or not. How can I do that if...' she hesitated before taking a deep breath. 'If you still...'

I was by her side before she could finish.

'Sofia,' I said, taking her hand. 'Let me speak. When I spoke to your father before I saw you this afternoon, I said there was no choice to be made between his good self and me. If you decide to be baptised and I was so fortunate as to become your husband, then we three would be a family, and one with more than enough love for each other. It may be that your dear Papa will have to stay in the ghetto if we are in Florence but that is not the case here. The future is always uncertain, but are we to turn away from love? Please, my dear, will you have me?'

There was a little silence then but when she looked

up at me with such a clear-eyed smile, it was enough for me to know her answer.

'I will. Oh William, I—'

I stopped her speaking in the only way I could. We clung together for a long time until she gently pushed against my chest.

'Are you carrying a book, William? Or is this a block of wood against your heart.'

'It was a block of wood once,' I said, taking the box from beneath my jerkin. 'Then I made this to keep a very precious lace cuff from harm. I will never part with it.'

'Such a beautiful thing,' she said, turning it over and over. 'It could only be made by you.'

'But now,' I said, taking it from her, 'we must not let it come between us.' And I placed it safely on the table before taking her in my arms again.

It was a while later that a firm knock at the door reminded us there was another world outside. Alice opened the door an inch.

'The landlord wants the room,' she said. 'I told him he'd have to wait first time, but he's come back and said he can't wait no longer.'

She shut the door with a slam.

Sofia was rather shocked. 'Do all servants behave like that here?'

'Please, my darling. Don't think badly of her. Her appearance and manners may be against her, but I swear the girl is honest. She has been a help to me lately and I'm hoping to improve her lot in some small way. If not for Alice here,' I said, opening the door. 'I would be taking my dinner in Flanders this evening.'

'Well in that case, Alice,' said Sofia. 'You have my warmest thanks for persuading me to see Mr Totman earlier.'

What a strange trio we were, walking back along Cheapside from The Feathers. Sofia, dark-eyed and dainty, dressed in something of a foreign manner, but even so, a beauty clearly worthy of regard. Alice, a little distance from us, in her too-big smock with an expression that told no story, although I'm sure a small smile turned her lip at times. And there I was, still in my travelling cloak but with the trace of kisses on my lips and such a lightness in my step I barely felt the cobbles. The shadows were lengthening, and all the windows in the fine houses of Cheapside twinkled like jewels in the low sun. Wasn't London the fairest of cities? Full of wonders to be pointed out?

AFTERWORD

It has been a remarkable year. Today we are walking in the opposite direction, down Cheapside, and then on to the docks where another farewell will take place. John is very happy with the success of his Booke of Songes and Ayres, which no doubt will become known as his First Booke, as he is already thinking of a second. Jane and the children are happy that John, following another trip to Germany, has been home for a long time and, although Robert is unhappy at my going this morning, I think he will get over it soon.

Signor Biscaldi, despite his obvious enjoyment of London's tastiest victuals, is happy to be travelling home again as he told me that he feels safer on the road. My present fear for him is that he may find that his escape route is once again too much of a squeeze.

Like her darling papa, Sofia is a happy traveller and I know she is excited to be visiting all the cities and towns along the way. Her enthusiasm is catching, and I am more than happy to be going with them. Much of my life will be spent travelling as I am part of the family business now. With her father's blessing, Sofia was baptised in April, and we were married soon after. John had slipped the key to Joseph's old house into my hand when Sofia and I returned from The Feathers on that day of miracles. It was soon transformed into a suitable London residence and thanks to the purchase of the neighbouring property, I was able to keep the workshop. We will settle there if blessed with children but that is for the future to decide. Meanwhile, the business makes demands on us, and we are returning to Florence.

Alice, who once knew nothing about the role of a lady's maid, still knows very little, but we could not leave her behind. She has grown upwards and outwards, and looks healthy, even pretty when she smiles, which is not yet often enough. At the sight of the big ships, she pales.

'Me across the sea,' she mutters and shakes her head.

I try to reassure her that we will return, but she looks at me as if I am a simpleton.

She's right to doubt me. Don't I remember well my own fears when setting out with John to unknown lands, and I was charged with keeping him safe?

How differently I feel now, such that even if the sea does go up and down, my mind and heart are settled. I wonder about old Mistress Dowland. My obligations to her are all done. Was she right to entrust her son's safety to me? I think not, as trouble came to me as much as it did to him. Marvels happened too though, not least the meeting with my beloved wife.

Ah, but John now, it is hard to say farewell, as I will miss him more than anyone. He would hear no word of thanks for the house, or his part in reconciling Sofia with me. For much of this short walk he has been extolling the virtues of Denmark. Quietly, he asks if I ever hear how Lady Anna has fared, to let him know. Worry for him surges through me, but with the merest glance at Sofia, it is quelled. When he grasps my hand, I wish him success and happiness in everything he does. For a moment he looks grave, perhaps too full of feeling to speak, but then with a slight shrug, almost as if casting off a cloak or relinquishing a burden, he smiles and wishes the same for me.

ACKNOWLEDGEMENTS

Considerable thanks must go to Jane Skinner, Karen Edwards and Margaret James for their sharp eyes, to Su Bristow, Richard Lee and Ben Morgan for their wise words, to Berni Stevens for another perfect cover design and to all of them for their unwavering and hugely appreciated support.

The Luthier's Promise is based on a letter, now in Hatfield House, that was written by the composer and lutenist, John Dowland, to Sir Robert Cecil in 1595.

Very little is known about the life of John Dowland, despite his fame. I owe much to the research undertaken by Diana Poulton in her comprehensive work: *John Dowland, his Life and Work published in 1972*, although it contains no mention of an adopted brother.

ABOUT THE AUTHOR

Cathie Hartigan

Cathie lives in the historic city of Exeter, Devon. Many years ago she trained as a music teacher at Dartington College of Arts and her love of music is reflected in all her novels.

She is the founder of the Exeter Novel Prize.

With Margaret James she co-authored:
The Creative Writing Student's Handbook
The Short Story Writer's Workbook
The Novelist's Workbook

www.creativewritingmatters.co.uk

BOOKS BY THIS AUTHOR

Secret Of The Song

Music, mayhem and murder in a gripping dual time story set in contemporary Exeter and Renaissance Naples.
'a mystery story, subtly constructed and many-layered, and it won't let you down.' 5*
Shortlisted for the Hall and Woodhouse DLF Prize

Notes From The Lost

In 1943, two soldiers escape from a train in the Italian mountains behind enemy lines. Only one makes it home and it's not to a warm welcome and happy ever after.
In 2000, Ros sets off on a trail to discover the truth. What she discovers is that everyone, including herself, has something to hide.
'a beautiful, complex and deeply moving novel.' 5*
Shortlisted for the 2020 Selfies.

Printed in Dunstable, United Kingdom